CW01668239

The Love Dilemma

Tracy Corbett

RUBHA

Dedicated to the original Tap-dancing Fairy.
Still think about you, Lou. Still miss you.
Louise Newcombe 1974-2006

Chapter One

ELENA

Thursday, 22nd May

There weren't many things that would cause Elena Romero's body to flood with stress hormones when she was focused on work. She was a skilled practitioner, calm and reassuring. 'Assertive', as her youngest sister, Luisa, referred to her—although usually in a tone that suggested it wasn't a compliment. But when her phone flashed with a silent message from Luisa that said *Urgent—get home now!* it was enough to threaten the onset of heart failure.

Hiding her panic from her patient, Elena checked the time, relieved to note the treatment session was almost over. 'How does that feel now?' she asked, hoping thirty minutes of intensive massaging had alleviated the pain of recurring sciatica.

The woman eased into a sitting position. 'You're a miracle worker, even if you're also a sadist. Seventy-five quid for the pleasure of being tortured is not my idea of fun.'

'No pain, no gain.' Elena's phone flashed with another message.

Where are you? We need you here!

The use of the word 'we' meant her other sister, Sofia, must also be involved in whatever drama was unfolding at home, and for Sofia to be absent from work, it meant the situation was serious enough to warrant asking for more time off—something her employers were becoming increasingly unhappy about. Maybe if they had care responsibilities themselves they might feel differently. Unless you'd experienced the trials of looking after a poorly loved one, it was hard to comprehend the constant exhaustion and demands.

Elena scrolled through the electronic calendar on her laptop. 'Same time next week?'

Her patient groaned. 'If I must.'

Elena tried to appear calm while the woman located a credit card and paid for her treatment. Transaction completed, Elena was finally able to grab her phone and escape. If the emergency at home was serious then she'd have to cancel her afternoon appointments, which wasn't ideal. Reputation was key to success, and she wasn't the only physiotherapist in Notting Hill. The competition would seize any opportunity to steal her business, but family came first, so she'd do what needed to be done.

Her patient was occupying the single-person lift as it creaked downwards towards reception, so Elena skipped down two flights of stairs and pushed through the fire door, almost bumping into a sign-writer stencilling a new name on the glass door of the ground floor office.

The impressive Georgian building had been converted

into commercial offices a few years back. The landlord, Hugh Spencer-Harrison, ran his counselling services from the middle floor, and if she'd known the ground-floor tenant was moving out, she'd have spoken to Hugh and asked if she could switch offices, so her ailing patients didn't have to negotiate the stairs or use the unreliable lift each time they visited. But it was too late now, the space had been taken. She'd just have to hope that whoever Daniel J Jackson was, he might be open to swapping offices with her. It was a long shot, but nothing ventured, nothing gained and all that.

Slamming the door behind her, she raced down the path and clattered through the iron gate as she headed towards Portobello Road. The market ran every day except Sundays, so the area was always buzzing, and she had to swerve around the mass of pedestrians filling the pavements.

It was normally a four minute walk from Portobello Road to Lancaster Road, where her family lived. When she exercised at night, she could cover the distance in less than two minutes. On a bustling market day, running wasn't an option. Swerving at speed was the best she could manage, apologising to shoppers as she knocked into them, and trying not to crash into any of the stall holders.

Glancing at her phone, she was relieved to discover no further messages. Sofia would normally be straight on the phone if there was an issue concerning Luisa's health, so receiving a message from Luisa herself was an anomaly. Her youngest sister was usually incredibly stubborn when it came to asking for medical help.

Maybe Sofia was sick? Had something happened to her middle sister? It was a horrible thought. Sofia had been the only other person keeping the family afloat in recent months since their mum's unexpected death from an aneurism. It was a horrendous event that had been compounded by Elena splitting from her long-term boyfriend Felix. Being dumped for a better job was bad enough. Being left a week after her mother's funeral was beyond cruel. Talk about cold-hearted.

With Felix gone, she'd struggled to pay the bills on their rented flat alone. So when Papi returned to Colombia to sell off his business interests and improve their financial situation, moving back into the family home to help Sofia look after Luisa had seemed like the sensible decision—even if giving up her independence had been a wrench. She was thirty years old and back living at home. Life was not going to plan.

Elena darted between two stalls selling bric-a-brac and Indian scarves, ignoring the stall holders' invitations to sample their produce. The smell of freshly baked goods made her stomach rumble. The lure of *pain au chocolat* would normally be tempting if she wasn't responding to an emergency.

Skidding around the bend, she entered Lancaster Road —or Rainbow Row, as it was commonly known. Architecturally, every house was identical. Three-story town houses, built in the 1820s, each one with a set of steps leading to a colourful front door and a prominent bay window at the front with a balcony above. The only thing setting them apart was the colour—each one was painted a different shade, from shocking pink to sandstone beige. There were blues, greens, pastels, each one reflecting the character of the people who lived inside—or, at least, the people rich enough to own such prestigious dwellings. Current house prices in the area topped three million. The only reason the Romero family owned such a fancy pad was because her maternal great-grandparents had bought the property back in the 1940s and passed it down through the generations.

Reaching the front door, Elena tried to ignore the flaking cerise paintwork around the doorframe. Whatever the gaudy colour said about them as a family, she wasn't sure, but the disrepair certainly told a story. Money was tight. Papi wasn't currently earning and the properties in Colombia had yet to sell. Luisa's health prevented her from working full-time, and the increasing cost of living wasn't slowing down any time soon, which left Elena and Sofia as sole earners in the family.

Almost kicking down the door, Elena raced inside. 'I'm home!'

A scream rang out from above, followed by thundering footsteps running across the landing. Elena had assumed the emergency was medical, now she was wondering if they had an intruder. In which case, she needed to arm herself.

Grabbing a bread knife from the kitchen, she jumped the stairs three at a time, grateful for the power in her legs from regular circuit training.

There was no sign of anyone on the first floor where the bedrooms were, so she followed the banging up another floor to where Luisa had her art studio. The sight that greeted her was surreal.

Sofia was clinging onto one of the large sash windows and holding a mop head, trying to dislodge a distressed pigeon from the rafters, who was flapping about and head-butting the wall.

'The cavalry has arrived!' Luisa threw her arms in the air, before performing a comedy double-take when she spotted Elena's weapon of choice. 'Err ... why are you carrying a bread knife?'

'I heard screaming, I thought you were being attacked.' She placed the knife on the floor, out of harm's way.

Luisa grinned. 'What were you going to do, slice them to death?'

'It was all I had time to grab.' And then she noticed Luisa's outfit. 'What on earth are you wearing?'

'A tent.'

'Because?'

'Sewing Bee transformation challenge, turning an old canvas into a wearable garment.' Luisa did a spin. 'Like it?'

'You call that wearable?'

Luisa shrugged. 'It's practical, it keeps the paint off.'

'Is anyone going to help me?' Sofia was balancing on top of a wooden chair.

'Sorry!' Elena headed over to the window, shaking off the sight of her youngest sister wearing an orange two-man tent. 'Please tell me the pigeon isn't the emergency.'

Luisa looked disgruntled. 'Of course it is! I mean, look at the state of my studio. Bird shit everywhere.'

Elena flashed Luisa a loaded look. 'You called me home from work to deal with a pigeon?' It was hard to comprehend that Luisa was twenty-five years old, she looked and acted much younger. But Elena figured that was the curse of being poorly. How could anyone grow up when they constantly needed looking after?

Luisa folded her arms. 'Sofia isn't faring so well. She needed help.'

'I assume you sent Sofia the same urgent message?'

'She certainly did.' Sofia wobbled on the chair. 'And when I'm done catching this blessed pigeon, we'll be having a discussion about the meaning of the word *urgent*.' She sounded uncharacteristically flustered. 'This is not my idea of urgent.'

Elena glared at Luisa before kicking off her trainers. 'Mine either.'

'What should I have done then? Let the little bastard fly around shitting on everything until you came home tonight? Ruining Mum's brocade curtains? Gifted to her by her ancestors on their deathbed?'

'Quit with the dramatics.' Elena climbed onto the cabinet, the only piece of furniture not removed from the room to allow Luisa space to be creative. 'I'm not about to get sentimental over a set of curtains.' She looked at Sofia. 'What's the plan?'

'I have no plan.' Sofia gave Elena an exasperated look. 'Catching pigeons is not my forte. I do not have RSPCA training. My ability to deal with rogue birds is non-existent.'

'RSPB,' Luisa corrected. 'RSPCA deals with animals.'

Sofia bit her lip. 'Are you going to throw something at her, or shall I?'

'No one's throwing anything at me,' Luisa replied, perching on her artist's stool. 'I'm fragile. I have ailments. It's discriminatory to throw things at the disabled. I have rights.'

Elena might have responded with a rude gesture, had Luisa not started coughing. A reminder that however infuriating she was, her health issues were very real. 'Make yourself useful and turn off the lights.'

'Err ... why?'

'The poor thing is traumatised. It has no idea how to get out, any more than we know how to capture it. Birds flock towards the light, if we open the window and turn off the lights, it might fly towards the window and free itself, saving us the stress of trying to grab it.'

Luisa went over to the light switch. 'Who knew you were so knowledgeable about birds.'

Elena rolled her eyes. 'I'm a woman of hidden talents.'

The lights went out.

Sofia lifted the sash window and climbed down from the chair, still managing to look stunning despite her dishevelled ponytail and flushed cheeks.

Sofia had inherited their father's Latino characteristics, her dark skin was both flawless and luminous. Along with her curvy figure, fluttery brown eyes and pouty mouth, it was a devastating combination, something her sister seemed oblivious to. She never seemed to notice when someone did a double take or openly gawped at her. Elena had never worked out whether her sister's indifference to looking like a cover model was endearing or annoying. The fact that she currently had bird shit on her blouse didn't detract from her appeal, although it did smell.

'I need to change.' Sofia slipped her feet into her work courts, elevating her to almost five feet. 'Expect a lecture,' she said to Luisa, before marching over to the door and disappearing from the room.

Luisa looked puzzled. 'What did I do?'

'You made her worry for no good reason.'

'Well, I didn't mean to. ... And what about the pigeon?'

'We leave the pigeon alone.' Elena padded over to the sink to wash her hands. 'It's more likely to fly out without an audience.'

'What about my artwork? I need to finish my painting, I'm in the creative zone.'

'Tough. I'm not spending another moment chasing down a pigeon.' Elena dried her hands and put her trainers back on. 'Besides, it's lunchtime. Take a break. With any luck, by the time you're done, the pigeon will be gone.' She picked up the knife and held open the door. 'Come on, Picasso. Let's go.'

Pouting, Luisa removed the paint-splattered poncho and dramatically dragged herself from the stool. 'If I must.'

Unlike Sofia, when Luisa pouted it was more petulant teenager than sexy siren, no doubt a result of being the youngest of three and mollycoddled since birth. Not that Elena begrudged her, Cystic Fibrosis was a cruel illness that dominated all of their lives. She was entitled to pout.

Luisa followed Elena down the wide staircase, past the family photos hanging on the walls, depicting a happy and loving unit. A unit blown apart by death and absence. It was still hard to accept how their lives had changed overnight. One moment they were planning a family trip to Bogotá, the next they were arranging their mum's funeral. Three months down the line and it was still difficult to see a way out of the sadness.

Luisa nudged Elena's shoulder. 'Are you angry with me?'

'Not angry. Frustrated.'

'Because I can't deal with wayward pigeons? I did try, but I got breathless and had to stop.'

Elena paused on the stairs, guilt overriding any grievance she might feel.

Luisa picked at her split nails, discoloured from excessive steroid use. She looked so morose and her skin was paler than usual. She had the same dark hair and brown eyes as her sisters, but her skin was lighter, her skinny frame more a result of her medical condition than genetics. 'I hate being so limited.'

Elena's heart pinched. 'I know.' She touched her sister's arm. 'And we don't mind helping you. But maybe next time explain what the problem is, so we don't have a heart attack trying to get home so fast.'

'Fair enough.' Luisa looked sheepish. 'Sorry. The pigeon made me panicky. He had evil eyes.'

Elena leaned against the banister. 'Evil eyes?'

'Yeah, and a bad attitude.'

Elena couldn't help grinning. 'Are you being just a little dramatic?'

'No, you weren't there. He waited until I'd almost reached him every time before he flew off. That's deliberately provocative, he was toying with me.'

Elena's laugh faded when Luisa rubbed her chest. 'Do your lungs need clearing? I have time before my afternoon appointments. I can give you physio, if you need it.'

'I'm fine. It's just another infection.' Luisa walked off before Elena could react.

It took a moment before Elena recovered enough to chase her sister downstairs. 'You have another infection? Why didn't you say anything?'

'It's hardly shocking news. Infections are my thing.'

'But you know how quickly things can deteriorate.'

Luisa raised her hand. 'Stop fussing. I'm fine. It's no big deal.'

Easy for her to say, she wasn't the one who constantly worried. 'Are you taking antibiotics.' They always had a supply in stock, along with masses of steroids and various drugs to help thin the mucus from her airways and enzymes to help her absorb fat and nutrients. They had more medication in stock than Boots the Chemist. Luisa often joked that she'd make a great drug dealer—*Breaking Bad* comes to Notting Hill.

'Of course I am. I'm not stupid.' Luisa shook away Elena's attempt to take her hand.

Sofia appeared from the kitchen, her hands on her hips.

'Care to explain why there's a man asleep on the sofa in the conservatory?'

Luisa shrugged. 'I guess he hasn't woken up yet?' She sauntered into the open-plan living area as though it was no big deal.

Elena looked at Sofia with raised eyebrows. 'There's a man in our conservatory? Has he been there all night? I didn't see him this morning.'

'Neither did I.' Sofia marched into the glass extension at the back of the house, Elena close behind. 'And he's minus his trousers.'

True enough, a trouser-less man wearing a designer polo shirt and ludicrous underpants was sprawled on the floral sofa, snoring gently, his mouth wide open.

Elena fanned her face and recoiled from the smell. 'Jesus, he reeks of booze. Who is he?'

'No idea.' Luisa was curled up in the wingback armchair as though nothing was amiss. 'Ryan. No ... Bryan. Or was it Leon? I can't remember. He's some guy I hooked up with last night. We got wasted. Clearly a lightweight. No stamina, some men.'

Elena looked at her youngest sister. 'Do you remember inviting him home?'

Luisa chewed her lip as if trying to remember. 'Not exactly. It's all a bit hazy.'

Elena pointed at her sister, before remembering she was still holding the bread knife and lowered her hand. 'Do you need reminding of the dangers of bringing home strange men?'

Luisa pulled a face. 'He's not strange ... well, apart from the Superman underpants, which, I agree, aren't exactly a turn on. And he was far from super-human last night. From what I can remember, the whole thing was a bit of a disappointment.' Luisa's wrist went limp. 'If you get my drift.'

Sofia folded her arms. 'He could've robbed us, Luisa. Or worse.'

'Hardly,' Luisa scoffed. 'Look at him, sleeping like a baby.'

The man made a loud snorting sound.

'See?' Luisa pointed at him as he clutched a silk pillow to his face, like a toddler clinging hold of a cuddly toy. 'He's a man-child. Nothing to be afraid of.'

Sofia shook head. 'Looks can be deceiving. You've no idea what he's capable of.'

'I discovered what's he's *not* capable of,' Luisa said, with a sigh. 'And stop fussing. It's not like I'd complain if either of you brought a bloke home.'

Sofia tugged the silk pillow away from the man's grasp, making him grunt. 'We'd never bring anyone home,' she said, shaking dribble away from the delicate antique fabric.

Luisa lifted an eyebrow. 'And that's why you're so uptight all the time. Maybe you should try it. Anyone would think you were ninety-seven, not twenty-seven. Live a little.'

The man snorted again, jolting as if his snoring had woken him.

Elena lifted the bread knife as a warning, ready to defend her sisters if he turned violent.

He grunted a few more times, rolled onto his back, and then rubbed his face, stirring from his semi-conscious state.

Elena stepped closer, Sofia did the same.

After several yawns, breaking wind and scratching his crotch, the man opened his eyes and slowly took in his surroundings, clearly confused as to where he was.

What he made of the collection of brightly-coloured

Colombian artefacts, mixed in with the exposed wooden beams, rustic brickwork and quintessential English floral furnishings, she had no idea. But his expression changed the moment his gaze landed on Sofia, his eyes widening at the sight of her standing over him with her hands on her hips.

'Morning, sweetheart.' His sleepy gaze focused on her breasts. 'You're even more gorgeous this morning than you were last night. I can't believe I pulled a babe like you.'

Sofia's eyes narrowed. 'You didn't.'

'That would be me.' Luisa waved from the armchair, unperturbed by the man's slight. 'She's way out of your league, mate. Don't even think about it.'

The man did a double-take, looking uncomfortable as the events of the previous night caught up with his brain. His expression turned wary as he clocked the expression on Elena's face and the bread knife in her hand. 'You planning on using that?'

'Depends.' Elena stood her ground. He was right to be afraid. *Very afraid*, as Wednesday Addams would say. 'Time to leave.'

Swallowing, he sat up and ran a hand through his messy hair. 'Anyone seen my jeans?'

Sofia picked them up from the floor, holding them at arm's length as though they were contaminated and threw them at him.

Elena gestured to the door. 'And get a move on. You've outstayed your welcome.'

'Any chance of a coffee before I go?' He winked at Sofia as he shrugged into his jeans and fastened the fly.

Elena kicked his trainers towards him. 'None whatsoever. Move it.'

The man had barely shoved his feet into his trainers before Elena and Sofia escorted him from the room like a couple of nightclub bouncers extracting a patron for bar fighting.

'Do you want my number?' he said to Sofia in a low voice.

'No, she doesn't!' Luisa yelled, heaving herself up from the armchair. 'And neither do I!' With the flip of her middle finger, she headed for the kitchen. 'I'd say thanks for a great night, but we both know that'd be a lie. More like *Droopy*man than Superman.'

The man flinched.

Elena and Sofia ushered him towards the front door.

'Are you sure you don't want my number?' he said to Sofia, stepping over the threshold.

Sofia pretended to contemplate his offer. 'Goodness, let me think. It's tempting, wouldn't you agree, Elena?'

'Oh, I would.' Elena leant against the doorframe. 'He's a catch, after all. Why wouldn't you want a man who wears Superman underpants and hooked up with your sister last night?'

Sofia sighed. 'It's a dilemma, that's for certain.'

The man looked between them. 'You're being sarcastic, right?'

'What do you think?' Elena slammed the door in his face. 'Idiot.'

And Luisa wondered why they didn't date. Elena's bad experience with Felix hadn't put her off love entirely, but she'd vowed to stay clear of uptight men in suits—and definitely immature idiots wearing children's underwear.

Sofia headed for the kitchen. 'What a charmer.'

Elena followed her. 'A real peach.'

When they arrived in the kitchen, they pinned Luisa simultaneously with a loaded look. Her sister seemed clueless as to the level of worry she caused them. Added to the stress of running the house, grieving for their mum, and missing Papi, it was hard to hold it together some days. Luisa's antics were not helping.

Luisa adopted a defensive stance. 'Don't look at me like that, you're not my bloody parents. It's no big deal.'

Elena shoved the bread knife back in its stand. 'Luisa, you've just been telling me you've got a chest infection.'

'So?' She opened the freezer door and removed a tub of ice cream.

'So, getting drunk and bringing home random men is not ideal.'

'Why? I might die tomorrow.' She opened a drawer and unearthed a spoon. 'Unlike you two, I'm not prepared to waste what little time I have being all goody-two-shoes and doing nothing other than working and fretting. Talk about *dull*. Some of us want to enjoy life.' Nudging the drawer shut with her hip, she flounced into the lounge.

Elena clenched her fists, resisting the urge to bang her forehead against the wooden countertop. 'Did she really just say that? We're working our bloody socks off, trying to pay the bills and keep a roof over our heads and look after her, and she has the cheek to accuse us of being *dull?*'

Sofia folded her arms. 'And just when I was starting to feel bad for yelling at her.'

Chapter Two

DANNY

Friday, 23rd May

Daniel Jackson gazed up at the opulent properties lining St Luke's Mews in London's prestigious Notting Hill and shook his head, stunned by what he saw. The extent of the Spencer-Harrison family's wealth still amazed him, despite having been a part of their lives for nearly two decades. He couldn't believe this was where he would be living for the next few months. It was beyond belief.

Although he'd lived in the UK for eighteen years, London wasn't a city he was familiar with. He'd mostly lived in the South East, moving from one town to another to further his career and living from paycheque to paycheque. He was used to noisy neighbours and arguments over street parking, not rooftop balconies and sophisticated security systems. It was like something from a futuristic movie.

'The residents are going to think we're burglars,' his

brother said, glancing at one of the perfectly maintained and yet deserted courtyards. 'Curtains are twitching. It's only a matter of time before the police show up and arrest us for trespassing.'

Danny suspected the people who lived in these properties didn't own anything as mundane as curtains. They probably had remote-controlled silk drapes, handmade in a rural village in Morocco by eccentric, yoga-mad monks.

Imagining himself living here was almost as surreal as his student days when he'd stayed at the Spencer-Harrison's stately home in rural Berkshire. It was a far cry from most student accommodation, but then most people didn't have a best friend whose father sat in the House of Lords.

When he'd won a place at Oxford University to study law, he'd foolishly assumed his parents' disapproval of his life choices would lift and he'd finally win their respect. That hadn't happened. Instead, they'd withdrawn financial support and he'd abandoned any ideas of returning to Orange County, resigning himself to a new life in the UK with his surrogate family—people who actually gave a damn about him.

Danny checked his watch. 'Hugh should be here soon. Stop looking so nervous, it's making you look guilty.'

'I feel guilty.' Connor dug his hands in his jeans pockets. 'And I haven't done anything wrong. But that doesn't always count for anything, does it?'

Danny placed a reassuring hand on his brother's shoulder, knowing that being accused of something he hadn't done was an emotional trigger for him. Connor had discovered first-hand that justice didn't always follow a false accusation. 'We're here legitimately,' he assured his brother, hoping to convince himself in the process. 'Stop worrying.'

'Tell that to the woman giving us the evil eye.' Connor nodded to the property behind. 'I don't think we're the right kind of resident for this area.'

Danny flattened a crease in his T-shirt, wishing he'd worn one of his work suits instead. He felt competent in his work attire, even if it wasn't practical for lugging about packing crates. 'We could be millionaires, for all she knows. People shouldn't judge by appearances.'

'But we're not millionaires, are we?' Connor's voice was barely a whisper, as though he was fearful of being overheard.

'No, but Hugh is. And he's invited us to stay, so that makes our presence legitimate.' Danny checked his surroundings, taking in the immaculate planters attached to the iron balconies, each one bursting with greenery, no doubt manicured by gold-medal-winning Chelsea designers, whose hourly rate probably exceeded Danny's monthly income. There was an unusual absence of trash, as though nothing dared blight the view—not a garbage bin in sight.

The tension gripping his neck eased slightly at the sight of his mate's car pulling into the courtyard. 'Here's Hugh now.'

Connor glanced behind him. 'He might be too late. The woman's on the phone, she doesn't look impressed. Expect sirens.'

The midnight blue Jaguar eased silently to a stop, and a grinning Hugh Spencer-Harrison emerged from the vehicle looking like something from GQ magazine. 'Gentlemen, you found our little pad okay.'

Danny raised an eyebrow. 'Little?'

'Compared to the Chelsea town house, it is.' Hugh gave a good-natured shrug. Lights flashed on his fancy car as it silently locked and he made a beeline for Connor, enveloping him in a crushing hug. 'I've missed you.'

Connor hugged him back, the bond between them as strong as ever.

Being landed with caring responsibilities for a five-year-old at the tender age of nineteen had upended Danny's life in a way he couldn't have imagined. Sharing the load of that responsibility with Hugh had been the only reason he'd coped. Eighteen years later, and the bond had been cemented by love and tragedy.

'Ready for the grand tour?' Hugh strode over to the front door, mastering the art of smart casual in his designer chinos and polo shirt. The Breitling watch on his wrist glinted as it caught in the sun's reflection.

Danny only had two looks: work smart, or work casual. They were basically the same thing, with or without a waistcoat.

Connor only had one look: student casual. Which was hardly unusual when you were twenty-two and yet to enter the world of employment. Danny didn't begrudge his brother his lack of responsibilities; adulthood had a lot to answer for.

Danny took after their father, tall and solid, his colouring lighter than his brother's. Connor took after their mother with his slender frame, and had inherited her dark eyes and jet-black wavy hair, which almost reached his shoulders. Despite his love of loose-fitting jeans and baggy hoodies, Connor still made an impact. He'd been a cute kid who'd grown into a handsome man, even if he didn't realise it. His self-confidence had taken a hit of late.

Danny certainly felt like the poor relation as they followed Hugh into the elite mews property.

'Open-plan living area,' Hugh said, gesturing to the

expanse of white stretching ahead. 'Kitchen to your right, staff quarters to your left.' The space was accented with glass and chrome, and magazine-styled to perfection. Clean lines, large designer pieces of furniture and exotic plants filled the floor space. Forget cosy rugs or family photos, this was like a show home, as if no one had ever lived there.

Connor gazed upwards, his mouth opening in awe as he took in the grand glass mezzanine above. 'Wow.'

Danny made a mental note to avoid cooking anything messy for fear of ruining the white floorboards. They'd eat in the garden.

'There are four double ensuite bedrooms upstairs, and a self-contained garden room on this level.' Hugh handed Danny a set of keys. 'There's no lift, annoyingly, so I'm assuming you'll need to take the garden room with your hip problems.'

Danny flinched at the mention of his injury, and also at the mention of a lift—even the lack of one. He wouldn't have used the elevator anyway, not after what happened ten months ago. He grew sweaty just thinking about getting trapped inside one again.

He glanced at Connor to see if Hugh's comment had caused his brother any pain, but Connor seemed fine—even if he did have his hands tucked under his armpits, as if he was afraid of touching anything.

'Can I check upstairs?' Connor looked mildly intrigued at the prospect of staying in such a fancy crib.

Hugh gave him a slow smile. 'Make yourself at home. The place is yours.'

'Temporarily,' Danny added, still uncomfortable at accepting help from his friend, however grateful he was. 'And don't jump from the balcony,' he joked, and then instantly regretted his insensitivity when Connor flinched. 'Sorry, poor attempt at humour.'

'Don't worry about it. I'm used to bad dad jokes.' Connor's smile didn't quite reach his eyes.

Danny watched his brother disappear upstairs, before dropping his head in his hands. 'Shit … shit … shit.'

'Still walking on eggshells, I see.' Hugh patted his back.

Danny raked his hands through his hair. 'I'm an idiot.'

'Understandable, in the circumstances.' Hugh glanced towards the spiral staircase, no doubt checking Connor was out of earshot. 'How's he doing?'

'I have no idea,' Danny said, sighing. 'Sometimes he opens up and talks to me, and other times it's like the drawbridge is down and I can't reach him. It's torture.'

Before Connor's arrest, they'd always been so close, a team, facing adversity together. Conversation had been easy and open, and now every topic seemed to be peppered with emotional landmines waiting to detonate. Danny felt overwhelmed by it all.

'It's a normal response, given what's happened,' Hugh assured him.

'But it's not Connor.' Danny walked over to the panoramic window and stared at the communal garden below with its stone water fountain and manmade bridge. 'Or not the Connor he used to be. I want my brother back. The energetic, lively kid who never stopped smiling.'

Hugh joined him by the window. 'You realise that's an unrealistic expectation? And he's not a kid anymore, he's a man. This will take more than a band aid and a kiss to make it better.'

'I know.'

'It'll take time to process what's happened. There's no quick fix.'

'I know that too.' Logically he knew that, but the interim was torture.

Hugh rested his hand on Danny's shoulder. 'All you can do is be supportive and patient.'

'Thanks, doctor.'

Hugh laughed. 'You should be grateful, I normally charge extortionate rates for my counselling services.'

'Which is how you can afford a place like this.'

'Oh, this isn't mine,' he said, casually looking around. 'This is part of the family's portfolio. An investment property.'

Danny avoided eye-contact. 'It won't be with a couple of freeloaders staying here.'

'You're my guests.'

'I'd feel more comfortable if we paid rent.' He hated feeling like a financial burden.

'Out of the question.' Hugh squeezed Danny's shoulder. 'And don't insult me again by mentioning it, or we'll be falling out.'

Danny attempted a smile. 'We never fall out.'

'So don't break tradition now.'

Danny swallowed hard. 'Thanks again for helping us. As soon as the house in Henley sells we'll look to buy somewhere locally.'

'No rush.' Hugh eased Danny to face him, holding him by the shoulders. 'And no thanks required. You're family. Not by blood, but in all other aspects. I cleaned up enough toddler accidents to warrant being an honorary uncle. You're doing the right thing. A change of scenery will do you both good. He'll bounce back soon enough.'

Danny hoped so. The last eighteen months had been agony. Moving area was a desperate attempt to draw a line under everything that had happened and enable them to move on. He knew persuading Connor to return to uni wouldn't help things, even if his brother quitting before taking his final exams was heart-breaking. But Hugh had been right. Connor's mental wellbeing was more important than obtaining a degree. Hopefully a new start away from anyone who knew what had happened was the key to them both recovering.

Danny met Hugh's watchful gaze. 'He's lucky to have you in his life. We both are.'

Hugh tilted his head, a questioning look on his face. 'Not sleeping?'

Danny frowned. 'Why d'you say that?'

'You only get sentimental when you're tired.'

Danny pushed Hugh away. 'Bugger off.'

His friend laughed. 'Spoken like a true Brit. It's only taken two decades, but we've beaten the Americanisms out of you. If I can just get you to use a knife and fork properly, I'll be a happy man.'

Danny rolled his eyes. 'I'll never understand your obsession with cutlery. You're the only person I know who owns a scallop fork.'

'Etiquette, darling. It's not a proper dinner banquet without a cucumber server and grape shears. Have my parents taught you nothing?'

Danny grinned, appreciating his mate's efforts to lift the mood.

Hugh picked up a gadget and aimed it at the huge glass doors, which slowly began opening. 'Besides, you're not the only person who complains, James hates it too. He's never recovered from my mother mistaking him for staff when they first met. It was the veterinary van that confused her, she thought he'd been hired to geld the horses. It was quite the mix up. He still feels the need to lower his eyes and curtsey whenever he sees her.'

Danny followed Hugh onto the veranda. 'Poor man had no idea what he was taking on marrying you, did he?'

Hugh grinned. 'He knows now.'

Smiling, Danny looked over the edge of the veranda. Cushioned below was one of London's hidden gems, a secret walled garden enjoyed only by the residents of the mews. A canopy of large trees and the sound of running water from the fountain added to its tranquillity.

A beat passed, before Hugh asked the inevitable. 'So, how are you doing? And don't insult my intelligence by telling me you're fine. You couldn't possibly be fine, so don't bother lying to me.'

Leaning on the railing, Danny stared into the pond, watching a bird flapping its wings. 'I guess that's the downside of having a shrink as a best mate.'

Hugh smiled. 'I prefer to think of it as a bonus.'

'I know. And so do I, really.' Danny knew things would have been much worse without Hugh's support. 'I couldn't have coped these last few months without you. But it means I can't pretend everything's okay. You know me too well.'

Hugh's arm slid around Danny's shoulder. 'There's nothing you can say that will shock me, so don't hide. It's important Connor seeks help from an independent practitioner, it wouldn't be appropriate for me to treat him, but it's different with you.'

Danny frowned. 'How so?'

'Because I know darned well you wouldn't see anyone if it wasn't me, so you're stuck with me. The good news is, I'm free of charge, discreet, and non-judgemental. Plus, I love you, so you know I have your best interests at heart.'

Danny eased himself away from his friend's hug. 'Right.'

Hugh laughed. 'Poor Danny. Still suffering from intimacy issues and you're almost forty.'

'I blame my parents. And I'm thirty-six.'

'I blame your parents too. And yet the metaphorical umbilical cord was severed eighteen years ago when you left the US.'

'Only because they died.'

Hugh shrugged. 'True.'

Danny often wondered how things might have turned out if his parents had lived. Would he have returned home to the US? Made amends with them? Healed the rift? He certainly wouldn't have become a surrogate parent at age nineteen and swapped partying with uni mates to making school runs and visiting dinosaur museums. He'd still been a kid himself, forced to grow up too soon and take responsibility for caring for another human being. He'd never resented Connor or regretted becoming his guardian, but he still mourned the loss of his youth and being able to have fun and be reckless and free. All that had changed overnight. One day he was lying in bed recovering from a hangover, the next he was answering the door to social workers and receiving the news that would change his life forever.

Hugh's tone turned sombre. 'Either way, you can't blame your current aversion to relationships on your parents' influence, it's your own choice entirely.'

'Don't I know it.' Danny's body stiffened, as it always did when thoughts of Maisie Marshall seeped through the gaps in his carefully constructed defences. 'Love is dangerous. People get hurt.'

Hugh let out a lengthy sigh. 'You love Connor.'

Danny turned to his friend. 'And look what that's done to me.' He rubbed his chest. 'I'm an emotional wreck.'

'And yet when faced with the scenario of potentially losing him, you went to extraordinary lengths to save him. You need love in your life as much as the next person.'

'Connor is enough.' Danny felt himself flush. 'And you ... of course.'

'You *love* me?' Hugh feigned shock. 'The impenetrable Daniel Jackson loves me? No, stop, I can't deal with this outpouring of emotion. Reign it in, for goodness sake, you'll have me in floods.'

Danny turned away, embarrassed. 'Stop taking the piss. I'm trying.'

'I know you are, and I love you for it.' He kissed Danny's cheek. 'Even if you are infuriating.'

Connor appeared behind them.

'Ah, the man of the moment.' Hugh turned to smile at him. 'Like what you see?'

Connor nodded eagerly, looking a lot younger than his twenty-two years. 'There's a swimming pool in the basement.'

Hugh tutted. 'Well, of course there is. We're not savages.'

Smiling, Danny shook his head. 'Prick.'

Hugh grinned. 'Spoken like a true Brit.'

Chapter Three

SOFIA

Thursday, 29th May

Sofia's pulse quickened as the train pulled into the station and she searched the mass of bodies swarming through the carriage doors. Her heart was thumping so hard she was surprised the other commuters couldn't hear it.

She strained her head as more bodies squashed into the space, causing the passengers to grumble and shift into non-existent gaps.

Just when she feared he wouldn't be on the train, the woman in front shifted position and she saw him. He was standing in front of her, one hand holding onto the rail, his body jerking with the movement of the train as it pulled away.

It was an illogical feeling. She knew nothing about this man, what his name was, what his voice sounded like, or whether he was kind and considerate, or a nasty thug. And yet a pull within her made her want to reach out and run her hands through his wavy black hair. Not that she'd ever dream of approaching him—she was far too introverted, admiring from a distance was as far as her bravery went.

She glanced discretely at him from her seat, trying not to draw attention. He was so close she could read the Superdry label on his jacket, see the depth of his brown eyes and admire the soft hair framing his jawline. He was only a few inches taller than her, and like her, he avoided eye-contact with the other commuters.

It only made her like him more. He wasn't rugged, like the men her sister Luisa favoured. He was beautiful. There was no other word to describe the paleness of his skin and the flutter of his long lashes. He was mesmerising. And she'd got it bad.

But he didn't look her way. He didn't even register her existence—like he hadn't on the other four days since he'd started sharing her morning commute.

Why was it that men she wasn't attracted to approached her, but the men she'd like to talk to never did? Luisa's theory was that Sofia intimated men. Her sister claimed Sofia's outward appearance didn't match her reserved personality, referring to her busty curves and slim frame as 'porn-star attributes', which Sofia had never found complimentary. Clothes fitted her snugly, which often drew men's gazes downwards, and invited salacious suggestions, which made her uncomfortable. In contrast, if the men she wanted to notice her caught her eye, they'd become flustered and look away, as if fearful of being inappropriate.

Proving her point, the train pulled into White City and the man disappeared without a backwards glance. She tried to find him amongst the wave of bodies crowding the platform, but he was gone.

Sighing, she rested her head against the seat, her mind awash with 'what-if' scenarios. If she was brave like Luisa, she'd have flirted with him and asked for his phone number. If she was confident like her elder sister, Elena, she'd have struck up a conversation with him and discovered whether he was as adorable as he seemed. Instead, she'd cast him wistful glances and looked away before he'd spotted her staring at him.

Sofia wasn't timid when it came to other areas of her life. She had an extensive client portfolio at the media firm where she worked, and she line-managed a team of five people. She was assertive and confident in her abilities, a natural team leader—according to her colleagues, anyway.

She was the same at home. Despite being the quietest of the three sisters, she held her own when it came to family dynamics. She'd adopted the parental role since their mother had died and Papi had returned to Colombia, stepping up to look after Luisa and helping to run the family home. She didn't mind, she was homely by nature, content to spend her time cooking, reading, and listening to music. An evening on the sofa watching a romantic film was preferable to hitting the bars in town, and she had been voted by her sisters as the one 'most likely to settle down'.

The trouble was, until four days ago, she'd never met anyone she could see herself 'settling down' with. She wasn't going to achieve her dream of living 'happily ever after' if she didn't have the nerve to say hello to a man, was she? Besides, he probably had a girlfriend. Why wouldn't he? He was gorgeous, and she was getting carried away by an unrealistic romantic ideal.

When the train pulled into North Acton station, she squeezed past the bodies crammed into the carriage and exited the train, ignoring the man whose arm brushed against her chest. It wasn't the first time. Sadly, she doubted it would be the last.

It was only a short walk to Park Royal. She liked the opportunity to exercise her legs and clear her mind.

She was soon entering the lift in the plush building where she worked and heading up to the top floor where her office was situated. She wasn't artistic, like Luisa, or sporty like Elena, and a job in media hadn't been her dream career, but everyone had been excited for her when she'd won the hotly contested graduate role, so she'd faked enthusiasm in the hope that time would lead her onto something more appealing. Five years had passed, and she was still waiting.

Sofia knew she should be grateful. She was proud of achieving so much at twenty-seven, and yet she couldn't shift the weight in her chest that had landed when their mum had unexpectedly died. A feeling compounded when Papi had disappeared back to Colombia. She missed them dreadfully and her life had felt slightly empty ever since.

'Miss Romero?' The sound of her name stopped her from entering her office. One of the HR secretaries scurried towards her. 'Miss Romero, your presence is required at a meeting on the fourth floor.'

Meetings on the fourth floor were never a good sign, and neither was the prefix of 'Miss' when using her name—formal titles were only used when trouble was afoot.

Sofia tried for a smile. 'I have a staff appraisal this morning.'

'Mr Ackroyd needs to see you immediately. He's waiting in his office.' The secretary rubbed her palms on her skirt, seemingly panicked at the idea of not following Mr Ackroyd's instructions. 'If you'll follow me.'

Sofia hung up her coat in her office and placed her bag in her desk drawer, sliding her phone into her skirt pocket.

She needed a moment to compose her thoughts, even if she'd anticipated this moment coming. Senior management hadn't been happy with her attendance record of late. Perhaps today was the day things switched from informal reprimands to an official warning.

'Cancel my appraisal meeting, would you, Rupe?' she said to her colleague as she passed his desk, aware that her team had wary looks on their faces. It seemed as though they expected the worst too. 'Hopefully I won't be long.'

Ignoring a few raised eyebrows, she was escorted across the office as if being led to the docks by the prosecution. Neither of them spoke as they entered the lift and travelled down to the fourth floor.

Silence greeted them as they exited the lift and she was shown into an interview room where three people were already seated around a large table.

Giles Ackroyd, the Head of HR, stood up when she entered. 'Thank you for joining us, Miss Romero. I assume you know my colleague, Mr Smithson—he'll be taking minutes of the meeting. And this is Rosemary Pitts, solicitor and CEO of our parent company.' He gestured towards a stern looking woman in a grey trouser suit.

Sofia's unease increased. Her employers were bringing out the big guns.

Giles Ackroyd pointed to a chair. 'Take a seat, Miss Romero.'

Sofia sat down, folding her hands in her lap to hide their shaking.

Clearing his throat, Mr Ackroyd returned to his seat and pulled a file towards him. 'This meeting has been arranged to address the issue of repeated absences from work, a situation that seems to have deteriorated over recent weeks. I note you were absent again yesterday?'

Sofia nodded. 'I had to attend a treatment plan meeting with the medical team looking after my sister.'

He looked up from the file. 'Which resulted in you failing to attend a meeting with one of your clients?'

Sofia flinched. 'I rescheduled the meeting before I left.'

'Something I'm led to believe you'd already done twice before?'

There was no point denying it. 'Yes.'

Giles Ackroyd exchanged a look with the CEO, as if gaining her consent for what was coming next. 'When we spoke about this situation two weeks ago, I pressed upon you the need for your career to be your priority and informed you that action would be taken if further absences occurred.'

Sofia's mouth had gone dry, but the water jug was out of reach, no doubt done on purpose to make her suffer. 'I assure you I take my work very seriously, and I try to provide my clients with the best possible service. However, I also have care responsibilities for my younger sister, who has a serious medical condition, and there are times when I have to deal with emergencies arising from her complex needs. She currently has a chest infection.'

'A chest infection?' The CEO's tone questioned the seriousness of the situation.

Sofia met the woman's glare. 'My sister has Cystic Fibrosis, a condition that affects her lungs and digestive system. This often requires intravenous antibiotics and additional oxygen if she doesn't respond to oral medication.'

Her three accusers exchanged awkward looks.

'While we sympathise with your situation, Miss Romero, you must appreciate we have a business to run.' Giles Ackroyd poured himself a glass of water, failing to offer Sofia one. 'Client welfare must take precedence, and we cannot ignore these repeated absences and not take action. We must treat staff equally, and this behaviour would not be tolerated by any other member of the organisation.'

The CEO nodded her agreement.

'You're a valued account manager, but your tardiness is affecting your productivity. For that reason, we're forced to start formal disciplinary proceedings. This isn't something we take lightly, but it's something we feel is necessary to maintain the level of professionalism we strive for as a company.'

Sofia licked her dry lips, trying to prise them apart. 'I understand that, and I'm truly sorry for causing such disruption. However, I've worked for the company for five years and until my mother's death four months ago, I hadn't taken a single sick day, or taken any unauthorised time off. This is a temporary situation and one I hope will be resolved when my father returns from Colombia.'

Mr Ackroyd tilted his head. 'And when will that be?'

Sofia's cheeks grew warm. 'I don't know.'

'A week? A month?'

'I honestly don't know. He's dealing with a business matter.'

It was hard not to feel let down by Papi. Sofia adored him, they all did, they were a close-knit family, and their mum's death had shattered them all. She understood his need to free up monetary assets, but he'd been gone over two months and showed no signs of returning. His daughters were suffering too, but he didn't seem to understand that. Or if he did, it wasn't enough to expedite his return.

Mr Ackroyd remained unsympathetic. 'You cannot expect the company to continue allowing repeated absences with no reassurance the situation will be resolved any time soon.'

Sofia glanced at the other two, hoping for an ally, but she was met with stony-eyed glares. 'I appreciate that, but the staff handbook states that compassionate leave can be granted for registered carers, which I am.'

'The policy relates to immediate family only,' the CEO replied, as if anticipating the point being raised.

Sofia looked at her. 'My sister *is* immediate family.'

The CEO opened the handbook and read from a section bookmarked with a post-it note. 'Immediate family is classed as a child or parent of the employee. It does not extend to siblings, grandparents, or other extended family.'

Sofia had hoped these rules were open to interpretation. 'My sister has no parents to look after her. She relies on me. Can't you make an exception in this instance?'

Mr Ackroyd sighed, as if weighed down by the difficulties of being head of HR. 'I'm afraid our position remains unchanged. The company offers a comprehensive benefits package, which we feel is reasonable and generous. Introducing discretionary decisions would only encourage other staff to take advantage of the rules.'

The weight in Sofia's stomach grew heavier. So much for them showing her some compassion.

'This meeting constitutes a first official warning,' Mr Ackroyd continued, picking up his pen. 'If your attendance doesn't improve with immediate effect, the company will have no option but to issue a second official warning. After which, your contract of employment will be terminated.' He closed the file. 'Notes of this meeting will be sent to you and a copy placed on your personnel record. You have the right to appeal any final decision, which must be submitted in writing within seven days of your dismissal.'

Sofia felt tears welling. Things had escalated quickly if they were talking about dismissal.

'Do you have any questions relating to the process?' The CEO's tone was abrupt.

Sofia shook her head. There was no point prolonging the agony. 'I have no questions.'

Giles Ackroyd stood up. 'Thank you for your time this morning, Miss Romero. I sincerely hope no further action is required. We would be sorry to lose such a valued employee.'

They didn't sound sorry, they sounded judgemental and mean.

Leaving the room, she wasn't sure what to do with herself. Collapsing in a heap and crying wouldn't help, so she aimed for the water cooler by the lift.

A tight throat made swallowing hard, but she forced down the water and took a few deep breaths, trying not to panic. She couldn't afford to lose her job. The house might be mortgage free, but there were bills to pay. Bills that her and Elena barely managed to cover between them. Losing an income would be a huge problem for all of them.

Any hope of remaining calm evaporated when her phone vibrated in her pocket and she read the message.

Breathing not good. Called an ambulance. Admitted to ICU. Bruised from several attempts to insert cannula. Feeling tearful. Need my sister. Can you come to the hospital?

Sofia sagged against the water cooler.

How on earth was she supposed to prioritise work when her sister needed her so badly?

Chapter Four

ELENA

Wednesday, 4th June

The smell of roasting coffee filled the morning air as Elena headed down Portobello Road, making it impossible for her to walk past the barista van without succumbing to temptation. It wasn't as if she hadn't earned it, she'd already been for a run this morning, and a caffeine hit was reward for her efforts.

Shifting her phone to the other ear, she leaned against the side of *Portobello's Gold* jewellery shop as she waited for the queue to disperse. She didn't want her fellow Notting Hill residents to overhear her conversation with Luisa and learn about her sister's latest health issues.

'Did you get any sleep last night?' she asked, knowing how much Luisa loathed being in hospital.

'It's impossible to sleep with so much noise. Machines beeping, patients groaning, and incessant coughing. If I don't get parole soon I'll go insane.'

Elena felt for her sister, she wanted her home too. Hospital stays were scary for the whole family, not just Luisa. There was always the underlying fear that one day her sister wouldn't make it home. 'Have your oxygen levels improved?'

'Not really. The doctor said my SATS are still too low for him to discharge me. My fingernails are an attractive shade of blue, and that's without gels.'

Elena rubbed her forehead. Things were not improving as quickly as she'd like. Sometimes Luisa responded to treatment and was out of hospital within a couple of days. Other times it seemed like her body was resistant to the drugs—or, more likely, her body wasn't up to fighting off the infection, a more worrying scenario. 'Is your breathing better?'

'Until I move about, and then it's like I'm a hundred years old. There's only so much lying in bed watching Netflix I can take.' She made a raspberry sound. 'Anyway, I'm bored talking about my health. Entertain me. What are you doing?'

A group of women had been served and were now moving away from the van, shortening the queue. Good. Elena was running late. 'I'm on my way to work. I have a new client booked this morning, post-op ACL repair.'

'Please tell me he's a six-foot rugby player with thighs the size of tree trunks.'

Elena laughed. 'Sorry to disappoint. Sixty year old woman who fell over on a bus when it braked sharply.'

'Dull.'

'I'm sure she'd agree, three weeks on crutches is no fun.'

'Have you no hot new patients to tell me about? Not even a mildly attractive banker with a sprained ankle?'

'Not as yet, but the day is young, who knows what

accidents might occur.' The queue moved again and Elena caught sight of a man who seemed to be taking in his surroundings. 'Although there's a nice-looking man queuing for coffee at the van.'

'Excellent. Details, please. I currently have no love life stuck in here, so I need to live vicariously through you. Age? Height? Actor resemblance? Give me the lowdown.'

Elena never judged men by looks alone, but her sister needed distracting, so she played along to ease Luisa's suffering. 'He's tall, medium-build, late thirties, and reminds me of ...' she squinted, assessing his dirty blond hair, prominent cheek bones and square jaw. 'Ryan Reynolds.'

'Ooooh, maybe it's actually him?' Luisa sounded excited. 'He might be filming in the area.'

'Nah, he just looks a bit like him. He has the same mischievous eyes.'

Luisa laughed, which was a great sound ... until she started coughing and Elena had to hold the phone away until the fit subsided.

'Is he alone?' Luisa eventually asked, still wheezing.

Elena checked the queue. 'He appears to be.'

'What's he wearing?'

'A dark grey three-piece suit.'

'Oh, god, not another suit.'

Elena winced, as she always did at the mention of 'the suit'—or rather, her boyfriend of five years, Felix.

It was difficult to get her head around everything that had happened over the last four months. Up until January, everything had been fine. Or at least, she thought it had been fine, but then Felix announced he'd accepted a new job in Manchester and was relocating. He didn't want them to split up, and hoped she'd move with him, but when she pointed out she couldn't leave Luisa, they'd argued over where her loyalties lay. He'd accused her of pandering to her family, and she'd accused him of putting work before family. They were mid-argument when her phone rang with the news that her mother was being blue-lighted to the nearest emergency department.

Felix didn't come with her to the hospital that night. He did attend her mother's funeral two weeks later, but left the next day for Manchester as planned, unwilling to delay the start of his new job. Was it any wonder she was bitter?

'Not all men who wear suits are like Felix.'

Luisa scoffed. 'I've yet to be convinced. Does he look judgemental?'

Elena watched the man smile at a small child and pick up the kid's toy for him, which had fallen from his buggy. Elena couldn't blame the mother when she offered him a flirtatious smile—she was feeling a little warm herself.

'Who knows,' she said with a shrug, admiring his straight spine. He had good posture, the physio in her noticed these things.

She'd always defended Luisa's accusation that Felix was 'boring', he just wasn't as playful or demonstrative as they were. His family were accountants and actuaries whose idea of a good night out was watching the opera and attending polo matches. They'd never appreciated the Romeros' love of dressing up as Hobbits to attend a *Secret Cinema* event, or pedal-boating on the Thames in the pouring rain for the hell of it.

It was only after they'd broken up that she'd been able to analyse the relationship properly. In hindsight, maybe they weren't as compatible as she'd imagined. She hadn't enjoyed being coerced into attending highbrow quizzes, and he'd found her love of pillow fights too 'silly'. As for public displays of affection, they were 'unnecessary' and 'inappropriate'. He wouldn't even hold her hand in public. Realising all this didn't make the breakup any less painful. It still smarted that he'd chosen his career over her.

Elena sighed, still adjusting to the change in her relationship status. 'What does judgemental even look like?'

'Rigid posture, sombre expression, doesn't laugh when someone trips up the kerb. Someone who looks at everyone with a critical eye, as if expecting them to nick their wallet.' Luisa didn't lack imagination, that was for sure.

The man reached the front of the queue and ordered his coffee. 'This guy seems chilled enough. He's smiling at the barista, so that's something.'

'I need convincing. Follow him and see where he works. If he's an another actuary, run a mile.'

The queue had disappeared, so Elena headed over to the van and ordered a cappuccino with extra chocolate sprinkles. 'I'm not following a strange man,' she hissed into the phone.

'Why not? Some of my best dates have resulted from a spot of stalking.'

Elena rolled her eyes. 'I wish you wouldn't tell me these things. Like I don't worry about you enough. Your lack of personal safety is alarming.'

'Think of it as living on the edge. A terminal illness removes any fear of being bumped off via other means.'

Elena stepped away from the van, lowering her voice. 'Your condition isn't terminal. It's life-limiting.'

'Which is a polite way of saying I'm unlikely to reach forty.'

'People with CF live longer every year. The latest treatments are amazing.' Elena needed to believe this as much as Luisa did.

'Then why am I stuck in hospital on an IV drip? Every infection leaves me weaker, no point denying it. And how did we get onto my health again? Stop depressing me, woman. Tell me about the hot Ryan Reynolds lookalike.'

Elena strained her head to see where he'd gone. 'Well, he's now heading down Portobello Road. He's walking slowly, looking at the stalls and pausing when something catches his eye. I'm guessing he's not local, he seems a bit overwhelmed by all the chaos.'

'Good. Maybe he needs a tour guide. Go offer to show him the sights. Or better still, push him in front of a bus. Cause an injury so he needs to see a physio and then offer him your card.'

The barista indicated Elena's coffee was ready, so she went to fetch it. 'Your mind is a strange and scary place, Luisa Romero. Only you could come up with such a crazy idea. And besides, there's nothing romantic about attempted murder.'

'On the contrary. Men like assertive women. Have I taught you nothing?'

Smiling, Elena headed away from the van. 'There's a thin line between being assertive and being a certified nutter.'

'Semantics. ... Have you lost sight of him?'

'No, he's turning off the main road, heading towards ...' Elena stopped and watched the man opening the iron gate. He favoured his left side slightly, pausing to rub his right hip before continuing. Interesting. Maybe he did need a physio after all?

'Elena? ... What's happening? Has he been run over? Mugged? Fallen down a manhole? What?'

'He's heading into the building where I work.'

'You're kidding me.'

Elena watched as he unlocked the door and disappeared inside. 'He must be the new tenant.'

'Bullseye. Time for action. Go introduce yourself. Smile, flirt, suss him out, and then phone me immediately with the lowdown. I want details, including his star sign and his marital status. Okay?'

Elena laughed at her sister's ludicrous demands. 'I'm not interrogating the poor man. Especially as I need to get on his good side.'

'Did you say bedside?'

Elena shook her head, still laughing. 'I'm hoping he'll swap offices with me.'

'So go be charming. Disarm him with your feminine wiles and get what you need. Also, get his phone number.'

'Speak later.'

'Can I stay on the line and listen?'

'No.' Elena headed for the building.

'Spoilsport.'

Hanging up, Elena went inside the three-storey Georgian town house and instead of heading up the stairwell to her treatment room, or taking the claustrophobic lift, she tapped on the glass door of the ground floor office.

'Hello?' She pushed open the door. 'Anyone here?'

And there he was, looking as striking as he'd been on first sighting. It hadn't been wishful thinking, then.

He was over by the window, minus his jacket now, looking at the London views while sipping his coffee. As he turned to face her, she noticed a glint of something promising in his brown eyes, visible through a pair of black square-framed glasses. He looked surprised to see her standing in the doorway, his dirty-blond eyebrows lifting slightly at the sight of her.

'Hi, I'm Elena,' she said, marching into the room with

an air of confidence she hoped presented her as a woman to be taken seriously. 'Elena Romero. I work on the third floor. Physiotherapist. You must be Daniel J Jackson, the new tenant.'

'Pleasure to meet you, Elena.' He extended his hand to meet hers. 'Call me Danny.'

His hand was soft and toasty warm from where he'd been holding his coffee carton. She felt an instant tingle, which wasn't unpleasant. It'd been a while since she'd been attracted to anyone—she'd almost forgotten what it felt like. 'Are you settling in okay?'

'Getting there. I've nearly finished unpacking.' He gestured to the crates on the floor, filled with dense-looking legal publications. 'It's a great space. I like the big windows. I've always had a thing for period features, it amazes me the buildings here date back so far.'

She was pleased to note the shelves were empty and the desk clear. She wouldn't be inconveniencing him too much by asking him to move offices. 'I thought I detected an accent. American?'

He nodded. 'Although the folks back home think I sound British now.'

He had a nice voice, rhythmical and easy-going. 'How long have you lived here?'

'Eighteen years.'

'Nearly as long as me. My family moved here from Colombia when I was eight.'

He took a sip of coffee. 'You speak Spanish?'

She nodded, her eyes drawn to his full mouth when he licked away a smudge of coffee. 'Although not so much these days, mainly when I'm talking to Papi. My youngest sister was only a toddler when we moved away, so she's not fluent. She gets grumpy if she can't understand what we're saying and hates the idea of missing out on gossip.'

He smiled. 'And is she?'

Oh, inevitably.' Elena grinned. 'It's fun to wind her up. Isn't that what sisters do?'

'I wouldn't know.'

'Shame. Sisters are great ... most of the time.' She wiggled an eyebrow.

He laughed and held her gaze for a moment, his eyes lingering before shifting away. It seemed she wasn't the only one doing a spot of checking out.

What did he make of her, she wondered? She'd never been girly or beautiful like Sofia. She wore her dark hair short and she'd inherited her mother's sporty physique, but she was comfortable in her own skin and happy with her lot. Feeling strong and empowered was more important than looking like an Instagram hottie.

What she did possess was a killer smile ... or so she'd been told, so she unleashed it on him, hoping to stun him into complying with her request.

Bingo. His eyes widened and he ran a finger around the neck of his shirt, as if the garment was suddenly too tight.

She stepped closer, ramping up the intensity. 'The thing is ... seeing as how you haven't finished unpacking ... how would you feel about switching offices with me?'

His smile faded.

Had she been too abrupt? She needed to get in quick and explain. 'Only, I'm on the third floor. There's a lift, but it's cramped, and most of my patients have injuries or mobility issues, so using the stairs is a problem. Sometimes the lift isn't working either, and that causes a problem, as you can imagine. It would be really helpful if I could switch to this space on the ground floor and you take the third floor. Would that be possible, do you think?'

He placed his coffee carton down on the empty desk. 'I'm afraid not.'

She moved even closer, keen to win him over. 'It's a great space, bigger than this area.'

'I don't need more space.'

'The views are fantastic too,' she said, pointing to the large sash windows. 'You look right across the green adjacent to Portobello Road. It's stunning, especially in the spring when the cherry blossoms are out.'

'Sorry, but I'm happy where I am.'

That was it? She waited a beat, wondering if he'd elaborate, but he didn't say another word. He just looked at her, his expression devoid of any emotion. Was he a robot? 'Even though I've explained about my patients' needs?'

'I also have clients, and ground-floor access would suit my business better.'

'But your clients don't have health issues.'

'Some do.' He headed over to the door.

This wasn't going as planned. 'Why don't you come up and see the space before making a decision?'

'No, thanks.'

She lifted her hands in exasperation. 'That's it?'

He opened the door. 'That's it.'

Why wouldn't he consider her request? She'd given him a perfectly reasonable argument to support her request and he was dismissing it without so much as an explanation. 'Can I ask why?'

He pushed his glasses up his nose. 'I've already explained why. It would be inconvenient for my clients and ...' he gave a short shrug, '... because I don't want to.' He continued holding the door open, an unsubtle hint for her to leave. 'Anything else I can help with, just let me know.'

She stopped in her tracks. Was he serious? She searched his face, noticing his slightly forced smile. He couldn't have been more unhelpful if he'd tried, but it was clear he wasn't backing down. With a sarcastic rolling of her eyes, she brushed past him and exited his office. 'Thanks for nothing, Daniel J Jackson.' The J stood for *Jerk*, obviously.

'Thanks for popping by. Maybe see you around.' He closed the door behind her.

Not if she could help it. She hoped he dropped a heavy crate on his foot while unpacking his stupid boxes. It would serve him right. Unhelpful man.

So much for thinking he might be accommodating and understanding. No such luck.

Her phone rang as she stomped up the stairs towards her office. 'Hi, Luisa.'

'So, how'd it go? Is he as hot as we'd hoped?'

'Absolute non-starter. A complete and utter ...' she checked behind her, just to make sure he hadn't opened the door, '... *suit*.'

Luisa sighed. 'What a disappointment.'

Elena trudged up the stairs.

Her sentiments exactly.

Chapter Five

DANNY

Wednesday, 4th June

The moment Elena Romero left his office, Danny kicked a waste paper basket across the room and sunk onto his work chair, dropping his head into his hands. Frustration and shame consumed him. Why the hell hadn't he just told her the truth?

Pride, that's why. His stupid male ego had prevented him from telling her about his injury. Instead, he'd been rude, uncooperative and acted like a complete dick.

So much for a fresh start and making a new life for himself. He'd managed to alienate his fellow tenant on day one. All because he was embarrassed.

Why was he embarrassed? The truth was almost too humiliating to admit. It was because she was attractive. Talk about pathetic. He was thirty-six, for crying out loud. The sight of a gorgeous woman should not interfere with rational behaviour. He was a feeble human male, unable to admit to a weakness in front of a hot woman.

He scrubbed at his face, trying to erase the shame.

It's not like she'd even judge him for it. The woman was a physiotherapist, she treated injured people all the time. Admitting he had a stiff hip wasn't exactly a big deal. It wasn't like he was admitting to murder.

Running his hands through his hair, he stood up, sending the office chair skidding across the wooden flooring. This was ridiculous. He needed to man-up, apologise, and tell her why he wasn't able to swap offices with her. Once she knew the truth, she'd understand his reasoning. Simple. But leaving things to fester would only make the situation worse and cause an atmosphere between them, which would make co-inhabiting in the building a nightmare. He needed to resolve this immediately.

Stretching his neck from side to side, he strode purposefully towards the door and into the lobby area.

Blood pounded in his ears at the mere sight of the elevator door, so he headed for the stairway and began ascending. Pain kicked in after four steps. By step ten his hip was on fire. By stair fifteen the joint had seized up entirely and he couldn't lift his leg.

Sagging against the wall, he waited for his breathing to settle before descending the stairs, coming down backwards, using one leg at a time, like someone three times his age.

By the time he was back in the lobby, he was faced with two options. Give up, return to his office and find a phone number for her clinic. Or overcome his fear of confined spaces and use the elevator.

It had been eighteen months since his nightmare had first begun, followed by a year of allegations, police interviews, stress and worry, throwing both their lives into utter turmoil. Faced with prosecution and jail time, Connor had reached breaking point and couldn't see a way out of his situation. The idea of Connor feeling so hopeless and alone that he'd contemplate ending it all was pure torture.

The fear Danny had experienced as he'd tried to reach his brother that night would haunt him forever. The thought of losing his beloved brother was unbearable. He hadn't cared about injuring himself in the process, or the sleepless nights that had followed. His only focus had been on reaching Connor in time and making sure he was safe, looked after, supported and pulled back from the brink. Focusing on his own recovery could wait. Supporting Connor couldn't.

He stared at the elevator door, his palms already clammy.

The only way to overcome his fear was to face it head on. He punched the elevator button, and when the door clanked open, he stepped inside. The shake in his hand as he pressed the button for the third floor was bearable, expected, a mere inconvenience—he could do this. But as the shake increased, morphing into a tremble that reverberated up his arms and ran through his body, it became hard to breathe.

As the door started to close, his panic levels increased. Black spots appeared before his eyes and he felt lightheaded. Instinctively, he jammed his foot in the gap to prevent the door closing and clamoured at the door, almost ripping off finger nails as he levered it open.

He became aware of the stairway door opening and Elena Romero stepping into the lobby to greet a woman who had come through the front door, but it wasn't enough to counterbalance the force of his weight being propelled forwards.

The sound of Elena's yelp as he smacked into her hit him as hard as the pain in his hip as he tumbled to the floor, taking Elena down with him.

'What the hell?' she said, thumping his chest. 'Get off me!'

When he failed to immediately move, she shoved him with all her weight, sending him rolling away.

'I'm sorry,' was all he could manage, before almost fainting. Sweat was dripping off him, his was mouth dry, and his vision had blurred.

'Are you drunk?' she barked, getting to her feet.

He shook his head, wishing the tightness in his chest would ease.

'I should report you to the police for assault.'

'Pleased don't.' He'd had his fill of police to last a lifetime. 'I just ...'

'Just what?' she snapped, rubbing her ankle. 'I'm waiting for an explanation.'

His brain was refusing to send correct signals to his mouth. He wanted to explain, to tell her about his injury, his aversion to confined spaces, to assure her he wasn't dangerous, but all that came out of his mouth was a long, shaky groan.

'That's it, I'm calling the police.'

'Please don't.' Danny lifted his hand, willing his panic to subside, which it only did when he heard Hugh's voice cutting through the mayhem.

'Danny? What's happened?' The next thing he knew, Hugh was by his side, one hand grasping his, the other stroking his face. 'It's okay. You're okay. Just breathe.'

'What's wrong with him?' Elena's tone was less abrupt now. 'Is he ill?'

Hugh paused, as if debating how much to say. 'It's

temporary, he'll be fine. You can leave. Don't worry, I'll deal with him.'

'Are you sure? Do you need me to call an ambulance?'

'It's fine, really. I've got this.'

'Well ... if you're sure. I hope he's okay,' she said warily, still rubbing her ankle.

'Thanks for your understanding.' Hugh smiled up at her and Danny could only envy his mate's ability to be charming and in control.

Unlike him, who was a quivering mess on the floor.

Elena crossed to the woman who'd been waiting, wide-eyed and understandably confused. 'I'm sorry about that. I'm Elena, let's head up to my clinic. We'll use the stairs.' She glanced at Danny with a concerned look before leading the woman away.

Hugh waited until Elena had disappeared before turning his attentions to Danny. 'Look at me,' he said, using his assertive counsellor's voice. 'Take a few slow breaths.'

Danny focused on Hugh and the way his blue eyes expressed kindness and concern, the electric light above highlighting the red in his hair.

'That's it,' Hugh said encouragingly. 'You're doing fine. Everything's going to be okay. It's over now.'

'I ... tried to use the ... elevator,' Danny said faintly.

'Well, that was dumb.' Hugh gave him a stern look. 'We've spoken about this. Counselling first, action later, remember? Trauma recovery takes time.'

'I thought I could overcome it.'

'Of course you did, you're male and stubborn. You see this situation as a weakness rather than a reaction to a horrific event. You need to stop expecting everything to return to normal overnight and accept the road to recovery is a slow one.'

Danny rubbed his chest, the wheezing easing slightly. 'Sorry.'

'No apology necessary. Can you stand up?'

'I think so.' Danny got to his feet, leaning against Hugh for support. 'You smell expensive.'

'Good to know.' Hugh led him into his office and eased him onto a chair. 'That's it, I've got you. Slowly does it. Drop your head between your knees.'

Danny did as he was told, feeling a dull thump in his temples as he leaned forwards.

Finally, his heart rate began to slow, the shaking in his limbs subsided.

Hugh rubbed his back. 'That's it, take it easy. I've got you.'

Feeling less faint, Danny sat upright and rubbed his clammy face. His shirt was drenched in sweat. 'What must she think of me?'

'It wasn't a great first impression,' Hugh said dryly, reaching for a water bottle lying on the desk and handing it to Danny. 'Drink.'

'That wasn't our first meeting. The first one was even worse.'

Hugh raised an eyebrow. 'How so?'

Danny unscrewed the water bottle lid. 'She asked me to swap offices with her, I refused.'

'Understandable, given the circumstances.'

'Except I didn't explain the circumstances. I just said no, and rudely.' He took a long swig of water, wishing it was neat gin.

Hugh frowned. 'You didn't tell her about your injury?'

Danny shook his head.

'Or the claustrophobia?'

'Nope.'

Hugh perched against the edge of the desk, one Armani boot crossed over the other. 'Can I ask why?'

Danny shrugged. 'Male pride?'

Hugh rubbed his temples. 'For an intelligent man, you can be infuriatingly dense at times.'

'Tell me something I don't know.' He took another swig of water. 'The moment she left I realised I'd been a dick, so I was trying to get upstairs to apologise and explain, but ... well, you know the rest.'

Hugh sighed. 'The good news is, the damage isn't permanent.'

'I don't see how. She hates me. She thinks I'm a drunk.'

'She'll see reason.'

'You saw the way she looked at me.'

Hugh smiled. 'Elena Romero is one of the kindest, loveliest people I know. Believe me, once she knows the truth, she'll not only forgive you, I guarantee she'll want to help you.'

Danny recoiled. 'That's supposed to make me feel better? I'm humiliated enough.'

'Would you prefer her to stay angry with you?'

Danny flinched. 'No.'

'Then you have no option but to come clean. Pride be damned.'

'Easy for you to say.'

'And easy for you to do.' Hugh rested a hand on Danny's shoulder. 'You just need to show her your true self.'

Danny looked into his mate's delusional eyes. 'God help her.'

Hugh gestured to the water bottle. 'Drink, please.'

Danny downed the rest of the water.

'How are you feeling now?'

'Idiotic.'

'I meant, physically.'

'Fine.' He rubbed his chest. 'I hate feeling like this. I never used to be so flaky.'

Hugh got up and closed the office door. 'Time for some home truths.' He pulled up a chair so he was positioned directly in front of Danny. 'You grew up in a household where love and approval were conditional. Showing emotion was considered weak, and you were constantly criticised and reprimanded for not being who your parents wanted you to be. Your only option was to leave home at eighteen and fly halfway across the world to escape their influence.'

Danny breathed in another waft of Hugh's aftershave. 'Something I've never regretted.'

'I know, but then your life was thrown into chaos with the devastating news that your parents were dead and you were the sole carer of your five-year-old brother.'

Danny's stomach clenched at the memory.

Hugh rested his elbows on his knees, narrowing his gaze. 'This was followed by a decade of hard work, sacrifice, and channelling your energies into ensuring Connor didn't suffer and had the best upbringing possible. And your efforts succeeded—Connor is smart, sensitive, and kind. He's a credit to you.'

Danny blinked hard, trying to stem the threat of tears.

'I never once saw you falter, or doubt yourself during that time. You instinctively knew what Connor needed and you were there for him. But I also never saw you properly grieve for the life that was taken away from you, or the loss you'd suffered. You never cried, got angry, or complained. And to anyone watching from the outside, you were in total control. I kept looking at you thinking, one day it's going to hit him.'

Danny's eyes dropped to the floor. 'And we both know when that happened.'

'Exactly. My point is, nearly losing Connor was a trigger for a whole other load of shit you hadn't really dealt with. Everything that had led up to that point hit you. A meltdown was unavoidable. You think you're failing, you're not. You're finally letting go of all that pent up emotion. It needed to come out at some point. And now it has. You'll come out of this stronger and better for it. Trust me.'

'I hope you're right.'

Hugh held out his hands. 'When am I ever wrong?'

Danny laughed. 'Infuriatingly, never.'

'It's a skill, I know.' Hugh leaned forward and kissed Danny hard on the forehead. 'I've got your back, okay?'

When someone tapped on the door, Danny pulled away from the embrace and frantically wiped his eyes. He wasn't expecting any clients, and whoever it was, he didn't want them to see him like this.

Hugh got up and opened the door. 'Hi, Elena.'

Danny inwardly cringed. Couldn't she have waited until after he'd pulled himself together?

'My patient had to cut our session short, so I thought I'd check everything was okay before heading back up.'

'That's kind of you.' Hugh opened the door fully so Elena could see Danny. 'As you can see, he's doing okay.'

Danny didn't feel okay. He was damp from sweating, his eyes were sore from the effort of not crying, and his shirt was dirty from falling on the floor.

An awkward silence filled the air.

Hugh raised an eyebrow, trying to convey a message to Danny to *say something*.

Danny opened his mouth, hoping for an eloquent speech. 'Sorry,' was all that came out.

Elena looked unimpressed. 'Right.'

Hugh sighed. 'Is there anything you'd like to add, Danny? Perhaps let Elena know what you were trying to do?'

Danny's stomach flipped. He felt like he was in front of the headmaster being reprimanded for being cheeky to a teacher. 'I wanted to apologise for not swapping offices with you.'

Elena nodded slowly. 'Okay.'

'And to offer an explanation?' Hugh urged, narrowing his eyes at Danny.

'I'm claustrophobic,' he muttered, like a sulky teenager.

Hugh's stare intensified, his hand gesture indicating more was needed. 'And?'

'And I have a bad hip. I can't climb stairs.' There, he'd said it.

Elena looked between Hugh and Danny. 'You couldn't have just told me that?'

Danny closed his eyes. 'Apparently not.'

Another pause hung in the air.

'Well, thanks for explaining.' Elena sounded uncertain. 'At least I understand now. I hope you feel better soon.'

Hugh gave her a warm smile. 'Thanks for stopping by, Elena. It was kind of you. Hopefully we can put this behind us and make a fresh start as colleagues and friends.' The optimism in his voice was laughable.

Elena's expression conveyed her own doubts about this. 'I'd better get back to my work. Don't worry about the office swap, I get it. We'll stay as we are.'

Hugh waved her off. 'See you around, Elena.'

Elena forced a smile. 'Sure.'

Danny managed a weak smile.

There was a long pause after Hugh closed the door.

When he eventually turned to face Danny, his arms were folded across his chest, and Danny knew a bollocking was coming.

'That went well.' Hugh leant against the door.

Danny dropped his head in his hands and wished he could erase everything that had happened and start the day again.

If only.

Chapter Six

ELENA

Wednesday, 11th June

Elena had spent a busy morning treating a group of teenage rugby players at a local private school, leaving her exhausted and smelling of deep heat and an overload of testosterone. There was something disconcerting about treating six-foot mountains with muscles as solid as concrete, only to discover they were barely fourteen years old. Where did they breed these kids? It was a tough gig and physically demanding, but it paid well, and she enjoyed dealing with sports injuries. A fit person responded to treatment a lot better than an unfit person. Not exactly rocket science, but it was in stark contrast to the contract she had with a local care home, where the sessions progressed at a snail's pace and were far more sobering. Getting older was no fun.

Having grabbed a sandwich from one of the stall holders on Portobello Road, Elena headed back to her clinic, glad to have a free afternoon to catch up on paperwork. She might even get to finish a bit earlier this evening and pop in to see Luisa on her way home. Her sister's discharge from hospital had been delayed yet again following another failed attempt to treat her infection. Elena was trying not to panic, but it was hard to watch Luisa deteriorating. She felt so helpless.

It might help if Papi responded to the numerous messages she'd sent him, but it had been radio silence all week. What was going on? He was testing her patience.

As she entered her work building, she noticed the door to Daniel J Jackson's office was open. She hadn't seen him since their bizarre encounter a few days ago, when he'd appeared to be having some sort of anxiety attack.

She supposed she should feel sorry for him, and maybe she would do, if he'd been honest with her. How hard was it to admit he had a bad hip and didn't like enclosed spaces? A simple explanation would have saved them both the embarrassment of him having a meltdown and her twisting her ankle when he'd bundled into her.

Felix had been the same. If he was ill he'd never wanted a fuss, and would bat away any attempt to 'nurse' him, as he called it. But when she didn't make a fuss, he'd complain she was 'ignoring him'.

Elena rolled her eyes at the memory.

She was done tolerating emotionally immature men.

She was about to push through the doorway leading to the stairs when she spied a woman sitting in the solicitor's office. The woman had her back to the door, so the view was obscured, but Elena could see enough to recognise the petite frame and long, glossy, dark hair. The shock made her let go of the door, causing it to swing back and nearly smack her in the face.

When the woman laughed, Elena marched towards the office door, which she immediately regretted when her sore ankle twinged. It was a toss-up as to which was more surreal—the sight of her sister dabbing her wet eyes with a man's handkerchief, or Daniel J Jackson perched on the edge of the desk, his shirts sleeves rolled up, and looking all hot and charming as he smiled down at her sister.

'You've been so kind,' her sister said, sniffing back tears. 'I can't thank you enough.'

'It was the least I could do. I'm sorry you're so upset.'

'Why's she upset?' Elena's voice made them both startle. 'What did you do to her?'

Daniel Jackson stepped away from the desk with such a jolt he knocked over a wastepaper bin. 'I didn't do anything,' he said defensively, lifting his hands.

'You must have done something. My sister's in tears and you're the only person here.'

Sofia caught Elena's arm to stop her advancing. 'It's nothing to do with him.'

Elena looked at her sister's beautiful face, bathed in sunlight streaming in from the large window. She looked angelic. She also looked forlorn. Her mascara was smudged, and her eyes were puffy, neither of which detracted from her beauty.

'You don't need to defend him, Sofia. He has a history of injuring women.'

'That's hardly fair,' he objected, frowning at her.

'But not untrue.' She pointed at her ankle. 'I'm still walking with a limp.'

He looked mortified. 'Did I do that?'

Was he for real? 'I twisted my ankle when you rugby tackled me to the floor.'

'I didn't rugby tackle you,' he said, his foot catching

the upturned wastepaper bin as he moved forwards. 'I accidentally fell into you. It wasn't deliberate.' He sounded annoyed, which infuriated her further—she was the injured party here. 'I had no idea I'd hurt you.'

She folded her arms. 'Well, now you do.'

A tug on her arm made her glance down, only to find her sister glaring at her. 'What is wrong with you?' Sofia hissed, like Elena was the one acting unreasonably.

Elena baulked at the unfairness. She was not at fault here.

Daniel cleared his throat, dragging her focus away from Sofia. 'I'm sorry for hurting you. I had no idea. Are you okay?'

Elena gave him a dismissive shrug. 'I'll live. I'm more concerned about my sister and why she's been crying. More importantly, why's she sitting in your office?'

Sofia squeezed Elena's hand. 'Danny isn't the reason I'm upset.'

Her sister was on first name terms with him? 'How do you even know each other?'

'We don't, we just met.' Sofia offered him an apologetic smile. 'I was waiting in the lobby and Danny saw I was upset. He offered to make me a cup of tea while I waited for you.'

Elena's gaze switched between her sister's sad expression and Daniel Jackson's smug one. He might be innocent on this occasion, but she wasn't fool enough to trust him.

Her tone softened as she addressed her sister. 'Why were you upset?' And then she realised what time of day it was. 'Oh, crap. You've been fired, haven't you?'

Sofia's hands twisted in her lap. 'It's not like it came as a shock.' She got up and offered Daniel his soggy hanky back. 'Thanks for the handkerchief.'

'Keep it,' he said, shaking his head. 'I have plenty.'

Who carried a handkerchief these days? How gentlemanly of him. He had manners, at least.

Sofia flattened the front of her suit skirt, as if trying to regain her composure. 'Sorry to have taken up so much of your time.'

'It's not a problem,' he said kindly. 'I'm sorry about your job.'

'Thanks for the tea.' Sofia picked up two bags from the floor. 'Apologise for being so rude,' she whispered to Elena as she brushed past and disappeared into the lobby.

Elena flinched. Why should she apologise? But she knew deep down her sister was right. She owed him an apology, however disgruntled she felt. 'Sorry,' she mumbled, before chasing after her sister.

'Sorry again about your ankle!' he called after her.

Ignoring him, she grabbed one of the bags from Sofia and headed up the stairwell. 'I should've warned you about him, sorry.'

Sofia followed her upstairs. 'What's there to warn me about? He's a darling.'

Elena shot her sister an exasperated look. 'A darling? Hardly. He's ... weird.'

'Unlike you to be judgmental.' Sofia lifted her skirt hem, making it easier to climb the stairs. 'And what's so bad about being weird? We're weird.'

'We're weird in a good way,' Elena said, taking the second bag from Sofia, who was already panting from the climb. 'Unlike Daniel-the-*Jerk*-Jackson, who's weird in a certifiable way. The man is creepy.'

'Don't be ridiculous.' Sofia fanned her face. 'And what does the J really stand for?'

'I told you, it stands for *Jerk*.'

'You're being mean.'

'Mean?' Elena stopped ascending, allowing the throb in her ankle to subside. 'First encounter, he was rude to me. Second encounter, he caused an injury. I can't wait to see what he's got has planned for our next meeting. Full on assault, no doubt.'

Sofia overtook her on the stairs. 'Ah, now I get it. You *like* him.'

'Are you kidding me?' Elena raced to catch her sister up, ankle be damned. 'I do not *like* him.'

'Why else would you be so defensive? Admit it, you're attracted to him.'

'I certainly am not,' Elena scoffed, appalled at the idea. 'And besides, he's met you now, so I don't stand a chance.'

Sofia held onto the railing. 'So you do like him?'

'No, I just meant—'

'It wasn't me he was staring at.'

Elena felt a wash of heat hit her cheeks. She must be getting warm from the climb, she was usually fitter than this. 'Rubbish.'

'And it wasn't me who made him blush, or knock over the bin.'

'Which just proves my point.' Elena reached the top step and unlocked her office. 'The man is a health hazard and should be avoided at all costs.'

Sofia followed her inside. 'I'm glad you fancy someone. It'll do you good to get back out there, especially after the hurt Felix caused you.'

Elena dumped the bags onto the couch. 'I do not fancy *The Jerk*.'

'His name's Danny. And I think you do.' Sofia slid onto the couch. 'Why deny it? He's lovely. Handsome, kind, and he clearly has good taste if he fancies you.' Her sister's smile was open and beguiling. 'What's not to like?'

Elena pointed at the bags. There was no way she was admitting she found Daniel Jackson attractive, not after the debacle of her last relationship. She clearly had questionable taste when it came to men. 'What have you brought?'

'Don't change the subject.'

Elena folded her arms. 'Have you resorted to shoplifting? Is it a reaction to being fired? Is that it? Have you gone on a spending spree?'

Sofia laughed. 'Fine, I'll stop ribbing you about *Danny*.' She kicked off her high heels and curled her tiny feet under her. 'The bags contain costumes. Luisa was upset at missing out on last night's Secret Cinema event, so I thought we could surprise her with a re-enactment of *The Mummy*. I got these from the charity shop.'

Elena tipped the contents of the bags onto the couch. 'Let me guess, you're playing the part of the demure Egyptologist, Evelyn. You have that whole sultry librarian thing going on.' She picked up a wide-brimmed hat. 'A reserved exterior masking a smoking hot body.' The discovery of a white Victorian blouse and long black skirt confirmed her theory. 'Who am I? The dead high priest, Imhotep?'

Sofia rummaged through the garments. 'Like I'd do that to you,' she said, handing Elena a brown leather gun holster. 'You're Rick O'Connell, the swashbuckling hero and slayer of the undead.'

Elena inspected the holster. 'Cool.'

'It's fitting, really, seeing as how you saved our family ... even if your behaviour just now was far from heroic.'

Elena tied the man's scarf around her neck. 'My reaction was justified. I thought he'd upset my sister.'

'But he hadn't. And you don't normally behave like a crazy person. It was very out of character, which is why I think you like him. He ruffles your feathers.'

'Nonsense.' Elena avoided eye-contact with her sister. 'What did you get for Luisa?'

Sofia picked up the Cleopatra wig. 'Anck-su-namun, the sexy unhinged priestess.'

'She'll love that.'

'I've downloaded the film onto my iPad. We can stop for cinema snacks on the way, Luisa will have a fit if we turn up without popcorn.'

'True.' Elena held up the tan-coloured jodhpurs. 'So, what happened at work?'

Sofia sighed. 'I was dismissed.'

'Well, I guessed that, but what happened exactly?' She kicked off her trainers. 'I need details.'

'I was called into Mr Ackroyd's office and told my position was being terminated with immediate effect for repeated and unauthorised absences.'

'Just like that? That's outrageous.'

'Not really. I'd been given two verbal warnings. It's not like I didn't know the outcome when the hospital called the other night to say Luisa was struggling. The moment I left work to be with her, I knew I'd be dismissed. Especially when I arrived at the hospital and saw Luisa on that awful machine. There was no way I was leaving her.'

Elena's heart pinched at the reminder. 'Yeah, it wasn't great.'

It had certainly been a traumatic few days. The hospital had hooked Luisa up to a machine that blasted air into her lungs to help clear the fluid and mucus build-up, as her body was struggling to do the job itself. But it was an intense experience and Luisa had become agitated and kept trying to remove the face mask, saying it was making her hot and panicky. The hospital had called Sofia in the hope that having a loved one with her might ease Luisa's anxiety. So they'd dropped everything and headed to the hospital, resigned to a long night ahead. When it became clear Luisa could be on the machine for several hours, they'd decided to take shifts. Elena stayed overnight and Sofia took over early the next morning, meaning she hadn't gone into work.

Elena shimmied into the snug jodhpurs, pulling them up her legs. 'I wish I'd swapped shifts with you now and covered the day instead.'

'It wouldn't have made any difference. You'd have had to cancel your appointments and lost income—either way it meant sacrificing one of our careers. Better mine than yours. Although I'm not looking forward to my exit interview on Friday, being fired is humiliating enough without being subjected to a post-mortem.' She unzipped her skirt and let it fall to the floor. 'Hopefully I'll find another job soon.'

'You shouldn't have to find another job, it's outrageous that your employer treated you this way. It's discrimination. You shouldn't be punished for being a carer.'

Sofia fastened the long black skirt around her waist. 'I agree, but what can I do? I didn't meet their criteria for being a carer.'

Elena dragged her physio tunic over her head and slung it on the couch. 'Then we challenge their definition of carer.'

'What's the point? Being a carer isn't covered by statutory legislation, it comes under contractual law, which means the company can apply whatever rules they wish. I don't have any grounds for challenging the decision.'

'Of course you do.' Elena slid her arms into the white granddad shirt. 'Someone has to set the precedent, why not you? You've been there five years and have an exemplary employment record. You need to force them to accept that as Luisa's carer you're entitled to the same dispensation as other carers.'

Sofia tied the polka dot scarf around her neck. 'And how do I do that?'

Elena squeezed her feet into the brown leather boots. Despite being a size too big, it was still a push to get her swollen ankle inside. 'I don't know, but there's bound to be stuff online.'

'When I told Danny I'd been dismissed he asked if I was going to raise a grievance and appeal the decision. He said if that failed, I could apply to have the case heard at an Employment Tribunal. A judge would decide whether the employer had acted reasonably or not.'

Elena didn't like the idea of Daniel Jackson knowing about their business. She got to her feet and reached for the leather gun holster. 'You told him what happened?'

Sofia buttoned up the Victorian blouse. 'Not in any detail. I just said I'd been dismissed from my job and he said if I felt I'd been treated unfairly there was action I could take. We didn't discuss specifics, just the process.'

'Right.' Elena was relieved, although why, she wasn't sure. Perhaps it was because he seemed like the judgemental type, and she could do without his disapproval. She'd had enough of that with Felix.

There was another emotion lurking beneath the surface too: guilt. Elena should have known that further time off would result in her sister's dismissal and she should have insisted on staying with Luisa herself. She was a bad sister.

Sofia tucked in her blouse. 'He mentioned an organisation called ACAS.'

'ACAS?' Elena typed the details into her phone. 'Advisory, Conciliation and Arbitration Service. They're an independent body who receive money from the government to help resolve employment disputes.' She was begrudgingly grateful to Daniel for pointing them in the right direction. 'We should give them a call.'

Sofia slid on the waistcoat. 'Even if I do get my job back, it doesn't solve the issue of Luisa still needing care.'

'But if your employer accepts you're a carer they'll have to allow you time off. We've got nothing to lose by calling them, it's a free service.' Elena came over to her sister. 'You need to fight this, Sofia. Don't take any crap, your employers are out of order.'

Sofia puffed out her cheeks. 'Okay, I'll call them.'

'Good, now how do I look?' Elena adopted a manly stance and then karate-kicked the couch, making her ankle twinge. 'Ouch.'

Sofia laughed. 'You look perfect. Like an adventurer off to explore the Egyptian desert.'

'Excellent.' Elena picked up the wide-brimmed hat and placed it on Sofia's head. 'And only you could make this outfit look sexy. Did you bring overcoats?'

Sofia looked puzzled. 'No, why?'

'We have to ride the tube dressed like this?'

Her sister's face fell. 'I didn't think of that.'

Rolling her eyes, Elena pocketed her phone and held

the door open for Sofia. 'The things we do for our sister. Come on, let's get this over with.'

They headed downstairs and into the lobby, stopping to laugh at their reflections in the long wall-mirror. Any hope of escaping without encountering Daniel Jackson disintegrated when his office door swung open and he stopped dead in surprise. 'Wow, okay. I wasn't expecting that.'

Elena's hands went to her hips. 'Yes, can I help you with something?'

'No, I'm all good.' His eyes travelled the length of her body. 'Nice outfit. I hope that's not a real gun.'

She patted the plastic revolver. 'I might feel safer if it was, for next time a man rugby tackles me.'

His eyes narrowed. 'Harsh, considering the man's actions might not be intentional.'

'Well, he would say that, wouldn't he?' Elena met his intense stare head on, she refused to be intimidated. 'And intentional or not, the result is the same. I could barely get this boot on.'

His gaze travelled lower. 'I'm not surprised, they look quite ... snug.' His voice was slightly husky now. His head was tilted to one side and she wasn't sure she could interpret the look on his face. More puzzling still, he'd barely looked at Sofia. When Sofia was in the room, Elena was used to being invisible.

Far from breaking eye-contact, he continued staring.

Why was he looking at her like that? This was like Felix all over again, wasn't it? A man disapproving of any behaviour deemed 'inappropriate'.

So what if they were dressed in ridiculous outfits? Why shouldn't they be? It was for a good cause, the mental well-being of their beloved sister. What this man thought of her was insignificant. His opinion was irrelevant. She didn't give two hoots what Daniel-the-*Jerk*-Jackson thought of her.

With a swish of her hips, she headed for the front door. 'Come along, Sofia,' she said, beckoning for her sister to follow. 'We have men to slay.'

Danny's eyes grew wide.

Chapter Seven

SOFIA

Friday, 13th June

Acute embarrassment consumed Sofia as she concluded her exit interview and was escorted from her work premises like a disgraced employee caught with her hand in the cash box. After leaving so abruptly on Wednesday, she had hoped to say a proper goodbye to her colleagues and explain why she'd been dismissed. But the security guard stood over her the whole time as she'd stuffed her measly belongings into a cardboard box, cutting short any chance of conversation.

Having stripped her of her laptop, entry card, and office keys, the security guard checked each item off a list, inspecting them for damage. If his intention was to make her feel like a hardened criminal, then he'd succeeded. Humiliation burned at her cheeks. Her only crime was being a carer. It seemed unfair that she was treated in the same undignified manner as if she'd been fired for gross misconduct.

Feeling conspicuous, she stood on the busy London pavement trying to compose herself and ignore curious glances from passers-by who were no doubt wondering why she was crying. She hadn't loved her job, but she had enjoyed working with her colleagues, and she'd felt a sense of satisfaction in doing her role well. Leaving under a cloud wasn't good for her self-esteem, and it certainly didn't bode well for her future prospects. Would another employer be sympathetic to her situation, or would they see her as a liability too? She supposed she was about to find out.

Wiping her eyes, she picked up the cardboard box containing her personal items and headed for the train station. In hindsight, she should have left behind the large spider plant, which was threatening to poke her eye out and spill soil over her beloved photo of her parents. Why hadn't she thought to wear flats? But she'd needed a barrier, and wearing her suit and heels helped to disguise her fragile state.

North Acton station was still busy, despite the rush hour being over. She nearly dropped the box twice as she negotiated the steps and turnstiles leading to the platforms. The relief she felt when her train arrived a few minutes later almost reduced her to tears. A feeling that was exacerbated when she spotted an empty seat by the window and was able to slink away from view and hide behind the box for the journey home.

No one liked an audience when they were upset, and she wanted nothing more than to get home, have a good cry, and console herself with hot chocolate and a heated blanket. She'd face reality tomorrow. Today, she wanted to feel sorry for herself.

The hardest part had been hiding her dismissal from Luisa. She didn't think it was fair to burden her sister when she was so poorly, so she'd pretended everything was okay when she'd visited the hospital over the last couple of days and kept quiet about having spent yesterday afternoon on the phone to an ACAS adviser in the hope of getting her dismissal overturned.

Luisa's health had improved enough that her sister had been taken off that awful lung machine and she was slowly responding to intravenous antibiotics. It was early days, but Sofia was keeping everything crossed that her sister would be out of hospital soon.

When a loud clanking noise filled the carriage, Sofia was so lost in thought, it took a moment to register the painful screeching of brakes. The sudden change in momentum propelled her forwards and she dropped her box, sending it crashing to the floor as the train juddered to a halt.

A brief silence followed, quickly replaced by chaos as the other passengers began complaining and trying to find out why the train had stopped.

Sofia collected her things from the floor and returned them to the box, which was now dented. Adjusting her skirt, she dragged herself onto the seat and glanced out of the window. They appeared to be stranded between stations.

The other passengers in the carriage began to look around, as if noticing their fellow commuters for the first time. A collection of puzzled, confused, and frightened expressions gazed back at her.

And then she saw him, the man from her morning commute. He was standing in the aisle looking directly at her, a concerned look on his face. Her heart rate sped up, she gasped, and the air left her lungs in a whoosh.

And then he began walking towards her.

'Are you okay?' he asked, crouching down to pick up the photo of her parents from the floor. She hadn't even noticed it had fallen out. 'I hope it's not broken.'

As she reached to take the photo from him, their fingers brushed and she had an awful feeling her sudden intake of breath was loud enough for the whole carriage to hear. Before she could chastise herself for behaving like a character from a regency novel, a guard appeared from the next carriage and strode down the aisle.

'There's a fire in the signal box at Notting Hill Gate. The train can't move until it's repaired.'

'Do you know how long the repairs will take?' a man further down the carriage asked.

'No idea. They're doing everything possible. I'll let you know as soon as I know something.' The guard raised his hands defensively and edged out of the compartment.

Sofia had been glad of the interruption, it had given her a moment to compose herself. The man she'd wanted so desperately to talk to for so long was finally sitting in front of her, asking her if she was okay, and giving her the prime opportunity to strike up a conversation.

She had to act quickly—if she remained gawping at him like a stunned goldfish he'd conclude she was a weirdo and leave, and then her chance would vanish. She was an adult, for goodness sake, and she needed to start behaving like one.

'I'm Sofia,' she said, holding out her hand as if he was a business colleague, before realising her mistake and withdrawing it. 'Sorry. Bad morning, I'm a bit stressed.'

'That's okay, it's not every day you get stranded on a train. I'm Connor,' he said, mirroring her action and holding out his hand.

Grateful, she shook it. 'I'm Sofia. I've already said that,

haven't I? Sorry, I'm not usually so strange.' Which might have reassured him if she hadn't still been holding his hand, clinging on like he was a life raft and she was drowning. But his hand was so warm and soft, and she didn't want to let go.

'I don't think you're strange at all,' he said softly, seeming unfazed by her clutching hold of his hand. His brown eyes were even more mesmerising close up, and so shiny she could see her own gormless expression reflected back at her.

Thankfully, the guard re-entering the carriage broke the awkwardness, and allowed her the opportunity to remove her hand.

'Sorry, folks, no chance of getting the signal box working. Got to get you off the train here, you'll have to make your way to the station by foot. It's only about a hundred metres, it's perfectly safe. Staff will be there to assist you. If you could all get off the train as quickly as possible.' The guard jumped onto the tracks. He made it look so easy.

Connor offered Sofia his hand and nodded towards the doorway. 'Shall we?'

She let him pull her to her feet. 'I'm not wearing the right shoes for jumping out of a train,' she said, grimacing down at her heels. 'If only I'd known, I'd have worn trainers.'

He unhooked the rucksack from his shoulder. 'I have some in my bag,' he said, opening the flap. 'They might be a bit big, but you're welcome to wear them.' He handed her a pair of retro Nike basketball boots, white with a red trim. 'My dad's American,' he said, offering her a shy shrug. 'He likes to get me stuff to remind me of my roots.'

'That's nice of him,' she said, admiring the boots, which were still huge compared to her tiny feet. 'My father's

Colombian, he buys me pan-pipes and yellow knitwear and wonders why I don't wear them outside the house.'

Connor laughed, and she thought it was the most beautiful thing she'd ever heard. 'He sounds like quite a character. Is that him in the photo?'

'Yes, it was taken on holiday in Cartagena.' Thoughts of Papi made her wistful, so she sat down and kicked off her heels. 'My younger sister doesn't always enjoy his flamboyance. She finds his habit of serenading strangers in restaurants and starting congas at parties embarrassing.'

'And you don't?' He took her heels from her and placed them inside his rucksack.

'Don't get me wrong, I'm just as embarrassed, but he makes me laugh too much to mind him making a spectacle of himself. It's only when he starts matchmaking that I object.' She slid her feet into the boots and tied the laces. 'Then it gets really embarrassing.'

'Who does he try and matchmake you with?'

'Any eligible man he can find. Waiters, co-workers, random men in bars. His shame has no limits.'

Connor ran a hand through his dark hair. 'I'm sure the men don't mind. They probably can't believe their luck.' And then his cheeks flushed and he glanced away. 'Is your mum from Colombia too?'

Stupidly flattered, she shook her head. 'No, she's English ... or rather, she was. She died a few months ago.'

His face fell. 'I'm sorry. You must miss her.' The compassion in his eyes melted her a little.

'I do.' She stood up and inspected her bright white feet. 'I look like Minnie Mouse.'

He laughed. 'Better than jumping in heels.' He slung his rucksack over his shoulder and picked up her cardboard box. 'Ready?'

She followed him over to the exit, trying not to look down at the awaiting drop. She'd never realised how big the gap was before, trains were really high up.

Without any hesitation, he threw his rucksack onto the tracks, and having placed her cardboard box on the carriage floor, leaped from the train like one of those free-runners.

Retrieving her box and placing it next to his rucksack, he turned to her, his arms outstretched. 'Your turn.'

Her legs suddenly felt wobbly. Whether it was from the impending jump or from the sight of him offering to catch her, she wasn't sure.

He beckoned for her to jump. 'Come on, I've got you.'

'I'll squash you.'

He smiled. 'No, you won't. You'll be fine. Just don't look down.'

Easier said than done.

She glanced at him, standing below ready to catch her, and focused on the softness of his handsome face, as opposed to the hard landscape beneath him waiting to snap her ankles.

'Sit on the edge and ease yourself forwards if you're worried about the drop,' he said, reassuringly.

She shuffled towards the edge. 'I hope you know what you're taking on?' she said, using the sight of him with his arms outstretched as a distraction from the falling distance below.

'Trust me,' he said, looking at her intently. 'I promise I'll catch you.'

Oddly, she did trust him, which probably wasn't logical, or smart, or in her best interests. What other choice did she have?

Closing her eyes, she pushed herself away from the ledge.

Twenty minutes ago, she'd never spoken to this man. Now she was lying in his arms, feeling the shape of his slim body through his soft hoodie, the heat of his skin, and fantasising about taking his face in her hands and kissing him until she was breathless.

Their faces were inches apart. It was like time had ground to a halt, pinning her in place, silencing everything around her. And honestly, she could have stayed like that all day, gazing into his face, imagining them together. The breeze carried his scent towards her and for a moment she felt a little dizzy. This man was like a drug. What made it worse was that he seemed utterly oblivious to the effect he was having on her. His eyes were wide, and innocent, and kind, and they looked at her with concern ... but no hint of flirtation, or desire. She was smitten and he was ... well, nonplussed.

Batting away her disappointment, she let him lower her to the ground and she moved away to collect her cardboard box.

Maybe he thought she was too old for him? But there couldn't be much of an age gap between them, a few years at most. He looked early twenties, and she was only twenty-seven, so not a huge difference.

'Let me,' he said, taking the box and hooking his rucksack over his shoulder. 'Are you okay to walk to the station?'

'I think so.'

They followed the other passengers down the tracks towards a group of railway staff waving red flags.

She felt Connor glance at her, as if maybe he was searching for safe conversation. 'How will you get to work?' he asked, hoisting up the box. 'Can you take the bus?'

'I'm not going to work today.' And then realising she

didn't want to admit she'd just been fired, added, 'I ... decided to take the day off. I'm heading home. What about you?'

'This is my stop.' He pointed to the White City sign attached to the wall. 'I'm volunteering at the local community centre today. It's only a couple of minutes' walk from the station, so I should be there in time for my shift.'

She hadn't expected that. 'What kind of volunteering?'

'Whatever they need me to do,' he said, with a shrug. 'Today I'm coaching a walking football session for men trying to lose weight.'

'Really? What a great thing to do.' She had to tread carefully over the uneven ground, she was in danger of tripping up, even in trainers. 'I envy people who are sporty. I'm definitely not, I can't catch, and I can't throw, and as for running ...' she was about to add that her boobs hurt when they bounced up and down, but stopped herself in time. Too much information. 'Anyway, it's great that you're helping out.'

'I'm not that sporty myself,' he admitted, seemingly shy to admit as much. 'I'm more of a spectator, but they don't seem to mind. I do a lot of cheering them on and fetching water when they run out of breath. Stuff like that.'

They reached the end of the tracks and were directed up a flight of work-access steps onto the platform. She was desperate to know more about this sweet, lovely man who volunteered and helped rescue floundering women. 'What do you do when you're not volunteering? Do you work? Or are you still studying?'

His eyes dropped to the floor. 'Neither.' Swallowing awkwardly, he walked over to a bench and placed the box down, his back to her.

Feeling like she'd struck a nerve, she followed and sat

down, leaning down to unlace the trainers he'd loaned her. 'I didn't mean to pry.'

'You didn't. I'm taking a breather after a difficult time in my life, trying to work out what to do next.' His voice was so quiet she barely heard him above the station noise.

She wanted to tell him she was doing the same thing. Her life had been upended and she knew all about needing to take some time to regroup. But this wasn't the moment for confessions. The platform was filling with flustered passengers from the abandoned train, asking the staff questions about their onward journeys. The announcements blaring out from the speakers above killed any intimacy between them.

Removing her shoes from his rucksack, he handed them to her. 'Don't forget these.'

She slipped her feet into her court shoes and stood up. 'Thanks so much for loaning me your trainers. Think of the damage I'd have caused jumping in heels.' Her laugh sounded a little strained. 'I hope you're not late for your shift.'

He glanced at the large digital clock on the arrivals board. 'I'm okay. How about you?'

'I'll be fine.' She held out her hand. Might as well end things the way they started. Formally. 'Thanks so much for helping me. You're a true gentleman, Connor.'

He took her hand, not shaking it this time, but gently holding it. The impact of his touch was just as powerful as it had been the first time. 'Maybe see you around.'

'I hope so.'

But he'd let go of her hand and was walking away.

He didn't turn back, even though she waited, hoping he would.

She continued watching until he'd disappeared from view, like a ghost vanishing into the grimy London air.

He hadn't asked for her phone number, or discreetly found out what her surname was so he could search for her on social media. Nothing.

She'd been so desperate to talk to him, convinced they'd hit it off, and they had ... hadn't they? It wasn't her imagination. So why didn't he want to see her again?

Maybe he already had a girlfriend.

Or worse ... he just didn't fancy her.

The disappointment was crushing.

Chapter Eight

DANNY

Monday, 16th June

It was hard to decide which was more challenging: helping Connor coach basketball to a bunch of uncoordinated teens who'd never played the game before, keeping awake when he'd barely slept, or faking feeling happy and supportive of Connor's volunteering efforts, when in truth he'd rather crawl back to bed with a bottle of Jack Daniels and nurse his sore hip.

'No running with the ball!' he yelled at a lanky kid stomping about in heavy work boots. 'You need to dribble.' The kid looked confused, so Danny picked up a spare ball and demonstrated. 'See? Bounce the ball when you move.'

The kid slammed the ball down, causing it to ricochet off his chunky boot and hit another kid in the face. The second kid retaliated by throwing a punch and the pair started brawling. It was the third skirmish so far and they were only thirty minutes into the session.

'Break it up!' Danny shouted, sprinting over and pulling them apart. 'Basketball is a non-contact sport.' Who was he trying to fool?

Why he'd agreed to help coach such an unruly bunch of youths he had no idea. This couldn't be good for his blood pressure. Connor wasn't faring much better, he wore the same expression he'd had when their cat had died.

'Let's try drills instead,' he said, stopping the game before it descended into a bar fight. 'Line up either side of the court. Take it in turns dribbling up to the basket and shooting.' He threw the ball at the kid with the work boots. 'You first. And next time, bring sneakers.'

The kid pulled a face. 'You what?'

He'd been in the UK for nearly two decades and yet some habits were hard to break. 'Trainers. You can't play ball in steel-capped boots.'

The kid wiped his nose on the sleeve of his already dirty hoodie. 'These are all I 'ave.'

Danny felt momentarily bad for the lad—his threadbare combat trousers and scruffy haircut indicated money was tight. 'Then use mine,' he said, kicking off his Nike Air Jordans, 'but keep those on,' he added, stopping the kid from removing his holey socks. 'You can return them at the end of the session.'

Having handed out the rest of the basketballs to the group, Connor jogged over to Danny. 'It's not going well, is it?'

'It's fine.' Danny forced a smile as he gripped Connor's shoulder. 'It's the first session. They've never played before, it's bound to be challenging. Give it a few weeks and they'll be spinning the ball around like LeBron James.'

Connor raised an eyebrow. Okay, maybe that was a stretch too far.

'Have faith,' he said, his smile convincing as he handed Connor the last ball. 'Shoot a few hoops and show them how it's done.'

'It's not like I can play, either,' Connor said, sounding dejected.

'You're still better than any of them, and you underestimate your skills, you have good technique.'

'But I have no height,' he said, jogging off to join the line of kids waiting to score baskets.

Danny suppressed a sigh. It was true that his brother wasn't the tallest player on the court, but he still ran rings around the other lads.

Despite shouting instructions from the side-lines, what followed wasn't a pretty sight. Balls hit the hoop rim, smacked into the lights above, and threatened to smash the surrounding windows. They'd be lucky to make it out of there with the place still intact. The community centre was falling apart as it was, this session might finish it off for good.

When Connor glanced over, his face filled with panic, Danny gave him a thumbs up, urging him on and being the encouraging supportive role model he'd never had in his own life.

As far as Danny was concerned, hiding the true extent of his feelings from Connor was a necessity—even if it was a contentious point between him and Hugh. It was something they regularly disagreed on. Hugh was an advocate for transparency, he encouraged honesty and promoted 'sharing' as a way of maintaining mental stability.

Danny knew it made sense. A mentally healthy person talked about their feelings, asked for help, and admitted when they were struggling. Mental health issues were no longer a taboo subject—as evidenced by the posters lining the walls of the community centre, promoting various support groups from dementia coffee mornings to Active Mind classes. There was nothing to be embarrassed about. And he wasn't, not really. He'd just never been forced to assess his own mental health before. Now he had, he'd been found wanting.

Padding over to the bench seat in his socked feet, Danny held the steel work boots at arm's length. They smelled rancid. Probably how his sneakers would smell at the end of the evening.

A ball rolled towards him and he threw it back to the group, encouraging the lads to keep going, even though Connor was the only one to have scored a basket so far.

Slumping onto the bench seat, he folded his arms, consumed by tiredness and the ache in his hip.

He'd always been too busy to assess his mental state before. His life revolved around work, caring for Connor, and running a home. Focusing on his own needs had been a luxury he'd never had time for. It was only when his life had imploded last year that he'd discovered he wasn't as mentally robust as he'd imagined. Something he'd been forced to admit when he'd had a meltdown at work the other day and embarrassed himself in front of the woman he shared office space with. The memory made him cringe.

The image of Elena Romero's disgusted expression staring at him like he had two heads distracted him so much that he barely ducked in time when a ball flew past and smacked against the wall behind him.

He cupped his hands around his mouth. 'Great work, guys! Keep it going!' He wasn't sure who he was trying to convince, but the American in him refused to be negative. 'Good team work!'

Therapy was all the rage in the States. It was

commonplace, even considered essential. It was something healthy, sane, and rational people did to maintain balance and sense in their lives. He understood the theory. If you broke your leg, you got it plastered. If you had a migraine, you took pain killers. And if you had the urge to scream, cry hysterically, and battle against a daily urge to wrap your brother in a blanket and never let him out of your sight, you sought psychiatric help. Only a fool would allow their suffering to continue to the point of insomnia and acute claustrophobia, and still deny they had a problem.

He was that fool, it seemed.

'Let's add in some passing!' he shouted to the group, trying to mitigate against their low boredom threshold. 'Make your run-up in pairs. Throw two short chest passes across the court before making a lay-up.'

Two kids smacked into each other. Several lost control of their balls. One pass was so vicious it nearly broke his partner's nose. Danny grimaced. Well, this was a fun way to spend the evening. The things he did for love.

Connor caught a wayward pass and made an almost impossible shot, skimming the ball off the backboard before it swished into the net. Danny resisted the urge to fist-pump his boy. He was the coach—showing favouritism wouldn't be appropriate.

The fact that Connor wasn't his kid only made things more conflicted. He'd brought him up, fed him, clothed him, overseen his education and ensured he was safe, healthy, and sociable. Biologically, he was Connor's brother. Emotionally, he was Connor's parent. He felt pride, love, and an attachment so strong he'd sacrifice his own life to ensure Connor was okay. And he almost had.

When Connor was young, his needs were obvious. As a

twenty-two year old adult, things were becoming more complex. Each time Danny felt he should step away from being parental and start being brotherly, he was consumed with guilt and panic. What was his role now? He had no idea. All he knew was that he felt like he was failing.

'Okay, let's switch it up. Vary the throws between bounce passes, chest passes and overhead lobs.' A ball crashed into a skylight above and Danny flinched, waiting to see if the glass shattered. 'Keep it at head height, guys!'

Danny checked his watch. Another fifteen minutes to go. He could barely keep awake as it was, he hadn't slept at all last night.

Hugh attributed Danny's insomnia issues to 'unresolved emotional trauma'. Not exactly shocking news. He didn't need a psychology degree to understand how his parents had messed him up.

He was the only child of strict, religious parents, and the Jacksons hadn't approved of physical affection or praise. Instead, they had governed the home with rules, punishments, and constant disapproval. Nothing met their exacting standards, and whatever Danny did, it was wrong, no matter how hard he'd tried. So he'd stopped trying. He developed a thick skin, ignored their criticisms, threats and punishments, and withdrew from family life and focused on school instead, counting down the days until he could escape.

'Nice job, guys!' Danny clapped his hands, determined never to be as negative as his parents had been.

To say he'd felt alone during his early life was like saying the pope was mildly religious. His parents weren't deliberately cruel people. They'd never hit him, starved him, or withheld medical treatment. He just wasn't loved, not in the conventional way a parent usually loves their kid, anyway.

And then Connor had come along. An unwelcome inconvenience that, far from softening his parents' approach to parenting, had only increased their frustrations. Danny had felt little love for his parents, but he'd adored his baby brother, so from the age of fourteen, he'd become the kid's main carer. He'd changed diapers, fed him, bathed him, read stories and taken Connor to the park. He'd bounced him on his knee while he did his homework, responded to his crying in the night when his parents failed to wake up, and only relinquished his responsibilities when his parents hired a child minder—a miserable woman called Anya, who matched his parents' style of cold-hearted discipline.

Leaving home at eighteen was supposed to be liberating, a chance to escape his unhappiness and create a new life for himself. He'd applied to universities all over the world, eager to move as far away as possible. There was only one problem: leaving four-year-old Connor behind. The guilt he'd felt was crippling.

The timer on his watch beeped, indicating the end of the session.

Danny did his best to hide his relief. 'Great session, guys! Time to wrap things up!' He jogged onto the court, sliding about in his socked feet as he collected the balls. 'Same time next week.'

When he'd played ball at high school in the US, a session would end with high-fives, back-slapping and positive reinforcements from the coach. These kids trudged off the court with their heads down, looking uninspired and bored. Maybe they wouldn't show up next week. He could only hope.

No. He didn't mean it. Connor needed a focus in his

life, and helping others was a great way of rebuilding self-esteem. According to Hugh, anyway. So if this was helping Connor, then Danny would do whatever was necessary to support him.

The group disappeared from the hall, some mumbling begrudged thanks, others ignoring him completely. London kids were a tough crowd.

He went over to Connor with the net for the balls. 'Not bad for a first session.'

Connor gave him a look. 'It was terrible. I feel like I've let the centre down.'

'Don't be daft, of course you haven't. Come here.' He drew Connor into a hug. 'The centre were looking for ideas about activities to engage local youths and you suggested basketball. It was a great call. Sport unites people.'

Connor pulled away. 'They didn't look united.'

Danny opened the bag so Connor could load the balls. 'Starting something new takes time. Some of these kids have probably never played sport before, or been encouraged to join in with group activities. They have low self-worth. Give them time. We need to build their trust. Don't give up yet.'

Connor dropped a couple of balls in the bag. 'Admit it, you hated it.'

Danny feigned shock. 'Are you kidding me? I had a great time. I love coaching ball to miserable teenagers. What's not to love?'

Connor laughed and went off the collect the remaining balls. 'I appreciate you helping me. I wasn't confident enough to run the first session on my own.'

'But you will do, give it time. You'll get there.'

Connor returned with the last of the balls. 'Can I ask you something?'

'Sure, you can ask me anything.'

'Why have you never got married?'

Danny dropped the bag he was holding, spilling balls onto the court.

Where had that come from?

Connor was looking at him, waiting for an answer. 'Was it because of me?'

Danny flinched. 'Of course not. Why would you think that?'

Connor stopped one of the balls rolling away. 'I don't know, really. It's not something I've thought about before. It's always been you, me, and Uncle Hugh.' He picked up the ball and started spinning it in his hands. 'Lately I've been wondering why there's been no one else in your life. I know you've been on dates and stuff, but you never bring anyone home. Why is that?'

Danny's head was in a whirl, it wasn't a subject that had come up before. He could have done with some warning.

He rubbed his forehead. 'Where's this coming from? Do you feel like you've missed out or something? Like you're lacking a mother figure?' This had been Danny's biggest fear, that somehow he wouldn't meet Connor's emotional needs.

Connor sighed. 'It's not that, but you've been on your own all these years. I wondered why, that's all. Your life revolves around me, and I guess I've taken that for granted. I've never stopped to think about what you might want.'

Connor was worried about him? Just when he thought his guilt couldn't get any worse. 'I'm not single because of you, Connor. Never think that.'

'Then why? Have you never wanted someone in your life?'

Oh, boy. This was not a conversation he was prepared

for. How could he even begin to explain why he avoided relationships? He took a breath, trying to compose his thoughts.

In hindsight, Hugh was right. Hooking up with Maisie Marshall when he first arrived at uni was the ultimate revenge for years of repressed emotions. Maisie was loud and fun, a real party girl. She wore short denim skirts over ripped fishnet tights with tie-dyed baggy T-shirts, and smoked weed using one of those cigarette holders from the nineteen-thirties. She was fiercely intelligent, loved debating politics, and was at the front of every student rally, no matter the cause. It had been liberating to be around someone so unafraid of judgement or consequence. Maisie Marshall was fearless. She was also a drug addict.

Danny forced himself to look Connor in the eye. 'I've never met anyone I've liked enough to continue seeing, that's all. There's nothing complicated about it, it's just never happened for me.' Which in part was true, there'd been no one since his uni days he felt strongly enough about to tempt him back into a relationship. Once had been enough.

'What, never? You've never fallen for anyone?'

Oh, he'd fallen all right. He'd been so in love with Maisie he'd ignored the warning signs for months. He wasn't sure whether it was his naivety, an unwillingness to see what was staring him in the face, or Maisie's expertise at hiding her addiction that stopped him from facing the truth. Probably all three.

Knocking back shots at parties with a joint in her hand wasn't shocking, it matched the other students' behaviour. It was only once the initial honeymoon period had worn off that things had switched from loving and tender to arguing and accusations. Paranoia, lying, deceit, stealing money from him, hiding bottles under her bed, track marks on her arms, burnt foil wrappers in the bin. And yet for weeks he ignored it and found excuses to justify her erratic moods. It was only after a fight in which she'd accused him of cheating on her and punched him in the face that he'd walked out, his parents' voices ringing loud in his ears, reminding him what a stuff-up he was. Whether he would have gone back to Maisie and tried to help her, he'd never know.

Connor dropped the ball in the net. 'So you've never been in love?'

Danny knew his anguish was visible, so there was no point lying. 'I was once, back in my uni days. It didn't end well.'

Connor looked intrigued. 'What happened?'

Danny's mind rewound to that night seventeen years ago when the police had shown up at his student digs. He'd assumed Maisie had got herself in trouble again. She'd already been arrested for jumping off a moving train, trashing the rest room at a bar, and smacking a security guard in the face with her shoe.

So when he opened the door and saw the sombre expressions on the police officers faces he suspected the worst. A feeling compounded when he heard the words 'fatal accident' and one of the officers asking him if he wanted them to call someone to be with him. It was only when they mentioned the Orange County Coroner that he realised they weren't talking about his girlfriend, but his parents back home in the US.

The following night Maisie Marshall overdosed. It was only later the following day he'd discovered several missed calls from her on his phone—calls he'd never picked up.

In the space of twenty-four hours he'd lost both his

parents and his girlfriend, and was now the sole carer of his five-year-old brother. He wasn't sure he'd ever fully recovered.

Shaking away the memories, he tried to conceal the pain he felt inside. 'We ... we were very different people, that's all. We wanted different things. It was never going to work out.'

Connor took the bag from him. 'And there's been no one since?'

'No, there hasn't.' Which was at least the truth. Occasional hook-ups, a few repeated dates, but nothing meaningful or lasting, his heart couldn't take it. 'But I'm okay with that, it's not something that bothers me.'

Connor's eyes fell to the floor. 'Right.'

'Where's this coming from?' He reached out to touch his brother's arm. 'You've never asked me about relationships before, why now?' And then he spotted the colour in Connor's cheeks. 'Have you met someone?'

Connor carried the bag of basketballs over to the storage cupboard. 'We need to lock up.'

Danny followed him. 'You have, haven't you? Connor, you can tell me. It's okay. What's her name?' He mentally slapped himself. 'I mean, *their* name.' He shouldn't assume.

Connor had collected various friends over the years, a mix of sexualities and genders, but to his knowledge his brother had never been in a serious relationship. He was either very discreet, or not interested. Maybe there was another reason—was Connor afraid to admit who he was dating?

Oh, hell. Danny caught him up. 'Seriously, Connor. It's okay. Whatever you tell me, it's fine. Are you seeing someone?'

Connor locked the storage cupboard door. 'There's no one. It was nothing, just a brief moment.'

Danny followed him around the room, slipping in his socks, trying to keep up as Connor collected discarded rubbish. 'It can't have been nothing if you're asking me about girlfriends, and why I'm not married.' He caught Connor's arm. 'It must have been something, what happened?'

Connor stopped walking. 'I met this woman ... and ...'

Danny's heart was racing. 'And?'

Connor's eyes lifted to his. 'It felt like I'd been hit by a train.'

Danny swallowed. 'In a good way?'

Connor rubbed his chest. 'Like I'd forgotten how to breathe.'

Oh, bless him. 'Okay, and did she feel the same way?'

'Maybe, I don't know. Probably not. It doesn't matter.' Connor was off again, stacking chairs and avoiding eye contact.

Danny knew he had to tread carefully. Connor used to be so easy to talk to, an open book, a chatty teenager. They'd never had problems communicating until that night when everything changed. Now one ill-advised comment could bring the shutters down and it would be radio silence. 'Why doesn't it matter?'

'She wouldn't like me if she knew what'd happened, would she?'

So that was it.

Danny didn't think his heart couldn't shatter any more than it had, but another piece broke away and disintegrated into dust.

Taking his brother by the shoulders he turned Connor to face him. 'Listen to me. You did absolutely nothing wrong. You were falsely accused. The police dropped the charges and you were innocent of any wrongdoing. You know that. We've talked about this, it was unjust, and badly handled, and you're not at fault.'

Connor shook his head. 'Mud sticks, though. You saw the social media posts, no smoke without fire.'

'That was trolling, Connor. Cruel, ill-informed people making judgements about stuff they know nothing about.'

'But people believed it.' His voice cracked. 'They treated me differently afterwards. Students at uni stopped talking to me, they pointed and whispered. I heard the rumours, even after the case was dropped. It'll never go away, not fully.'

Danny was struggling for breath, and they weren't even in an enclosed space. 'Listen to me, Connor. What happened was grossly unfair, but never think for one moment it was a reflection on you as a person. You're good, and kind, and loving, and you'd never do anything to hurt anyone. Anyone who knows you believes that completely.'

'What about the people who don't know me? Are they going to believe the truth? Or what they read online? Seems to me people are happy to believe the worst.'

'Then you don't want those kinds of people in your life.'

'You're right. I need to be more like you and protect myself. Steer clear of love and relationships and be content being alone. If I don't let anyone close, then they can't hurt me, can they? It's safer that way.' Connor turned and walked off.

Shit.

Danny rubbed his temples, sinking under the weight of realisation.

Connor wasn't alone because of what had happened to

him, he was afraid of love because that's the lesson he'd been taught by his guardian. He was a rotten parent.

Danny jogged over to the bench seat, searching for his sneakers. The heavy work boots were missing too. The lanky kid had nicked his shoes? *Jesus!* Now he had to walk home in socks, on top of everything else.

He grabbed his jacket and raced after Connor, his hip burning like hell.

Chapter Nine

ELENA

Wednesday, 18th June

As soon as Elena saw the 'adult content' warning sticker on the colouring book, she knew she had to buy it for Luisa. Her sister was bored out of her mind in hospital and complaining about the lack of creative outlets to occupy her time. Complaining was a good sign, it meant Luisa's health was improving, even if trying to keep her stimulated was exhausting work. It wasn't possible to set her up with oils and an easel, but a colouring book containing extremely rude words and some crayons would be perfect.

Thanking the stall-holder, Elena weaved her way through the crowd of shoppers filling Portobello Road as she headed for work. She was tired this morning, struggling to shake off a restless night peppered with bad dreams about her mum dying and her break-up with Felix. Both losses had occurred simultaneously, so they overlapped in her mind, one memory triggering another. She knew she needed to recover from her losses and look to the future, but how could she do that when Luisa was in hospital, Sofia was unemployed, and Papi was showing no signs of returning home? Her own needs would have to wait.

When she spotted Daniel Jackson ahead of her, she paused by the iron gate, waiting until he'd disappeared inside the building before following him inside. She didn't need another irritant adding to her unsettled state this morning.

Thankfully, she'd been spared any further bizarre encounters with the man she shared a building with. His office door was either firmly shut, the lights were out, or he'd left work by the time she'd finished dealing with her list of patients. Either way, she'd managed to avoid seeing him for a week, and that was something she was extremely grateful for.

So to find herself niggled with guilt was a puzzlement. She had nothing to feel guilty about. The man infuriated her. He clearly had issues, and her life was filled with enough drama without adding his into the mix.

Her plan to ignore him and focus on her own troubles was the sensible course of action. It was solid. Understandable. Logical, even. Guilt be damned, she would not be drawn into his issues, of which he appeared to have many.

This rationale was almost enough to sweep her past his closed office door towards the stairs and escape any unwanted encounters. But then she remembered his kindness towards Sofia, and she found herself pausing by the stairwell, her hand hovering above the door handle as if controlled by an external force.

With a resigned sigh, she backtracked and walked over

to his office door, rapping against the glass before she could sense-check her actions.

When the door swung open, she was hit by a waft of aftershave, which was almost enough to derail her, but she held her ground, refusing to be intimidated by his grouchy expression, or the way his pale lilac shirt fitted snuggly under his striped grey waistcoat.

'Oh, it's you,' he said, his tension easing slightly. When she offered him a strained smile, he lifted a suspicious eyebrow. 'Do you need something?'

'No, but you do. Can I come in?'

There was a moment's pause, almost as if he was weighing up his response. He looked tired, and there was a weariness hanging over him like a shroud, as if the effort of standing upright was too much for him.

She tilted her head in a questioning manner. 'Is that a no?'

He stepped back and held the door open, his expression wary.

'Thank you.' She entered his office and dumped her bag on the visitor's chair. 'I'm here because you're in pain.'

He looked confused. 'Why d'you say that?'

'It's obvious.' She folded her arms, showing she meant business. From their brief interactions so far she knew he'd be resistant to accepting help, so she was ready to play hardball. 'Am I wrong?'

She took his silence as confirmation.

'Good. Denying it would be pointless and a waste of my time. I'm taking time out of my day to help you, so I'm not going to take any crap. Are we clear?' She wasn't usually so abrupt with patients, but there was something about Daniel Jackson that brought out the combative side of her.

He ran his hands into his hair. 'Has anyone ever told you your bedside manner needs work?'

'No, and it's your hip that needs work,' she said, shrugging off her jacket. 'Do you have a diagnosis?'

He shook his head. 'No.'

'Have you received any treatment for it?'

'No.'

'Have you consulted your GP?'

He hesitated, seemingly uncomfortable by her direct line of questioning.

Tough, she needed to know what she was dealing with. 'Well, have you?'

'No.'

'Can I ask why not?'

'No.' He turned away, and then immediately turned back. 'Where's this coming from? I've never asked for your help. Why the sudden interest in my health?'

'You're right, you didn't ask for my help. And if I'm being honest, I don't relish the idea of helping you—'

'Then why are you here?' he snapped, dropping his hands. 'Why bother?'

'Because you were kind to my sister,' she said, unfolding her arms in an attempt to soften her stance. 'Your advice proved useful. She contacted ACAS and they're helping her, and I'm grateful for that. So I figured it was only fair to reciprocate and offer to help you in return.' One good deed deserved another, and all that.

He walked over to the window. 'You don't need to help me. I'm fine.'

'Are you?' She looked around his office, noticing the lack of unpacking and an open box of paracetamol lying on his desk. 'You don't seem fine.'

'Well, I am.' He stared out of the window, his shoulders like granite.

'Are you really fine? Or are you just stubborn?'

He swung around to face her. 'Is this how you usually talk to your patients?'

'My patients aren't usually resistant to getting help. They're smart enough to realise they need treatment.' Well, most of them. She'd lost count of the number of patients who'd failed to complete their treatment or continued with their exercises. Not everyone valued their health as they should. 'Call me crazy, but here I am, offering to help you despite your rudeness.'

His incredulous expression was almost laughable. 'You think *I'm* rude?'

'Yes, but I'm willing to overlook that.' Her wide smile seemed to confuse him even more. She was a little confused herself, her mind was conflicted about her motivations for helping him. 'Do you want my help, or not?'

He stepped away, banging into the window behind. 'No, I don't.'

'Don't say I didn't offer.' She headed over to collect her things, hoping he wasn't so stubborn he'd actually let her leave.

'Wait.'

He'd had her worried there for a moment. She kept her back to him, her hand resting on the door handle. 'Is there something you wanted to say?'

'I don't want your help ... but I accept I might need it.'

She could only imagine how much he'd hated admitting that.

Suppressing a smile, she turned to face him. 'Drop your trousers.'

'Excuse me?' His expression was priceless.

'You can't use the lift or stairs to visit my clinic, so I need to examine you here.' She locked the office door. 'And I can't do that with you fully dressed. I need to assess your hip joint.'

'I'm not taking my trousers off.'

She knew better than to push it. 'Will you at least take your waistcoat off?'

He looked like he wanted to refuse, but sulkily conceded. 'If I must.'

She averted her eyes as he unbuttoned his waistcoat and slid it from his shoulders. 'And untuck your shirt.' Her mouth had become a little dry as he pulled his shirt from his trousers, revealing a flash of skin. She wasn't usually affected by men undressing, she'd seen enough bare bodies over the years to become immune to the sight of a naked man. Strange that Daniel Jackson of all people should unsettle her. 'Shoes off too, please.'

'Why do I need to take my shoes off?'

'So I can assess your gait.'

He stepped out of his shoes. 'This is so weird.'

It was, but then she was used to being called weird–it was a word Felix had often used to describe her. He'd never meant it as an affectionate term, more a cruel judgement.

She moved the visitor's chair to create more space. 'Walk around the room for me.'

He did as she asked, pacing up and down the confined space.

'Lift your shirt so I can see your hips moving.' She wasn't asking him to do anything unusual, but for some reason the situation felt far from medical. It must have been down to the setting. If they were in her clinic it would be different, more professional and less ... distracting.

He turned and walked towards her. 'Is this really necessary?'

'Absolutely.' She watched him turn, his balance slightly out. 'Is this a long-term deterioration of the hip joint, or the result of an injury?'

'An injury.'

She crouched down so she could see the line of his hips. 'When did it happen?'

'Nine months ago.'

Not ideal, it was easier to treat a fresh injury. 'What happened?'

He stopped walking. 'I don't want to go into details.'

She glanced up, waiting for him to face her, but he stayed turned away. 'Keep walking, please.'

It took a moment before he responded.

She studied his hip movement and the way his step was shorter one side. 'I don't need all the details, but I do need something to go on. Was it a fall? An impact injury? Did you twist the joint?'

The muscles in his jaw clenched. 'I jumped from a height and landed heavily.'

'How high up were you?'

'About two metres.'

'What surface did you land on, soft or hard?'

He visibly flinched, as if plagued by painful memories. 'Concrete.'

It was a miracle he hadn't broken his pelvis. 'I imagine that was incredibly painful.'

He shot her a sarcastic look. 'You could say that.'

She softened her tone. 'And what happened after you fell?'

He frowned. 'How do you mean?'

'Did you receive any medical attention? Was an ambulance called?'

'No, I …' He glanced away. 'No medical treatment. I needed to … to help someone else. Their needs were greater than mine.'

She waited, allowing him time to gather himself, the memories were clearly still raw. 'And it's been painful to walk ever since?'

He rubbed his arms, like he was cold. 'Some days it's worse than others. It's mostly stairs I struggle with.'

'May I?' When he nodded his agreement, she went over and placed her hands on his hips. 'Is it a sharp jabbing pain, or a dull ache?'

'A dull ache.' There was such anguish in his voice she wondered if he was talking about his hip, or his heart. Whatever had happened that night, it had certainly left a scar.

She gently compared the joints. 'Worse when you weight-bear?'

He nodded.

She moved around to his back and lifted his shirt. 'Was this incident the start of your claustrophobia issues too?'

He didn't immediately answer. 'Is that relevant?'

She rested her fingers at the top of his spine, checking the feel of each vertebrae as she moved downwards. 'Studies have shown a link between physical and emotional trauma. They often feed off each other. Depression can exacerbate physical pain.'

'I'm not depressed.'

'And yet you have an acute injury you haven't sought medical help for.'

'I've been busy. It doesn't mean I'm depressed.'

She felt the muscle in his left buttock spasm as she ran her thumb over the area. 'Do you take pain medication?'

'Sometimes.'

The rigidity of his supporting muscles indicated he was using other muscles to carry the weakness in his hip. 'Daily? Weekly?'

'You don't need to lecture me about not getting treatment, okay? I had my reasons.'

'I'm sure you did.' She moved to his side, unruffled by his testiness, pain made people grumpy. 'And I'm sure they were valid reasons, but continuing to live in pain while relying on drugs to get through the day isn't ideal. You may find your claustrophobia issues subside once the pain reduces, so to refuse help might be classed as—'

'Stupid?'

She met his gaze. 'Not in your best interests.'

'Very diplomatic.'

She stepped away from him. 'I appreciate we haven't got off to the best start, but the physio in me struggles to watch someone suffering when I know treatment would help. The question is, are you going to continue being stubborn and deny yourself the opportunity of feeling better, or are you going to accept my offer of treatment?'

He closed his eyes. 'How much will it cost?'

'No charge.'

His eyes shot open. 'I have to pay you.'

'Oh, you'll pay,' she said, pinning him with a look. 'Just not with money.'

One eyebrow raised. 'Should I be alarmed?'

'As the author Adam Kay put it, *This is Going to Hurt*.' She stunned him with one of her beaming smiles. 'Besides, the sooner you're healed, the sooner I can persuade you to swap offices with me.' She held out her hand. 'Lift your right knee to the height of my hand, please.'

He lifted his knee. 'Is that why you're doing this?'

In truth, she had no idea why she was doing this, her logic was severely skewered. All she knew was that she wanted to ease this man's suffering.

'Like I said, you helped Sofia, so I'm helping you.' It was the only reasoning she had, so she was clinging hold of it. 'It's what civilised human beings do. Lower your knee and transfer your weight to the right hip.'

She slid her hand over the joint and around to his buttock. When she glanced up she realised he was staring at her, the lenses in his glasses misting over slightly from the heat in the room. She supposed it was rather odd to have a strange woman gripping your arse.

'Why are you looking at me like that?'

'I can't work you out. One moment you're bitching at me, the next you're incredibly nice. Which is the real you?'

'Can't I be both? Part vixen, part angel?'

His gaze dropped to her mouth. 'You're no angel.'

It was probably down to the non-medical space, why else would the hairs on her arms be lifting? 'Why is it men feel the need to pigeonhole women into types? A smart man would realise that people, regardless of gender, are complex creatures made up of many facets. I have layers, not all of them nice. Straighten up for me and lift your left knee.'

He did as instructed.

She checked the angle of his hip. 'Can you go any higher?'

He lifted his leg a fraction, grimacing as he did so.

'Stop there. I don't want you pushing into pain.' She met his worried gaze. 'Not yet, anyway.'

'There's that expression again. It unnerves me.'

'I can't think why?' She attempted an innocent look. 'Besides, how would you like it if I made an assumption about you based on our interactions so far? Would that be a fair assessment of your character?'

'No.' He lowered his eyes. 'I'm not at my best right now.'

'Exactly. So I'll withhold my opinion until I know you better.' She tapped his knee. 'Lower your leg and drop your weight to the left side.' The stiffness in his hip was visible. She pointed to his trouser fly. 'It would help if you unbuttoned. You can leave them on, just ease the waistband down a bit.'

He kept his eyes locked on hers as he slowly unzipped his fly. 'Enough?' It was his turn to play games.

'Plenty,' she said, disguising her lumpy swallow as she slid her hands into the top of his trousers. His skin was very warm and smooth. 'So, who is Daniel J Jackson? I know you're a solicitor, and you're originally from the US, and you've lived in the UK for eighteen years, but what else? What lies behind the suit?'

'You tell me. You're the one undressing me.'

'Oh, please,' she scoffed. 'Believe me, if I was undressing you, you'd know about it.' She regretted her choice of response when his eyes widened with surprise—and if she wasn't mistaken, a touch of heat. 'I meant figuratively,' she said, digging her thumb into his pelvis and killing any hint of desire.

'There's not much to tell,' he said, grimacing through the pain as she assessed the extent of scar tissue.

'I don't believe that. Everyone has layers.'

'Not me. I'm pretty basic,' he said, clenching his jaw. 'What are your layers?'

Sensing he needed a distraction from the pain, she

indulged him. Nothing too personal, just enough to convince him she wasn't the enemy. 'Well, I'm part English, part Colombian, so I'm a complex mixture of demure containment and fiery exuberance. You've met both versions, I believe.'

'I think I read about you in a book once.' He lifted an eyebrow. 'It was called Jekyll and Hyde.'

'Funny.' Except it wasn't. Felix's criticisms about the flaws in her 'split personality' still niggled.

She dropped to her knees, her hands still on his hips.

The look on his face was priceless. 'Err ... what are you doing?'

She glanced up, her expression pure innocence. 'What do you think I'm doing?'

'I think you're being deliberately provocative.'

'As if I'd do such a thing. I'm a professional, I'll have you know. How else can I assess the alignment of your hips unless I'm at eye-level?' She trailed her hands down his legs, feeling each quad muscle twitch as she passed over it.

'You were telling me about your layers,' he said, his voice strangulated. His head was angled upwards, his eyes were staring at the ceiling, and his hands were bunched into fists. He reminded her of Dr Bruce Banner as he tried desperately not to turn into The Hulk.

'Well, I alternate between wanting a raucous night out to craving a quiet night in. I love spicy food, but I equally adore egg and chips, and I go stir crazy if I don't regularly exercise. I believe in the certainty of science, but the escapism of creativity.'

'Like dressing up in weird costumes?' He laced his hands into his hair, gripping hard, until he realised his trousers were about to fall down and frantically grabbed for the waistband.

Ignoring a flash of baby-blue underwear, she stood up. 'It's a family thing.'

He pulled his trousers up. 'Your whole family dresses up?'

'It's something we've always done.' She smiled at the memory of her mum seated at the sewing machine, humming along to music as she finished their costumes, working late into the night.

He frowned at her. 'Why?'

'Probably to avoid reality,' she said with a shrug. 'You've heard the saying, when life gives you lemons, make lemonade. Well, in our version we dress up in elaborate costumes and become make-believe characters, who conquer the world, have adventures, and experience loads of fun. ... Bend over and rest your hands on your knees, please.'

He blinked in surprise. 'Is that necessary?'

'I wouldn't ask if it wasn't.'

'Can I zip up my pants first?'

'Not yet.'

Letting out a frustrated sigh, he bent forwards. 'What are you trying to escape? Did you have a troubled childhood or something? Did your parents argue all the time?'

'Crikey, no.' She stood behind him and checked his coccyx. 'I had an amazing childhood, it was heaps of fun. And my parents never argued ... well, they did sometimes, but it never latest long. Arguing inevitably ended up with them heading for the bedroom. We learnt never to disturb a closed door, my parents had a very passionate relationship.'

'I envy you.' He stood up with a groan. 'Sorry, that was really insensitive. I know your mum died ... I just meant not all couples have what they had.'

'It's okay, I know what you meant. Do you have any pain in your groin?'

He looked genuinely horrified. 'Please don't examine my groin.'

She wanted to assure him any physical reaction to her touching him was perfectly normal. She treated hormonal teenagers, for crying out loud. Somehow she didn't think this would appease him. 'Is it okay if I examine your glutes?'

He bit his lip. 'If you must. Can I stay upright?'

'Yes.' She moved around to his back. 'What about your parents, what are they like?'

His shoulders stiffened. 'Deceased.'

'Both of them?' She was stunned into silence for a moment. 'Goodness, I'm sorry.'

'It was a long time ago.'

She placed her hands on his lower back and checked his symmetry, her animosity dissolving with each new fact she discovered about him. Knowing how much she missed her mum, the idea of losing both parents was unimaginable. 'Do you have any other family?'

'A brother.' He held onto the front of his trousers, as if fearful they were about to fall down again. 'So, if you had such a great childhood, why did you need to escape reality?'

'Sick sister,' she said, running her hands down his glutes. 'It's why we moved to the UK, so Luisa could get the treatment she needed.'

The muscles in his backside clenched tighter. 'Is she better now?'

Elena shook away an image of her sister lying in her hospital bed hooked up to various machines and drips. 'It's a permanent condition, so she'll never be totally okay. There are good days, mixed in with a load of really bad ones ... which is why we make the most of every day and do stuff like dressing up. It helps.' She pressed her thumb into the muscles either side. 'Any pain when I do this?'

'No.' He stepped away, keeping his back to her. 'Can I zip up my pants now, please?'

'Yes, you may. Want the verdict?'

Fastening his top button, he turned to face her. 'Hit me with it.'

'I'd like to refer you for scans to be certain, but I'm pretty sure you've damaged the ligament at the head of your femur which attaches to the hip socket. I can give you exercises to improve flexibility, but there's a significant build-up of scar tissue around the area, which is hampering your movement and exacerbating the pain.'

'Is that something that can be treated?'

'Yes, but I warn you, it'll be painful. We basically have to re-injure the hip by breaking down the damaged tissue. You need to prepare yourself for a few painful massages and stretches while the injury heals and regains its elasticity. Your hip will be quite sore for a while.'

He rolled his eyes. 'Great.'

'Short-term pain, long-term gain, as I say to my patients. This is the best way of reversing the damage.' She headed over to the chair and picked up her bag, her impression of Daniel Jackson having altered over the last half hour. She wasn't quite sure how she felt about that. 'But scans first to confirm my diagnosis. Any questions?'

He looked a little shellshocked. 'I don't think so.'

'Good, call me if you think of anything.' She placed her business card on his desk, before heading over to unlock the door. 'Oh, and your fly is still undone,' she said, hitting him with a smile as she exited his office, calm as you like, totally unfazed and in control.

Who was she kidding?

There was nothing calm about the thoughts filling her mind. Her hormones were doing backflips.

Daniel J Jackson was most certainly a 'suit'.

He was also hot as hell.

Chapter Ten

SOFIA

Friday, 20th June

It was the smell Sofia hated more than anything, that heady mix of toxic cleaning products and antiseptic, attempting to cover the aroma of failing health. The Royal Brompton was better than most, with its reputation for being at the forefront of specialist research for heart and lung disease. The historic building was peppered with modern technology and flashes of medical genius, and yet it was still a depressing clinical environment. The family had endured enough health centres over the years to develop an acute aversion to visiting such institutions. It was a comfort to know Luisa was in good hands, but the sooner they could leave, the better.

'What's taking so long?' Luisa flopped onto the narrow hospital bed and kicked her feet up. 'I need to escape before they change their minds again.'

'We're waiting on the pharmacy.' Sofia checked her phone for notifications. 'They're packing up your meds now. Hopefully, it won't be long. This time tomorrow you'll be home and eating home-cooked food and painting again.' She turned the page on the colouring book, her shock levels increasing with each new word. 'I still can't believe Elena bought you this. It's so ...'

'Rude?' Luisa laughed. 'That's why I like it. My favourite word is—'

'I can tell which one it is.' Sofia held up the brightly coloured expletive.

Luisa grinned. 'What gave it away?'

'The abundance of pink hearts.'

'I like the juxtaposition.' Luisa rolled onto her side. 'By the way, I heard from Papi last night.'

'You did?' Sofia snapped the book shut. 'What did he say? Where was he? Where's he been all this time?'

'He's been off-grid in Medellin with Uncle Roberto meeting with a potential buyer for the farm. They've been trekking through the jungle on horseback. They didn't see another person for days, apparently. They had to hunt for their dinner and ran out of fresh water at one point.'

'How very adventurous of him.' Sofia tried and failed not to feel disgruntled. 'It's dangerous territory out there. Apart from the harsh terrain, there are drug gangs to contend with. Supposing something happened to him?'

Luisa shrugged as she inspected her flaky fingernails. 'He can take care of himself.'

'That's debatable.' Sofia tucked the colouring book inside Luisa's hessian rucksack, purchased during their last visit to Cartagena before their mum had died. 'What did he say when you told him you were in hospital?'

Luisa looked away. 'I didn't tell him.'

'Why ever not?'

'Because then he'd feel like crap.' Luisa crossed her legs, sounding annoyed. 'And I don't want to add to his pain. Let him conclude his business dealings, or whatever he's doing, and then hopefully he'll come home and be Papi again.'

Sofia went over to the bed. 'Luisa, he needs to know how ill you've been. You should've told him.'

'Oh, like you told me you'd been fired?'

Sofia took a step back. 'You know about that?'

'Flinch all you want, Sofia Romero, but the truth works both ways.' Luisa adopted her sulkiest pose.

Sofia sagged against the bed. 'How did you find out?'

'Credit me with some intellect. You've been visiting me during the day and changing the subject when I ask about work. It didn't take a genius to realise you'd been fired.'

So much for protecting her sister. 'I didn't want you worrying.'

'Or feeling guilty. That's the real reason. You were fired because of me, weren't you?'

'It wasn't because of you—'

'Who was it then, Father Christmas?' Luisa's raised voice caused a passing nurse to look in, moving on when Sofia reassured her there was nothing to be alarmed about.

Sofia reached for Luisa's hand. 'No one made me do it. It was my choice to put you ahead of work.'

Luisa pulled her hand away. 'I'm too needy, that's what you and Elena tell me.'

'We've never called you needy.' At least, she didn't think they had. She experienced a sudden pang of guilt. 'But you do need family around to support you when you're ill. With Mum gone and Papi away, it's our responsibility to look after you. You'll always come first, and there's nothing you can say that will make us act otherwise.'

Luisa pouted. 'I don't need protecting.'

'I know, and I'm sorry. I was just delaying telling you until you were feeling stronger.'

Luisa folded her slim arms, large purple bruises visible beneath her vest-top. She still looked incredibly fragile. 'I hate causing so much angst.'

'Unemployment's not so bad,' Sofia said, searching for a positive. 'I've enjoyed spending time at home. You know me and household chores.' She tried for a smile, but Luisa wasn't easily won over. 'And I'm appealing my dismissal, so who knows, they might reverse their decision.'

Luisa hugged a pillow. 'I bet the house is ridiculously clean, all the cushions are puffed up, and you've relabelled the pasta jars.'

Sofia smiled. 'Busted.'

'You better not have tidied up my studio?'

'As if.' Sofia checked her phone when it pinged. 'Your meds are done. Ready to break out of here?'

Luisa scrambled off the bed. 'At last!'

As Luisa skidded around the corridor in her socks, thanking the staff and hugging nurses, Sofia packed up Luisa's things.

Despite being told the prescription was ready, it was still another hour before they left the hospital and headed for South Kensington tube station.

Luisa slid her arm through Sofia's. 'So, what have I missed? Fill me in on the gossip. Have you met any hot men I need to know about?'

Sofia sighed. 'Just the one.'

Luisa laughed, and then spotted the mournful

expression on her sister's face. 'Oh my God, you're not joking.' She tugged on Sofia's arm. 'Bloody hell! Tell me.'

'Nothing much to tell.' Sofia hadn't planned on telling anyone about Connor, but maybe sharing her tragic encounter might help her recover, as she'd done a lousy job so far trying to shrug off the humiliation. 'There was this man I saw on the train each morning I liked the look of, but he obviously didn't feel the same way.' They headed down the steps towards the turnstiles, Sofia supporting Luisa's weight.

'How do you know he didn't feel the same way? Did you talk to him?'

'Watch your step.' Sofia waited until a harassed man had bundled past before continuing. 'Yes, I talked to him. He helped me when the train broke down, and we spent a bit of time together.'

Luisa waited until they'd found seats on the platform before resuming her interrogation. 'And? Come on, don't leave me hanging.'

'And ... he was lovely.' Sofia cast her mind back, remembering the kindness in his brown eyes when he'd first approached her and rescued her photo frame from the floor. 'A bit younger than me. Kind of shy, and funny, in a gentle way. I felt something I'd never experienced before, like my mind was screaming at me, *This one. This is him. You've found him.* ... Crazy, huh?'

'Completely bonkers.' Luisa grinned. 'But also incredibly romantic, which isn't my thing, but I totally accept it's a dealbreaker for you. You're looking for a deep connection, someone you can be all lovey-dovey with. And why not? If we were all the same then we'd be chasing after the same guy, and think how awkward that would be, especially as they'd choose you every time, and then we'd be angry at you for not sharing, and we'd argue and fall out, and as sisters we need to stick together.'

Sofia laughed. 'Daft thing.' The train pulled into the station, the screech of brakes painful. 'But he didn't choose me, did he?'

She helped Luisa onto the train and searched for a vacant seat. The hospital wristband on Luisa's arm caught the notice of a woman, who vacated her seat. Thanking her, Sofia ensured Luisa was settled before leaning against the window, tucking Luisa's rucksack under her.

Her sister looked ponderous, her mind calculating a cunning plan. 'I need more details, so I can deduce if this man's worth pursuing.'

Sofia hoped the train noise would mask their conversation. 'Like I said, we chatted for a while. He helped me with my stuff and loaned me his trainers, so I could walk on the gravel.'

'Thoughtful.'

'It was, but then we got to the station and ... nothing. He seemed to withdraw, like he couldn't get away fast enough. That was it, he was gone.'

Luisa frowned. 'He didn't ask for your phone number? Socials? Any contact information?'

'Nothing.'

'Puzzling.' Luisa tapped her lower lip, the back of her hand covered in a large plaster from the cannula removal. 'Did you at least get his name?'

'His name's Connor.' She rested her head against the glass, trying to hold onto the fleeting memory of that day. 'He volunteers at the community centre near White City station, that's all I know.'

'Should be enough to track him down.' Luisa searched

the internet on her phone, her long hair masking her face. 'Here it is, we can get off at Wood Lane station. It's only a short walk, we can be there in seven minutes.'

It took Sofia a moment to realise what Luisa was suggesting. 'We're not going to the community centre, Luisa.'

'Why not?'

'Weren't you listening?' Sofia leaned closer, her voice a hushed whisper. 'He didn't feel the same way. I'm not going to embarrass myself chasing after a man who's not interested. I have some pride.'

Luisa tucked her hair behind her ears. She looked animated, something that had been absent lately. 'There's no way he's not interested, not unless there's something seriously wrong with him. You're the hottest woman I know. Look at you, you make Jennifer Lopez look positively dreary. You're smart, kind, and sweet. You're even funny ... although not in my league, obviously, but you have your moments. There's no way this man's not interested, not unless he's gay ... but even then I know several gay men who still would.'

Sofia shook her head. 'I get that you're being kind, but he just didn't fancy me. Not enough, anyway.'

'What d'you mean, not enough?' Luisa was like a dog with a bone. 'So he *did* fancy you?'

'I thought he did.' Sofia recalled the moment Connor had lowered her to the ground. 'There was this fleeting moment when I'd jumped from the train and he caught me, and he was looking at me, and I felt this connection. I honestly believed this was it. You know ... love. The real deal.'

Luisa's eyes were wide—mostly with horrified shock. 'Holy cow, you have got it bad.'

'But then the moment vanished and he disappeared, so it must've been my imagination.'

Luisa shook her head. 'There has to be another reason.'

'Maybe he already has a girlfriend.' The idea was painful and depressing, but it was one that kept popping into her head. Did his heart already belong to another?

'Only one way to find out.' Luisa twisted to read the tube map on the wall. 'Next stop, Wood Lane.'

'Luisa, we're not doing this.'

'Why not?'

'He'll think I'm deranged, and besides, you've just got out of hospital. We need to go home so you can rest up.'

Luisa tugged on Sofia's hand so hard they almost bumped noses. 'Listen to me. I've spent weeks stuck in that clinical room, listening to machines beeping, people crying, and watching patients die from the same condition I have. What I *need* is to live a little. I'm not stupid, it was touch-and-go this time, so don't you dare tell me to *take it easy*. Who knows how long before I'm ill again, so for the moment, while I'm feeling fine, we're going to have some excitement.' She got to her feet. 'And pursuing a potential love interest on behalf of my beautifully annoying sister is just the distraction I need. Have I made myself clear?'

Sofia picked up Luisa's bag from the floor, she knew when to concede defeat.

'Smart decision.' Luisa headed for the nearest door, sliding past the other passengers. 'Because unless you take a risk, you'll never see him again, and you'll be left wondering what might have been.' Reaching the exit, she rested her hands on Sofia's shoulders. 'This way you'll know one way or the other. Agreed?'

As crazy at it sounded, her sister had a point. 'Agreed.'

Who knew, maybe she wouldn't feel the same way

about him this time around? Perhaps her desire for love was fuelling her imagination and exaggerating her feelings. Maybe seeing him again wouldn't have the same impact.

As they exited the station and followed the directions to the community centre, Luisa took Sofia's hand. 'When we get there, let me take the lead. This is my area of expertise.'

Sofia slowed her walking pace. 'What area of expertise is that, exactly?'

'I'm much better at assessing a man's credentials than either you or Elena. I love you both dearly, but you're clueless when it comes to relationships.'

'Says the woman who goes through men like underwear.'

Luisa laughed, the effort causing her to catch her breath. 'And for very good reason. They don't measure up. In many ways, if you get my drift.' She wiggled her little finger, making Sofia smile. 'Life is short, and for me that's literal, not figurative, so I don't have the patience for time-wasters. I've become astute at working out who's worth bothering with and who should be tossed out with the garbage.'

Sofia had an image of Luisa interrogating Connor like Papi used to do in restaurants, questioning waiters as to their boyfriend suitability. 'Please don't embarrass me.'

Luisa patted Sofia's hand. 'Subtlety is my middle name.'

Sofia's heart sped up as they approached the redbrick Victorian building, with its leaded windows and high-peaked roof, a stark contrast to the modern buildings either side. 'This is it. We're here.'

There was no way Sofia would have agreed to this outing if she'd had prior warning, but her sister had ambushed her. She was fighting the urge to run. Supposing he didn't remember her? Or he ignored her? Or worse, he did recognise her, but he didn't want anything to do with her. Luisa was convinced this escapade would provide answers, but it could also to deepen Sofia's heartbreak.

The large wooden door thudded shut behind them with a loud crash as they entered the building. So much for an unobtrusive entrance, the whole of London would know they'd arrived.

It was eerily quiet inside and very cold, like the place had its own weather system. To the left was a small unstaffed reception area, and on the right was a noticeboard filled with outdated posters and sign-up sheets for various activities. Leaflets were haphazardly scattered across the table, along with a box labelled 'lost property'.

'There's no one here.' Sofia tugged on Luisa's arm. 'Maybe we should leave. I feel like we're trespassing.'

'Don't be daft, it's a public building.' Luisa headed for the inner door. 'The doors wouldn't be open if they didn't want visitors. We might as well look around now we're here.' She yanked open the door and almost walked into a man entering from the other side. 'Oh! You must be Connor.'

How Luisa knew it was Connor, Sofia had no idea. But when her sister glanced behind and winked, Sofia felt instant heat hit her cheeks.

So much for the impact having lessened. The air left her lungs, her legs wobbled, and she had to lean against the leaflet table to avoid fainting. What was wrong with her?

Her only consolation was that Connor appeared equally shocked. He jolted when he saw her and took an immediate step back. His expression switched from surprise, to joy, to anguish in a heartbeat, before settling into neutrality. 'Sofia? This is a ... surprise.'

She doubted that. He had that strained look of someone

whose family had arranged a surprise party for him and invited all his ex-girlfriends along.

'Hi, Connor.' She gave a little wave and then dropped her hand self-consciously. 'Is it okay for us to be here?'

'Of course.' He'd hesitated before answering, always a bad sign. 'This is a community space, it's open to everyone.'

'It's my fault.' Luisa had watched their exchange with a delighted, calculating look. 'When my sister told me about this place I insisted we visit. I'm Luisa.'

It took Connor a moment to drag his gaze away from Sofia. 'Nice to meet you. I'm one of the volunteers here.'

'So Sofia said.' Luisa's hand was behind her back, her thumb upwards. 'I'm interested to find out what's on offer. Art in particular. You have posters advertising classes.'

Connor ran a finger around the neck of his black T-shirt, like he needed air. 'The art classes aren't running at the moment, we're short on volunteers.'

'Oh, that's a shame.' Luisa pointed to the inner door. 'Can we look around? If you're not too busy.'

'Err ... sure, I guess I can show you around.' He held the door open for them. 'Through here is the main hall, we use this space for large groups, basketball, jumble sales, parties, that kind of stuff. Weekly Zumba classes have just started, if you like dancing.'

'Oh, I love dancing,' Luisa said, following him into the hall. 'But nightclubs rather than village halls, and only when very drunk. I'm assuming you don't run drunk Zumba classes?'

Sofia cringed. 'My sister's joking.'

Connor turned and smiled. 'I got that.'

It was the first genuine smile she'd seen since that day on the train, and her stupid little heart flipped at the sight of it. Her stupid little heart also whimpered when his smile faded and he turned away. This man was adorable, but he might also be a health hazard.

'We have a smaller room where we hold talking therapy sessions and a reading group,' he said, opening the door to a windowless room. It was soulless and painted beige, with scuff-marked walls from pre-existing posters and furniture. 'We have a couple of counsellors who run drug recovery sessions, and a weekly Alcoholics Anonymous meeting, but we'd like to introduce more activities for people dealing with mental health issues. There's high demand for support in the area and the local welfare team have a long waiting list.'

Luisa tilted her head inquisitively. 'Is that something you get involved with, Connor?'

His face drained of colour. 'No, I don't have any qualifications in that area.'

Luisa raised her eyebrows at Sofia, before following him out of the room. 'What's your role here, then?'

Connor led them through the main hall. 'I mainly fill in with sports activities and help with admin stuff. The manager's in his eighties and his health issues prevent him coming down, so things have slipped a bit.'

Luisa glanced at Sofia. 'And you're trying to turn things around?'

'As best I can.' He stopped by a fire exit door.

'That's very noble of you, Connor. Kind. Altruistic, even.'

Sofia poked her sister in the ribs, Luisa was laying it on a bit thick. Evidenced by Connor's weirded-out expression.

He pointed across the hall. 'We have a kitchen on the other side of the building and a café, but it's not open today.'

Luisa nodded. 'No one to run it?'

'Unfortunately not.' He opened the fire door and

stepped outside. 'We're advertising for more volunteers, so hopefully people will come forward. This is the courtyard. We run twice-weekly walking football sessions out here. We get a good turnout for that. The local GP surgeries refer patients to us who'd benefit from improving their fitness.'

The outside area was as dull as inside, bare cracked fencing panels ran the perimeter with rusty wire mesh above, and not a plant in sight.

Luisa headed for a wooden bench and sat down, her breathing shallow. 'It all sounds very impressive, Connor. Although the place is looking a little unloved, if you don't mind me saying.'

Sofia glared at her sister. 'Luisa.'

'It's okay, she's right.' Connor shoved his hands in his jeans pockets. 'We don't have the resources to do everything we'd like. The space needs a makeover, but until we get more volunteers we can't attract more hirers, and without income we can't do the work.'

Luisa rubbed her chest. 'Then it's your lucky day, Connor, because I'm currently on the lookout for an activity to occupy my brain and stop me from overthinking. I have Cystic Fibrosis, which is a physical condition rather than a mental one, but still depressing as hell. My wonderful sister here does a fabulous job looking after me, and I'm eternally grateful, but I'm hard work, even when I'm not ill, so an activity would be good for me ... and her.'

Sofia crouched next to her sister. 'Luisa, you've just got out of hospital.'

'Thanks for reminding me.' Luisa rolled her eyes. 'And as a result of lying on my arse for the last three weeks my lung function has deteriorated. The doctors recommended light exercise to improve my breathing, and as I loathe exercise with a passion, I'm thinking a spot of painting might be the answer.'

Connor looked puzzled. 'Painting?'

'I'm an artist.' Luisa smiled at him. 'And this place could definitely do with a lick of paint. Maybe even a couple of murals to liven things up. Interested?'

Connor looked between the sisters. 'Only if you're sure? We can't pay you, but we can cover materials. And if you need to stop because of your health, that's fine. Whatever you need.'

'That's very understanding of you, Connor. Isn't he a sweetheart, Sofia?'

Sofia ignored the mischievous glint in her sister's eye. 'Luisa, that's a big undertaking, and you haven't been well. It'll take time to rebuild your strength.'

'Which is why you're going to help me.' The glint in Luisa's eye exploded into full-blown shooting stars, lighting up her face with scheming joy.

Sofia blinked. 'I am?'

'My sister's between jobs at the moment,' Luisa said to Connor. 'My fault entirely, I'm a full-time occupation. She's amazing, by the way. I'm guessing you'd worked that one out for yourself?'

Phrasing it as a question left the poor man with no option but to confirm. 'I had, yes.'

His voice was soft and low, and it was impossible to read any meaning behind his words. Sofia had made that mistake before, she wasn't foolish enough to be hoodwinked a second time.

'Thought as much.' Leaning on Sofia, Luisa stood up. 'This is a perfect solution for everyone. The community centre gets a makeover, you get some extra volunteer support, and I get to splash paint around all day.' There was no denying her sister looked genuinely happy about the arrangement. Maybe a project would be good for her, even if it was meddling in Sofia's love life.

Sofia realised Connor was watching her. 'What about you, Sofia, what do you get out of this?'

'Me?' *Apart from seeing you every day?* 'I guess I'm about to find out.'

Chapter Eleven

DANNY

Wednesday, 25th June

As Danny filed the last document in a pre-trial bundle ready for court, someone knocked on his office door. He assumed it would be Elena—massage oil in hand, ready to pummel his body into submission. It was a strangely arousing thought, and highly disturbing. Elena Romero was not his type, not in the least. She was too exuberant. Too volatile. Too much of ... well, everything. Tectonic plates shifted when she was in the building, like her aura had its own galaxy and she defied the laws of astronomy. Being in her presence was not restful.

So opening the door to discover Connor standing in the lobby gave him a pleasant bolt of surprise.

Connor hovered slightly, still unsure of himself. 'Hey, how's it going?'

It broke Danny's heart to witness such lack of self-confidence, and he pulled his brother in for a hug. 'This is a nice surprise, I wasn't expecting you.' He kissed the side of Connor's head.

Unlike Hugh, Danny wasn't great with words, and he wasn't emotionally intuitive or able to offer insights and verbal comfort. All he could do was demonstrate his love for Connor with actions.

He held onto the hug, needing the physical contact as much as his brother did, before letting go and holding him at arm's length. 'Everything okay?'

'Uncle Hugh's invited me out for pizza. I'm meeting him here after work. Can you join us?'

Relief swamped him. There was no drama, just the need to socialise and eat. Normal stuff. Good stuff, healthy stuff ... well, aside from the pizza, but everyone had to live a little.

'I'd love to,' he said, genuinely disappointed. 'But I have an appointment booked for five-thirty. I'll meet you afterwards though, where are you going?'

'Cinquecento on Portobello Road.'

'Fancy. Save me some pizza, okay?'

'Will do.' Connor smiled, the hint of angst still evident in his dark eyes. He looked pale, but less haunted, which was enough of a lifeline for Danny to cling onto. Would the joyful innocence of the old Connor ever return? He hoped so.

Danny beckoned him through the door. 'Come inside, there's something I want to talk to you about.'

Connor followed him into the office, hands shoved deep inside his jacket pockets. 'Should I be worried?'

'Of course not.' Danny hesitated, unsure how to tackle what had been plaguing him. 'I keep thinking back to that conversation we had the other night at basketball, about relationships and stuff.' The discomfort had been keeping him awake at night—not that he slept much, but now he had the guilt of destroying his brother's belief in the whole 'happy ever after' to add to the long list of things he felt inadequate about. 'I'm sad you have such a negative view of love. Dating should be fun and exciting, not something to steer clear of.'

Connor frowned. 'And yet you have?'

Boy, the past was coming back to haunt him. 'I know, and maybe I was wrong to do that. Please don't punish yourself by missing out on something just because it might not work out. Love is a dice-roll, it's a chance you take. Better to try and fail than avoid it altogether.' He clocked the incredulous expression on Connor's face. 'You're right, I'm a hypocrite. I had a bad experience, and I've let it destroy any chance of trying again. I've actively steered clear of relationships, and that probably wasn't in my best interests, or yours. You mean the world to me, Connor. I want you to be happy, and I hate the idea of you walking away from something because of one shitty experience.'

Connor raised an eyebrow. 'You're saying I should believe in love?'

'Exactly.' Danny smiled, hoping to appear encouraging and a supportive older brother, rather than a tale of doom and gloom. 'Be open to it. Don't deny yourself the chance of seeing where something might lead.'

'Okay.'

Danny stilled. 'Okay? ... That was easy.'

Connor shrugged, his shoulders already hunched from the padded hood of his jacket. 'I mean, I will if you will.'

He might have expected a catch. 'Excuse me?'

Connor walked over to the visitor's chair and flopped down, his demeanour uncharacteristically defiant. 'I'll stop avoiding the possibility of a relationship—if you do.'

Danny silently cursed, his brother was too smart for his own good. 'It's different for me, I'm fine being single.'

'So am I.' Connor's innocent expression didn't fool Danny for one second, but he was prevented from challenging his brother by a tap on the door.

'Hello? Sorry, didn't mean to interrupt.' Elena stood in the doorway wearing her navy physio tunic and carrying a holdall. She looked tentatively between the brothers. 'Do you need to reschedule our appointment?'

'No, it's fine. I was just finishing up.' Unsettled, Danny ran his hands through his hair, feeling cornered from all sides. 'This is my brother, Connor.'

Elena waved. 'Hi, nice to meet you. I'm Elena.'

'Elena's my physiotherapist,' Danny added, feeling the need to explain the appearance of a gorgeous woman standing in his doorway, especially as Connor's eyes were flitting between Danny and Elena in a 'what's happening here?' kind of way.

Connor couldn't have looked more surprised if Danny had introduced her as his private escort. 'I didn't know you were getting treatment?'

Danny suddenly felt self-conscious. 'It's a recent thing.'

'Your brother's very stubborn,' Elena said, leaning against the doorframe. 'It took some persuading.'

Connor's eyes widened. 'I've been at him for months to get treatment. How did you convince him?'

'Coercion, mostly. I'm stubborn too.' Her smile was like a weapon, fast and wide, and able to shift dimensions and space. Danny took a step back, the woman scared him.

In contrast, Connor appeared relaxed and totally unfazed, as though she was just a woman and not the human equivalent of a lightsaber with the ability to disarm her enemies. 'I hope you know what you're dealing with. He's not good at accepting help.'

Danny blinked in surprise. Connor was teasing him? That was a new development.

'I'd gathered that.' Elena directed her smile at Danny, like a sniper about to unclip the safety mechanism on her Glock. 'To be honest, he's the one who should be worried.' She came into the office and dumped her holdall on the floor. 'I inflict pain.'

Did she have to sound so thrilled about it?

Danny loosened his shirt collar. 'If you've both finished assassinating my character—'

'This looks cosy.'

Danny turned to see his best mate standing in the doorway. Great, more witnesses. Would anyone else like to join them? Maybe he should sell tickets.

'Uncle Hugh.' Connor shot over and hugged him. 'This is Elena, Dad's *physiotherapist*.' He nodded conspiratorially towards Elena as though everyone except Danny knew what was going on. 'Can you believe it?'

Hugh looked amused. 'Stranger things have happened. I would tell him it's about time, but he hates it when I gloat.' He slung his arm over Connor's shoulder. 'Ready for pizza?'

'Yes, Dad's joining us after his pain-fest.'

Elena looked confused, no doubt wondering why Connor had called him *Dad*.

Before he could explain, Hugh burst out laughing, a big amused sound that made Connor grin and Danny take another step back. 'I'm almost tempted to stay and watch.'

Danny was done being goaded. 'You can leave now. Thanks for dropping by. Good night.' He gave Hugh a playful shove out of the door and clumsily kissed Connor's head before shutting the door behind them.

'Nice meeting you, Elena!' Connor shouted from the lobby.

'You too!' Elena called back, before turning to Danny. 'Ready for some fun?' She gestured for him to lock the office door.

A host of emotions flooded his brain as he snatched at the lock. Confusion at what was happening, relief at hearing Connor laugh, but most of all, annoyance at being caught with his guard down.

'Don't even attempt to intimidate me,' he barked, storming over to his desk, unable to hide the rage bubbling inside him. Feeling insecure had always been a trigger, making him angry and unreasonable, but he didn't care if his behaviour wasn't rational, he was sick of playing Mr Nice. 'I know your game and I won't be toyed with.'

Elena looked stunned. 'I have no idea what you mean.'

'Turn around,' he said, unzipping his fly. 'I'm changing into joggers, and they're *not* coming off.'

With eyebrows raised so high they almost disappeared into her hairline, she turned away and rested her hands on her hips. 'I think you have the wrong impression of me.'

'No, I don't think I do.' He stepped out of his suit trousers, his agitation levels rising when he realised he'd forgotten to remove his shoes. 'This is about revenge for you, isn't it? A way of paying me back for not swapping offices. Oh, for fuc—' He kicked off his shoes, yanking the trousers from his feet.

A beat passed before she spoke. 'Is that what you think?'

'Delighting in inflicting pain? Making me undress? Locking the door? I'm not dumb,' he said, evidence suggesting otherwise when he nearly pulled on his joggers back-to-front. 'You obviously get a kick out of trying to embarrass me. Well, I'm not having it. Pack it in. I'm not playing your games.'

There was another long, drawn-out pause. 'Are you done?'

He unbuttoned his shirt, hot from wrestling with his clothing. 'Yes.'

She turned to face him, her expression more tentative than he'd seen before. Good, she deserved to be on the back foot. 'May I address your accusations?'

'Go for it. I'm sure you have an answer for everything,' he muttered sarcastically, fumbling over his sleeve buttons.

She switched her weight from one foot to the other, as if steadying herself. 'Firstly, I don't enjoy inflicting pain, it's part of my job. I endeavour to read people and assess how best to manage the situation, as it can be incredibly challenging. I assumed ...' her hand went to her throat, '... wrongly, as it transpired, that you'd appreciate a more light-hearted approach, rather than sympathy. Apologies if I've inadvertently made you feel uncomfortable.'

Big of her. He removed his shirt, not caring that he was standing in front of her shirtless. Let her squirm and blush, she was the one playing games, not him.

She glanced at the door, possibly wishing to escape. He knew the feeling. Her fingers trailed down her neck and it was impossible not to watch as they lowered to her neckline. Her nails were short and shiny, matching her dark hair. Her whole appearance was wholesome and clean, with no obvious make-up, and she radiated health—although her current glow was probably caused by the heightened situation rather than exercise.

It took a moment for her flushed gaze to return to him. 'Secondly, the locked door is purely for privacy, no other reason. My aim is to preserve my patient's dignity at all times, and allowing someone to walk in during a session would be completely unprofessional.'

He couldn't argue with that—he wanted to, he just couldn't.

Her eyes skimmed over his bare chest, before lifting to meet his slightly less annoyed expression. 'Thirdly, I cannot treat an injury through clothing. Again, I try to deal with this in a jovial way to make it less awkward, particularly when it's a delicate area of the body. It certainly wasn't my intention to embarrass you, and I assure you I'm not playing games.'

He rummaged for his T-shirt in his bag, mostly to detract from the foolishness he felt.

She waited, her hands clasped in front of her, her head slightly bowed. 'If you feel I've been inappropriate in any way, I'm truly sorry. I take my job very seriously and I'm mortified that you consider my actions to be unprofessional.'

Shit. Why did she have to apologise? He'd expected a fight, not an apology. He wanted someone to take his anger out on, and she seemed like a worthy sparring partner.

More annoyed with himself than her, he shoved his T-shirt over his head. 'Great. I feel like a right dick now.'

Her chin lifted slightly. 'You're entitled to raise concerns about your treatment, and it would be wrong of me to dismiss those concerns, but I hope I've reassured you. As for the office swap, it was a poor attempt at a joke. It's clear why you couldn't agree to that, and I won't mention the subject again. You have my word.'

He supposed this was the English side of her character she'd spoken about, the demure posture, contrite expression and contained mannerisms. It was certainly a contrast to the

Latin side of her, that was for sure. He wasn't sure which was more unnerving. He knew where he stood when she was fighting back, maybe he should be more worried about this side of her—she was eerily calm, like a python poised to strike.

He came around from behind the desk. 'I overreacted, I'm sorry. You haven't been unprofessional, it's my own hang-ups making me defensive.'

'My only desire is to help. I have no agenda, there's no game playing, and I truly believe I can ease your discomfort. But maybe you'd feel more at ease with another physiotherapist? I can refer you elsewhere, if you'd prefer.'

'And go through this again? God, no. You'll do.'

A wry smile tugged at her shiny lips. 'I'm touched.'

He rubbed his neck. 'You know what I mean.'

She unrolled the mat onto the floor and knelt down, glancing up at him, her long eyelashes silhouetted against her eyelids. 'Are we good?' When he nodded, she patted the mat. 'Lie face down, please. I've taken a look at your scans and they didn't reveal any further damage, so we know what we're dealing with. Hopefully we can make swift progress.' She waited until he was in position. 'Comfortable?'

'As comfortable as I can be lying on the floor.'

She shuffled closer and he could smell something faintly floral. 'I'd like to begin with a light massage to warm up the muscles, would that be okay?'

'Go for it.' He knew he sounded irritable. He also knew he'd overreacted earlier, and neither admission was helping him relax.

Sighing, he rested his forehead on his arms as she lifted his T-shirt and began working her way down his back. Her hands were cold to start with, but grew warmer as she worked the muscles in his lower back. It was a strange sensation. Intrusive, personal, pleasurable. He could feel the tension in his muscles almost sigh as they relented and softened at her touch.

'Bad day?'

'Bad year,' he answered on reflex, followed by a grimace. There was something unravelling about being massaged, as though her fingers were dismantling his emotions as well as his muscles. 'I don't know what's wrong with me, I never used to be this sensitive. I get so agitated these days, I flip between wanting to punch someone and bursting into tears.'

'You wouldn't be the first to do either in my presence,' she said, her fingers sinking deeper.

He jolted at that. 'You've been punched?'

'Several times. It's a reflex reaction to pain. I don't take it personally, although I have learned to duck.'

He was genuinely shocked—he had no idea physiotherapy was such a precarious profession. There was no denying the treatment was painful, eye-wateringly so, but it wasn't unpleasant. He almost relished the torture, physical pain was easier to manage than emotional pain. 'I might curse, but I won't punch you.'

'Good to know.' She paused, and he felt something liquid run down his back. 'At our last session, we established that this change in your emotions coincided with your accident.' She shifted position and resumed massaging, her fingers digging in so hard he had to bite his hand to stop himself crying out. 'I mention this, because living with constant pain can affect everything, from how a person moves, sleeps, and socialises. It's often described as like being stuck inside a room with a low ceiling you can't escape from and you can never stand up in. The constant nagging pain acts like a dripping tap, slowly driving a person crazy.'

She'd described it perfectly, that's exactly how he felt.

Her hands travelled lower, the oil making her movements more fluid and his pelvis twitch in response. 'Your over-sensitivity is probably a result of the pain you're in and your body struggling to process it and allow you to function properly.'

'Maybe.' It was hard to focus on logic when he was fighting his body's reaction to her touch.

There was nothing remotely romantic about the situation, and yet it felt incredibly intimate. His sexual encounters over the years had been straightforward, short in duration, and basic in their aim—gratification without complication. He'd never allowed for anything more, no hand-holding, cuddling, candlelit dinners, nothing that would cross the line or cause confusion. He knew men who would act like they wanted more, a relationship, love, commitment, until they'd got what they wanted and then ghosted the person. He'd never done that, and he never would. It seemed deceitful and risked a messy ending. His interactions were like his business dealings, scheduled, emotionless, and with a fixed conclusion.

So to find himself lying in such a submissive position and allowing a woman, albeit a professional health worker, to wrestle away that control and cause such a physical and emotional reaction, was highly unnerving.

'Can you roll onto your back for me?'

He clenched his jaw. 'Not right at this moment.'

'That's okay. I'm just going to do some gentle stretches on your hamstrings, okay?' She sounded perfectly unflustered, and he guessed he wasn't the first man to react in such a way. She lifted his lower leg and pressed his heel into his buttock. 'Can I ask a personal question?'

He hoped it wasn't the obvious one. 'I can't promise to answer.'

She held the stretch and he was grateful for the pain, it diverted blood flow elsewhere. He suspected she'd used that technique before. Nice trick. 'Your brother called you Dad.'

He wondered what else she'd overheard. 'That's not a question.'

'Is that your way of politely shutting me down?'

'No, but my relationship with Connor is complicated. Biologically he's my brother, but I've raised him since he was five years old. So he views me as both his brother and his parent.'

She switched legs and began to inflict more pain on his other side. 'You told me your parents had died, but I had no idea you'd raised your brother. How old were you?'

'Nineteen. I'd only been at university a year, and suddenly I had to juggle childcare with my law studies.'

'How on earth did you manage it?' She sounded genuinely interested.

He often wondered himself. 'I couldn't have done it without Hugh's help. We've been best mates since I arrived in the UK. Most nineteen-year-olds would've run a mile, but he saved me. My parents cut off financial support when I left home, so Hugh's family took me in and helped me look after Connor.'

'Which explains why you're so close.'

'Yeah, we're tight. Hugh is family, always has been.'

'He's not your average counsellor, is he?' She sounded ponderous, and he knew why.

Hugh came from old money and held himself with the confidence of a man in authority. He attended polo events, his father sat in the House of Lords, and his family socialised with the powerful and elite, but his entitled exterior masked a heart the size of Mars. Hugh Spencer-Harrison was indeed a conundrum.

'Hugh used to be a stock broker and made a stack of money from it too. The role and lifestyle suited him.' But it had also impacted on their relationship, creating a period they referred to as their 'barren years' when they'd struggled to keep in touch and lacked time to meet up. 'I was as surprised as anyone when he gave it up to retrain as a counsellor. He's good at it, though. We've had a tough year and Hugh's been there for us both.'

'The ideal friend.' She eased his leg down. 'Are you okay to turn over for me?'

He checked his dignity was intact before rolling over.

'Take a deep breath and relax into the mat for me. I'm going to gently stretch out your hip, but you need to let me know if it becomes painful. Bend your left knee up for me.'

He allowed her to move him into position.

'Why did your parents cut you off?' It was an intrusive question, but her attention remained focused on his hip.

He supposed he couldn't blame her for asking—he'd mentioned it, after all. 'Because I chose to study law instead of dentistry.'

Her eyes briefly met his. 'That was it?'

'Pretty much.' There were other things, like their need to control everything, the fact that they valued appearances over happiness, and their general lack of empathy or compassion, but in the end it had come down to his fight for freedom and independence. They wanted to dictate his future, he wasn't going to comply. 'They wanted me to join the family practice. I said no, they made an ultimatum. You can guess the rest.'

She lifted his leg higher. 'Dentistry wasn't for you?'

'The idea of spending my days inside other people's mouths is not appealing.'

She smiled at that. She had an amazing smile, it was almost as distracting as the feel of her hands sliding down his thigh. 'Were you on good terms when they died?'

'Nope.'

'That's sad.' She moved to his other leg. 'Why did you choose to study law?'

'I like problem solving. I guess I like winning too. Setting up in practice gives me a sense of control and allows me to be there for Connor.'

'Maybe you'll have more time for yourself moving forwards, now he's an adult.'

'Maybe.' Why did that thought scare him so much? It hadn't occurred to him before, but maybe he needed Connor more than his brother needed him.

She attempted to ease his right knee to the floor and open up his hip, but it was stiffer than his other leg and resisted. 'You said it's been a bad year, are things still tricky?'

'We're getting there. It's complicated.' Made more so now that Connor had issued his own ultimatum regarding them both dating—maybe his brother had more in common with his parents than he'd realised.

'Complicated I get.' Elena tried the stretch again, checking his face for signs of pain. 'After my mum died, my father returned to Colombia to deal with a few business issues, and we haven't seen him since. We've just discovered he's been trekking through the jungle like some wildlife explorer, totally unaware that his youngest daughter's been in hospital for three weeks.'

'I remember you said she'd been ill. How's she doing?'

'She's home now, but it's hard work caring for a sibling, and Luisa's twenty-five. I couldn't have coped looking after her when she was five, she's enough of a handful now.'

'I've never regretted taking on Connor, he means everything to me.' When he winced, she eased off the stretch and lowered his leg.

'Doesn't mean it hasn't been hard work, or without cost. Am I right?'

He nodded.

There was such kindness and understanding in the way she looked at him that he felt quite overwhelmed. Damned emotions. He preferred it when he'd been numb. It was easier than riding the rollercoaster of extremes.

She sat back on her haunches. 'I'm guessing this accident of yours involved Connor too? I'm not going to pry, but it explains why you're so knotted up.' She tapped his thigh. 'And I don't just mean your muscles.'

His eyes burned hot. 'Are we done?'

'We're done.' She rolled effortlessly onto her feet and upright in a seamless motion. 'Same time tomorrow?'

Dismay filled his gut. 'So soon?'

'Initially. But then we can extend the gap and introduce a set of stretches for you to do at home. Need a hand getting up?'

'I'm good.' If by good he meant groaning as he flopped about trying to twist onto his knees and push himself up with all the fluidity of a ninety-year-old. 'Tell me it gets easier.'

Smiling, she rolled up the mat. 'Eventually. You might be sore tonight. Take paracetamol for the pain and drink plenty of water. A warm bath might help too.'

He'd yet to try out Hugh's fancy jacuzzi, tonight might

be the night. 'I'm meeting up with Connor and Hugh for pizza, you're welcome to join us.'

Why had he said that?

Inwardly, he cringed, praying she wouldn't say yes. She might read something into it and assume he was interested in her. Worse, Connor would definitely read something into it and rejoice at him 'dating' again. He waited for her answer, mentally crossing his fingers.

She zipped up her holdall. 'That's kind of you, but I have plans tonight.'

Thank God. He felt relieved ... Actually, he didn't feel relieved, and he had no idea why. 'Does it involve dressing up?'

She laughed. 'Not this time. We're supposed to be FaceTiming Papi in Colombia. Assuming he can get a signal and he doesn't bail on us again.' She sounded sad.

He went over and unlocked the door. 'Are things not good with your dad?'

'It's impossible to tell. He's still grieving for our mum, and that's affecting his decision-making. Poor man's devastated, so it's impossible to stay angry with him when he's struggling so much. At the same time, we're left to look after Luisa, which isn't always easy. I switch from missing him to being angry with him about a hundred times a day.' She hoisted her holdall onto her shoulder. 'We just want him to come home.'

'Do you think he will?'

'At some point. The question is when. The thought of living without either parent is horrifying.' She flinched. 'Sorry, I didn't mean to sound insensitive.'

'You didn't. I hope you get to talk to him.'

'Me too.' She joined him by the door. 'Enjoy your pizza.'

'Sorry again for ranting earlier.'

'All forgotten.' She paused as she stepped into the lobby. 'By the way, your T-shirt's on inside out.' Smiling, she disappeared out the main door.

Danny glanced down. Christ, he couldn't even dress himself.

He was in a worse state than he'd imagined.

Chapter Twelve

ELENA

Friday, 27th June

Elena held up her phone and walked around the room, ensuring she captured the full impact of the grand suite in all its glory. Never in her life had she stayed somewhere so exclusive, she was almost afraid to touch anything.

'Take a look at the bed,' she said, zooming out so her sisters could see the queen-sized frame. 'Four-poster, with matching gold headboard.'

'Do you think it's real?' Sofia asked. 'It looks so luxurious.'

'All that pattern's making my eyes hurt,' Luisa chipped in.

It was true the room was the polar opposite of minimalism. The colour palette was varying shades of champagne, with accents of deep gold and dark walnut. The carpet was one pattern, the wallpaper and furniture another design entirely. The suite footprint was larger than their entire downstairs, and the townhouse wasn't exactly small.

'And Hugh paid for the whole thing?' Sofia asked, as Elena showed them the glass chandelier dangling above the bed.

'His way of thanking me for being his plus-one.' Hugh's husband, James, was away at a conference, so he'd asked Elena to accompany him to an annual charity event he was on the trustee board for. It wasn't a difficult decision, accepting an invite to a Roaring Twenties dinner dance in one of London's most expensive hotels. 'Hugh has an appointment first thing tomorrow, so he's not able to stay overnight himself, but he wanted me to have the full hotel experience.'

'Let's see your dress.' Luisa's face was squashed next to Sofia's on the screen.

Elena stood in front of the standalone gilded mirror, angling her phone until she was in view. 'Can you see?'

'Oh, Elena, you look beautiful!' Sofia looked a little emotional as Elena swished from side to side, making the fringing on her flapper dress swing out.

Had she known the room's décor in advance she might not have opted for the champagne colour, she was in danger of disappearing into the wallpaper. The dress was classic twenties design, with a sheer neckline, leading down to a beaded bodice and trimmed with so much fringing she felt like a helicopter about to take off when she twirled around. With matching glittery headband, dangly earrings and gold T-bar shoes, she felt suitably glammed-up for a night out.

The outfit had felt like overkill in her bedroom at home, but in such palatial surroundings it hit the mark. Or at least, she hoped it did. Hugh was hiring a vintage tuxedo, so she needed to raise her style game.

Her phone pinged with a message. Hugh must have arrived, but her excitement faded as she read the message. 'Oh, you're kidding me.'

Sofia looked concerned. 'Is something wrong?'

'Hugh's been called to the hospital to deal with an emergency, one of his patients has been sectioned. He's not able to come to the event.'

'Oh, what rotten luck.' Sofia looked crushed.

'Can't you fly solo?' Luisa jostled with Sofia for prime position. 'You stand a better chance of pulling if you're on your own.'

'Believe me, I'd rather go solo, but he's sending a replacement *date*.' It was hard not to spit as she said the word. 'Daniel bloody Jackson.'

Luisa pulled a face. 'Who?'

Sofia nudged Luisa. 'The man she shares an office building with.'

'Oh, shit! You mean, the hot suit?' Luisa burst out laughing, which quickly resulted in a coughing fit. 'Priceless.'

Sofia rubbed Luisa's back. 'He's really not so bad, Elena. He was very kind to me when I met him. Maybe away from work he's a different person, more relaxed, and less ...'

There were several words Elena could have inserted into the pause. She opted for ... 'Difficult?'

'Exactly.' Sofia nodded. 'A social event in a nice hotel might bring out his charming side.'

'Or, he might still be a boring suit and expect you to use the correct fork at dinner, refrain from consuming any alcohol, and be tucked up in bed by nine p.m.' Luisa thumped her chest, trying to clear her airways. 'I'd ditch him, if I were you, and take your chances elsewhere.'

It was tempting, especially after their recent encounters. Tensions were at an all-time high. She wasn't sure what radiated between them that caused her skin to prickle and her pulse to thud—it was either acute sexual chemistry, or a bad allergic reaction. Both were highly dangerous and likely to result in a hospital admittance.

Her phone pinged again. 'Damn it, he's here. I suppose it's too late to fake a migraine?'

Luisa's firm, 'No!' collided with Sofia's, 'Yes!'

Sofia glared at Luisa. 'She can't leave him waiting, it would be rude.'

Luisa poked her tongue out. 'She owes the man nothing. Her date was with Hugh the hot gay therapist, she has every right to bail. Ditch the suit, I say. He's a lost cause.'

'Nonsense, he's not that bad, and if nothing else, it might make your working life a bit easier. What have you got to lose?' Sofia's hand covered Luisa's mouth when she attempted to interrupt. 'Smile, be positive, and enjoy the evening.'

Elena sighed. 'Fat chance. But yes, okay, I'll try.' She glanced at her mum's bangle-watch on her wrist. 'I'd better go, the event has started.'

'Keep an open mind,' Sofia urged.

'And keep your pepper spray close,' Luisa added.

Rolling her eyes, Elena blew kisses to her sisters. 'Have a good evening, the pair of you. Enjoy Bridgerton.'

Elena exited the bedroom and headed for the lifts, the heels of her shoes sinking into the plush carpet.

How on earth had this happened? What crime from her uneventful life was so scandalous that she deserved an evening with Daniel-the-*Jerk*-Jackson?

She pressed the button for the lift and watched in awe as two glass doors slid open without so much as a whisper. She stepped inside, nodding a hello to an older couple dressed in vintage clothing and clearly attending the same event.

As the lift descended, she reminded herself she'd promised to start calling her nemeses by his given name. This concession wasn't down to a sudden shift in her opinion of him, but more an acknowledgment that he wasn't quite the demon she'd first thought, and maybe ... just maybe ... she'd been too harsh in her judgement of him. The man had issues. He had a bad hip injury, a complex relationship with his brother-cum-son, and serious anxiety. She needed to cut him some slack.

That didn't stop him from being a suit. He just wasn't a jerk.

The hotel was filled with arriving guests. The mass of bodies, chatter, and music made searching for her *date* troublesome. Immaculately dressed staff carried trays of canapés and champagne flutes, and doormen dressed in gold and green livery lifted their hats as guests were shown through to the banqueting hall.

A tap on her shoulder made her startle.

'Sorry I've kept you waiting,' he said, as she turned to face her companion for the evening. 'I didn't get Hugh's message until I was leaving work.'

'I imagine it took Hugh some persuading to get you here,' she said, with a wry smile. 'You've probably spent the last hour trying to come up with an excuse not to attend.'

'Champagne?' he said, snatching two flutes from a passing tray and handing her one.

Nice dodge. Her assessment was obviously correct.

He tried for a smile. 'Might as well make the most of a

free night out. You look beautiful, by the way, that's a stunning dress.'

She accepted the offer of champagne. 'Thank you.'

'I didn't have time to collect Hugh's suit. This was the best I could do at short notice.'

He was wearing one of his dark grey work suits. However, the addition of a purple silk handkerchief poking out of his top pocket matching his tie, and a fitted waistcoat over a dark purple shirt, lifted his look from boring office to Tom Ford model. She'd be lying if she didn't acknowledge that he looked good. Too good.

She sipped her champagne, the bubbles tickling her red lips. She wouldn't have worn *Fever Red* lipstick of she'd know who her date was. With Hugh it would have been a fun part of her outfit and in-keeping with the whole flapper look: false eyelashes, beauty spot, and kohl-flicked eyes. But with Danny it felt dangerous, as though she was waving a red flag at an enraged bull. The way his eyes kept dipping to her mouth confirmed her theory, especially when he swallowed awkwardly and knocked back another mouthful of champagne.

'Is my company that awful?'

He frowned. 'Why would you say that?'

'You drank that champagne in less than five minutes. I guess inebriation is one way of getting through the evening.'

'I'm nervous.' He rubbed his forehead. 'I thought alcohol might help.'

His admission surprised her. 'Why are you nervous?'

He gestured to the inner doors. 'Shall we head through?'

Another dodge.

Puzzled, she followed him. 'You really didn't want to

come tonight, did you? How did Hugh persuade you? Bribery? Guilt? You owed him a favour?'

'All three. But it was Connor's ultimatum that swung it.'

She raised an eyebrow. 'Which was?'

'If I didn't come, our deal was off.'

'What deal?'

'He'll only start dating again if I do.'

She stopped dead. Of all the things she imagined he might say, that wasn't one of them. Intrigued, she took his arm and they headed into the noisy banqueting hall. 'And why don't you date?'

'Women scare me.'

'Pathetic.'

'I don't see you with a partner.'

Elena pinned him with her sweetest smile. She could fob him off with a lie, but that would hardly encourage him to open up about his own troubles, and sometimes the brutal truth was needed. 'That's because he left me, took a job in Manchester and walked away from a five year-relationship without so much as a single tear. It's rather cutting to discover a man is affected more by leaving his golf club than his girlfriend. So here I am, alone and bruised, and spending the evening with a man who's only here because he doesn't want to break a deal with his brother. Life's harsh. Am I complaining? No, I'm not.'

Her date blinked a few times, no doubt wondering whether she was serious, before handing her another flute of champagne. 'I think you need this more than I do.'

'Debatable.'

'He doesn't sound like a nice man.'

'He was perfectly nice, most of the time. He just didn't love me enough to stay. Such is life.' She walked off with a shrug, feigning more nonchalance than she felt. The rejection still stung. 'Coming?'

He joined her by the roulette table. 'So you're off men?'

'No, I'm just more careful about who I let into my life. No more suits.'

'Suits?'

She watched the croupier deftly spin the wheel. 'It's what my sister calls men who put their careers ahead of their family. Serious, rigid types with no sense of fun, who'd rather be working at the office than at home in bed pleasuring their loved one.'

He choked on his drink.

She patted his back.

Red twenty-five landed and the man opposite yelled with delight as he collected his winnings.

Danny frowned at her. 'Am I a suit?'

'More champagne?' she asked, following his lead by swerving the question and snagging another two drinks from the passing waiter. 'So, why doesn't Connor date?'

'He has trust issues. Plus, it transpires I haven't been the best role model in that department.' He turned back to the table.

She waited a beat. 'And that's why he made a deal with you?'

Danny kept his eyes on the wheel as it spun. 'We both date, or we both stay single. Which is fine by me, but not fair on him. I don't want him missing out.'

'Why is being single okay for you?' She nudged his arm. 'None of this "women scare me" bullshit. What gives?'

He turned to her, one eyebrow raised. 'What gives?'

'It's something my sister says. Let me rephrase, what's stopping you from meeting someone?'

'Fear.' When the woman next to him won and threw

her arms in the air, he nearly spilled his drink. 'Seriously, I don't have the energy to deal with the drama.' He moved away from the woman and towards a small stage where a magician was performing card tricks.

Elena followed him. 'Drama?'

'Yes, the drama. You avoid suits, I avoid drama.'

'And what's the definition of drama?'

'High-maintenance, emotional, irrational, complicated.'

'Ah, right.' Elena smiled. 'What was her name?'

Danny knocked back his champagne. 'Trouble.'

She laughed. 'Divorced?'

'Dead.'

She stopped laughing.

The magician pulled out a playing card from a man's top pocket and the crowd applauded. She studied Danny's profile: square jaw, defined cheekbones, his almost perfect eyebrows, even if his glasses didn't sit quite straight on his nose. 'You're not the luckiest bloke on the planet, are you?' Looks aside.

He gestured to a passing waiter. 'I'm the human equivalent of a black cat.'

'I thought black cats were supposed to be lucky.'

'Not in my experience.'

'Also dead?'

'Squashed by a tractor.'

She couldn't help laughing at the absurdity of it all. 'Christ, maybe I do need another drink. This is depressing stuff.'

Danny swapped his champagne for a glass of Jack Daniels. 'Now you know why I don't date.'

Elena declined more champagne and opted for a non-alcoholic fruit cocktail—she needed to keep her wits about her. 'Because they will either give you grief, mess up your perfectly ironed shirts, or end up dead?'

He nodded. 'That about sums it up.'

'Then it's just as well this isn't a date.' She clinked glasses with him. 'Cheers!'

He sighed and took a swig of whiskey. 'Hugh would've been a great date for you. He's more fun than I am. Sorry you drew the short straw.'

She watched his face turn serious. 'Do you ever have fun?'

'Depends on your definition of fun?'

She thought of all the fun times they'd had as a family before her mum's death. 'Letting go, being daft, laughing until your bladder gives way.'

'Based on that definition, never.' He drank more whiskey. 'Why are you looking at me like that? Stop it, I don't like that calculating look, it usually means pain is about to happen, and I've suffered enough, you said so yourself.'

She rested her hand on his suit lapel. 'I'm thinking this evening could be part of your ongoing therapy.'

He looked down at her hand. 'The answer's no. Whatever it is, no.'

'Appalling attitude. Talk about fatalistic. Here's the thing, we're at an amazing venue, we're dressed up, there's music playing, games on offer, and free alcohol. If you can't loosen up and have fun on a night like this, when can you?'

He didn't look convinced. 'What are you suggesting?'

'Nothing alarming, no pain involved. Just succumbing to the ambience and allowing those rigid muscles of yours to relax a little.' She squeezed his bicep. 'What have you got to lose?'

'My dignity?'

'Oh, please.' She punched his arm. 'I'm talking about a few games of poker and dancing the Charleston, not stripping naked and swinging from the chandeliers ... at least, not while sober.' She slipped her arm through his. 'Just think, you can return home dishevelled and tipsy and delight in telling Connor all about your exciting *date*. He'll be so proud.'

He swayed slightly on his feet. 'Why do I feel like I'm being manipulated?'

'Because Connor isn't the only one with trust issues. Like father, like son ... or rather, brother, whatever. Like I told you before, I have no agenda. My only goal is to help you get better, and that includes letting go of your inhibitions. You never know, you might actually enjoy yourself.' She held out her hand. 'Truce?'

Whether it was to stop her badgering him, or acknowledging the opportunity in front of him, she wasn't sure, but he shook her hand. 'Truce.'

'Good. Let's go party.'

It took an hour before his jacket came off, and another half hour before he loosened his tie, during which time they played two games of poker, and lost, four games of roulette, without a single red or black colour match, and failed to guess the correct suit in a game of chance with the magician. Danny Jackson really was the unluckiest man on the planet.

Throughout the mayhem of a noisy swing band, raucous laughter and uncoordinated dancing, Danny knocked back whiskeys, smiled like a lunatic, and gradually succumbed to the effects of excessive alcohol. It was hilarious to witness, and oddly endearing.

His attempt at the Charleston made them both laugh to the point of stomach ache, and he was a beat behind everyone else during the salsa—although he did redeem himself during the slow dances. With his arm around her waist and his other hand holding hers to his chest, she could almost feel the moment his body relented. The rhythm of his breathing mirrored hers, and the assuredness of his hold hinted at what lay beneath, and it certainly wasn't a rigid suit.

She couldn't remember dancing with Felix like this. Maybe because they'd started out as friends at university and gradually eased into a relationship. There'd never been heightened attraction, or a steamy honeymoon period that had eventually cooled off. Their relationship had been tepid from the start. Steady and serious. Boring, as Luisa would say. Maybe she was finally realising what she'd missed out on.

By eleven p.m. Danny had lost all trace of sadness, by midnight he was suitably dishevelled, and by one a.m. he was as floppy as an inflatable Santa on a windy night and unable to remain upright for any length of time.

If composed and suited Daniel J Jackson was hot, then his crumpled, slightly slurred counterpart was positively smoking. His self-deprecating humour was endearing, his inability to throw dice in a straight line was adorable, and his throaty laugh was unexpected and infectious. The real killer was the photo booth session.

'Your turn,' he slurred, placing a felt gangster hat on her head. With a pink feather boa wrapped around his neck, shedding glitter onto his glasses, he was a far cry from the serious man she knew from work. 'You look lopsided. Why are there two of you?'

'Probably down to the amount of whiskey you've consumed.' She caught him as he slid off the seat. 'Careful ... It's a wonder you're still conscious.'

A beeping noise counted down to another photo.

'Smile for the camera.' He twisted his head as the camera flashed and knocked foreheads with her. 'Sorry ... sorry ... I'm such a clumsy goose,' he said with a hiccup, patting her forehead while trying to stop her hat falling off.

Clumsy goose? He really was drunk.

The swivel chair shifted as he slumped forwards and dropped with a loud clunk, resulting in them both losing their balance and falling through the curtain.

They landed outside the booth on the plush carpet, a tangle of arms and legs, his body on top of hers. The gangster hat obscured her face and she had a mouthful of feathers.

Danny lifted the hat from her face. 'Peekaboo,' he said, making her laugh so hard she sucked in a breath and nearly choked on a feather. 'You have feathers stuck to your lipstick.' He gently blew on her face, trying to remove them, which was oddly arousing.

It was only when two staff members rushed over to check they were okay that she spotted a few guests watching with raised eyebrows. She supposed they were in rather a compromising position, lying on the floor entwined, Danny's fingers caressing her lips.

What has started out as daft and playful was in danger of tipping into something a lot steamier—especially if he didn't remove his left hand, which was cupping her breast.

Having assured the staff they were okay, she wriggled free from underneath Danny's body and rolled over to face him. 'You need to lie down,' she said, noticing the slightly glazed look in his eyes.

'I'm already lying down,' he replied, smiling at her and closing his eyes. 'Goodnight.'

'Oh, no, you're not sleeping here. Up you get.' She got to her feet and tried to drag him up. 'Time for bed.'

Danny leaned on her, spitting pink fluff from his own lips as he tried to remove the feather boa threatening to strangle him. 'Where will you sleep?'

'I'll take a taxi home.' She hooked his arm over her shoulder and led him towards the lifts. 'Come on, I'll take you to bed.'

'Is that a promise?' There was a hint of mischief in his eyes.

She patted his arm. 'Dream on, pal.'

His good humour disappeared when he saw the lift doors opening and she felt him stiffen beside her. 'Shit. I can't go in there.'

'Yes, you can. It's only two floors and the lift is huge—look at it, you could get a bed in there. You'll be fine. I'm with you. Nothing's going to happen.'

He resisted when she tried to ease him inside. 'Really, I can't.'

'Look at me,' she said, placing her hands either side of his face. 'You're going to be fine. You just need to trust me. Can you do that?'

There was a painful hesitation before he nodded.

'Good.' She leaned in and kissed him. It was a spur of the moment decision, based on feeling rather than logic. And there was nothing lasting or provocative about the kiss, it was just a fleeting gesture designed to distract him.

It did the trick, he looked a little stunned. She was a little stunned herself. His lips were warmer than expected, and much softer, and it was tempting to dive in for more. But then she'd be heading into dangerous territory, risking the evening turning from mild flirtation into steamy seduction. And she didn't want that. ... Did she?

'Easy does it,' she said, easing him towards the lift. 'Just a couple more steps and we're inside. Brilliant. You did it.'

He didn't look convinced.

When she reached for the button, he grabbed hold of her like she was about to throw him off a cliff.

'It's okay,' she said, using her best soothing voice. 'I'm here. You're safe.' She took his hands, trying to stem the shake. 'Look at me, nowhere else, keep looking at me.'

His pupils were huge behind his glasses, making his brown eyes darker than usual. His hands gripped hers so tightly it was painful. She was almost glad, the discomfort detracted from the sensation of his body pressed against hers, the smell of whiskey and aftershave, and the way his eyes kept dipping to her mouth.

When he leaned forwards she half wondered if he was going to kiss her. It would be her own fault. After all, she'd lit the fuse. This was what happened when you played with fire, she'd ignited trouble. And although her brain instructed her to turn away, her body was having none of it. Bring it on, her insides screamed, aching for the feel of his approaching lips pressing against hers. So she was almost disappointed when he didn't kiss her, and instead rested his forehead against her brow and closed his eyes.

'I got trapped inside an elevator.' His voice was barely a whisper and laced with enough trauma to kill any thoughts of kissing.

'I guessed that might be what happened.'

'I couldn't get out.' His breath sounded shaky. 'I couldn't get to Connor, and he needed me. He'd ... he'd sent me a message.' His voice cracked. 'A goodbye message.'

His words landed heavily, and Elena experienced a sudden sense of foreboding. She drew back enough to see the haunted expression on his face. Acute pain and suffering stared back, raw and unbridled.

'When the elevator jammed, I panicked. I had to get to him. The thought of losing him was ...' He squeezed his eyes shut, his breath hot on her face. 'I prised open the door and jumped. That's when I injured my hip.'

'That's awful, Danny. I'm sorry you had to go through that.' The lift eased to a stop and the doors opened, not a moment too soon. 'We're here. You made it. Can you move?'

He nodded slowly and let her lead him out of the lift, sagging against her as they headed down the corridor towards the room. When she glanced at him, alcohol and grief had overridden all the fun of earlier.

'Connor seems okay now,' she said carefully, unsure how to handle such a sensitive confession. 'I'm guessing you got to him that night?'

Danny stopped walking. 'He was just sitting there on the edge of the car park wall, staring at a bottle of pills.' A glazed expression clouded his face, as if he was transported somewhere else and no longer present. 'I've never been so scared in my life. I had no idea what to do. I know you're supposed to remain calm in situations like that and talk the person down, but I just grabbed him and pulled him away, it was all I could think of.'

Poor man, what an awful thing to experience. 'I'd have done the exact same thing if it had been one of my sisters.' She pointed to the bedroom door. 'This is the room.' She touched the door key to the sensor and helped him inside.

The room seemed different bathed in the glow of a single side lamp, less gauche and more sensual, the champagne colour warming and seductive.

Danny turned to face her. 'Do you have to go?'

She met his pleading gaze. Did she have to go? Good

question. It was late, she was tipsy, and he was standing before her looking sad and drunk and vulnerable. A highly dangerous combination. The kind of combination that could lead to a bad decision, an awkward working environment, and the end of their physio sessions.

She should leave. It would be the sensible thing to do.

But then she remembered he'd have to negotiate the lift again in the morning and she couldn't leave him to do that alone.

If there was another reason why she didn't want to leave, she refused to acknowledge it.

She pushed the door shut. 'No, I don't have to go.'

Chapter Thirteen

DANNY

Saturday, 28th June

Danny couldn't remember the last time he'd woken with a hangover. As the pain pounded through his skull and the light hurt his eyes, he remembered why he avoided over-drinking. It was self-torture. It took a while to focus on his surroundings, and even longer to recall how he'd ended up in a hotel room with Elena Romero.

She was nowhere to be seen, only the sight of her flapper dress hanging on the back of the wardrobe door provided evidence she'd even been there. Maybe she'd already left? He couldn't blame her. He couldn't remember much about the previous night, but the fleeting snapshots he could remember were enough to make him cringe. Had he really danced the Charleston? Fed Elena chocolate covered marshmallows? And crawled around on his hands and knees looking for her earring when he'd dislodged it trying to wrap a feather boa around her neck? It would be a blessing if she had left. It would save him a lot of embarrassment.

And then he heard singing coming from the bathroom and the sound of running water. His torture wasn't over.

Pushing himself against the large headboard, his shoved away countless pillows and rubbed his eyes. He wore nothing but boxers. His clothes were neatly hung up and his shoes were tucked under the dresser, perfectly parallel, as if on their best behaviour.

If he'd been the one responsible for removing his clothes they'd be lying in a heap somewhere, so he must have had help. He vaguely remembered them laughing and falling onto the bed when she'd tried to remove his shoes. It was a blank after that. Had anything happened? Had he been inappropriate?

The shower cut off, and a few minutes later Elena appeared in the doorway wearing one of the hotel's plush robes, her hair wrapped in a towel.

'Morning,' she said, looking fresh-faced as she searched in her bag, no hint of a hangover. 'Sleep well?'

'I guess I must have done.' If nothing else, the excessive alcohol had knocked him out for a few hours, that was something. 'Did I snore?'

She laughed. 'No, but you did mumble a lot. It was quite enlightening.'

He pulled the covers higher, covering his bare chest. 'What did I say?'

She rubbed face cream into her cheeks. 'I have a nice smile, apparently, and pretty eyes, but my perfume makes your nose itch.'

His forehead scrunched into a frown. 'Sorry.'

She smoothed the cream down her neck, her red nails

stark against her white robe. 'Why? For the most part you were flattering.'

He watched her unwrap the towel and rub her hair. 'I didn't ... you know, do anything I shouldn't have? We didn't ...?'

She paused rubbing, angling her head to look at him. 'You don't remember?'

He felt his cheeks heat.

'How to bruise a woman's ego ... And I thought you enjoyed it.' She slumped onto the bed, making the mattress bounce. 'I mean, you sounded like you enjoyed it, the people in the next room had to bang on the walls you were so loud. You said the earth moved. So for you not to remember is quite crushing.' Her hand lay flat on her chest, the robe gaping a little at the front.

His eyes dipped to her chest, he couldn't help it. 'You're teasing me, right?'

She threw a pillow at him. 'Of course I'm teasing. As if anything happened,' she said, with such an exaggerated eye-roll he couldn't work out whether he should be offended. 'I've ordered a breakfast tray and swimming shorts. Did you know they sell Rolex watches and cashmere loungewear in the hotel shop? I stuck with the basics as it's going on Hugh's account, I didn't want to take advantage.' She climbed off the bed and combed her hair.

'I can't face food.' His stomach lurched. 'And why have you bought swim shorts?'

'The food is for me. The strong coffee and swim shorts are for you.'

When someone knocked on the door, she bounced off the bed to open it and beckoned the waiter inside, stepping out the way of his trolley.

'Morning,' she said, her sing-song voice making Danny's head pound.

'Good morning, madam.' The young man's tone was dutifully subservient. 'Would madam like me to serve?'

'We're good, thanks.' Tipping him, she closed the door and chucked a paper bag onto the bed. 'I'm guessing that's your swimwear.'

'Again, why do I need swimwear? I'm going straight home.'

'No, you're not.' She poured him a coffee.

He lifted his eyebrows. 'Excuse me?'

She came over to the bed and handed him a delicate bone China cup. 'You passed part one of your therapy session by loosening up last night, but that was down to the alcohol. Today's challenge requires you to relax while sober.'

He sipped his coffee—it was good stuff. 'I don't understand.'

'The room's booked all day.' She headed over to the trolley. 'We have complimentary access to the hotel's facilities. If you think I'm missing out on a spa day, think again. They have a range of treatments on offer. I don't expect you to indulge in anything too intrusive, but reflexology will do you the world of good, plus they have an outside jacuzzi.' She took a bite of croissant, spilling crumbs down the gape in her robe.

He stilled, coffee cup halfway to his mouth. 'I'm not doing a spa day with you.'

'Why not? It's Saturday, do you have other plans?'

'No, but—'

'Then no reason to refuse.' She poured a glass of juice. 'I guarantee this will help you relax, why would you turn that down?'

If his brain wasn't soaked in alcohol he might be able to think up a valid reason. 'It's not my thing.'

She tilted her head. 'Have you ever had a spa day?'

'No, but—'

'Then how do you know you won't like it?' Her hand went to her hip. 'As your physio, I'm recommending it. Plus, if you say no, I'll leave, and you'll be left to negotiate the lift on your own. And we're several floors up, so you can't use the staircase either.'

He could tell by the smug look on her face that she knew she'd won. 'That's blackmail.'

She took another bite of croissant. 'I'm clever like that. So, are we going to the spa?'

'Do I have a choice?'

'No, but let's pretend you do. More coffee?'

'I'm good, thanks.' He watched her devour the rest of the croissant, resisting the urge to wipe a flake of pastry from her lower lip. He wasn't sure what was happening between them, but the idea of spending more time with her didn't scare him as much as it should. The fact that he wasn't scared was terrifying.

He reached for his phone and messaged Connor to say he'd be home late.

Connor's one-word reply almost made him choke on his coffee. *Date?*

Danny typed a reply. *Therapy session.*

Connor shot back a reply. *With Elena?* A series of emojis followed, including hearts, crossed fingers, and a couple kissing. *Lucky you.*

Not lucky, she scares me.

Feel the fear and do it anyway. Another message followed straight after. *Have fun. Don't be shy. Use precaution.*

Danny replied. *Not funny.*

He glanced up and realised Elena was watching him.

'Everything okay?' she asked, tilting her head.

'I was letting Connor know I'd be late home.'

'Did he tease you about being on a date?'

The shock nearly made him spill his coffee. 'How did you know that?'

She perched on the corner of the bed. 'You told me about your dating pact last night.'

He placed the coffee cup on the bedside stand. 'I did?'

'You don't remember?'

He rubbed his forehead, trying to think. Did she have to sit so close? Knowing she was likely naked underneath the robe was distracting enough, he didn't need the temptation of her soft skin and floral scent dangled in his face. 'I'm wondering what else I said now.'

She wiped a drip from the edge of the juice glass. 'You told me about getting trapped inside a lift, and how you feared for Connor's safety.'

He pushed the covers away, suddenly hot. 'I ... I shouldn't have told you that.'

'And yet you did, which means it's still an issue for you. Unresolved trauma, as they say.'

'You sound like Hugh.' He pushed out of bed, needing some space and feeling slightly nauseous as his head spun faster than last night's roulette wheel. He made a hasty exit from the bedroom.

The bathroom was huge and shiny and an assault on his eyes. Stripping off his shorts, he stepped into the shower and let the hot water punish him for his loss of control. Spilling his secrets was not the best way to support Connor. For some reason he kept opening up to Elena and talking about stuff he shouldn't: private stuff, stuff better kept to himself.

But was it? He couldn't deny he felt lighter afterwards, less taut around his temples. Maybe Hugh had a point and talking about his vulnerabilities made them less disabling.

Rubbing his hair dry, he jolted when the paper bag containing his new swimwear smacked against his back. 'You'll need these!' Elena called from the bedroom, not actually entering the bathroom, thankfully.

He pulled on the new designer swim shorts and one of the hotel's swish robes, sliding his feet into a pair of disposable white slippers. As he glanced in the mirror, he almost didn't recognise himself. Downing three glasses of water, he cleaned his teeth before re-joining Elena in the bedroom. 'I look stupid.'

'You'd look more stupid visiting a spa in your suit. Once you're there and relaxing you won't care what you're wearing, believe me. Ready to go?'

'What floor is the spa on? I only want to use the elevator once.'

'Fair enough.' She unhooked her dress from its hanger, making her robe gape further as she reached up. 'We'll take our stuff down with us and store it in the lockers. That way, you can leave afterwards without retuning to the room. Okay?'

Her expression was so kind he felt an instant tightness in his throat. 'Thank you.'

She folded her dress. 'What for?'

'For putting up with me. I'm being difficult.'

'No, you're not.' She busied herself packing her overnight bag. 'You like being in control, I get it. New situations unnerve you. I imagine you've spent the last seventeen years holding things together and ignoring your own needs. Understandable, but not conducive to a stress-free existence.'

He was hit by a pang of guilt. 'Please don't think I'm complaining. I'd do anything for Connor, he's my family, he needs me.'

'Of course he does, just as you need him. The idea of losing him is terrifying, believe me, I know only too well how hard it is watching someone you love suffer and feel so helpless. I've experienced it enough times with Luisa. Sometimes sharing the pain with someone who understands can be helpful.'

'Please don't tell anyone.'

She stopped packing. 'Is that what you're worried about?'

'Connor's so sensitive about the whole thing, he'd be mortified if he knew I'd told you.'

She came over and rested her hand on his arm, close enough that he could smell the fabric conditioner on her robe. 'I'd never tell a soul, you have my word. But Connor's not the only one affected by this. Constantly worrying about another person's wellbeing is exhausting. You need an outlet too.' He noticed she still had a flake of pastry balancing on her lower lip.

'I have Hugh,' he said, staring at her mouth.

'And now you have me.' She licked her lip and dislodged the flake of pastry. 'You're not sure whether that's a good thing, are you? What do I need to do to prove I'm trustworthy? I told you about my ex leaving me, didn't I? You don't think that was humiliating to admit?'

'I guess.' It felt strangely surreal to be inside a hotel room wearing nothing but a robe, and almost chest-to-chest with another person also wearing nothing but a robe. Especially when that person was incredibly attractive and was looking at him intently, her skin glowing, her eyes filled with compassion. 'You said he left for a job?'

She sighed and returned to packing her things. 'Not even a great job, a routine actuary job in Manchester. He felt like it was a step on the career ladder and too good an opportunity to pass up. He assumed I'd move up there with him, it never occurred to him I wouldn't go.'

'Of course you wouldn't go, you'd never leave Luisa.' He picked up his suit and shoes, and realised Elena was looking at him. 'What?'

'He never understood that. Strange that you do.'

'You put family first,' he said, with a shrug. 'Same as me.'

She zipped up her bag. 'Who'd have thought we'd have something in common.'

'Shocker, I know.' He opened the bedroom door. 'Can I ask you something? Am I really a boring suit?'

She wheeled her case over to the door, smiling. 'You weren't last night.'

'And today?'

She paused. 'Jury's out. We'll see how you cope with the spa.' With a wry smile she headed into the corridor. 'So, how did this whole dating thing come up with Connor in the first place, what triggered it?'

They headed for the elevators, and he could already feel the pounding in his head increasing. 'He met someone he liked. Really liked. I've never seen him so love-struck.'

Elena pushed the button for the ground floor. 'What happened?'

'Nothing. He missed his chance. He was afraid of showing her who he was, and admitting things haven't been great for him lately. He feared she'd reject him if she knew about his mental health issues and what led to them, so he bailed before he got hurt.'

'That's sad.'

The doors opened with a soft ping and he stared into the abyss ahead.

As if sensing his encroaching panic, Elena slipped her arm through his and eased him forwards. 'Focus on what you can control,' she said, her voice reassuring. 'The movement of your legs, your breathing, and the sound of my voice. Nothing is out of your control. You've got this.' She turned him to face her. 'You were telling me about Connor.'

The doors closed and he could feel his pulse racing—it was like the walls were closing in on him. 'I feel responsible for his insecurity. I don't exactly take risks myself.'

'It's never too late to start.' She held eye-contact with him. 'And why are you so anti-relationships? Surely not just because of one bad experience?'

'It was a doozy.'

'Well, you'll never convince Connor to be brave if you don't lead by example.'

His palms were clammy, his neck prickling. 'Hugh says the same thing.'

'Hugh's a smart man, you should listen to him.' She squeezed his shoulder, her expression encouraging, as if he was being super courageous and not shaking like an abandoned wet dog. 'How did you two meet?'

Danny's mind tumbled back to his arrival in the UK and travelling by train from Heathrow to Oxford. He'd never felt more scared in his life. Everything looked so different, the roads were busier, the sky greyer, the sunlight less yellow. His excitement had wavered, making him wonder if he'd made a colossal mistake in leaving his home country. And then he'd arrived at the campus and headed into the grand hallway with all the other newbies, unaware his life was about to change.

'First day of uni, Hugh was signing up students for freshers' week. He was loud and confident and wearing ridiculous yellow and blue striped trousers. I'd never heard someone with an accent like his, I thought he was putting it on. And then he heard my accent and slung his arm around me, kissed my cheek, and promised to look after me.'

Elena laughed. 'Love at first sight, huh?'

'Bizarrely, yes. No one had ever been that demonstrative with me before, or been so comfortable showing affection. Hugh was someone I didn't know I needed, and he's someone I never want to live without.'

'That's quite the bromance, you know.' She tapped his hand and nodded to the opening glass doors. 'Ground floor. You made it. And I didn't have to kiss you this time.' He must have looked surprised, because she rolled her eyes and half-pushed him out of the elevator. 'Good to know it wasn't that memorable. Thanks for that.'

Was she kidding? He'd felt the same way when Hugh had kissed him all those years ago, as if a puzzle piece had slotted into place and filled a gap he hadn't known existed. And just as he'd felt then, he knew things would never be the same again. He wasn't about to admit that though—she already had the upper hand, she didn't need any more ammunition.

He followed her into the spa centre, a calming space painted pale green and with soft music playing in the background. The lights were dimmed, candles flickered in small alcoves spaced along the walls, and staff dressed in dark green tunics drifted from room to room like practised silent film stars, unobtrusive and serene.

Elena pointed to a laminated list on the counter. 'See if anything takes your fancy.'

It was like reading from a menu in a foreign restaurant. He had no idea what a botanical facial was, or a shimmering body ritual—it sounded slightly satanic. 'You mentioned a jacuzzi, can we start with that?'

'You don't want a melting body massage?'

He shook his head. 'I don't like being touched. Not by strangers,' he added, when she raised an eyebrow.

'Jacuzzi it is. I'll meet you the other side of the changing rooms, you'll find lockers inside.'

'Have you been here before?'

'No, but most spas are similar, although none quite as elite as this. I'm excited to try everything.'

He watched her almost skip away, admiring her ability to set aside her worries and enjoy the present. He could learn a lot from Elena Romero, he realised.

The changing rooms were virtually empty, and he stored his clothes away and followed the signs to the outdoor jacuzzi, passing a large sauna, the gym, and a huge sunken bath.

On reaching the outside, the sight ahead shocked him. The area had been landscaped to look like the geothermal spas in Iceland, with protruding rocks, a waterfall, clouds of ice, and a series of small wooden bridges leading between the various pools of water. The whole area was shrouded in mist, with steam drifting up from each pool like something from a mystical land.

Elena appeared from the changing area, her shocked expression indicating she was equally impressed. 'Oh, heavens,' she said, squeezing his hand. 'I didn't expect this.'

He stared at their entwined hands, unsure of what to

make of such unabashed intimacy. Witnessing the wonder on her face made him smile, and it was impossible not to relish the moment.

'Which one to choose?' she said, looking around.

'You decide.'

'Let's explore.' She let go of his hand and headed over one of the bridges, looking over the edge and pointing out clusters of unusual flora. 'This one,' she said, reaching a sunken pool hidden beneath the rocks. 'It's nice and private. You'll feel more secluded here.'

He wondered if she craved privacy too, a lot of women did, but when she dropped her robe and made her way into the water, showing absolutely no signs of feeling self-conscious in her skimpy bikini, he was left staring open-mouthed.

'The water's so warm,' she said, twisting to beam at him. He wished he could take a photo of that exact moment—the smile spread across her face, her arms trailing over the water, and the way she seemed so comfortable in her own skin. Letting go of the rope handle, she slowly sunk below the water, like a graceful mermaid entering an enchanted sea.

Christ, his hangover was making him poetic.

Shaking his head, he removed his robe and joined her in the water, which was hotter than he'd expected and soft and slippery, like it was drenched in baby oil.

Elena was still submerged, the water's surface as still as the surrounding rocks. He was just getting concerned about her safety when she broke the surface, smiling and looking like some kind of sea goddess. She pushed her wet hair away from her face and floated effortlessly in front of him, perfectly at home in the water.

'You like swimming?' He balanced himself against the smooth rock face.

'I do,' she said, her arms moving slowly to keep afloat. 'We spent a lot of time at the beach in Cartagena when I was young. Papi travelled there for business, so he'd take us with him and we'd spend the days on the beach. I'm guessing you haven't been there?'

He shook his head.

'It's such a beautiful place, nestled inside an ancient walled city. Peaceful by day, pulsating club scene by night. New Year is something to experience. I've never seen such colour and life, it's intoxicating.'

'I thought you were young when you lived there?'

She swam over to him. 'Age isn't so relevant in Cartagena, everyone parties the same. The streets are filled with tables outside the restaurants circling the city square, ready for the nightly entertainment. Early evening it would be dance troupes and magicians, followed by singers and folk dancing, and then by midnight it would switch to salsa and merengue.'

'That explains why you looked so comfortable dancing last night,' he said, alarmed when her hands dipped under the water and rested on his hips.

'It's part of Colombian life, everyone dances, young and old. No one's allowed to sit out. If you try someone will pull you onto the dance floor. Ease your leg up for me.'

He let her lift his leg, recognising the stretch they did in his physio sessions. It felt easier to do in the warm water. 'Do you miss living there?'

She held the stretch, allowing the muscles around his joint to soften. 'I miss the warm weather, even though where we lived wasn't that hot. Bogotá is nearly nine thousand feet above sea level, so it's cooler than the rest of the country. But they don't have seasons like we do over here, it's the same pretty much all year around. It's still warmer than London most days.' She repeated the stretch, her hands slippery on his skin. 'I miss horse riding in the mountains, and the friendliness of the people. There's none of this silence on the trains with people staring at their feet. In Colombia everyone chats to everyone, with lots of animation and hugging. I miss that.'

'Sounds idyllic.'

'It wasn't all perfect,' she said, with a sigh. 'There's lots of poverty in the country, and no welfare system or national health service. Seeing homeless kids on the streets was never easy. There's still a drug smuggling problem, although it's pushed more to the rural areas these days, and crime is high in certain places. Politically it's quite unstable, but I love the place and it's where my roots are.'

'Will you go back to live there one day?'

'Nope, the UK is home now, and Luisa's very much a Brit. She'd never cope with the culture, she's a proper *Londoner*,' she said, exaggerating the accent. 'What about you, would you ever live in the US?' Without warning, she lifted his foot and began massaging it.

He tried to concentrate, but it was tricky when his foot kept nudging against her breast. 'No, for the same reason as you. Connor was five when he left, and like Luisa, he's very much British. I was never happy in the US, and although that had nothing to do with the country, the UK is home now. I fit here, and I'd miss Hugh too much.'

Her fingers circled his ankles, running over his soles in such a way it felt as though she was reaching every part of him. Unlike him, she showed no awkwardness at touching him in such an intimate way. 'Why weren't you happy in the US? Was it because of the rift with your parents?'

'That was part of it. They weren't a lot of fun.'

Her fingers dug deeper, spreading the joints in his toes. 'Did you ever have fun?'

'I did at school, I guess. But my home life was very serious. Not much laughter.'

'I couldn't cope without laughter in my life.' Her hands slid up his shins, a sensation completely unlike the torture of their physio sessions. 'Did things change when you came to the UK?'

'From the moment I met Hugh,' he said, glad to focus on the past and not on the current sensation of Elena's hands sending shock waves up his legs. 'That first year at uni was crazy. Hugh and I partied all the time, joined every organisation we could, and barely had time to study.'

It seemed like a lifetime ago now, a different version of himself.

'Hugh's family are titled, so we'd go to polo matches and horse racing at weekends, getting drunk and causing mayhem. I spent the whole time wondering when someone was going to bollock me for misbehaving. But Hugh's parents behaved even more shockingly.'

He remembered their antics fondly, the eccentric purchases, and random guests staying overnight, from politicians to famous musicians. Everyone was treated equally and welcomed with kindness and acceptance, including him. No wonder Hugh was such a rounded individual, he'd had great role models.

'And then it stopped when Connor came along,' he said, with a sigh.

Elena switched to massaging his other foot. 'No more laughter?'

He let his head rest against the rock face behind. 'Not for a while. Thanks to Hugh and his family things were better than they would've been. After a while we found our rhythm. Weekends became about Legoland and football matches, Pizza Express and early nights. I thought it would be the death of my friendship with Hugh, but it wasn't. He joined in, dressed up as a pirate for Connor's birthday, organised days out, and became part of our family.'

Elena smiled. 'If I didn't love Hugh before, I do now.'

'I know, he's a special guy.' Danny smiled, partly at the memory of Hugh, but mostly because having your feet massaged was oddly arousing.

Was she being deliberately seductive? Her body language gave nothing away, she massaged his feet as though she was doing a chore, like the washing up. Just as well really.

His thoughts returned to Hugh. 'The year we graduated uni he arranged a road trip around Europe for the three of us during the summer holidays. Six weeks spent inside a cramped camper van. Connor never stopped smiling. We snorkelled, visited museums, and camped on beaches. It was a turning point for us, looking back. Things became less challenging after that. When we returned, Hugh headed off to be a stock broker in the City, and Connor and I moved into our first home.'

She lifted his feet into her lap and massaged them simultaneously. 'Do you feel you've missed out?'

'Not really. I mean, I had my party days at uni, and although I wouldn't have chosen to become a parent at nineteen, I haven't been unhappy. I've enjoyed looking after Connor, I've got a good career. I'm sad about certain things that've happened, but I have no regrets. It's only this last year that things have been difficult. Prior to that we had a great life. At least, I think we did.'

'Hey, don't doubt it.' She squeezed his feet, making his eyes widen. 'Watching you and Connor together is gorgeous. You have a solid relationship, and things will improve, I promise. Like I said before, enjoying the good moments will help you cope with the shitty ones. So today is about self-care. No parental worries, or dwelling on injuries, just a day to let go and indulge in something pleasurable. Are you enjoying your massage?'

'It's okay.'

She raised an eyebrow. 'Just okay?'

He wasn't about to admit it was the best thing he'd experienced in a very long time. 'It's unexpected.'

'I'll take that as a positive.' She resumed massaging. 'See what can happen when you stop being resistant? You discover a new pleasure. And you were so certain you didn't like being touched.' She wiggled an eyebrow. 'Kind of nice, isn't it?'

He relented with a nod. 'You're not a stranger.'

'Not anymore.' She grinned, as if knowing how much he was enjoying it. 'It's even better if you close your eyes.'

'I'm okay as I am.'

'Still don't trust me?'

'I'm trying,' he said through gritted teeth.

'Try harder.'

She tugged on his legs and the next thing he knew he was underwater, sinking into the warm water and losing his hearing as the muffled sounds of the waterfall drifted away.

Elena's hands slid up his torso and encircled his waist, taking his weight and allowing him to float to the surface. Her body was underneath his like a human airbed, her head resting next to his, her arms around his chest. The sky above was obscured by mist and steam, and as the sound of the waterfall returned, he succumbed to the moment, unwilling to fight it.

As his eyes closed, and his fingers intertwined with hers, he found himself drifting into a state of utter contentment.

For the first time in as long as he could remember, he felt ... relaxed.

Chapter Fourteen

SOFIA

Tuesday, 1st July

Choosing what clothes to wear for a day splashing paint about shouldn't have been that complex. Overalls were the obvious choice, despite the itch of thick canvas scraping against Sofia's skin as she'd zipped up the navy jumpsuit and folded the hem over to make them shorter. The garment was too tight across the bust, highlighting the very different body shapes of her and her sister. Work overalls suited Luisa's lithe frame, they hugged Sofia in all the wrong places.

Ordinarily, it wouldn't matter. She'd never considered herself overly vain, but then she'd never been in the situation of trying to attract the attentions of a man whose interest remained undecided. She was entering new territory.

The second issue they encountered on leaving the house was a hostile taxi driver who refused to allow tins of paint inside his cab. Their arrival at the community centre was delayed by forty minutes while they waited for their kindly neighbour to drop his children at school and return to transport them to their destination in his fancy off-roader. His son regularly threw up during car journeys, so he wasn't bothered by a few tins of paint, he'd assured them.

When they eventually arrived at the community centre, there was no sign of Connor. They had to make their way through the main hall with their equipment, incurring strange stares from the parents who'd gathered for the 'music and play' session. Several of the children grew curious at the sight of paint-rollers and brushes being carried through the hall, and became excited at the idea of playing with paint—their parents, less so.

Luisa sped up, her reaction to small children on a par with someone facing open heart surgery without an anaesthetic. 'Weird little creatures,' she mumbled, as they crossed the hall.

In contrast, Sofia only saw cute, smiling toddlers running about, full of energy and squealing with laughter. When one little girl waved at her, she couldn't help smiling.

'Do not engage,' Luisa hissed, urging her sister to move faster. 'They'll suck out your soul first chance they get.'

'They're children, not demons, Luisa.'

'They don't fool me, I've seen The Midwich Cuckoos.'

'That was a work of fiction,' Sofia reminded her sister, as she followed her into the meeting room they'd been assigned to paint.

Following their earlier visit to the community centre, Luisa had searched for contact details online and they'd exchanged emails with Connor about arrangements for their visit. Luisa had instructed Sofia that by the time they finished today, Sofia needed to be in possession of Connor's personal contact details too. Sofia was still undecided whether having Luisa act as matchmaker was a gift or a hindrance.

The meeting room was stuffy and smelled dusty, but at least it had been cleared of furniture—apart from two plastic chairs. The grubby carpet tiles couldn't have been any dirtier if they'd spilled several tins of paint over them.

'You start sugar-soaping the walls,' Luisa said, plonking herself down on a plastic chair. 'My mural design needs work.' She opened her sketch pad and began chewing on the end of her pencil, lifting her feet to rest on the spare chair.

Sofia unrolled plastic sheeting across the floor. 'I get all the good jobs.'

'Preparation is key,' Luisa said, without looking up. 'Fail to prepare, prepare to fail.'

Sofia rolled her eyes—her knees were already feeling the discomfort of kneeling on lumpy carpeting. 'Very inspiring.'

The door opened and Sofia's heart gave a little kick as Connor appeared. He was wearing a denim-coloured hoodie and baggy cargo trousers, his wavy black hair framing his soft features. He looked adorable. He also looked stressed. There was a weariness about him that tugged at her insides.

'Hi,' he said tentatively. 'Do you have everything you need?'

'I think so.' Sofia sat back on her heels. 'There's a hardware shop nearby, so we can pop out if we need anything.'

'You'll need to change clothes if you're going to help,' Luisa said, glancing up at Connor. 'Painting's messy work, you look far too neat. Nice hoodie, by the way.'

Connor ran a hand through his hair. 'I can't help, I'm afraid. I'm trying to sort out the accounts this morning. We've got no income coming in, and I've no idea why.' He gave a half-hearted shrug. 'Sorry.'

'That's a shame. We were looking forward to your company.' Luisa's eyes darted between Sofia and Connor mischievously.

Sofia climbed off the floor, feeling at a distinct disadvantage being so low down. 'Don't you have an accountant to deal with the finances?'

'There's no money to pay an accountant. The manager dealt with everything, but he's too ill to do anything at the moment. I've offered to take over, except I don't know what I'm doing.'

Luisa clapped her hands, making them both jump. 'Sofia will help you. She used to be an account manager.'

Sofia glared at her sister. 'I thought you wanted me to start sugar soaping?'

'Oh, that can wait,' she said, dismissing her sister's concerns. 'Besides, I'm still working on my design. Go and be useful, I'm happy sketching.'

Sofia turned to Connor. 'I'm no expert.'

'Bullshit.' Luisa pointed her pencil at Sofia. 'She has a business degree and uses budget software to manage the household expenses. She's a maths geek. If anyone can fathom numbers, it's Sofia.'

The concern on Connor's face lifted. 'I'd really appreciate your help.'

Sofia tried to keep her expression neutral. 'Looks like I've been redeployed,' she said, glancing at Luisa, who wiggled her eyebrows and mouthed '*get his number*'.

Praying Connor hadn't seen her sister's unsubtle gesture, they left the room, with Sofia wishing she'd brought a change of outfit. The rigid material between her legs rubbed together with such friction she was worried the overalls might ignite. She felt self-conscious enough as it was.

'Is your sister feeling better now?' Connor asked, as they headed down the corridor towards the main hall. 'She'd just come out of hospital last time I saw you.'

'Luisa's health is never great, even at the best of times, and this latest infection gave us a real scare, but she's slowly improving, thanks.'

'She looks very frail.'

'I know. The problem is, she loses weight when she's ill, and because of the issues with her digestion, it takes forever to put the weight back on. If she gets another infection while she's still weak, she can deteriorate really quickly. It's a real worry.'

'It sounds it.'

They entered the main hall and were hit by a wall of sound, children screaming and laughing as they acted out the moves to the 'Wheels on the Bus'. It was a cute sight, and one that gave Sofia a pang of longing. However much she wanted a decent career, she also wanted a family one day.

Connor glanced at her. 'Has your sister always had this condition? Sorry, I don't know much about it.'

'That's okay, not many people do. Cystic Fibrosis is a rare genetic disease. Why Luisa has it and the rest of my family don't is down to statistics and bad luck. Luisa drew the short straw. She'll always have it, even if she gets a new heart and lungs.'

Connor looked shocked. 'Is that what needs to happen? A transplant?'

'Possibly.' Although it was something the family hoped

wouldn't be needed, and something Luisa was adamant she didn't want. 'She's on a new combination of drugs, which the doctors are hoping will improve things. It's a waiting game.'

They reached the end of the hall and Connor opened a door. 'She's very brave. I mean, she doesn't act like an ill person, does she? Sorry, that sounds stupid.'

'It's okay, I know what you mean. Luisa's incredibly resilient and she has a great attitude, most of the time. She copes better than I would in her situation. She makes jokes and fools around, but sometimes the mask slips and you can tell underneath the bluster she's scared.'

'I would be too.' He led Sofia into a small office with similar décor to the meeting room, beige walls, cheap furniture, no natural daylight. 'She said you used to be an account manager?'

'I was, yes.' Sofia knew it was time to confess. Besides, she had nothing to be ashamed of, as Elena kept reminding her. 'That day I met you on the train, I'd just been fired from my job. That's why I was a bit of a mess.'

'You weren't a mess,' he said, the shake of his head making his hair sway. 'Not that I saw. I guess that explains the box of stuff you were carrying.'

She tried for a self-deprecating smile. 'And the crying too. I wasn't at my best.'

'Why were you fired?' He visibly flinched. 'Sorry, none of my business.'

'I don't mind you knowing. It was a bit raw at the time, and I was embarrassed, that's why I didn't say anything. I feel differently now, I'm more aggrieved by the situation. They fired me for taking time off to look after Luisa.'

He ran a hand through his hair. 'That doesn't seem fair.'

'It's not, which is why I'm challenging the dismissal on

grounds of disability discrimination. I'd been in the job five years. It's only recent months I've needed time off after Mum died and Papi had to return to Colombia. I've worked numerous weekends and extra hours getting my work done, but that didn't seem to count for much.'

His smile was kind. 'Luisa's not the only who's brave. You are too. Challenging authority isn't easy.'

Her hand rested on her chest. The cramped room was making her feel warm. 'I can't expect Luisa to fight if I don't fight too. Life isn't always easy, and sometimes you have to find the courage to stand up for yourself.'

He looked ponderous. 'I guess so.' His frown disappeared with a shake of the head, and he pointed towards a small desk. 'This is the ancient computer the manager used to do the accounts. There's a filing cabinet over there with folders containing receipts, and stuff. I've looked though it all, but it doesn't tell me much.'

Sofia sat in front of the computer, her knees banging the underside of the desk. 'You said there's no income, so let's start with the hall hirers. There should be hire income, if nothing else. Where will I find a list of users?'

Connor leaned on the desk next to her and wiggled the mouse. 'There's an excel spreadsheet containing all the information.'

As the screen slowly came to life, she glanced at his hands, noticing his bitten right thumbnail. It was the first imperfection she'd seen. In a way, she was glad, it made her feel less critical of her own failings.

'I can't remember the last time I used a desktop computer,' she said, trying to keep the conversation going. There was still an awkwardness between them, but she'd promised Luisa she'd persist and find out for certain whether Connor was attracted to her or not. However mortifying that might be.

'I'd never used a desktop before,' he said, opening a folder. 'I wondered why nothing happened when I tapped the screen.'

Sofia smiled, her humour fading as the excel spreadsheet opened with multiple tabs and endless columns. 'Heavens, this is how they manage their accounts?'

'Basic, huh?' Connor pulled up a chair next to her, so close she could feel his warmth. She noticed a small scar on the back of his hand. Another imperfection, and another story from his life she'd yet to discover.

Re-focusing, Sofia scanned the excel document and clicked on one of the tabs. 'This looks like a list of hirers. It's showing invoice dates, but they don't appear to have been updated for six months.'

'That's when the manager stopped coming down.'

'That explains why the income's dried up. No one's been invoiced. What about outgoing payments?' She clicked on another tab, which revealed the same, a list of overdue payments showing in red text. 'It's a wonder you haven't received demand letters.'

'We might have, I wouldn't know. They go to the manager's home address.' Connor was watching her, and she could feel the intensity of his stare. 'How bad is it?'

'Hard to tell. It'll take me a while to go through this. Is the manager likely to return?'

Connor shook his head. 'He's in his eighties and suffers with kidney failure. His wife says he's on regular dialysis.'

Sofia turned to Connor, needing to understand more about how everything worked. 'So who employs him? Who actually owns the community centre?'

'The building was gifted to the community by Tobias

Hislop on his death in 1901.' He nodded behind her. 'That's him there. He built the place in memory of his wife.'

Sofia looked at the ornate plaque hanging on the wall, the painting above depicted the image of a charming man with a large grey moustache. 'Not exactly the Taj Mahal,' she said, studying the painting. 'But he was obviously quite the romantic.'

'They say his wife's ghost is still present in the building.'

Sofia raised her eyebrows. 'The place is haunted?'

'Not haunted, so much. She appears in the form of a Red Admiral butterfly. I don't believe in ghosts, but it's strange the same butterfly appears throughout the year, even when there's snow outside. There's no logical explanation for it.'

Sofia couldn't explain it either. 'Have you seen this butterfly yourself?'

He nodded. 'First session as acting manager it landed on my shoulder while I was booting up the computer.'

'Maybe you should've asked it how the accounts worked.'

Connor's sudden laugh hit her with force. 'It might've made life easier. Especially as it's supposed to be a sign of approval. She only appears if she likes you, apparently.' He sounded amused and she liked the lighter tone in his voice.

'I'll try not to take it personally if I don't see her then.' Sofia's world was becoming stranger by the minute. 'Are there any other supernatural beings I need to know about?'

'None that I know of. The community centre's run by committee, made up of parish and town councillors, church personnel, and local elected members. Some of them might as well be dead for all the help they give, but technically they're alive.'

Sofia let out a sigh. 'What a complicated arrangement.'

He watched her closely. 'Any suggestions how we manage things?'

She liked him using the word 'we'. 'Firstly, we need to get you co-opted as official manager with the authority to make decisions and run the accounts. We'll also need permission to purchase a proper accounting package. The current system is woefully inadequate. I can then transfer the data and produce up-to-date accounts. It'll then be a case of paying bills and invoicing hirers, and introducing an automated billing system that's not so reliant on any one individual. Ideally, you need two bank signatories. I'm not sure what the tax situation would be for a set-up like this, I'll have to look into it.'

Connor looked tentative. 'Would you be the second signatory?'

'Me?'

His cheeks coloured. 'I don't have anyone else to ask who knows about this stuff.'

Sofia considered the question. Teaming up would mean them spending more time together, that was a definite plus. They could get to know each other, explore whether there was a real attraction ... but that came with risk. Supposing there wasn't a connection? And did she really have the time? She had Luisa to consider. But then, what had she just been saying about life being too short, and needing to be brave? She should listen to her own advice. 'I guess I could, but the committee might want to appoint someone already linked with the centre.'

'I doubt it. When I've tried talking to them about this they don't want to get involved. Most of them have been coerced onto the committee by the organisations they work for. They'd welcome someone like you taking charge.'

He looked so hopeful, that she felt stupidly flattered. 'I'm no expert.'

'You know more than me. Please?' His hand rested on hers—as if she wasn't flustered enough. 'At least until you get your job back.'

She refused to flip out just because a man she fancied was touching her. 'My appeal might not be successful.'

'It will be if there's any justice in the world.' His face was so close, a pleading look in his eyes. She hadn't realised she'd stopped breathing until he slid his hand from hers and his eyes fell away. 'I don't know why I said that. It's not like life is fair. People don't always get justice, or if they do, they have to fight to prove their innocence. It's hard not to feel helpless when you've been treated unfairly.' He chewed on his right thumbnail.

She wanted to touch him, but it felt like the moment had vanished. 'Well, you know to start with I wasn't going to fight my dismissal. I was too humiliated, I just wanted to hide from the world and feel sorry for myself.'

'What changed your mind?' He lowered his hand, as if annoyed with himself for biting his nail.

Sofia answered honestly, sensing he needed reassurance. 'People reminding me I have value. That I didn't deserve to be treated badly, and that accepting an injustice doesn't just harm me, but anyone facing similar unfairness in the future. Sometimes you have to make a stand. If nothing else, if I don't clear my name, I'll struggle to get another job.'

'I guess you're right.' He looked unsettled by something.

'In the meantime, it'll do me good to be productive. So yes, I'll help you.'

His face broke into a smile. 'You will?'

Her daft little heart did a somersault. 'Well, I'm more qualified to do this than I am sugar-soaping walls.'

A loud thud made them both jump. Standing in the doorway was a little girl wearing pink dungarees and a large bow attached to her beaded cornrows. Before either of them could react, she charged into the room and banged into Sofia's legs. 'Helloooo! I'm Cora, I'm fwhee years old.'

Sofia laughed. 'Well, hello, Cora. I'm Sofia, and this is Connor.' The little girl beamed at them. 'But you're not supposed to be in here. Where's your mummy?'

'There you are!' A harassed looking woman stood in the doorway, her milk-stained shirt buttoned up wrong. 'Cora Davey-Johnson, get back here this minute! I need to change your brother's nappy, and I can't do that with you running off. Get over here now!'

Connor lifted his hand. 'Hi, I'm Connor, I'm the acting manager today. You're welcome to leave her with us while you deal with your baby. The toilets aren't very spacious, so it might be easier for you without this little helper.' He gave Cora a knowing look that said, *Yes, I'm talking about you*, to which she replied with a toothy grin.

The woman looked at him like he was an angel sent down from mummy-heaven. 'You sure?'

'Of course. The toilets are next to the café. We'll be right here when you get back.' Connor smiled at the woman, open and kind, and Sofia found herself swooning a little too.

Cora lifted her arms, jigging about and eager to be picked up.

Connor swung her onto his lap, with no suggestion he imagined children to be blood-sucking vampires in disguise. Sofia couldn't help feeling relieved. He was no Luisa.

The mother also looked relieved, but for entirely

different reasons. 'You're a lifesaver. I won't be long. Be a good girl, Cora. No tantrums!' She hurried away with her screaming baby, as though fearful Connor might change his mind if her daughter kicked off.

'Curly hair!' Cora grabbed a handful of Connor's hair. 'Bow!'

Connor pretended to be confused. 'Bow? What bow? I don't see any bows.'

'Bow!' She yanked the pink bow from her hair and shoved it towards Connor. 'Bow!'

'Oh, *this* bow.' He clipped the bow into his hair and gave her a big grin. 'Does it suit me?'

Cora squealed and clapped her hands.

Sofia couldn't help laughing. He looked so cute with a huge pink bow in his hair, and completely comfortable, as though he wasn't bothered what he looked like, which just made her like him even more.

'Do you think it would suit Sofia?' Connor unclipped the bow and reached across to clip it in the side of Sofia's ponytail. His fingers grazed the side of her face as he secured the bow. 'That's better, Sofia's much prettier than I am.'

Sofia's face heated another few degrees.

Cora let out another squeal and patted Connor's face with her chubby hand. 'Song!'

'Song? Demanding, aren't you?' He pretended to think about it. 'What shall I sing? Nirvana? Wolf Alice? Wet Leg? Who's your favourite band?'

Sofia was laughing. 'You'll have a shock if she says Royal Blood.'

Connor blinked at her in surprise. 'You know Royal Blood?'

She gave a small shrug. 'I saw them at Reading festival last year, they're one of Luisa's favourites.'

He looked impressed. 'You go to festivals?'

'Mostly to keep an eye on Luisa,' she admitted, in case she gave the wrong impression and he thought her a hardened festival-goer. 'Honestly, I'd rather watch the coverage on TV. I'm not a fan of mud.'

He grinned. 'Or blocked loos?'

'Definitely not blocked loos. Or drunken partygoers falling into my tent.'

'That might have been me,' he said, his easy smile fading a few seconds later, as if remembering something. 'Although not last year.'

She noticed his frown. 'You didn't go last year?'

He shook his head, but didn't offer an explanation.

'Topsy and Tim!' shouted Cora, bouncing up and down on Connor's lap.

His frown lifted as he focused on the little girl. 'I don't know that one. How does it go? Can you sing it for me?'

'It's a TV show,' Sofia admitted. 'I caught Luisa watching it in hospital recently.'

He cocked an eyebrow at her. 'Are you sure you're not a fan too?' His playfulness made her laugh.

She lifted her hands in surrender. 'Guilty.'

His smile made her insides turn liquid. 'D'you know the theme tune?'

She shook her head. 'Sorry, no.'

'Then it'll have to be Incy Wincy Spider.' Connor cleared his throat and began to sing, using his hand to crawl up Cora's arm, deliberately tickling her, and making her squeal.

Sofia watched in amazement as this shy man

entertained the little girl, his haunted expression replaced by childish playfulness. She was as smitten as Cora, watching him add in actions to the words and change his voice to match the different characters. She could hardly believe it.

He was just hitting his stride when the mother returned from the toilets. 'You're a natural,' she said, looking less harassed now her baby had stopped crying. 'I could do with you at bedtime.'

Sofia thought the same thing ... and then mentally kicked herself. Thank goodness she hadn't said anything out loud.

Connor stood up and placed Cora on the floor, passing her chubby hand over to her mother. 'Bye-bye, Cora. Next time Nirvana? Okay?'

'Okay!' Cora clearly had no idea what she was agreeing to. 'Byeeee!'

The family disappeared amongst more laughter and mayhem, briefly returning when they realised Cora's bow was still attached to Sofia's ponytail.

Connor was still smiling when his phone rang. He reached across for it, checking the caller ID, before looking at Sofia. 'It's the chair of the committee. Okay if I take this? I can ask about the software we need and the other stuff we discussed.'

Sofia got up. 'Sure, go ahead. I'd better check on Luisa, anyway. I have sugar-soaping duties.' Plus, she needed to cool off a bit.

'Leave me your number,' he said, as she reached the doorway. He gestured to a pack of post-it notes on the desk. 'So I can let you know what they say. You'll need my number too if we're going to work together ... right?' He sounded tentative and waited for her nod of approval before scribbling down his number and handing her the post-it note.

Sofia knew she shouldn't read anything into it, but this failed to stop her pulse increasing.

Having written down her number, she left Connor talking to the committee chair and returned to Luisa in the meeting room.

Luisa looked up when Sofia entered, still sprawled between two chairs, and still sketching. 'Well, how did it go? Were you successful?'

Sofia showed her sister the post-it note. 'Mission accomplished.'

Luisa threw her arms in the air. 'Houston! We have lift off!'

Chapter Fifteen

ELENA

Saturday, 5th July

If Elena wasn't working on a Saturday, she was usually helping Sofia with household chores, resolving one of Luisa's dramas, or, if she was really lucky, able to indulge in a long run. Since her mum had died and she'd moved back home, it was rare she had a completely free day.

Luisa was holed up in her studio engrossed in a secretive art project, and Sofia was trying to decipher the instructions for a new accounting package she'd acquired. So with both sisters occupied, it meant Elena could accept the offer to attend the Spencer-Harrison's annual charity boat race in rural Bucklebury, a tiny hamlet nestled in leafy Berkshire.

Surprisingly, the invite for today's outing hadn't come from Hugh, but Danny. *To prove I'm capable of having fun*, his message had read, which was intriguing, as she hadn't thought Danny capable of fun unless coerced into it.

She'd briefly hesitated before accepting, wondering if spending another day in his company was such a good idea. It might set fire to the spark of attraction she already felt sizzling beneath her skin, and that wouldn't be in anyone's best interests, least of all hers. But the lure of a day boating was too appealing an opportunity to pass up.

Danny's instructions that she wore 'something red' and brought 'spare clothes' with her had also piqued her curiosity. She'd opted for red and black yoga leggings and one of her maroon Bamboo running tops, her rucksack filled with jeans and a fleece as replacements.

Having changed trains at Paddington, the journey out of London was speedy, and they were now approaching Thatcham, where Hugh had agreed to pick her up. It wasn't an area of the country she was familiar with, so she followed the other passengers onto the station forecourt in the hope of spotting Hugh's fancy car.

There was no sign of Hugh. Instead, a woman wearing a waxed green Barbour jacket was waving frantically and beckoning Elena towards a beaten-up Land Rover, covered in mud.

Glancing behind, Elena expected to see whoever the woman was waving at, but when she turned back, the woman let out a shrill whistle and pointed directly at Elena. 'Over here!'

Feeling dubious, she headed towards the woman, who could easily double for the late Queen in an episode of The Crown. Headscarf, wellington boots, and a horde of hounds occupying the rear of her Land Rover.

'You must be Elena? Just as Danny described. Gorgeous gal.' The woman's handshake was ferocious. 'Virginia Spencer-Harrison. Hugh's mummy.'

How Elena didn't laugh, she had no idea. 'Lovely to meet you. I was expecting Hugh?'

Virginia unearthed a handkerchief from the sleeve of her jacket. 'Drama with one of the rafts. I volunteered to collect you. No bother, needed to drop off the vicar at the church, so combined tasks.' She wiped the door handle and opened the door for Elena. 'Hop in.'

Easier said than done. The Land Rover was so high off the ground Elena was grateful for her core strength as she hoisted herself onto the rock-hard bench seat. 'It's kind of you to collect me, I could have got a taxi.'

'Nonsense.' Slamming the door, Virginia marched around to the driver's side and climbed in. 'Although we do need to motor somewhat. Gates open in ten mins. Ruddy tradesmen have been causing me grief all morning. The portaloos were only installed forty minutes ago. Can you believe that? Left Nigel directing the barbecue truck down the lane. Lord knows where it'll end up if I'm not there to oversee.'

Elena's head was spinning. First from the information being fired at her, and then because they pulled away with such force she had to grip the door handle to avoid sliding off the seat. Something she had to repeat each time they skidded around a bend. Off-road rally drivers would struggle to compete with Virginia Spencer-Harrison, she was a formidable woman.

'I hear you're sorting out our Danny?' Virginia said, overtaking a line of cars like she was in a grand prix. 'Knocking him into shape, so to speak. Good job, I say. Men can be so obstinate. Must be doing a top job, the darling chap's looking more frisky on his feet. Got a real bounce in his step this morning.'

Elena considered herself fairly robust, but she gripped

the seat when an oncoming car honked and swerved to avoid being hit. 'I'm glad the physio's helping.' Behind her, the dogs barked and scurried about.

If Virginia noticed the other driver's agitation, she didn't let on. 'He couldn't take part in last year's boat race, the man could barely walk, poor darling. And what with everything that happened ... well, no need to spell it out. Enough said. This year he's back to being on top form. Excellent, I say!'

Elena blinked. 'Danny's competed in this event before?'

'Every year since we've known him. Even when Hugh was holed up in the City, Danny would bring Connor down to compete. Unbeaten for several years too, they were. Smashing team. We're very proud.'

Elena's rucksack toppled over when they rounded a bend. 'He said you were close.'

'We love those boys like they're our own.' Virginia sounded so proud. 'Still makes me hoot to think of the jinks Hugh and Danny got up to at uni. Lord, the scrapes we had to bail them out of.' She shook her head, her smile affectionate. 'I could tell you some tales.'

It was hard to imagine straight-laced Daniel J Jackson getting into scrapes, he seemed far too uptight. But he clearly had layers, and if Elena was interested in him romantically, she'd be keen to explore those layers further. As it was, she needed to keep a lid on her feelings. No good would come from fantasising. 'He said you helped him when he became Connor's guardian?'

'Poor lamb. Broke my heart.' Despite the narrow lanes, the speedometer quivered at sixty miles per hour as they hurtled down the lanes. 'Blood might be thicker than water, but Danny and Connor are part of our family. No two ways about it.'

Elena ducked when a low hanging tree smacked against the window. 'Lucky them.'

'He hasn't smiled much this last year, but he certainly looked chipper talking about you at dinner last night. You've made quite the impression.' Virginia winked, her focus unnervingly drawn away from the road. 'I can see why.'

Elena couldn't imagine Danny singing her praises. 'I expect he said something along the lines of me being a bully who inflicts pain.'

'Ha! Something like that.' Virginia slammed on the brakes with such force Elena nearly head-butted the console. 'I shouldn't worry too much, he didn't look unhappy about it. Quite the opposite.' She wound down the window and screamed at a young lad in a flat cap. 'Gates!'

Above the wrought iron gates was a sign for the house, Bucklebury Manor.

They'd arrived. Seemingly in one piece. Just.

The long, winding driveway was impressive. The canopy of trees above created an atmosphere of suspense as they approached the house—and what a house. Tall, wide, aged red brickwork, with tall sash windows giving the impression of watchful eyes. The sunlight bounced off the panes, making them appear to blink disapprovingly at any approaching interlopers.

Far from decelerating at the sight of the house, Virginia continued at speed, only braking once they'd almost toppled sideways, sliding around the ornate water fountain, and sent gravel flying up everywhere.

Elena lurched forwards like a crash-test dummy, rubbing her neck as they eventually skidded to a stop.

'Right, off to supervise the hubby.' Virginia snatched at the handbrake. 'Make yourself at home. No standing on ceremony here.' She slung open the door and launched herself from the Land Rover.

Elena exited in a slower fashion, unnerved at the prospect of injuring herself jumping from such a height.

Virginia spotted Connor in the distance and let out another of her shrill whistles to attract his attention. 'Connor! Connor! Come hither, boy!'

Connor jogged over, his face breaking into a smile when he saw who was with Virginia. 'Hi, Elena.'

'Be a darling and show Elena to Danny's room. Get this gorgeous gal settled.' Virginia opened the rear of the Land Rover and the hounds leaped from the vehicle with such enthusiasm Elena feared for the safety of her extremities, but they bounded away across the front lawn, heading into the distance.

Elena slung her backpack over her shoulder. 'I'm not staying overnight, Virginia. Just here for the day. I don't need a room.' And she certainly didn't need to share one with Danny.

'You'll need somewhere to dry off and change after all the shenanigans. Can't have you leaving here bedraggled, can we?' Virginia laughed, and Elena wondered what on earth she'd agreed to.

'This way.' Connor gestured towards the front door.

The inside of Bucklebury Manor matched the outside. Shabby period furniture filled the grand drawing room, the mismatch of chairs and couches facing the brick fireplace. A wide stairway led upstairs, past oil paintings of impressive stags and men in tweed jackets.

Connor smiled shyly. 'I'm really glad you're here. My brother's excited to see you.'

Elena felt a pang of unease, and knew she had to avert

any potential misunderstanding. 'A day boating on a lake at a stately home? Who gets to do that? Although I'm realising my idea of gently bobbing about on the water might be naive.'

Connor raised an eyebrow. 'Didn't anybody warn you?'

Elena paused. 'Warn me about what?'

'Oh, nothing.' Connor looked shifty.

Elena gazed up at a family portrait, amused at the sight of Hugh in a kilt, and continued up the stairs. 'So, tell me about this boat race? What are the rules?'

'There are no rules, it's just about who crosses the finish line first.'

'No rules? How anarchic.'

Connor shrugged. 'That's the aristocracy for you. It's a different world out here.'

Evidenced by the ancient tapestries on the wall. 'Is this place home for you?'

'Kind of.' Connor led her down a landing lined with wooden pillars, busts of various heads perched on top. 'I feel at home here, and I get treated the same as the other family members, so yes, it's home. I couldn't live here all the time, though. It's full on.'

Elena spied a stag's head on the wall. 'I can imagine.'

'Plus, the internet connection's rubbish.'

Elena laughed. 'Travesty.'

'This is the room.' Connor opened the door and let her enter first.

It was large, with a four-poster bed, and contained more shabby period furniture than your average museum. 'Fancy.'

'Are you dating my brother?' Connor's question caught her off guard and she turned to look at him, surprised by his frankness. 'He's evasive when I ask him, but he talks about you a lot, so I figure he must like you.' His cheeks coloured and he looked uncertain, as though he knew he was crossing a line, but desperately wanted reassurance.

Elena kept her response playful. 'I'm guessing some of what he says isn't flattering, so you're confused, right? Understandable, we didn't get off to the best start.' She dumped her rucksack on a wingback chair. 'It was all-out war.'

'But you like him?' He sounded uncertain.

Elena went over to Connor. Whatever her feelings towards Danny, she knew Connor was struggling with his mental health and she needed to tread gently. 'Yes, I like him, but we're not dating. I'm his physio and he's my patient. It's true we've moved past wanting to maim each other, and I'd like to think we've become friends, but it's nothing more than that. Sorry.'

Connor chewed on his thumbnail. 'Why not?'

'It's just not that kind of relationship,' she said, with a shrug.

Danny wasn't the right man for her, and she certainly wasn't the right woman for him. She'd ignored the warning signs with her ex, dismissing Luisa's concerns that Felix was too rigid for her, too staid and uptight. And her sister had been right. She needed to learn from her mistakes, and wait for passion and energy and laughter to come along. Someone who would be playful and daft, and dress up for Secret Cinema events. Danny was a nice man, but he wasn't demonstrative or free-spirited. And she was far too 'dramatic' for him, she'd drive him nuts. He needed calm and serene and controlled, all the things she wasn't. It would never work ... or so she kept trying to convince herself. Something that might be easier to do if she didn't find him so attractive.

Connor didn't look convinced either. 'I know he seems grumpy, but he really isn't like that. His sadness is my fault. Underneath, he's funny and kind, and he loves deeply.'

No wonder Danny adored Connor so much. 'You have a lovely relationship.'

Connor frowned at his bitten thumbnail and lowered his hand. 'I don't want him to be alone. He needs someone like you.'

Elena felt a tightness in her chest. 'You don't know me.'

'I know you make him flustered.'

Elena laughed. 'And that's a good thing?'

'I've only ever seen him disinterested before. Hugh says he needs someone to rattle him a bit, make him lose control and live a little. You seem like someone who—'

'Rattles people?' She rolled her eyes. 'Maybe you do know me after all.'

'Will you keep an open mind?' His expression was pleading.

'Maybe.' She nudged his arm, not wanting to dwell on thoughts of her and Danny as a couple, it was too conflicting. 'For now, I'm here to compete in this barbaric boat race, with no rules, so business first, pleasure later. Lead me to the slaughter ... as Iron Maiden would say.'

Connor's face brightened. 'You like Iron Maiden?'

'Like's too strong a word. My Papi's partial to a spot of heavy rock. I'm more Lewis Capaldi than Bruce Dickinson.'

Once they were outside and heading towards the lake, the relative quiet of the manor house disappeared. The vast lawn area was scattered with pitched tents and picnic tables with Fortnum & Mason hampers. Children raced around, chased by frantic adults trying to rein them in. Elena wondered if the word 'lake' was an exaggeration. Would it turn out to be a large pond, or a grand water feature?

But no, it was indeed a full-blown lake, large enough to accommodate ten teams of four people and their makeshift boats. Tall reeds and grasses lined the water's edge, with floating water lilies dotted about the surface sparkling under the sunlight. There were several wooden jetties leading down to the water, and a rope bridge provided access to a summerhouse on the other side.

The eccentricity didn't stop there. The chaos extended far beyond anything Elena could have imagined. Each team had a base camp, filled with supporters waving banners and dressed in their teams colours. A few teams had adopted suitable wet-weather clothing and added a scarf or hat in their colour of choice. Others had created elaborate outfits made from cardboard and plastic sheeting to make them look like Marvel characters, which looked amazing, but which she doubted were sea-worthy.

In addition to the crowds gathered to support the race, there was a large barbecue station, a pop-up bar serving jugs of Pimms, and the infamous portaloos, complete with changing cubicles and a drying-off area filled with towels and spare sets of socks. It was all very well-organised and totally surreal.

'There's our team.' Connor pointed to a red awning erected over a set of garden chairs.

'Now I get why I was asked to wear red,' she said, her muted top subdued compared to Hugh's onesie and Danny's bright red T-shirt embossed with the words *Team Usain Boat* in gold lettering. He was wearing black jogging bottoms with red piping down the sides and a red baseball cap, a far cry from his pristine work suits. Both outfits paled into insignificance compared to the man wearing red army fatigues, complete with Rambo headscarf and plastic rifle. 'Who's that?'

'Grandpa Nigel.' Connor unzipped his jacket, revealing a red T-shirt the same as Danny's. 'He gets his outfits made in the village.'

'Impressive.' Elena definitely felt underdressed. Had she known the dress code was 'eccentric', she'd have made more effort—it wasn't like she was averse to dressing up. Stupid her for thinking this was an actual sporting event.

They reached the group and Elena spotted their 'boat'—a large, square contraption made from bamboo poles and packed with hessian and straw.

Danny jogged over. 'You made it!' He stopped short, as if he wasn't sure how to greet her, hesitating between a kiss and an awkward hug.

She pointed at the raft, ignoring her body's reaction to seeing him. 'Will that thing even float?'

Danny lifted his shoulders. 'Technically.'

She pinned him with a look. 'What does technically, mean?'

'We tested it, and technically it floated.'

There was something he wasn't telling her. She searched his handsome face for signs of mischief. 'Did you test it with crew onboard?'

His nose crinkled as if he'd been found out. 'Kind of.'

'Kind of?' Her eyes widened. 'What does that mean?'

Connor threw his jacket over a garden chair. 'We tested it with two of the dogs on board, and it stayed afloat.'

Elena looked between Connor and Danny. 'And that constitutes a robust safety check?'

Danny nodded. 'Compared to some years, yes.'

'One year we sank at the start line.' Connor looked unperturbed at such a confession.

Elena threw her hands in the air. 'Well, great, guys. Good to know.'

Danny nudged her arm. 'I thought you'd approve, you're always on about taking risks.'

'There's taking risks and there's blatant insanity,' she said, nudging him back, and realising Connor was watching them, a hopeful look on his face. She needed to dial down the flirting. 'How many of these vessels make it to the finish line?'

Danny ran a hand into his hair. 'Depends. Two years ago just two. We won.'

'Oh, great odds.' Elena ignored their laughter. 'And last year?'

Their laughter faded.

Danny glanced at Connor. 'We didn't compete last year.'

Connor didn't utter a word, his eyes remained downcast as he placed a red team baseball hat on his head. 'Ready to go?'

'Sure thing.' Danny went over and squeezed Connor's shoulder.

Hugh appeared, all smiles and enthusiasm. 'Our team is complete,' he said, squashing Elena in a bear hug and rocking her from side to side. 'But you look far too neat.' He tutted at her sensible sports clothing. 'This is not the Oxford and Cambridge boat race.'

'Well, I get that now. Something that would've been helpful to know before I left home.' She rolled her eyes.

'I forget not everyone knows how depraved this event gets,' he said, placing a team baseball cap on her head. 'Okay, team, let's go!'

The four of them each took a corner of the raft and carried it down to the water's edge, aiming for their allotted start position. It was heavier than expected, and this did nothing to reassure Elena that the contraption would stay afloat. She glanced at Danny, who was watching her, a wry smile on his face.

'If you think about it, it's kind of like a spa day,' he said, trying to hide his smile. 'You've got your mud wrap, your bathing area, and even a seaweed facial. All things you love. And you're such a strong swimmer, it's not like you'd be in danger if you fell in.' There was a glint in his eye, as if her falling in would be the highlight of his day.

Elena realised she was being set up. 'This is revenge, isn't it? You want me to fall in the water.'

Danny scoffed. 'Revenge is a bit harsh. It's more about taking your advice. Have fun, you said. Let go and take a risk, you said. I'm just making sure you follow your own advice, and it's not all talk.'

Connor was grinning, enjoying watching the pair of them sparring.

'You were in on this too, weren't you?' she said to Connor, who tried to look innocent and failed. 'Hugh as well?'

Hugh lifted his chin. 'No comment. On the grounds I may incriminate myself.'

Elena ignored their laughter. 'I'll ensure my wrath is equally distributed if this ends badly. Expect repercussions.'

They just laughed harder.

Despite being duped, she was smiling too. After all, she'd laid down the gauntlet and challenged Danny to prove he was more than a 'suit'. She'd poked the bear and he'd retaliated. Fair play. And besides, he'd picked the wrong woman to test. If he thought she'd be daunted, he was woefully mistaken. Schoolboy error. She was not easily intimidated.

Their start position was in the centre. The boats either side ranged from small plastic tubs to grand contraptions with masts and makeshift sails. Elena wasn't sure how much engineering went into the designs, she suspected the aesthetic was more important than functionality.

They'd kept her in the dark deliberately. Sneaky lot. She might have been thrown momentarily, but she'd adjusted now and was determined to show Daniel J Jackson just what he was dealing with. He'd be the one left with mud on his face.

Having lowered the raft into the water, Hugh saluted. 'I hereby launch this vessel. Go forth, *Usain Boat,* and do your crew proud.'

'And don't sink,' Connor added, crawling onto the vessel on his hands and knees. 'Where d'you want me?'

Danny tied the raft's rope around a pole to stop them drifting off. 'Hugh on starboard, Connor on port. Keep your paddles aligned and follow my rhythm for strokes. Elena, you'll be at the back controlling the rudder and keeping us on course.'

Elena openly laughed. 'There's a rudder?'

Danny feigned offence. 'Of course there's a rudder, we're not amateurs. This is not our first rodeo.'

'You could've fooled me.' She searched for the elusive rudder, if there was one, it was hidden beneath the water. 'Who actually made this contraption?'

'It's not a contraption, it's a finely tuned racing dingy.' Danny offered her his hand.

'Yeah, looks it.' She took his hand and stepped gingerly onto the raft, which was about as stable as jelly. 'I get the spare clothes request now. The chances of us making it across this lake without sinking seems highly unlikely.'

'Such mutiny,' Hugh said, clutching his chest. 'We've only ever sunk once.'

'Twice,' Connor corrected. 'You're forgetting the year the Smyths capsized us.'

'Was that the year Patty Tompkins had to be resuscitated?'

Elena's hands went to her hips. 'I know what you're doing, guys. And it won't work. I'm no amateur either.'

Smiling, Danny stepped onto the raft, increasing the instability. 'Risky enough for you?' he said, holding Elena steady as the waves from another team's boat hit them. 'It's not too late to quit. Nigel's on standby to take over. I'm sure you won't be offended if a seventy-year-old man has to step in and replace you.'

'Fighting talk,' she said, their chests bumping together with the movement of the swell. 'But it's not me who has anything to prove. You're the one adamant to show me you're willing to take risks. Let's see what you're made of. ... Just don't reinjure your hip,' she added, not wanting to goad him to the point of reversing his good progress.

'My hip's fine,' he said, kissing her cheek. The action made him freeze, and she wasn't sure who was more stunned, her or Danny. He blinked a few times, and then attempted to cover his embarrassment. 'Don't worry about me. You worry about yourself.'

Elena pulled a face and pretended to be appalled, which was highly immature, but better than admitting she'd enjoyed being kissed—especially as Connor was watching them, and the kiss had done little to dampen his ideas about them dating.

A loud whistle sounded, followed by a muffled voice shouting through a loud hailer announcing one minute until the start of the race. This was followed by the crowd cheering and people racing towards the water's edge to support their team. There must have been a hundred people surrounding the lake, holding up banners, most of them unsteady—probably due to the amount of Pimms they appeared to have consumed.

Danny took up position at the front of the boat. 'Okay, let's go, team!'

Hugh and Connor balanced on their knees either side of the raft, their oars positioned above the water, ready to plunge. Elena knelt down and felt for the rudder, a large plastic thing shaped like a shark's fin, which she couldn't imagine steering a bath toy, let alone a raft with four people on it.

The whistle sounded again, giving them a ten second warning. The crowd counted down, speeding up as their eagerness took over. And then they were off ... or not, as it transpired.

'Untie the rope!' Danny yelled at Elena, who did as instructed.

They still didn't move.

Danny scrambled into the water and waded around to the rear of the raft to push them away from the reeds. His cheeks turned pink in reaction to the cold and he sucked in short breaths as he heaved against the raft, trying to shift them into the water.

Elena's gaze was drawn to his wet T-shirt clinging to his chest. 'I would offer to help, but there's no way I'm getting into that water voluntarily.'

He tried to smile, but it looked painful. 'Lightweight.'

His arm muscles flexed as he pushed harder, adding another distraction and playing havoc with Elena's concentration.

Danny dragged himself onto the raft, drenched and

smeared in pond algae, soaking her in the process. She might have complained if he didn't look so happy about it. He was laughing, his body animated, and it was the first time she'd seen him truly undone. Daniel J Jackson wasn't just a rigid control freak—beneath the suit was someone capable of being silly, ridiculous, and utterly unrestrained. It was annoyingly endearing.

They drifted further into the lake, almost colliding with another boat. It was mayhem. None of the boats travelled in a straight line—they drifted in all directions, worse than rush hour on the M25. The crowd screamed encouragement, like they had bets on The Grand National, not a charity event.

Despite their best efforts, *Usain Boat* veered off to the left and ended up in the same lane as another boat. As the two vessels collided, the opposing skipper shouted accusations of 'skulduggery', before losing his balance and toppling head first into the water.

Elena clutched hold of the slippery bamboo poles beneath her, trying to steady her balance and steer them back on course, but the rudder was useless. As she'd suspected, it was purely for show.

Around them, one by one the boats either sank or careered into the side banks, unable to reverse, their race over.

Only two remained, *Usain Boat* versus *A Yacht of Fun*.

Connor and Hugh paddled frantically, spraying everyone on board with more water than they were shifting. Danny was on his knees at the front, yelling instructions that no one followed. Elena held on as best she could, unable to influence the outcome and trying not to fall into the lake.

Waiting for them at the finish line were Virginia and

Nigel, jumping up and down like schoolchildren and screaming for them to '*go faster!*'

Elena shifted the rudder, aiming for the finish line, but a gust of wind sent them hurtling towards *A Yacht of Fun*.

'Excellent work, Elena!' yelled Virginia through a loud hailer. 'Sabotage the opposition!'

Elena couldn't take any credit, every tactic did the opposite thing than she'd intended.

It was a close finish, with both boats attempting to cross the line at the same time.

The captain of the opposing boat jutted out his punt in an attempt to derail them, a devious move. He lost his balance and joined the other competitors in the water. His team groaned with despondency, overridden by cheers from the *Usain Boat* supporters.

They were poised to cross the finish line first, aided by a sudden gust of breeze. A blast from a horn announced their success. The crowd cheered. Danny punched the air, and Connor and Hugh flopped towards each other and hugged—a manoeuvre that destabilised the raft further.

The momentum shift was enough to split the raft in two, and Elena watched in horror as the tethering came apart around her and freezing water gushed over her legs.

Connor and Hugh fell overboard with a loud splash.

Elena sucked in a breath and squealed as the cold seeped through her leggings.

Rallying herself to the challenge, instinct kicked in, and her core strength came to her aid. She was not going to get wet.

Steadying herself, she pushed onto her knees and then her feet ready to jump ashore. She'd show these men how it should be done.

But before she could jump, Danny grabbed her leg and shouted, 'It's okay, I've got you!'

Far from saving her, he smacked into her, and they slid off the raft and hurtled towards the water faster than Keanu Reeves saving Sandra Bullock from a runaway bus.

There was nothing Elena could do other than close her eyes, hold her breath, and brace herself for the impact of being submerged into the dark, cold, and very murky lake.

Chapter Sixteen

DANNY

Saturday, 5th July

Danny knocked hesitantly on the bathroom door. Elena had been gone a long while and he was worried she might have drowned in the huge standalone bathtub. It was an unlikely scenario, she was a strong swimmer and she'd survived being capsized in the lake, so a bathtub was unlikely to outwit her, but he felt the need to check on her anyway.

He could hear faint mumblings through the door and the splash of water.

'Elena?' He tapped gently. 'Are you okay in there?'

The splashing paused. 'I'm fine.'

She didn't sound fine, she sounded grumpy. He couldn't blame her, no one appreciated ending up in a muddy lake. He guessed he should have warned her. Getting wet was inevitable, but keeping that information from her hadn't been fair.

'Are you sure? Only you don't sound fine. Is there anything I can help with?'

A weighted silence followed. 'Not unless you're an expert in removing mud.'

He should have realised. When she'd emerged from the lake, dripping wet and wiping mud from her face, he'd half expected her to yell at him. Instead, she'd laughed and thrown a lump of mud at him, told him he was a 'clumsy goose', and refused his offer to help her up the slippery grass bank. He had a vague recollection of using the same phrase when they'd been drunk at the roaring twenties event, so he figured it was a fitting insult.

He leaned against the doorframe, his hair still damp from having showered in the downstairs family mud room, installed for the specific purpose of removing dirt after dog walking, horse riding, and boating accidents such as today. 'I spent many Sundays after football matches removing mud from Connor's hair, clothing and boots. Mud does not faze me.'

Another lengthy pause. 'Fine.'

'Fine? As in you'd like to me come in and help you?'

'I suppose so. The door's unlocked.'

He opened the door, hesitating before stepping inside. Bathrooms at Bucklebury Manor were not like the average bathrooms found in a new build property. They were large rooms, with open fires, ancient plumbing, and ornate clawfoot tubs centred in the middle of the room. The shower units downstairs were for practicality, but the Spencer-Harrisons liked to bathe in luxury.

Steam filled the room, smearing the gilt mirrors and glass panels on the large sash window. The lights were dimmed and two candles cast flickering light across the room. His senses were hit by a combination of lavender, rose, and coconut milk.

Elena was submerged in the water, sunk low enough to conceal everything except her head and hands. The abundance of bubbles were threatening to overspill the rim.

'Warmed up now?' he said, heading over and kneeling behind her.

'I think so, although I can still smell algae.' Her hair looked even darker wet, and it contrasted against the white porcelain bathtub. She reminded him of Cleopatra, bathing in coconut milk, as opposed to asp's milk. 'The shampoo's on the floor. I've washed it three times, but the mud won't shift.'

'The trick is to crumble it away, rather than washing it out,' he said, laying a towel on the stone flooring and gently extricating the mud from Elena's hair. 'Like you do when making pastry, rubbing the lumps until they disintegrate. If you try pulling that's when it's painful.'

'As I've discovered.' She let out a sigh, the movement causing the water to slurp up the sides of the tub. 'You're very knowledgeable about mud. Also pastry making.' She sounded amused, which was better than grumpy.

He continued removing mud from her hair. 'Essential requirements of being a parent.'

'You said Connor played football. Was he a sporty kid?' She sounded doubtful, and he knew why. Connor was a gentle soul, more suited to the arts than physical roughhousing.

'Not really. He went through a phase of trying to fit in at school by playing sports, but his heart wasn't really in it.'

'He's not a good team player?' She didn't sound critical, just curious.

'It's not that, he's just not competitive. Although he is

good at basketball, but he lacks the killer instinct. He was happier helping out with school plays and fundraisers than competing in sports. He was more popular with the teachers than the students. Connor was one of those kids who liked taking responsibility and helping people, rather than being the centre of attention.'

'Nothing wrong with that. Those are good traits to have.'

'I agree.' He ran his hands over her hair, checking for clumps of mud. It felt strangely intimate to be touching her in such a way. It was usually the other way around, and he wondered if she felt as undone as he did when she touched him. 'Plus, helping others is good for him. I've noticed a real difference since he's started volunteering. I'm hoping we've turned a corner.'

'He seemed to have fun today.'

'Yeah, he likes spending time here. This place is a safe haven, no one judges him or asks awkward questions, he's loved unconditionally.' He squirted shampoo into his palm and rubbed his hands together.

Elena lifted her arms and blew the bubbles away. 'The Spencer-Harrisons are quite a unique family.'

'That's one way to describe them.' He kept his gaze away from the sight of her body, visible though gaps in the bubbles, and began massaging her hair, sliding his fingers over her scalp, ensuring all the mud had disappeared.

'I like them.'

He smiled. 'I thought you might. Lift your head for me.'

She lifted her head, resting on her elbows on the sides of the bath. 'Why do you say that?'

'They're uninhibited. They don't care what people think. They live life according to their own rules, and they never allow anyone to shame them or deter them from being their authentic selves.' He didn't add that they reminded him of Elena. She had the same positive outlook on life, always energised, and not seeming to care what other people thought.

'It sounds like you envy them almost, which is interesting.'

'How so?'

'Well, you like the Spencer-Harrisons for being unrestrained and free in the way they live their lives, and yet you choose the opposite, opting for restraint and control. Why is that?'

'Lower your head in the water so I can wash off the shampoo.' As he rinsed her hair, he thought about her observation. He'd never really spotted the contradiction before, but she was right, as she usually was. He acted one way, but admired something different.

She disappeared under the water, running her hands through her hair and sloshing the water. When she remerged, she twisted to face him and rested her chin on the edge of the rim. 'Well?'

He shrugged. 'Habit, I guess. My childhood was governed by control and rules, so it's ingrained in me. The one time I allowed myself to let go and take a risk it ended badly. And then Connor came into my life, and I was forced to grow up quickly and act responsibly. I suppose it seemed easier to live guardedly than throw caution to the wind.'

'Even if your instincts say otherwise?'

He frowned at her. 'Why do you say that?'

'The few times I've seen you smiling and looking truly happy have been when you've not been in control and you've allowed yourself to let go. It seems to me living cautiously might be what your head dictates you should do, but it isn't what your heart actually wants.'

'It's not just about me, is it? I couldn't be reckless with Connor's safety or happiness. He comes first.'

'No, but he's no longer a child in need of constant protection. He's a man now. Can you pass me that towel?'

Danny got to his feet and fetched a towel from the railing. 'Connor's still fragile,' he said, holding the towel open for Elena and averting his gaze. 'He needs me. Keeping him safe is my priority.'

She stood up, sending water sloshing around the bathtub, her body covered in suds. 'I get that, but it seems to me your life has been governed by two extreme ideals. The pendulum has swung between stifling rules and heightened drama that ended in disaster, nothing in between. No blend of calculated risk, or opportunities to push boundaries in a safe environment.' She stepped out of the bathtub and took the towel from him, wrapping it around her. 'With such heartbreak clouding your judgement, it's hardly any wonder you're afraid of letting go, which is a shame, as when you do, the light that shines from you is almost blinding.'

His eyes shifted to hers, he was stunned by her words.

She nodded to the door. 'You can go now. Thanks for removing the mud, you're indeed very skilled in that department.' She smiled. 'As you mentioned pastry-making, I'm hoping cooking is another skill you possess. Boat racing is hungry work, any chance of some food?'

He ran a hand through his hair. 'Sure, no problem. Head down to the kitchen when you're done.'

'Thanks.' Turning away, she lowered the towel to dry herself, revealing a flash of glistening skin that did nothing to dampen his confusion. Once again, she seemed totally at ease with her body and it was hard to stop himself staring.

Common sense forced him to turn away and exit the bathroom, needing an escape from the heady scents adding to his unsettled state. Elena had highlighted the contradictions in his life. In the process, she'd created another one. His feelings for Elena Romero. His head said steer clear, his heart disagreed entirely.

Twenty minutes later, Elena appeared in the open-plan kitchen wearing jeans and a fleece. Her short hair had dried wavy and she was wearing the chunky socks he'd left out for her, no shoes.

'You look warmer,' he said, adding chopped garlic and chilli to the saucepan and making the ingredients sizzle.

'I feel warmer. Cleaner too,' she said, looking curiously around the room.

The space was an odd mix of modern and period. The ancient blackened Aga stood against the exposed brick wall by the fireplace, contrasting with the American-sized fridge-freezer next to it. The solid oak table filling the centre dated back to the seventeen hundreds, and combined with modern utensils and appliances, it made for an eccentric room.

'I had to douse myself in body lotion to erase the smell of algae,' she said, seating herself on a breakfast stool by the table. 'I hope Virginia won't mind me using her toiletries.'

Danny added tomatoes to the saucepan, trying not to imagine Elena smothering herself in body lotion. 'She said use anything you needed, so don't worry.'

She rested her elbows on the table. 'Where is everyone? It's eerily quiet.'

'Village pub. They showered downstairs before heading off.' He reached for the olives. 'Enjoy the quiet, give it a couple of hours and they'll be back here, loud and demanding, and most likely plastered.'

Elena smiled. 'Connor too?'

'He'll have a couple of beers.' Danny stirred the sauce.

'He's never been a big drinker, less so since he's been on medication. Alcohol doesn't mix with anti-depressants, and he becomes very morose.'

Elena looked concerned. 'Do you need to be with him?'

The kettle boiled and Danny poured hot water into a pan. 'Hugh's with him, he'll make sure he's okay. Connor knows drinking isn't a great idea, so he'll monitor himself. He's sensible like that. Self-aware, his counsellor says.'

Elena rested her chin on her hands, the sleeves of her fleece covering her fingers. 'A lot of people are resistant to getting help, so the fact he's seeing a counsellor and taking medication is a definite positive.'

Danny added pasta to the boiling water. 'That's what Hugh keeps telling me. He's doing everything he can to get better, and I need to be more positive and not hover around him all the time. Hugh says it puts too much pressure on him, and I need to give Connor space to work through his issues and just be there when he needs me.'

'Which is fine in theory, but not so easy to do in practice.'

'Exactly.' He liked that she understood, she was very emotionally intuitive, as Hugh would say. Danny gave the sauce a stir and came over to the join Elena at the table. 'I'm sometimes guilty of making the situation more intense than it needs to be, so I'm making a concerted effort to keep my distance.' He set the timer on his phone for three minutes. 'Hence why I'm here cooking for you and not at the pub.'

'For which I'm very grateful, it smells delicious. And don't be too hard on yourself, it's an impossible situation to get right. Believe me, I know.'

'Wine?' When Elena nodded, Danny poured two glasses. 'Your sister?'

'If we do too much for her, we're accused of

mollycoddling. If we back off, then we're not there for her.' She took a sip of wine and rolled her eyes. 'We never get it right, and we've been trying for years. You learn to go with the flow and not take anything to heart. Luisa's dealing with something the rest of us will never understand, so if she gets angry, or upset, or unreasonable, so be it. She needs someone to take out her frustrations on, and as her family, it falls to us to take the brunt. I believe it's what they call unconditional love.'

Danny nodded. 'Tell me about it.'

'Doesn't mean I don't want to pummel her with a pillow sometimes. She drives me bloody crazy.'

Danny laughed. The timer sounded on his phone and he got up to drain the pasta. He was aware of Elena watching him as he stirred in the sauce and grated parmesan cheese on top. Having wiped the rim, he added a sprig of basil and placed the bowl in front of Elena. 'Hope it's not too spicy for you.'

'I'm half Colombian, spice is my thing.' She pushed her sleeves up and looked appreciatively at the bowl of food. 'It smells delicious, and it looks like something served in a restaurant. I suppose I shouldn't be surprised.'

He searched out cutlery. 'Why does that sound like a criticism?'

'I'm just teasing,' she said, with a smile. 'I'm envious, really. My food tastes okay but looks a mess. I've never mastered presentation. This dish is as pristine as one of your designer suits.'

He handed her a fork. 'Funny.'

She took a bite of food, her face failing to hide her enjoyment.

He felt smug. 'Good?'

'Very good. I'm getting a nice hit from the chilli. Okay, I

take it back, there's nothing bland about this dish. It's delightfully hot.' She winked at him and took another bite.

He tasted the sauce, pleased with the seasoning. 'Still think I'm a boring suit?'

'I'll admit you have layers.' She took another mouthful, her eyes fluttering closed with delight, which gave him a stupidly warm feeling. It shouldn't matter that she liked his cooking, but it did. 'You're a man of many talents, I stand corrected.' Her smile turned mischievous. 'Still think I'm a drama queen?'

He lowered his glass. 'I never called you that.'

She laughed. 'It's what you implied.'

'Maybe, but not without good reason. You're very ...'

She waited, one eyebrow lifted. 'Choose your words carefully,' she warned, pointing her fork at him. 'I'm armed, remember?'

'My point proven. Threatening me with a fork.'

Smiling, she returned to eating. 'I'm only dangerous when provoked.'

'And I seem to provoke you without even trying.'

'True.' She seemed to think about this. 'Although, not so much anymore. I didn't understand you before, I do now. I may have been a little quick to judge.'

'Oh, you think?'

'Just as you judged me. So come on, what were you going to call me.' She took another bite of pasta, washing it down with a hearty glug of wine. 'You started to say, "You're very ..."? Very what? What am I?'

'Gorgeous.' It was out of his mouth before he could sense-check his answer. He wanted to slap himself.

Thankfully, she didn't believe him. 'Liar. That's not what you were going to say.'

'I'm not lying. You are gorgeous. And quirky, and

thoughtful, and I like spending time with you. No one's more surprised than I am.' It was more than he'd intended to reveal, and he shut up when he saw the shocked expression on her face.

Her fork was paused halfway to her mouth.

He'd overstepped, exposed his feelings and needed to backtrack. 'Of course, you're also combative, coercive, and terrible at steering boats, but no one's perfect.'

She resumed chewing on her pasta. 'I guess we were both wrong.'

He got up, unsure how to erase the sudden tension filling the room. 'Would you like more pasta?'

'I'm good, thanks. It was delicious.' She pushed her bowl away.

'No problem.' He covered the remaining pasta sauce and placed it in the fridge for Connor and Hugh to eat later if they were hungry. 'What time's your train?'

'Not for a while yet.' She checked her phone. 'An hour or so.'

Having loaded the dishwasher, he topped up their wine glasses. 'What would you like to do while you wait? We have board games in the drawing room, or a pool table in the games room.'

Her expression was still watchful. 'Do you have photos?'

'Photos?'

She nodded. 'Photos of you and Connor and your life here. I'm intrigued. I like looking at family photos, they reveal a lot about a person. They fill in the gaps.'

His eyebrows lifted. 'There are gaps?'

'There are.' She hopped off the stool. 'And bring wine.'

With a shrug, he picked up the bottle and did as instructed. 'Whatever you say.'

They made their way up to his room on the first floor. Embers still glowed from the fire he'd lit earlier and he added more kindling to boost the heat. The fire crackled and hissed as the flames caught hold.

'The only hard-copy photos we have are kept in here,' he said, heading over to the chest of drawers and searching through the piles of memorabilia Virginia insisted on keeping. 'I don't have any photos from my life in the US, and everything from the last ten years I have stored on my laptop, but there are photos here from when Connor was young.'

Elena stood in front of the fireplace warming her hands. 'Why don't you have any photos from your childhood?'

'It didn't occur to me to take any with me when I left home. After my parents died, the house contents were sold as part of the estate. I've no idea what happened to any personal items. Maybe my aunt took them, I don't know. She dealt with the estate sale.'

Elena looked confused. 'You didn't return home to deal with everything?'

'There was no point. I wasn't made executor or included in the will, so I had no jurisdiction over anything, it would've been pointless.' He found what he was looking for, an old photo album tucked at the back of the drawer. 'Besides, I was a skint student who suddenly had a five-year-old kid to look after.'

'Your parents didn't include you in their will?'

'Nope.' He carried the album over to the couch facing the fireplace. 'Everything was left in trust for Connor when he turns twenty-five.'

Elena joined him on the couch. 'How do you feel about that?'

He thought about it. 'I don't know really. We weren't

close, as you know. I think they cut me off in the hope it would make me conform, but I was never interested in their money, I only wanted love from them, and that was something they were incapable of giving.' He rubbed his temples. 'Actually, that's unfair. I think they did love me, they just weren't good at showing it. They were advocates of the tough-love approach, which I guess works for some people, it just wasn't right for me. Who knows whether they would've changed their minds in time. I don't begrudge Connor, though. I'm glad for him. He deserves it.'

Elena curled her legs under her. 'How did your parents die?'

'Car accident. They clipped a barrier and flipped off the road into a river.'

She gasped. 'Oh, Danny, that's awful.'

He nodded, feeling the familiar heavy weight pressing against his chest whenever he thought about the accident. 'We never got on, but it didn't stop me loving them and hoping things might turn around one day.'

Elena shook her head. 'Considering your upbringing, it's amazing how different you are with Connor. No one could accuse you of not showing him love or kindness.'

'It's what you said earlier about the pendulum swing, I guess. No way was I going to allow Connor to suffer like I did, so I became the opposite of my parents. Every opportunity I had I showed him he was loved and wanted. Our situation wasn't ideal, I had no money, and I was clueless about parenting, but I knew he'd suffered a huge loss and needed to feel loved, and that was something I could definitely do.'

Her hand settled on his shoulder. 'You're quite an extraordinary man, you know that?'

'Not really.' He opened the album, revealing a set of photos he hadn't seen for years.

Elena shuffled closer so she could see. 'Talk me through them.'

Photos of days at the beach and picnics at the lake stared up at him, the tape securing them to the pages faded and yellowing. 'These are from our first summer spent here after Connor arrived in the UK. I owe Hugh and his family so much, they took us in and included us in their lives.'

Elena pointed to a photo of Connor in Spiderman swimmers. 'He was such a tiny thing, look at those spindly legs.'

Danny smiled. 'All skin and bones.' There were times when he still saw Connor as that fragile little boy, and had to remind himself it was no longer who Connor was. He was a man now, capable and resilient, even if he was vulnerable at times.

'He was a beautiful child.' Elena turned the page and laughed. 'Is that you?'

'That was taken New Year's Eve. Virginia insisted on booking a childminder so Hugh and I could attend one of their infamous lavish parties. It was black-tie event, but I didn't own a suit, so Nigel loaned me one of his velvet smoking jackets.'

Elena laughed. 'Did you pull?'

'Several times, I was a hit with all the ladies aged seventy and above.'

'I can imagine,' she chuckled, resting her chin on his shoulder. She was so close he could feel her warm breath on his cheek. 'Even then you looked good in a suit. You look happy.'

'I look drunk. I threw up all the next day.' He turned another page. 'These are from our trip around Europe.' A series of photos showing Danny, Connor, and sometimes Hugh, posing by the camper van, diving off rocks, eating pizzas and visiting waterparks. 'And these were taken the day we moved into our first home.' It was strangely emotional seeing them carrying boxes into their tiny starter home, especially when Danny was still so young himself.

'You're smiling in every photo.'

He stared at the photos. 'I hadn't noticed that before.' She was right, he looked carefree and excited. 'It was a happy time, despite everything.'

As he turned another page, a loose photo slipped from the album.

Elena picked it up before he realised what it was, and it was a moment before she spoke. 'I'm guessing this is the woman you referred to as trouble?'

He took the photo of him with Maisie from her. It had been taken outside Brixton Academy after watching a band. 'How did you know it was her?'

'The look on your face is a mixture of love and fear.' She squeezed his shoulder. 'You said she died too? What happened?'

He blinked at the photo, Maisie's blue hair and black nails matching her gothic dress. 'She died of an overdose the same week as my parents.'

Elena closed her eyes. 'Oh, Danny.'

He tucked the photo inside the cover, unwilling to torture himself by looking at it any longer. 'We'd split up a few days before. She hadn't taken the break-up well and begged me to take her back. I ignored her calls. And then everything happened with my parents and Connor arrived, and the next thing I knew ... she was gone too. It was a grim time.'

'Why had you broken up?'

Danny closed the photo album and placed it on the floor. 'I couldn't deal with her addiction issues. It wasn't just the drugs, it was the lying and the stealing, and the mayhem that surrounded her. It was exhausting and very—'

'Dramatic?' Elena's sad smile told him she understood where his aversion to living a disorderly life came from.

He nodded. 'It didn't stop me feeling like I'd let her down. I still feel guilty now. I wanted to help her, I loved her, but I was out of my depth.'

'And then you had Connor to deal with and the death of your parents.' She sighed. 'To think I called you a suit.'

He turned to her. 'You weren't wrong, I am emotionally restrained.'

'No, you're not.' She shook his shoulder. 'No one could love Connor and Hugh, and the Spencer-Harrisons, like you do and be emotionally restrained.' Her arm slid around his shoulder. 'Your parents didn't show you love, and yet you loved them back. The woman you loved abused your love and made your life hell. It's not a suit you wear, Danny, it's armour.' She gave him a squeeze. 'You've been burnt, so you've built a protective barrier, only allowing those close who you know and trust, which is absolutely understandable ... but I imagine incredibly lonely.'

He was unable to stop the choke in his voice. 'I am lonely.'

With that, no further words were said. They just stared at each other.

The light had faded outside, only the glow from the fire prevented complete darkness, accompanied by the crackle of flames. He watched her watching him, an unanswered question hanging in the air between them.

Elena Romero was beautiful, kind, and giving. Why hadn't he seen it before? He reached out and touched her hair, letting his fingers trail down the side of her face. Her skin was warm and so soft it was like velvet.

She caught his hand before he could lower it and brought it up to her face, guiding his thumb across her open lips and making his breath hitch. Her eyes were fixed on his, intense and searching as she kissed the tip of each finger. She tilted his hand and kissed his palm, and then his wrist, creating a thud in his blood.

And then she sat forward and lifted her fleece over her head, discarding it on the floor, leaving her wearing only a blue vest-bra. Still her eyes never left his as she knelt up and straddled him on the sofa, lifting his T-shirt over his head and pushing him against the cushions.

She took his hands and slid them slowly up her thighs, settling them on her backside, before lowering herself until her chest touched his.

Her hands caressed his chest, trailing across his skin, and exploring his body. She kissed his forehead, then his eyelids, and finally each cheek, before twisting to gain access to the side of his neck, where she licked the twitching nerve there and flicked it with her tongue.

His body convulsed in response as wanting surged through him. His hands gripped her backside and he pulled her towards him, needing to feel her against him, closer, wanting to taste every part of her. Her hands laced into his hair and she pulled his head back to kiss him, pressing against him, moving her lips against his and sending him over the edge.

In one movement, he lifted her and flipped her on her back, still between her legs and needing to kiss her. It was frantic, and urgent, and when her hands slid beneath his jeans and drew him closer, her nails raking over his skin, it left him with no option but to submit any control and unravel in a way he hadn't done for nearly two decades.

Chapter Seventeen

ELENA

Sunday, 6th July

Elena blinked as weak daylight filtered through the gap in the heavy drapes and cast a sheen across the four-poster bed, illuminating the outline of the body next to hers. Pillows had been discarded, the sheets were rumpled into a creased mess, and the comforter was wrapped around one of the posts.

As she lay there, stretching out her tendons and reminding herself how she'd ended up in bed with Daniel J Jackson, she waited for regret to kick in. Sense and propriety had flown out of the window, replaced by a clawing need. All the promises she'd made to keep her distance and not cross the friendship line had disappeared even before her lips had melted into his. And she'd made the first move, it was her own fault. Need had overridden restraint and she'd succumbed, urged on by the way he'd seemed to crave her. It had been intoxicating.

As for retaining professionalism, she'd broken the cardinal rule and slept with her patient. She'd expected to feel remorse this morning, mixed in with a dash of shame, all-consuming guilt, and a smidgeon of annoyance at her lack of moral restraint.

Instead, she felt surprisingly buoyant. Her body was buzzing, boneless and floppy, and fizzing with heightened sensitivity. To think she'd accused Daniel J Jackson of being a boring suit. The man was a revelation.

The mattress shifted softly as he rolled over, smiling sleepily as his eyes met hers, the sheet wrapped around his bare midriff. 'You're awake.'

'I am.' She trailed her fingers down his arm, enjoying discovering each new nuance. His chest hair was soft, and he had a slight cleft in his chin she hadn't noticed before. Without his glasses on his brown eyes appeared lighter, flecked with hazel. 'How did you get this?' she asked, touching the curved scar on his bicep.

'Failed attempt at a tattoo.'

She peered closer. 'How come?'

'It was during our tour of Europe,' he said, with a sigh. 'We were on the island of Kos and we'd booked a childminder to look after Connor for the evening. After a night spent drinking too much Ouzo, Hugh came up with the brilliant idea to get matching tattoos. He coped fine. I fainted after thirty seconds.'

Elena smiled. 'What was it supposed to be?'

'A heart with Connor's name on a scroll. The tattooist only managed one section before I passed out.'

'You never got it finished?'

He shook his head. 'I suffered the humiliation of a half-finished tattoo for years before deciding to get the thing lasered off.'

Elena grinned. 'Made worse as Hugh had the completed tattoo, I'm guessing.'

'Exactly.' Danny shifted onto his elbow and rested his head on his hand. 'I didn't notice any tattoos on you last night. Do you have any?'

'Looking closely, were you?'

'I thoroughly investigated every inch.' His smile was laced with a confidence she liked. 'I don't have the words to describe the hotness of your body.'

She laughed. 'Hotness? Is that a real word?'

'If it's not, it should be.' He gave her a playful smile and she felt her insides twitch in response.

Her fingers continued down his arm, enjoying the way her touch made the hairs on his skin lift. 'In answer to your question. No, I don't have any tattoos. Luisa has loads, though. Although most of them are small and are hidden under clothes. She has a dolphin on her ankle, reflecting her desire to travel. A shooting star on her hip, in the hope if there is a heaven she'll end up there, and a series of Japanese symbols down her back about the promise of a utopian afterlife.'

'Deep.' He frowned. 'And sad.'

'I know.'

It was a ritual played put many times over the years. Luisa would return home with a new tattoo, her parents would pretend to be outraged and scold her, Sofia would act shocked, and Elena would laugh and tell her youngest sister they'd spelled something wrong, causing Luisa a moment's panic until she realised she was being wound up.

'Luisa pretends the tattoos are part of her desire to rebel, but there's more to it than that. She has so little control over her life that she needs to exert control when she can.' Elena sighed. 'I get that, it's a miserable existence for her sometimes, and if getting inked helps her cope, then why not. She claims we're conservative by comparison, but her choice of tattoos reveals the pain she suffers underneath the bravado.'

He nodded slowly. 'Sofia doesn't have any tattoos?'

Elena laughed. 'Tattoos are not Sofia's thing, she's the conventional one in the family. Well, conventional compared to me and Luisa. Sofia's always been the sensible one, the one who stopped her sisters from getting into trouble.'

He looked intrigued. 'Like what?'

Elena shrugged, enjoying the way the movement sent his eyes lowering to her chest. 'Nothing terrible. Luisa needs a chaperone on nights out to ensure she doesn't drink too much and end up in an undesirable situation. And with me, it's more about controlling my temper and moderating my responses when provoked. Sofia has an annoying habit of pointing out when I've overreacted ... which, before you say it, I'm well aware I can do sometimes.'

He grinned. 'You make up for it in other ways.'

She gave him a seductive look. 'Care to elaborate?'

His hand slid under the sheet and grasped her hip, sliding her towards him in one seamless motion.

There was an ease to their movements she found surprising, as they were opposites in all other aspects, and yet it seemed their bodies were in perfect harmony.

He pulled her on top of him, his hands holding her hips and easing her closer as he kissed her. It had been a long time since she'd experienced such an instant connection with someone. It usually took her a while to warm up, it certainly had with Felix. But with Danny it was like her burners were on full power from the off.

She laced her hands into his, moving to pin his arms

above his head so she could regain the upper hand. He groaned in response to her tilting her hips.

Her skin was heating up, her toes tingling with pleasure as he moved under her. It wasn't so much consenting as her body demanding, needing him more than she'd ever needed anyone. It might have been alarming had she allowed her mind to enter the debate. As it was, she shut out all coherent thought and simply let her body take charge.

He sat up, lifting her with him so she was astride him, his face level with hers. There was a moment's pause, where he looked at her with such tenderness she melted a little and ran her hands through his hair, breathing him in, at which point he twisted her onto her back and slid between her legs. It was a glorious feeling, warm and shuddering, making her breath hitch and tightening her insides as he moved against her.

And then someone knocked on the door.

Before either of them could respond, the door opened, and Connor appeared. 'Breakfast is rea ...' his voice trailed off, his shock apparent by his backwards step. 'Shit! Sorry. I had no idea. Sorry. Shit!'

By the time Danny had rolled off Elena with a groan, Connor had fled the room, the door banging shut behind him like the punchline to an unfunny joke.

Danny covered his face. 'Tell me that didn't just happen.'

Elena shuffled up the bed. 'Okay, it didn't happen.'

He rubbed his face. 'Shit.'

She swung her legs off the side of the bed. 'I guess that's my cue to leave.'

He caught her arm. 'I'm sorry, Elena.'

She turned to look at his stricken face. 'It was hardly your fault.'

'I didn't lock the door.'

'He still would've guessed what was happening.'

'Yeah, but not in such graphic detail.'

'He'll get over it.' She patted Danny's hand and slid off the bed, searching for her clothes.

'Will he? Our family isn't like yours. What was it you said about your parents making up when they'd argued and disappearing into the bedroom? That never happened in our house. My parents had separate bedrooms for a start. I've always kept that part of my life away from Connor.'

'Which you've admitted might not have been such a great idea,' she said, locating her underwear. 'Isn't that how this daft dating pact came about? A failure of communication about healthy relationships?' She pulled on her jeans. 'You being intimate with a woman is perfectly normal, and maybe now he's seen it, he'll feel empowered to do the same.'

He flopped onto the bed. 'I wish I shared your confidence.'

'The last thing he needs is for you to act embarrassed, or be awkward about it. The best thing you can do is to laugh it off. Go downstairs and show him everything's fine and this was just a bit of fun. Two adults hooking up. It doesn't have to be a big deal.'

Danny shot off the bed, striding over, his stark nakedness confronting. 'Is that how you feel, like this isn't a big deal?'

'Whoa, calm down. I have no idea what this is,' she said, softening her voice. 'Maybe it is just a one night thing, maybe it's something more, who knows. Now's not the time to get all deep and meaningful. Connor's the priority here.' She rested her hand on his chest. 'Whatever's happening between us can wait. My advice is get dressed, go to breakfast, act normal and show him there's nothing to freak out about. You're the role model, remember?'

Danny's forlorn expression was heart-breaking. 'You make it sound so easy.'

'Well, of course it won't be easy,' she said, with an ironic laugh. 'You'll be cringing inside like you want to die.'

'Oh, good to know.' His indignation made her smile.

'But you don't let on, okay? Fake it.' She let her hand slide lower down his abdomen. 'Like I did several times last night.'

He caught her hand. 'You did not.'

She lifted an eyebrow. 'Sure about that?'

'I'm sure.' He pulled her closer. 'And if I wasn't feeling absolutely mortified at having Connor walk in on us I'd prove it ... again.'

She reached up and kissed him. 'Save that thought for next time.'

He looked unsure. 'There'll be a next time?'

'If you play your cards right.' She gave him a playful pat. 'Now go get dressed, breakfast is waiting.'

Elena waited until she was hidden away inside the spacious bathroom before allowing her true emotions to surface. Groaning, she collapsed in a heap on the floor and lay with her hands covering her face, wishing she could perform a Harry Potter spell and apparate somewhere else.

She'd told Danny what he'd needed to hear and down-played the humiliation of being sprung by Connor. In truth, any chance of convincing Connor she wasn't dating his dad-stroke-brother would be pointless, and it was her own fault.

Knowing she couldn't hide forever, she got up, washed, and put on some make-up in the hope of appearing unruffled. Despite the 'hotness' of last night—to use Danny's wording—dating Danny Jackson was still a bad idea. It was too soon after Felix, and they were incompatible in temperaments. That was bound to cause problems down the line. They both had family dramas to deal with, and he …

She stared at her reflection in the mirror.

He … what?

All the misguided assumptions she'd made about Danny were false. She'd been clinging hold of reasons that no longer existed. The truth was, Daniel J Jackson was a sweetheart. He was sensitive and generous, and they enjoyed a laugh together. There was nothing majorly wrong with him, however much it pained her to admit. So was dating him really such a bad idea?

She resumed brushing her hair.

Plus, the man had moves, he'd made her toes curl last night. He'd been attentive and assertive, and how she'd ever thought he was selfish, she didn't know. His whole focus had been solely on her, ensuring she was having a good time. Not many men did that. His needs had come second, literally.

Feeling slightly calmer, she packed her bag, ready for a swift exit after breakfast, and headed downstairs.

Any hope of quiet discretion evaporated when a butler-type appeared and ushered her into the 'morning room', where the family 'awaited her arrival'.

The room was long and rectangular and bathed in light flooding in from the huge leaded windows. The space was filled with a long, solid table, decorated with vases of fresh flowers and candelabras. Virginia and Nigel sat at either end of the table in true blue-blood tradition. Connor was seated opposite, flanked either side by Hugh and Danny.

A man she didn't recognise rose from his seat when she entered and gestured for her to sit next to him.

'Hi, I'm James,' he said, extending a hand. 'Hugh's husband.' He was tall and slim with fiery red hair and light blue eyes that creased with amusement. He knew what had happened, she could tell. Why else would he be suppressing a grin? 'Nice to meet you, Elena. I've heard a *lot* about you.'

Hugh covered his laughter with a cough.

'Oh, I can imagine,' she said, sitting down, assessing the atmosphere in the room.

Virginia and Nigel looked like their usual formidable selves, dressed in country casual tweed and ready for a day spent riding, shooting, or whatever other sport the elite enjoyed.

Hugh was making a hash of trying to contain his laughter, and Connor looked vaguely hopeful, as if embarrassment had given way to the idea that maybe Danny had found 'love'.

In contrast, Danny looked like someone had burned all his expensive suits on a bonfire and he'd been made to wear polyester for the rest of his days. Poor man.

'Morning, lovely gal!' Virginia summoned the butler over to top up her coffee. 'Sleep well?' Her question caused Hugh and James to stifle more laughter.

They thought it was funny, did they?

Elena glanced at Danny, who looked mortified. His hair was rumpled, his cheeks were flushed, and if they'd been alone she might have dragged him back to bed. It was tempting, her inner thighs were still twitching.

Connor was looking at her with trepidation, like he wasn't sure if she was mad with him or not.

Elena had two options. Suffer like Danny, add to the awkward embarrassment filling the room, and leave

Bucklebury Manor with her tail between her legs ... or face the situation head on.

'I didn't get much sleep, no,' she said, nodding when the butler offered her coffee. 'I hope we didn't disturb anyone last night? We were rather noisy.'

Danny choked on his sausage.

Connor gasped, and Hugh and James burst out laughing.

'Goodness, what were you getting up to?' Nigel said, oblivious to the situation—which caused Hugh and James to laugh harder.

'Oh, all sorts.' Elena sipped her coffee. 'It was quite the body workout. Luckily, I'm reasonably fit. Danny's hip took a bit of a pounding, though.'

Danny's knife clattered onto his plate, making everyone jump.

A weighty silence hung in the air.

'I guess that's what happens when you try playing a game of *Twister* after too much alcohol. Utter carnage.' She accepted a plate of scrambled eggs from the butler. 'This smells delicious.'

She could almost feel the collective sigh.

Nigel dabbed his mouth with a napkin. 'Thank heavens. For a moment there I wondered what you were going to say.'

Everyone laughed, some more genuinely than others.

Elena turned to Nigel, aiming for wide-eyed innocence. 'What did you think I meant?' She glanced around the room, incurring a 'stop it' look from Danny as their eyes met. Anyone would think he wasn't enjoying the joke. She hit him with a beaming smile. 'Could you pass the ketchup please, Daniel?'

It was enough to break the tension and everyone

resumed eating their food. All traces of apprehension had vanished from Connor. Virginia and Nigel remained clueless, and Hugh and James continued to share indiscreet glances.

When she caught Danny's eye, he shook his head, pretending to be annoyed, but she knew he wasn't really mad. Her gamble had paid off. Instead of an awkward situation, the tension had lifted and normal chatter resumed.

She asked James about his work as a vet, and laughed at his funny anecdotes, usually involving the animals' owners. Hugh talked about his ideas for setting up a weekly session aimed at encouraging men to talk about their feelings, and Nigel talked a lot about his rod, which Elena realised after a few raised eyebrows referred to his love of fly-fishing. Neither Connor or Danny said much during the exchanges, incurring inquisitive looks from Virginia, who wanted to know why they hadn't eaten more.

After the table had been cleared, Virginia clapped her hands and shooed everyone from the room.

'Chores to do, places to be,' she said, patting Elena's shoulder as she moved behind her. 'Let me get the blessed dogs sorted, and then I'll drop you at the station. Unless you want to stay on? More than welcome to join us for the day, the laddies are heading off fishing.'

Elena stood up. 'That's kind of you, Virginia, but I should be getting back.'

'Righto.' Virginia gave Nigel a shove when he got in her way at the doorway. 'See you out front. Get Danny to show you the stables before you go, he said you liked horses. Join us any time for another jaunt. Always welcome.' She blew kisses at Elena as she marched off down the hallway.

'Hope to see you soon,' Hugh said, winking at her as he

headed upstairs. 'You must come for dinner. James does enjoy a couples' night.'

James kissed Elena's cheek. 'I can see why Danny adores you.'

'That's it, I'm leaving!' Danny headed for the front door. 'Not remotely funny, guys.'

Hugh and James laughed and disappeared upstairs.

Connor still looked hesitant, and Elena felt bad for him.

She waited until they were alone before heading over to him. 'I'm sorry about this morning. Bit awkward, huh?'

He ran a hand through his dark hair, reminding her of Danny. 'I shouldn't have barged in. I'm sorry, I had no idea.'

'Why would you after what I said yesterday about Danny and I just being friends? It's my fault. But I'm guessing it's left you a little confused?'

He shrugged, looking younger than his years in his *Wolf Alice* T-shirt. 'I get it. Friends with benefits, right?'

It was brutal, but probably accurate. She puffed out her cheeks. 'It could be, but it might be more, I don't know. I'm not sure yet, is that okay?'

He shoved his hands in his jeans pockets. 'Is it okay if I hope it is more?'

She smiled. 'Always look on the positive side, is my motto. You've got to be in it to win it, right? No point quitting before you've even tried.'

His frown lifted as if he'd been struck by something. 'I hadn't thought about it like that.'

'Whatever happens, I promise to be upfront and honest about how I feel, and I'll never do anything to deliberately hurt your brother. You have my word.'

Connor nodded. 'I know.'

'I'd better find Danny.' She squeezed his arm. 'Take care, Connor.'

She headed outside and found Danny waiting for her on the gravel pathway.

'I'm not sure whether to kill you or thank you,' he said, striding off towards the stables.

She had to run to catch him up. 'It worked, didn't it? Besides, we've nothing to be ashamed of. We're adults.'

'I know. And you're right,' he said, glancing at her. 'If it weren't for Connor I might find it funny. Everyone else certainly did.' He sounded peeved, and it made her smile.

'I just spoke with Connor and he seems fine. You never know, this might be the incentive he needs to start dating. Wasn't that the deal? You date, he dates. Simple as.'

Danny stopped by the stable door. 'Are we dating?'

She gave him a nonchalant shrug. 'Maybe.'

He folded his arms. 'Are you going to make a decision anytime soon?'

She struggled not to laugh. 'Maybe.'

'That's all I get? Maybe?'

She tapped her temple, pretending to think about it.

Rolling his eyes, he opened the door and headed inside. 'Anyway, it's more complicated for Connor.'

She followed him inside and was hit by the strong scent of leather and manure. 'Why's it more complicated? Because of his depression?' She hadn't expected so many horses, there must have been twenty lined along the walkway in individual boxes. 'I think people are more open-minded these days, less likely to judge. I hope so, anyway.' She stopped and petted a pale grey horse with mismatched eyes.

'It's the cause of Connor's depression that's the issue.' Danny rubbed his face, opening and closing his mouth a few times, as if debating whether to say something. 'Please don't tell anyone this,' he said, glancing at the door to check they were alone. 'But Connor's depression is a result of being accused of assaulting a female student while he was at university.'

Elena's shock must have been obvious.

'He didn't do it,' he added quickly. 'But for a while we struggled to prove that.' He sagged against the wall. 'The police were adamant they'd got the right person and made an application to The Crown Prosecution Service to press charges. It was only when another student came forward about an earlier assault that the police reviewed the evidence and realised it was a case of mistaken identity. DNA traces from the first attack confirmed it was the same man and an arrest was made. Charges against Connor were dropped, but only after months of stress and worry.'

Elena went over and hugged him tightly. 'No wonder you've both been so unhappy. What a nightmare.'

He hugged her back. 'I honestly thought they were going to lock him up. I couldn't bear it. I was supposed to protect him. I knew he was innocent, but I couldn't prove it. I've never been so scared in my life.'

Elena pulled back to look at Danny, an understanding forming as to his control issues. 'Is that why Connor did what he did, the night he ... you know?'

Danny nodded. 'He didn't think he could cope with prison.'

'I don't think I could either,' she said, quietly. Whatever she'd imagined had caused Connor such sadness, she'd never dreamed of anything so horrendous.

'Even after the charges were dropped things weren't great. There was no apology from the police, no compensation as the case hadn't gone to trial, and even when we submitted a formal complaint, the police were found to have acted appropriately.'

'That's outrageous, the whole thing sounds totally unfair.'

'Unfair doesn't make it unlawful.' He stepped away from the embrace and went over to one of the horses. 'It didn't stop there. We struggled to get newspaper articles revoked, and it's almost impossible to get content removed from social media once it's out there. The information was correct at the time of publication, so it's not libellous. Everywhere Connor went people would either question him, make judgemental comments, or assume he was guilty of something.'

She went over and rested her hand on his back. 'Is that why he left uni?'

Danny nodded. 'He needed a clean start. We both did. The whole thing was exhausting.'

'Has it helped, moving to London?'

'I think it has. I hope so, anyway.' He looked at her. 'Meeting you has certainly helped me.'

Breaking eye-contact, she went to the next stable. Inside was a smaller, scruffy-looking pony. 'No wonder you worry about Connor so much. Your concern for him makes more sense now.' She reached over and stroked the pony's soft nose.

'It's not as bad as it was. He's less fragile now, less angry, and the volunteering has definitely helped, but when it comes to relationships, I think it's damaged his confidence.'

Elena turned to him. 'How so?'

'He's afraid of being accused of something. It's made him nervous about getting close to anyone.' He joined her by the stable door. 'And then there's the whole no-smoke-without-fire issue. There's stuff about him all over social media, and he worries someone finding out what happened before he's had the chance to explain will prejudice them against him.'

Elena felt sad for them. 'It's not a conversation anyone wants to have, but if a person understands what really happened, surely they'd believe him? I don't know Connor that well, but even I know he'd never hurt anyone.'

Danny stilled. 'You do?'

'Absolutely. But I also know life isn't always fair like that. Part of the reason Luisa avoids relationships is for similar reasons. Either she hides her illness, which never works, as the moment anyone gets close it becomes blatantly obvious she has health issues. Or she tells the guy the truth, and even if they say they're okay with it, they inevitably ghost her.' She leaned against the stable door, resting her head on her folded arms. 'She's stopped bothering now, sticking to flings instead. It's sad, but I can't blame her. So I kind of get Connor's reluctance to put himself in that position.'

'Me too, which is why trying to convince him to date is so hard. I probably wouldn't date either if I was in his situation.'

She turned and placed her hands on Danny's chest. 'Even more reason why you need to support him and encourage him to be open to the idea of dating. What's the saying? Better to have tried and failed than never to have tried at all. Not every woman will judge him, they'll be someone out there who'll see the real him and never doubt the truth, I'm sure of it.'

'I hope you're right.'

A car horn sounded.

Virginia appeared in the stable doorway, dogs in tow, all barking and unsettling the horses. 'Ah, here you are! Engines running, lovely gal! Let's go!'

Elena reached up and kissed Danny. 'I've had a great time this weekend. Thank you for inviting me. It's been fun.' And then she remembered the muddy lake. 'Mostly.'

His voice softened. 'Will I see you again?'

'Of course. It's back to work tomorrow, I'll see you in the office.' With a smile, she jogged off to join Virginia.

'That's not what I meant!' he called after her.

Waving him goodbye, she climbed into the Land Rover and buckled up, anticipating another speedy driving adventure with Virginia.

As they sped away, she turned back in time to see Danny exiting the stables, looking troubled.

After all he'd been through, it wouldn't be fair to mess him around. She needed to make a decision about whether she was ready to start dating again, and soon. Both their hearts were at stake.

Chapter Eighteen

SOFIA

Tuesday, 8th July

Sofia winced as she stood up, stiff from being crouched down for too long in the same position. This was her third consecutive day working at the community centre and her energy levels were flagging. She'd spent all weekend painting the walls and ceiling of the meeting room while Luisa worked on her mural, and it was physically demanding work.

During the occasional break, she'd loaded more data into the new accounting software package and created invoices for the community centre hirers. It was mentally exhausting work, and entirely fruitless in terms of her plan to get closer to Connor, as he'd been away the whole weekend visiting family.

Tempting as it had been to message him, she'd deleted her words each time she'd tried to compose a message. She was a coward, as Luisa had unhelpfully pointed out, telling her to 'stop procrastinating and message the damn guy'.

It was easy for Luisa to be blasé when she wasn't the one whose happiness was on the line. One false move and it could be game over. Sofia didn't want to blow her chance, and messaging a guy when you weren't certain he felt the same way would only open her up to further rejection, and she wasn't ready for another let-down.

Arching her back, she stepped away to check her work. Luisa had stayed home today as her breathing had become wheezy, so Sofia had persuaded her to rest up.

Turning slowly, Sofia had to admit the room looked good.

Happy with the result, she began rolling up the paint-splattered floor covering, feeling the bass thump of Latin beats emanating through the walls from the main hall where the Salsa class had begun. Her hips moved involuntarily to the rhythm.

When the door opened, she immediately stopped dancing and jolted upright, as if she'd been caught doing something she shouldn't. Her heart skidded a little at the sight of Connor entering, and her embarrassment levels increased another notch. It had only been a few days since she'd last seen him, but she'd missed him.

She covered her blush by pretending to rub paint from her cheek.

'Hi,' he said, glancing a smile her way, before admiring the décor. 'Wow!'

'Doesn't Luisa's mural look great?'

'It's amazing,' he said, shaking his head in awe. 'I was expecting a basic makeover, not a Picasso masterpiece.'

She watched Connor move closer to the design, his head tilting as he took in the oak tree with the words 'You are not alone' inscribed beneath. Giant purple butterflies flew from the tree, captured mid-flight, one wing true to form and the other filled with phrases, such as 'Be kind' and 'Think positive'. The design seemed simplistic on first viewing, but once you looked closer, all of Luisa's clever intricacies came to life, the hidden hearts, the beckoning hands, and the bright yellow sun emerging from behind a dark cloud.

Connor moved around the room, his hands tucked inside his faded jeans pockets, his eyes taking in the brushstrokes. 'I can't believe you did all this.' There was a catch in his throat. 'It's extraordinary.'

'Luisa did all the design work, I just filled in the gaps.' She nodded to her own handiwork, the sections of pale lilac and soft green emulsion, but it was Luisa's clever artwork that had completely changed the ambience of the room. 'We found some old curtains at a charity shop, so I made a couple of beanbags and a few cushions.'

'You made these?' Connor flopped onto one of the beanbags, letting his hands run over the leaf-green design. He picked up a cushion and held it to his chest. 'You're so clever.'

'It wasn't hard, I used my mum's old sewing machine.' It was her default setting to bat away his compliments, but inside she was squealing with delight that he liked her handiwork. She could almost hear Luisa's voice telling her to get a grip.

His fingers played with the velvet piping edging the cushion. 'I can't believe how different the room looks. I never imagined it would look this good. Thank you.'

With a shrug, Sofia returned to packing up. 'It's no big deal.'

'It's a huge deal,' he said, getting up. 'When you said the

place needed a lick of paint, I thought you'd just whitewash everything. I had no idea you'd go to so much effort. It's beautiful.' He touched her arm. 'Really. Thank you, Sofia.'

His voice softened when he said her name and she had to suppress a sigh. 'I'm glad you like it.' When the room started spinning, she realised she'd stopped breathing. 'How was your weekend?' She moved away in the hope she'd stop blushing and start inhaling oxygen. Passing out was not the best way to impress a man.

He looked thoughtful. 'Interesting.'

She unzipped her overalls and stepped out of them. 'Interesting in a good way?'

'Maybe.' He picked up a role of masking tape, averting his eyes. 'I nearly messaged you at one point.'

She stilled. 'You did?'

'I don't know why, really.' He looked embarrassed. 'The sun was setting over the lake and the colours reminded me of the sunset in that photo you had on the train the day we met, the one of your parents on holiday. I was going to send you a photo, but then I lost my nerve.'

A number of thoughts filled her head. Mainly, the fact that he'd remembered so much about the day they'd met and the photo he'd fleetingly seen of her family. She wanted to ask why he'd been nervous about contacting her. Did it mean he liked her? Dare she hope? Luisa would tell her to stop dithering and ask him outright, but instead she tentatively asked, 'Can I see the photo?'

He scrolled through his phone and held it out for her to see. 'It's not that impressive when I look at it now.'

'I think it's lovely.' The photo showed the fading sunlight glinting off the water, sparkling against the sky behind. 'Is that where you were visiting this weekend, where your family live?'

'Technically, they're not really family, but they're the closest thing to extended family I have. They look out for me.'

She wanted to ask more, but she also didn't want to pry. 'I don't think family is necessarily who we're born into, but those who we choose to have in our lives.'

'I guess you're right.' His face was close to hers, his eyes flitting between her and his phone, as if he wanted to look at her, but it caused him discomfort. 'How's Luisa?'

'Tired.' It was only then that she realised she was wearing nothing but a vest-top over her lacy bra. She'd discarded her sweater when she'd overheated. 'Her breathing was a bit off this morning, so she stayed home.'

He averted his eyes from her bare arms. 'Another infection?'

'More likely paint fumes. Hopefully it'll settle down soon.' She searched the room, hoping to locate her sweater in the process of tidying up. 'By the way, I dropped off the bank signatory forms this morning and all the community centre hirers have now been invoiced. The scout group paid immediately, so I cleared a couple of red demand bills. I hope that was okay?'

'Of course it was,' he said, helping her pack stuff away. 'But you don't have to do everything yourself, especially as you've been painting all weekend.'

Sofia shrugged. 'I like keeping busy. It stops me overthinking.'

He looked at her. 'Have you heard anything about your appeal?'

Unable to find her sweater, she wrapped the damp paint brushes in plastic. 'The company have refused my appeal on the grounds that no new evidence was presented, so their original decision stands. My ACAS adviser still believes I have a strong case, so my application is being considered for an employment tribunal hearing.'

'Sounds positive.'

'Maybe,' she said, with a grimace. 'My former employers are instructing solicitors, so I'll be up against a law firm specialising in these types of cases. Even with an ACAS representative it's going to be tough to win the case.'

He replaced the paint tin lids. 'What can I do to support you?'

'Nothing, but thanks for offering.' She smiled. 'Being here helps, it's therapeutic. I even got roped in to make tea for the craft group this morning.'

'You have been busy.' He held up her blue sweater. 'Is this what you're looking for?'

'Oh, there it is.' She took it from him. 'Thanks.'

He averted his gaze as she pulled the sweater over her head. 'You're not planning on catching the train home with all this stuff, are you?'

'No, I'll take a taxi home and come back for the rest tomorrow. The pile to the right is rubbish, so we can load it into the dumpster. When do you need the room cleared by?'

'I cancelled all the bookings this week, so there's no rush.' He picked up the bucket of brushes. 'Leave the rubbish, I'll clear that in the morning.'

'Okay.' She packed away the rest of the kit. 'Luisa's keen to start on the main hall next, but I told her paid bookings were more important for the centre's finances, so I wasn't sure when the work could be done.'

'Most of the bookings pause during school holidays, so maybe we can schedule the work to be done when the schools break up. I'll organise a working party to help.'

'In the meantime, maybe we can spruce up the office, it's quite a dismal working environment.'

'Tell me about it.' He added the scraper to the bucket of brushes. 'You know, it seems stupid you taking all this stuff home if you're planning to do more decorating. Why don't you leave it here, we can make room in the outside storage cupboard.'

'That makes sense.' She loaded up the paint pots in her arms. 'Lead the way.'

They headed down the steps into the main hall, where a group of dancers were attempting to Salsa. The instructor was having to raise her voice to be heard above the loud music.

Connor exited through the side door and balanced the brushes on the bench seat while he searched for the padlock key. 'Can you dance?'

Sofia waited until he'd unlocked the cupboard before passing him the paints. 'It's kind of compulsory when you come from South America. I remember dancing on my first day of pre-school, I still had a pacifier in my mouth.'

He laughed. 'How old were you when you moved to the UK?'

'Five, but we've visited a lot over the years. Papi's family still live there, I have numerous cousins and extended family all over the place. Everyone dances in South America, young and old, even at home. Birthday parties, barbecues, funerals, no matter the occasion, someone will end up dancing.'

Connor nodded to where the dancers were attempting underarm turns. 'Like they're doing?'

'Mostly merengue. It has a similar rhythm, but you move side-to-side as opposed to back and forth.' She glanced at him. 'What about you, can you dance?'

He shook his head. 'God, no. Not since school. I was left

traumatised after being made to dance in front of the whole school. It wasn't a great experience.'

She smiled as she handed him the bucket of brushes. 'How come?'

'I volunteered to help make scenery for a production of The King and I, but it turns out I ticked the wrong box and signed up for the chorus instead. The teacher was so excited to have a boy in the chorus I didn't like to back out. I was forced to wear pantaloons and dance with eleven girls, all older than me.'

Sofia laughed. 'Some boys might like that.'

'Not this boy.' He rolled his eyes. 'I couldn't remember the steps or keep up, so they had to adapt the routine to dance around me, which made me stand out even more. You know it's bad when people use words to describe your performance like *brave* and comment on how much *enthusiasm* you had. It did nothing for my street cred, I can tell you.'

She watched him secure the padlock. 'And you haven't danced since?'

'I can hold my own in a mosh pit, but it's not a pretty sight.'

Sofia held out her hand. 'Shall we have a go?'

He stared at her hand like she was holding a grenade. 'You've just told me you've danced since childhood, and you expect me to dance with you now? No way.'

'Why not?'

'Because you already intimidate me enough as it is, that's why not.'

She dropped her hand. 'I intimidate you? How on earth do I do that?'

He lifted his hands. 'Where do I start? You've fixed the accountancy problem. You've decorated a room like it's something from the Tate Modern, and you made matching cushions and beanbags. You're like Superwoman. It'd be like that school production all over again. Me looking like an idiot, humiliating himself in front of a goddess.'

He thought she was a goddess? 'And I thought *my* self-esteem was low.'

He frowned. 'Why would your self-esteem be low? You're smart, talented, and you look like ... well, you look like that.' He gestured to her face and body, and then ran his hands into his hair. 'I'm going to shut up now.'

Her hands went to her hips. 'Hasn't anyone told you not to make assumptions based on appearance? You're not the only one who's had their confidence knocked, and you're certainly not the only person who fakes feeling more positive than they really feel.'

He looked mortified and reached for her hand. 'I'm so sorry, Sofia. You're right, that was wrong of me. It's just you seem so confident all the time, but I was wrong to assume. Please forgive me.'

'People often make incorrect assumptions about me,' she admitted, staring at their entwined hands, and glad he hadn't let go yet. 'Dancing can help improve confidence, you know. It's empowering, and lifts your mood.' She lifted her eyes to his. 'Will you let me show you?'

He looked hesitant. 'I'm not sure.'

'We're in a community centre with a load of other novices. There's no audience, no one's paying us any attention, they're too busy concentrating on themselves to notice us.' She stepped into the hall and gently tugged on his hand. 'Come on, show me how *brave* you are.'

He laughed. 'Like that, is it? I admit my inner trauma and you take the piss.' He was smiling, so she knew he wasn't really upset as he followed her into the hall. 'Don't say I didn't warn you.'

Sofia led him to the back of the hall away from the main group, where the music wasn't quite so deafening. 'Take both my hands. We move forwards and then backwards, like this.'

He had no problems following the rhythm, and within a few beats he was mirroring her movements.

'Relax your arms,' she said, demonstrating. 'That's it. Now soften your knees and loosen your hips. See? Easy.' She lifted her arm and turned underneath, catching his hand as she returned to face him. 'You're a natural.'

'Is that a euphemism for *enthusiastic*?'

She laughed. 'You're doing fine. How does it feel?' She hoped he felt the way she did. Sparks were flying.

'Nice,' he said, his eyes were locked on hers.

'I dance at home sometimes, when I'm feeling a bit down,' she admitted, moving closer to him. 'I put on Papi's Latin playlists full blast and dance while I'm cleaning, or cooking. I always feel better afterwards. It helps shake off negative thoughts.'

He smiled. 'I'm starting to see the appeal.'

'Luisa feels the same way about painting, and my older sister uses sport to manage her anxiety. We all need an outlet.' She turned under his arm again, brushing against him as he assisted the move this time. He was definitely getting the hang of it. 'Do you have anything like that in your life? An outlet for your anxiety?'

He seemed to think about it. 'Not really, although volunteering helps. Working here lifts my mood, and I feel better after a shift than when I've been at home alone. My counsellor says I'm still healing from an "emotional injury", and it'll take time to recover. I need to be patient and kind to myself.' There was a hesitation in his expression, as though it had taken a lot for him to admit that.

'Is this the thing that happened to you last year?'

He nodded. 'Please don't ask me to explain.'

'I won't.' She changed direction, pleased that he followed her lead and moved seamlessly with her. 'But you offered to support me earlier, so the offer is reciprocated. If I can help you in anyway, I will. I won't judge, I'll just be there for you, whatever you need.'

'Thank you.' He looked sheepish. 'I'm sorry for what I said before.'

'No harm done.' She smiled at him. 'You're a natural dancer, by the way.'

'I think that's down to my partner.' His face softened, and she slowed her movements, making them smaller so the gap between them reduced.

They stayed like that for a long while, moving slowly, their eyes never leaving each other. She never wanted the evening to end.

'What's your happiest memory?' she said, their bodies now touching. 'You know, the time you revisit in your head when you want a reminder of how good life can be.'

He thought for a moment. 'I guess it would be the last summer before I went to university. My dad took an extended break from work and we travelled Europe for a few weeks. It was something we'd done the first summer after my birth parents died, but I was only five then, so I don't remember much. We decided to repeat the trip.'

Sofia was confused. 'Your parents died?'

He paused dancing. 'Haven't I mentioned that? It was a long time ago.' He shook his head. 'Anyway, my brother, who's fourteen years older than me, became my guardian. I call him Dad sometimes, because that's what he is, really. He's the only parent I've ever known.'

'Goodness.' It was a lot to absorb. 'And it's just the two of you?'

He nodded. 'Just the two of us. Plus, Hugh, my dad's best mate. That's who I was staying with this weekend, Hugh and his family. They kind of helped raise me.'

They resumed dancing, Sofia still processing this new information.

'Anyway, we went on this trip around Europe and it was amazing. We went scuba diving, canoeing, and hiking. We travelled by boat and train, and even hired scooters at one point. It was magical. When we came home I was so excited for uni, I felt ready to join the world and start my adult life.' His smile was genuine and endearing. 'Yeah, that's definitely my happiest memory.'

'I can see why.'

'What about you? What's your happiest memory?'

'Similar to yours, I suppose.' The music had switched to a slower rhythm and she settled her body against his. It felt right, natural. He wasn't much taller than her, so her chin rested perfectly against his shoulder. 'It was last summer, before my mum died. Luisa's health was good, and life was happy, no dramas. We spent two weeks staying with my grandparents in Colombia. They live in a small village near Medellin, it's quite rural and we spent the whole time horse-riding, swimming in the lake, and going on picnics. My grandparents run a farm, and they'd host these weekly open events for tourists and the locals, where they'd parade the bulls and demonstrate ranch skills. There'd be a huge buffet, with local specialities, like *ajiaco*, *sancocho* and *empanadas*. A band would play live music, and the staff would dress in traditional costume and perform dances for the guests.'

His eyes crinkled as he smiled. 'It sounds amazing.'

'It was.' Her heart ached a little at the memory. 'It was such a special holiday.'

'Have you been back since?'

'Not since Mum died. Papi's there at the moment, dealing with some business stuff. Although in truth, I think it's more about avoiding his grief than anything. Some people need to keep occupied, and he's one of them. I'd like to go back again soon, though. Maybe once I sort my life out and start earning some money again.'

His thumb ran over her palm. 'I hope you do.'

'In the meantime, I close my eyes and transport myself back to happier times and hold onto the belief that one day those feelings will return for good.'

Connor slowed to a stop and stared at her, his eyes dark and intense. 'Sofia—'

What he would have said, she'd never know. The music cut out, the lights lifted, and the group of dancers started clapping. The Salsa class was over.

They held eye-contact for a moment, before stepping away from their embrace.

'I'd better head home to check on Luisa,' Sofia said, savouring the last of his touch as her hand slid from his. 'I'm sure you need to lock up.'

'Can I see you home?' Connor said, walking over to the door with her.

'I'll be fine, but thanks for offering.' Before she could stop herself, she leaned over and kissed his cheek. 'I liked dancing with you,' she said, before almost running from the centre, unwilling to witness his reaction.

It hadn't exactly been the classiest of moves. More

clumsy teenager than grown adult. What must he think of her?

If she'd been unsure of her feelings before tonight, all doubt had now vanished. She was falling in love with Connor. It wasn't rational, but it was how she felt.

But did he feel the same way? It was evident Connor had issues to work through, and she needed to tread carefully. Had she blown it by kissing him?

Her phone pinged with a message.

It was from Connor.

She opened the message, her hands shaking.

I liked dancing with you too. x

Chapter Nineteen

DANNY

Monday, 14th July

It had been a distracting couple of days for Danny. He'd tried his best to concentrate on work and occupy his mind with business matters, but his thoughts kept drifting to reminders of Elena. He'd barely seen her since the weekend. She'd been in work the whole time, ensconced upstairs in her clinic, but she hadn't come down to see him, like she used to do. He might have taken this as a hard rejection if he hadn't witnessed the string of patients heading up to her clinic each day. She had a business to run, same as he did, and he had to respect that. And he did. He just ached to see her.

He couldn't even use the excuse of needing a physio session, as she'd made it abundantly clear it was no longer appropriate for her to treat him since they'd become 'romantically' involved. His hip was functionally nearly normally now, helped by his home exercise regime, so this wasn't an issue—even though not seeing her most definitely was.

'Send the trial bundle over,' he said to his client over the phone. When he heard the stairwell door open, he peered into the waiting area, hoping it would be Elena. But when she didn't appear and another patient exited the building, he suppressed a sigh and returned to his office. 'No problem,' he said to his client, not really paying much attention to what was being asked of him. 'Once I've read the details I'll get back to you with my response.'

Ending the call, he leaned against the window frame and stared at the views across Notting Hill.

His head was all over the place. It had been since the weekend when things had taken an unexpected turn with Elena. He'd known he was attracted to her, that wasn't the issue. It was the other stuff that had thrown him into turmoil, like wanting to talk to her, missing her company, and getting hot under the collar when he thought about what they'd done last weekend. He'd fallen for her big time, and it was scary as hell.

He'd always believed he'd resisted getting involved with anyone through choice. He could have had relationships, he'd just chosen not to. Now he realised that was bullshit. He'd hadn't been in a relationship because he hadn't met anyone since Maisie who he'd wanted to be in a relationship with. Not that he'd given anyone the chance—he'd kept his distance, avoided getting to know anyone, and actively blocked anyone who'd attempted to get to know him.

He'd tried to do the same with Elena, but it had proved impossible. Her confidence and humour, and her determination to infiltrate his defences had forced her way into his life. He was stuck, waiting to find out if she felt as afflicted as he did, or whether it was game over.

He rubbed his temples. What was wrong with him? He was sulking about and moping over a girl, tying himself in knots as to whether she liked him or not. The way he saw it, he had two options. Get over her and return to focusing on work and parenting, or ... grow some balls and ask her out.

Venturing into the heady world of dating scared the hell out of him, but the idea of losing Elena terrified him more.

Having made his decision, he marched into the waiting area and pressed the button for the elevator, fuelled by a determination to sort his life out. But when the elevator door pinged open it was like invisible hands closed around his throat and started choking him. He tried to move, but panic gripped him, unsteadying him and tightening his chest.

'Get a grip,' he told himself, but his legs refused to obey.

Bored of waiting, the elevator door seemed to sigh as it closed, tired of waiting for the flaky passenger to board. Danny jabbed at the button again, forcing the door back open.

'Two floors,' he told himself. 'It's just two floors.' Still, his legs wouldn't move.

Exasperated, he punched the wall, sending a flare of pain shooting up his arm and tilting the painting above. He should be over this by now. He'd done all the right things. He'd talked about his damn feelings, he'd carried out his hip exercises, he'd attended informal counselling sessions with Hugh. So why was he still unable to ride in a damn freakin' elevator?

He rested his hands on his knees, cursing loudly.

The stairwell door slammed behind him, making him jump. 'Are you okay?'

'Jesus!' Typical that Elena chose now of all times to show up. 'Don't creep up on me like that.'

'I didn't,' she said, indignantly. 'I came down the stairs in my usual fashion, no creeping involved.' Her hands went to her hips. It was a look he recognised. Assertive, challenging, hot as hell.

'Sorry.' He gave her a sheepish grin. 'You're right. No creeping involved.'

'I'm heading out to run a physio session at the local rugby club,' she said, her eyes darting between him and the elevator door, which had pinged open again, like it was telling tales and snitching about his lack of bottle. 'Were you coming up to see me?'

'Trying to.' He rubbed his hand, regretting punching the wall. 'As you can see, I failed.'

'Was there something specific you wanted to see me about?' She placed her medical bag on the floor.

'Yes.' He straightened, he could do this ... but then doubt crept in. 'No. ... What I mean is ... kind of.' He was the opposite of Elena. Cowardly, pathetic, fearful of rejection.

She nodded slowly. 'Helpful.'

He cleared his throat. 'Do you want to go on a date?' he said on a rush, fumbling his moment and inwardly cringing. 'Sorry, let me try that again. What I meant to say was ... would you like to go on a date with me ... sometime? You know, if you'd like to. No pressure, or anything.'

'A date?' Her expression wasn't easy to make out. She was either appalled, or trying to smother a laugh. He wasn't sure which was worse.

'Yes, a date. It's clear you've been avoiding me since the weekend, and I figured we needed to get together to decide what happens next. If anything.'

She took a moment before responding. 'I haven't been avoiding you, I've been busy working. I've had back-to-back patients all week.'

'I know, and I appreciate that, but you could've dropped by to say hi. And you haven't. So it's a fair assumption to conclude you've been avoiding me.' He sounded needy and pathetic, and he hated himself for it.

'I haven't been avoiding you,' she said, carefully. 'But maybe I did need some space to see how I felt after last weekend. I hadn't expected things to develop the way they did.'

'Me neither.'

'I didn't want to rush into a decision. For both our sakes.' She looked so composed and unruffled standing there in her pressed physio tunic, her hair neatly styled behind her ears, like the professional clinician she was. Her lack of emotion made the dead weight in his stomach sink further. He was in turmoil, while she was casually thinking it over, as if the decision was no more taxing than whether to have chicken or fish for dinner.

He tried again. 'I get that, but this isn't just about the way *you* feel. It's not a decision you get to make solo. I get a say in this too.' Now he sounded desperate, great. 'So, that's why I think we should arrange a date. More research is needed in order for us to decide what happens next.'

Her lips twitched. 'Research?' She was definitely trying not to laugh.

'It's the logical thing to do. We know we're attracted to each other, and we know there's chemistry between us. There are a load of positives.'

She openly smiled. 'I agree.'

'There are also a few negatives.' He flinched. 'Sorry, not negatives, I don't mean that. What I'm trying to say, and badly, is that we both made assumptions about each other in the beginning that have turned out to be incorrect. Or, at least, it's only part of who we are. We need to fill in the gaps and see if the good stuff outweighs the doubts.'

She shrugged. 'Okay.'

He waited a beat, but nothing more was forthcoming. 'Okay?'

'It's a solid plan. Dating is the logical next step, a way of working out whether this thing between us has mileage, or whether it was just a moment in time. A very nice moment, it has to be said, but it's not enough to base a long-term decision on.'

He swallowed awkwardly. 'So we're in agreement?'

She floored him with one of her killer smiles as she collected her bag and headed for the door. 'Tomorrow night, Bertie Blossoms. 7pm. Don't be late.'

'I won't.' He watched her open the door. 'Right. Good. Well, that's sorted. See you tomorrow.'

She'd almost stepped out of the door, before turning back and walking purposely over to him and kissing him, her bag dropping to the floor with a loud thud. He hadn't seen it coming and had no time to prepare. Her arms wrapped around him, her body leaned into him, and she kissed him with such force he almost fell backwards.

He'd barely had a chance to reciprocate when she pulled away. 'Don't beat yourself up about the elevator, okay? You'll get there.' And with that, she picked up her bag and disappeared out of the door.

He was left standing there like a gormless idiot, blinking after her. Well, okay then.

That was good, right? She'd agreed to a date and she'd kissed him. Things were looking up.

He headed back into his office, his head repeating this

latest encounter. Her kiss had set off a buzz in his blood like he'd been injected with neat adrenaline. He hadn't wanted it to end. He definitely wanted it to happen again. She'd agreed to a date. The ball was in his court, he couldn't fumble his chance.

Checking his phone, he saw Connor's message asking him where he was.

He checked the time. He was supposed to be at the community centre helping Connor run the basketball session. When had it got so late?

Cursing, he grabbed his jacket and frantically locked the drawers. This was what happened when you let a woman distract you.

Slamming the door behind him, he exited the building and headed for the tube station.

He wasn't a fan of the underground, especially during the tail end of rush hour. Too many escalators, cramped turnstiles, and a lack of fresh air. It wasn't as bad as riding an elevator, but it still made him feel edgy and tense, as though a panic attack loomed in his periphery, a hairsbreadth away.

It was still preferable to driving around London and paying the extortionate parking fees, though, so he dealt with it as best he could.

The training session had started by the time he arrived at the community centre, and he cursed himself for being late and letting Connor down.

'I'm so sorry,' he said, running across the hall to where Connor was handing out basketballs. 'Something came up at work.' He wasn't about to mention his encounter with Elena, or his failed attempt to ride the elevator. Connor had enough to deal with—like a group of unruly youths looking for an outlet from their boredom.

'No problem.' Connor gave him a short shrug. 'We're just starting the warm up.' He blew his whistle and walked onto the court. 'Okay, everyone! Let's get started. We'll begin with some layups. Split into two groups and alternate between sides. This side first. Go!' He blew his whistle and the group split into two, their body language only mildly more enthusiastic than last time.

The players began dribbling the balls up to the net, some with a modicum of skill, others with about as much coordination as drunken rhinos on ice.

Connor jogged back over to him. 'I think we need to work on passing skills.'

'Good plan.' Danny squeezed Connor's shoulder, thinking he looked more confident tonight. Volunteering was paying off. He also looked smarter, he had on his best jeans, and he was wearing the new top Hugh had got him from the NBA store in Carnaby Street. And then he caught a waft of scent. 'Are you wearing aftershave?'

Connor tried to look nonchalant. 'Yeah, a bit.'

Who wore aftershave to a coaching session? 'Special occasion?'

Connor shrugged, his focus on the players doing layups. 'Maybe.'

Danny knew he needed to tread carefully, he didn't want to blow it by bombarding Connor with questions. He remembered the dating pact they'd agreed on and decided this was his way in. 'You know, I asked Elena out on a date this evening. We're going to Bertie Blossoms tomorrow night.'

Connor turned to him. 'You're dating?'

'That's the hope. I figured there was no point sitting at home wondering how she felt, so I asked her out. No guarantee it'll lead to anything, but it's worth a shot, right?'

Connor tilted his head. 'Are you nervous?'

'Terrified.'

He smiled. 'Why? It's Elena.'

'Exactly, it's Elena.' He grimaced. 'She doesn't suffer fools. The problem is I really like her, and I'd forgotten what it's like to be so into someone you can't think straight, and it scares the shit out of me.'

Connor picked up a ball when it rolled over and threw it back to the lanky lad who had stolen Danny's trainers last time they were here. 'She's worth the risk.'

'Why else would I be putting myself through this? She fills a void I didn't know was there. There's a connection between us that makes me feel alive, and I guess it feels like it's worth the risk of humiliation.'

Connor smiled at him, like a proud parent. It was like they'd switched roles. 'I think so too. Elena's great.' He turned back to the group. 'Keep it going, guys!'

Danny tried to sound casual when he asked, 'So ... what about you?'

Connor kept his focus on the court. 'Me?'

'I'm guessing the outfit tonight isn't for the benefit of the basketball guys.' He waited a beat. 'Is it for someone specific?'

It was a moment before Connor nodded.

Danny needed to contain his excitement. Or was it fear? He couldn't tell. This was a big step, and either way he needed to stay chilled. 'Are you meeting her after the training session?'

'No, she's already here.'

'Already here?' Danny looked around the room. 'What, at the community centre?'

'She volunteers here. She's in the office sorting out the accounts.' Connor waved to the group to keep going, their energy levels were flagging already. 'She's the woman I was telling you about before, the one I met on the train.'

Danny tried to cast his mind back. 'And she volunteers here? That's quite a coincidence.'

'Not really. I told her I volunteered here and she turned up a few days later with her sister offering to help.'

'Right.' Danny's head had started to spin. This woman had tracked Connor down? She'd turned up where he volunteered and infiltrated herself into his brother's world. Should he be worried? 'And things have developed between you and this woman?'

'Not really.' He rubbed his hands together. 'I mean, we've got to know each other a bit, but nothing's happened.'

'But you'd like it to?'

Connor nodded.

'What's holding you back?'

Connor's expression was morose. 'She's way out of my league.'

'In what way?'

'She's stunning, like proper stunning.' Connor's face flushed red. 'And she's smart and talented, plus she's older than me. Not that it bothers me, but she's way more mature than I am. I feel a bit intimidated when I'm with her.'

Danny knew all about intimidating women. 'Does she feel the same way about you?'

'I don't know. It's like you said earlier about Elena, there's a connection between us, and I feel better when she's around. I thought she saw me as just a friend, but the other night we danced together and she kissed me. She seemed kind of embarrassed afterwards, but maybe that's because she regretted it, I don't know. She smiled at me when she arrived tonight, so maybe she does like me.'

'Quite the conundrum.' Danny rubbed his neck, trying to process everything.

'So, I'm thinking I should do what you're doing and ask her out on a date? See what she says. But if she says no, then volunteering together is going to be awkward.'

'She's more likely to say yes.'

Connor's expression was hopeful. 'How come?'

'You obviously made quite an impression on her. To the point where she came here looking for you. I'm no expert, but would a woman do that if she wasn't interested?'

Connor seemed to ponder this. 'Maybe she really did just want to volunteer?'

'Or maybe she wanted an excuse to see you again.'

Connor smiled. 'You think I should ask her out?'

'I think you should ask her out. It's a no-brainer.' He patted Connor's shoulder, praying this woman was as cute as his brother described and not trouble looming. Maybe he was projecting his own insecurities onto Connor—he wasn't exactly a dab hand at dating himself—but Connor was too vulnerable to deal with any avoidable drama.

They both reverted their focus to the training session and he helped Connor set up passing drills, getting the players to switch positions and move the ball around. The lanky kid was wearing Danny's trainers, showing no shame whatsoever at having pinched them last time. Still, maybe he couldn't afford his own.

An hour later, Danny was sweaty from training and regretting not changing out of his suit before the session started. His fault for showing up late.

Connor was congratulating the group on a good session and assuring them they were improving. His confidence levels had definitely improved, and he joined in the banter and joked with the group. Danny's parental worries subsided another notch. Things were finally heading in the right direction. Maybe this woman was a contributory factor?

Having bagged up the basketballs, Connor came over to him. 'Do you want to meet her before you leave? It'd be good to get your opinion.' He looked a tad uncertain.

'You sure? Meeting the parents is quite full on, you don't want to scare her off.'

'She's not like that, she's really family-orientated, and I think she'd like to meet you. I've talked about you a bit. But keep it causal, okay? Don't embarrass me. Don't say anything about me liking her.'

Danny gave him a look. 'I'm not an idiot, Connor. Of course I won't. Where is she, in the office?'

'This way.' Connor led him over to a small room and knocked on the door before entering. 'Hey, Sofia, this is my brother, Danny.'

Sofia? It took Danny a moment to process his shock. It couldn't be, could it? It wasn't exactly a common name. 'Sofia?'

The woman swivelled on the office chair to face him, her smile faltering when she saw him. 'Danny?' She looked as thrown as he was. She stood up abruptly, gripping the chair for support.

He tried to gather this thoughts. 'I had no idea you volunteered here?'

Connor looked between them. 'You two know each other?'

Danny turned to a confused-looking Connor, trying to keep a lid on his own panic. 'Sofia is Elena's sister.'

Connor looked like he'd been slapped. 'What?'

'We met one time when I was visiting Elena at work,'

Sofia said, wringing her hands together. 'Danny kindly gave me some advice about my dismissal from work.'

'You're Elena's sister?' Connor's voice had lost all its volume.

Sofia nodded, and then seemed puzzled by something. 'How do you know Elena?'

Connor opened his mouth to answer, but switched his panicked gaze to Danny, uncertainty clouding his face, as if he was unsure how much to say.

'Err ... they've met a few times in the office,' Danny chipped in, trying to help Connor out. 'When Connor's visited me at work.'

'Oh, right.' Sofia didn't look overly happy. 'Small world.'

And getting smaller by the second.

Danny's phone pinged with an email notification, causing him to glance briefly at the message. It was the employment tribunal papers for his latest case. Thinking about work at a time like this wouldn't normally capture his attention, not when he'd just discovered his brother had the hots for the sister of the woman he'd fallen for, but the email heading was enough to distract him. It contained the name of the opposition. The person he'd be attempting to annihilate in court.

The blood drained from his face faster than if someone had fitted a tap inside his brain. His pulse quickened, his palms grew sweaty, and it was as if someone was forcing him inside an elevator. This couldn't be happening.

His panic must have been visible, because Connor rushed over. 'Are you okay? What's wrong, are you ill?' He looked concerned, like he was worried Danny was having a heart attack.

'I'm not ill,' was all Danny could manage, before resting

his hands on his knees as he breathed deeply and tried to prevent passing out.

Christ, maybe he was having a heart attack after all.

Connor rubbed his back. 'You're scaring me. Do you need an ambulance? Talk to me, what's wrong?'

What's wrong? The name of his opposition was Sofia Romero.

That was what was wrong.

Chapter Twenty

ELENA

Wednesday, 16th July

Although Elena felt awful about Sofia losing her job and was outraged on her sister's behalf, it had also been a relief having Sofia on hand more to help look after Luisa. Elena had been able to focus on work without any family-drama interruptions. She'd stopped panicking every time her phone rang, and her stress levels had significantly decreased. She'd even had time to tend to her own needs, like going away for the weekend with Danny, something she wouldn't have been able to do while Sofia had been working full-time.

But all that could be coming to an end as a date had been set for her sister's ET hearing. Disgruntled employees normally had to wait months, but Sofia had accepted a last minute cancellation, which meant everything could be concluded in a few days. And if her sister was returning to work soon, it was time to step up and pull her weight.

Consequently, when she received a message from Sofia asking her to come home as there was a problem with Luisa, she didn't hesitate to respond. It was the least she could do. Plus it gave her another excuse to avoid seeing Danny ahead of their date tonight. The window for procrastination was closing and she needed to make a decision.

Having locked up her clinic, she headed down the stairwell, mulling over the situation, and glad to note Danny's door was shut. It saved her from making small talk ahead of seeing him later.

She hadn't been on a date since splitting with Felix in the New Year. It was all very well to actively steer clear of 'suits', but allowing the encounter with her ex to prevent her from finding happiness with anyone else was self-sabotage, and she was smarter than that.

She'd been cautious of Danny in the beginning, wanting to avoid repeating the same mistake, as only a fool would go for a guy with the same hang-ups. But Danny wasn't Felix, not by a long way. Underneath the suit was a guy who liked messing around, who wasn't a judgemental stiff, and who was, in fact, a frustrated rebel, subdued by life's cruelties. Once he let go and relaxed he had no problems showing affection, being daft, or laughing at himself.

Plus, he seemed to like her the way she was. He got frustrated with her, he didn't always agree with her, but so far he'd never asked her to be anything other than who she was, and that's where he trumped Felix, who'd always wanted her to 'tone it down'.

Overthinking usually resulted in more confusion, but on this occasion working through her feelings helped her to reach a decision. She was going to date Danny Jackson. She liked him. It was time to shake off her wounds and take control of her destiny.

Besides, if Danny ever infuriated her, she'd just do what she did yesterday and stun him into submission by kissing him. Arguing with him might prove to be enormous fun.

She ran down Portobello Road, swerving in and out of the stalls, happy with her decision. It felt right, a significant turning point in her life. She was heading back into the world of dating. And about time too, her sisters would say.

She was breathing hard by the time she reached Lancaster Road, her legs feeling the burn as she ran past the rainbow-coloured houses lining the street. Energised by her decision to welcome romance back into her life, she sprinted up the steps and burst through the front door, announcing her arrival. 'I'm home!'

'Up here!' Sofia's head appeared over the balcony.

Elena raced up the stairs. 'What's happened?'

'No idea.' Sofia looked flustered, her ponytail had come loose, her top was untucked, and she was missing an earring. 'Luisa's stuck inside her art studio and I can't get the door open. Something appears to be wedged against it. I've tried talking to her, but she's making no sense.'

Elena paused for breath. 'Is she ill?'

'I don't think so, but I'm not sure.' Sofia headed up the second flight of stairs. 'I waited for you before deciding whether we needed to call an ambulance.'

Elena followed Sofia up to the attic space. 'If we can't get the door open we might need the fire service as well.'

'Another reason why I waited for you.' Sofia glanced over her shoulder. 'She doesn't sound ill, more like drunk.'

'Drunk?' Elena baulked. 'At eleven-thirty in the morning?'

'I know.' Sofia stood aside to allow Elena past. 'I'm sensing something bad has happened.'

Elena banged on the art studio door. 'Luisa? ... Luisa! Open the door!'

'Go away!' Luisa slurred. 'You don't need to worry about me ... I'm fine.'

Elena rattled the door handle. 'If you're fine, then open the door and let us in.'

'No, I'm working. I'm in the artistic flow, and I don't want to break concentration. Come back later. You must never disturb the muse.' There was a thud, followed by a low groan.

Elena banged on the door again. 'Luisa, I'm going to keep banging on this door until you open it, and if you don't open it, I'm calling the fire service and getting them to break it down.'

'Go ahead, I like men in uniform.' Luisa hiccupped. 'It'll be exciting.'

'I don't think they'll see it that way.' Elena rattled the door handle again. 'Come on, Luisa. This is crazy, open the door.'

Silence descended.

When Luisa eventually spoke, her voice was low and muffled. 'I don't want to see anyone right now.'

Elena exchanged a worried look with Sofia. 'Why not?'

'I'm depressed.'

Elena softened her tone. 'Luisa, we're worried about you. ... Are you drinking?'

'Who cares, it's not like it's going to kill me.' She sounded belligerent. 'I'll be dead long before I get alcoholic poisoning.'

Elena beckoned Sofia away from the door so she could whisper without being overheard. 'You've no idea what's caused this?'

'Not a clue.' Sofia gave a shrug. 'I've been out here for over an hour, but she won't tell me what's upset her.'

'I can hear you talking about me!' Something hit the door, indicating Luisa must have thrown something.

'So open the door and let us talk to you instead. Please, Luisa.' Elena returned to the door and tapped again. 'Come on, talk to us, what's happened?'

'Maybe I like wallowing.' Luisa started singing an off-key rendition of the REM song *Everybody Hurts*.

Elena rolled her eyes at Sofia. 'Something must have upset you. Talk to us.'

'I miss Papi.' Luisa sounded grumpy. '*When you're on your own ... in this world*.'

'Yep, we miss him too. But until he comes home, we're all you've got.' Elena shoved her shoulder against the door, which wouldn't budge. 'How about opening the door and letting us in. We can wallow together.'

'*Everybody hurts ... sometimes*,' Luisa sang, followed by a lengthy pause before Elena heard the sound of something being dragged away from the door.

This time when Elena tried the handle the door opened.

Luisa was sprawled on the floor holding a near-empty bottle of wine. She was wearing her homemade artist's poncho, purple tights and bunny slippers. Her hands were covered in dried paint. 'I'm a tap-dancing fairy.' Luisa kicked her legs up and sent one of her slippers flying across the room.

Elena headed over. 'Okay, I'll take that,' she said, crouching down to remove the bottle from Luisa.

'I'm not finished!' Luisa tried to grab the bottle.

'You can finish it later.' Elena sat on the floor and crossed her legs. 'Talk to us, what's happened?'

Luisa pointed to her phone, which was lying on the table. 'Bastards want to cut me up.'

Sofia fetched Luisa's phone and lifted her sister's limp hand to activate the finger ID. Sofia's frown turned into a sigh as she read something on the phone. 'It's an appointment notification from the Brompton hospital.'

'Read what it says,' Luisa said, waving her hand about. 'Talk about insensitive.'

Sofia spoke softly. 'It's a review meeting with the transplant team.'

Luisa looked glum. 'My time's up. Transplant, or *diiieeee.*' She mimed being strangled and flopped backwards, playing dead.

'It means nothing of the sort.' Elena took her younger sister's hand and pulled her upright. 'It's just a review meeting to discuss your options. No one's implying anything has to happen yet. They just want to make sure you're aware of all your options for the future.'

Luisa slumped against Elena. 'I'm not having a transplant.'

'Okay. If that's how you feel, fine.' Elena squeezed her hand. 'But the hospital team wouldn't be doing their job if they didn't keep that option open, in case you change your mind further down the line.'

Luisa poked her tongue out. 'I won't.'

'Then don't go to the meeting, decline the offer. But getting drunk is not the best way of dealing with it.' Elena wished Papi was here. He was better at coping with a morose Luisa than they were, he had a knack of bringing her out of her slump.

Luisa wiped her nose with the back of her hand. 'What else can I do?'

'You can talk to us.' Sofia sat down next to Luisa. 'You know we're here to support you. Always.'

'You can't be running after me all the time, you have your own lives to lead. I'm a burden.' Luisa hiccupped on a sob.

'No, you're not. Never think that.' Sofia wiped tears away from Luisa's face. 'And the ET hearing is not for a couple of days. What will be, will be. The decision is out of my hands, it'll be down to the judge to determine what happens next. Whatever happens, I'll be okay.'

Luisa slumped against Sofia's shoulder. 'It's not just the ET hearing, I'm screwing up your love life too. You'd be at the community centre today if it weren't for me.'

Sofia's cheeks flushed a little. 'Like I told you, I'm happy staying home with you. I don't need to be there every day. Besides, I think it's better I keep my distance for a while.'

'Why?' Luisa sat up. 'Has something happened? Did you ask him out? Did he ask you out? Tell me.'

'Who are we talking about?' Elena wondered what she'd missed. 'Don't keep me in the dark.' She looked at Sofia. 'Have you met someone?'

Sofia nodded slowly. 'Yes, but it's complicated.'

'It's really not that complicated.' Luisa slapped her hand on the floor. 'Sofia's in love. She doesn't think he loves her back, but any dummy can see that he does. He's a smitten kitten.' Luisa giggled. 'Hey, that rhymes.'

'You're in love?' Elena couldn't believe it. She really had been out of the loop lately. 'That's amazing, Sofia. I'm so pleased for you.' She reached over and hugged her sister. 'It's about time you found a guy who sees how fabulous you are. This is the best news ever.' And then she paused. 'Hang on, why am I only hearing about this now?'

Sofia waved her hand dismissively. 'Like I said, it's complicated. And maybe I wanted to see how things panned out before I said anything.'

'But you told Luisa.' Elena tried not to feel aggrieved.

Sofia pulled a face. 'Luisa dragged it out of me, you know what she's like.'

'Yeah, you know what I'm like.' Luisa shoved Elena, before registering the insult. 'Hey, what d'you mean? What am I like?'

Sofia shook her head, making her solitary earring sway. 'Look, it doesn't matter. It's no big deal, and after last night I can't see it going anywhere. It's over, whether I like it or not.'

Elena hated the sadness clouding Sofia's face. 'What happened last night?'

Luisa shook Sofia. 'Yeah, what happened last night? Did you and Connor argue?'

Elena stilled. 'Connor? ... His name's Connor?'

Sofia nodded. 'And last night I met his brother ... Danny.'

The world seemed to tilt on its axis and slowly grind to a halt, as if it was waiting with baited breath for what came next.

Elena swallowed, praying it was a big fat coincidence. 'Danny ... as in?'

Sofia's nod confirmed the worst. 'Danny Jackson.'

Luisa looked confused, but then the penny dropped. 'Oh, you mean the bloke at work you have the hots for?'

'I do not have the hots for anyone,' Elena lied, as she tried to assess the scale of the problem in front of her. So what if they liked brothers from the same family? They were sisters from the same family. It was slightly awkward, perhaps, but not insurmountable. She looked between her sisters. 'This isn't a big deal. Why does it need to be a problem?'

Sofia sighed. 'Because I received my trial papers this morning, with the name of the opposing solicitor—'

'Don't tell me.' Elena squeezed her eyes shut. This couldn't be happening, not when she'd just spent the morning convincing herself Danny wasn't like Felix and was a decent guy. Taking a deep breath, she opened her eyes and looked at Sofia, waiting for the bombshell to drop.

Sofia's expression was gloomy. 'Still don't think we have a problem?'

Numerous thoughts tumbled into her mind, deafening her ability to think straight. She needed air. She needed to take action.

'Are you okay to look after Luisa?' she said, scrambling off the floor and heading for the door. 'There's something I need to do.'

'You're not going to do anything rash, are you?' Sofia called after her.

'Me, rash? Never!' Elena raced downstairs, the thud of her pulse in her temples an indication of her increasing anger.

It was this level of anger, fuelled by neat adrenaline and a smidgeon of regret, that pumped energy into her legs as she ran down Lancaster Road and back onto Portobello Road.

A tiny part of her brain urged her to slow down, to take a breath and not emotionally react to the situation. The bigger section of her brain urged her on, eager to unleash hell on the man she shared an office building with.

This was a betrayal of the worst kind, and he was not getting away with it. No one messed with the Romero family. At least she'd discovered the real him in time and had come to her senses before getting too invested.

The iron gate swung on its hinges as she pushed through it and ran up the path into the building.

What she would have done if he'd had a client with him, she wasn't sure. She was in such a rage she might still have burst into his office and attacked him with his stapler.

Thankfully, he was alone, and there was nothing preventing her from marching up to his desk and smacking her hands down so hard it made him drop his ink pen.

'When were you going to tell me, huh? On our *date* tonight? Was that the plan? Sneak it into the conversation and hope I wouldn't make a scene in a public place? Or maybe you were hoping I'd never find out and I'd remain clueless. Is that it? Keep quiet and hope it goes away?' She stood up. 'How stupid do you think I am?'

He removed his glasses and rubbed his tired-looking eyes. 'I'm guessing this is about the ET hearing?'

'Oh, you mean you're not certain?' She pinned him with a stern look. 'Why, are there other things you've also been keeping quiet about? Like, for instance, the fact that your brother is messing my sister around and making her miserable?'

'That's unfair. Leave Connor out of this.' There was a twitch in his jaw, as if he was clenching his teeth.

'So you did know?' She lifted her hands in an exasperated fashion, hoping to emphasise her disappointment. 'I am so stupid. I knew from the moment we met you were a selfish arse, a man who puts his own interests above others. The signs were all there, but instead of listening to my instincts, I allowed myself to believe there was more to you than that. That underneath the starched suit was a caring, honest man, who put decency above self-interest. How dumb was I?'

He replaced his glasses and stood up. 'Will you please calm down.'

'Calm down?' She smacked the desk again, causing him to take a step backwards. 'Oh, I'm sorry, am I being a little *dramatic* for you?'

He let out a breath. 'Frankly, yes.'

'Huh! And this is why it'll never work between us.' She began pacing the room. 'I have every right to be angry. You're representing the employers who dismissed my sister for having the audacity to put a loved one's care needs first. They disregarded common decency, fairness, and compassion, and treated Sofia appallingly. Five years she worked for that company.' She pointed at him from across the room. 'Five years, never taking time off sick, and constantly being praised for her commitment to her role. And yet the one time she needed them to show leniency following the death of our mother, they sacked her.'

'Can I—'

'No, you bloody well can't!' She stopped pacing, ensuring he could see the venom in her eyes. 'And this is the type of company you've chosen to represent, is it? An organisation who values the bottom line more than their employees' welfare. Wow, you must be so proud.' She began slow clapping. 'Congratulations, Danny. You really know how to live up to your name. Daniel-the-*Jerk*-Jackson.'

He came around to her side of the desk. 'Are you done?'

She folded her arms. 'What do you think?'

He took a breath. 'I think you've been waiting for this to happen ever since we met. You've been itching to find a reason to prove your theory right and show we're not compatible.' His shirt was unbuttoned at the neck, his tie was skew-whiff, and his waistcoat was buttoned up wrong. It was the first time she'd seen him looking less than perfect.

It wasn't enough to derail her anger. 'Well, we're not!'

'What a relief, eh?' It was his turn to open his arms. He sounded more upset than angry, even though his shoulders were bunched. 'You were proved right. So maybe it should be me congratulating you, instead of the other way around.' He took a step closer. 'But don't you dare walk out of here acting all self-righteous and somehow believing you're the wounded party here, and I'm some kind of evil Bond villain, because that's horseshit, Elena. And you know it.'

Elena stood her ground, refusing to soften at the sight of his shaking hands. 'You're the one trying to ruin my sister's life, not me.'

He shook his head. 'That's what you'd like to believe, isn't it? It suits your narrative. It justifies you laying into me. It never occurred to you to come in here and talk to me rationally, did it? To ask questions and let me explain my side of things.' His shoulders lifted in a huff. 'Oh, no, that would be too reasonable for you. Instead, you make assumptions, fire accusations, and decide I'm guilty of all charges without any tangible information, or any facts about the situation.'

She pointed a finger at him. 'Don't lawyer talk me.'

'Why, is it that too *logical* for you? Are you incapable of having a rational discussion without resorting to shouting?'

'Fine.' If he wanted to discuss the facts, then so be it. She lowered her voice to a reasonable level. 'Did you know about Connor and Sofia?'

He paused. 'Yes, but—'

'Are you representing Sofia's employers at the ET hearing?'

'I've been assigned the case, but—'

'So I haven't made any assumptions, have I?' She raised her eyebrows, but not her voice, forcing herself to remain 'rational', as he'd put it. 'These are the facts. You're a complete shit, and I'm justified in being angry. There, discussion over.'

'No, discussion not over,' he said, running his hands into his already ruffled hair. 'I only found out about Connor and Sofia last night. Just as I only discovered the name of the employee who'd been dismissed last night. This is not information I've been sitting on for weeks, Elena. I haven't been hiding anything from you, or lying, or being deceitful. I'm as shocked by events as you are, and I'm still trying to process everything.'

'Right.' She waited a beat, ensuring he had enough time to look directly at her before she spoke. 'So you won't be taking the case then? Now you know Sofia is the person you'll be up against, you'll do the decent thing and withdraw representation?'

His eyes closed and the twitch in his jaw reappeared. 'It's more complicated than that.'

'Just as I thought.' Any last remaining hope drained out of her. 'Despite all your protestations, when presented with the option to do the decent thing, you don't take it. So protest all you want, Danny, but you've just proved me right. You've displayed your true self.' She walked over to the door. 'You're nothing but a suit. And before you say it, you're right, I'm nothing but a drama queen.'

She imagined she'd feel an acute sense of satisfaction as she slammed the door behind her and exited the building, having made her parting shot—which, judging by the hurt look on his face, had landed with precision.

But it wasn't righteousness she experienced as she

headed home, her legs now weighed down by spent adrenaline, it was sorrow. Heart-breaking, aching sorrow.

Why? Because he'd been right. However much she denied it, she'd been waiting for an opportunity to prove her theory right. Daniel Jackson was just like Felix, a selfish arse who had chosen his career over her feelings.

So it wasn't satisfaction she felt, it was stupidity.

And to think she'd thought arguing with him might be fun.

Chapter Twenty-One

SOFIA

Thursday, 17th July

The stairs creaked as Sofia carried the breakfast tray up to Luisa's room. She didn't want to wake her sister in case she'd managed to get back to sleep. Waking up with a hangover was never fun, made worse when you had to endure forty minutes of nebulisers, pill-popping, and being pummelled on the back to clear your lungs. Was it any wonder Luisa had crawled back under the covers?

When she reached Luisa's bedroom, she placed the tray on the floor and gently opened the door to peer inside. Luisa was hidden under a mound of duvet, silent and still.

Sofia was about to back away, when Luisa mumbled, 'It's okay, I'm awake.'

'I thought you might like something sweet.' Sofia picked up the tray and carried it inside. It was a constant battle to get enough calories inside Luisa, but luckily her sister's sweet tooth made life slightly easier. 'Danish pastry and a hot chocolate.'

It was enough to stir Luisa from her slumber. 'I hope you brought Nutella?'

'I even added mini marshmallows to your hot chocolate.'

'I am being spoilt.' Her sister shoved away pillows and propped herself against the headboard. 'Not that I deserve it. I was a brat yesterday. Sorry.'

Sofia was minded to agree. Not that she'd ever say as much aloud, but Luisa certainly knew how to cause mayhem in the Romero household.

She waited until Luisa was settled before placing the tray in front of her. 'Getting upset is understandable,' she said, moving to open the curtains. 'And we understand dealing with your health situation is awful for you. I even get the drinking. It's not ideal, but I understand your need to blank things out for a while. The bit I object to is barricading yourself inside a room.' She kicked off her heeled boots and climbed onto the bed next to her sister. 'It's not fair on us, Luisa. We were stressed beyond belief.'

Luisa pushed her long hair away from her face. 'I needed to be alone for a while.'

'And we would've respected that, if you'd asked. But when we physically can't get to you, it scares us. Supposing you'd become ill, or hit your head, or passed out from the alcohol? You'd have been trapped inside that room, and who knows what might've happened. Think what that would've been like for us?'

Luisa let out a breath. 'Sorry.'

'Please don't do that again.' Lecture done, Sofia pointed to the tray. 'Are you going to eat something?'

Luisa bit off a mouthful of pastry, sending flakes

cascading down the front of her Dalmatian pyjamas. 'Yummy.'

Sofia relaxed against the headboard. 'Planning to share any with me?'

'Unlikely.' Luisa chewed on another mouthful.

Sofia smiled. 'Just checking.'

'You can have a marshmallow.' Luisa lifted the mug of hot chocolate. 'Just the one. Don't get greedy.'

'Generous.' Sofia scooped up a pink marshmallow and popped it in her mouth. 'I'm sorry about the transplant stuff. Do you want to talk about it?'

'Not really.' Luisa gulped a mouthful of hot chocolate. 'I'd rather not think about it, to be honest. I know you think I'm in denial, but it's tiring, and so bloody boring keep being reminded I'm on a short-term lease. It's like I'm never allowed to forget about it, as if someone's following me around with a ticking clock, counting down the days until I expire. Sometimes I just want to live a normal life and do regular stuff.'

Sofia sighed. 'I get that.'

'Like painting the community centre, I've really enjoyed that.'

Sofia was relieved all the hard work had paid off. If Luisa was happy and had enjoyed doing it, then great—even if her sister didn't sound overly joyous about it. 'I wished you'd been there the other day to see everyone admiring your mural and talking about how incredible it was. I was really proud of you.'

Luisa sipped her hot chocolate, her body language dejected. 'That's nice.'

'And there's loads more to do.' Sofia tried to sound encouraging. 'So hopefully that'll help lift your spirits.' She realised too late that her words only made Luisa slump more. 'Luisa, what's wrong? I thought you wanted to do more painting at the centre?'

'Yeah, about that.' Luisa's face scrunched up, like it did when she was about to reveal the fallout from one of her mad escapades. 'I'm not sure we'll be going to the community centre much more, if ever.'

Sofia frowned, confused by her sister's words. 'Why would you say that? I thought you enjoyed it there, didn't you just say as much?'

'It's not that I didn't enjoy it.' Luisa handed her the tray. 'Take that for me, will you.'

Sofia climbed off of the bed and placed the tray on the floor. 'Then what?'

Luisa looked conflicted. She grabbed a pillow and hugged it to her chest. 'I wasn't drinking yesterday just because of the hospital message. I mean, that was part of it. Most of it, I guess, but—'

'Something else upset you?' Sofia perched on the edge of the bed, careful not to crease her rust-coloured Ghost dress. She'd made an effort with her appearance this morning in anticipation of seeing Connor later.

Luisa nodded, and Sofia realised there was something seriously bothering her. 'I found something out. Something bad ... about Connor.'

'Connor?' Sofia jolted as if she been given a static shock. What could Luisa have possibly found out about Connor?

Luisa beckoned for Sofia to take her hand. 'I didn't mean to, but I was looking at the photos on the community centre website to plan out my next mural, and I kind of got distracted.'

Sofia's mind had gone into turmoil. 'Distracted how?'

Luisa's guilty expression was a sure-fire indication she'd

done something she shouldn't have. 'I googled Connor's name.'

Sofia stood up, retracting her hand and sending a pillow toppling from the bed. 'Why would you do that?'

Luisa shrugged. 'Boredom, I guess. Nosiness. Intrigue.'

Sofia ran a hand over her blow-dry, another thing she'd done in her quest to shift her relationship with Connor from the friend-zone into romance. 'You shouldn't have done that, Luisa.'

'I know.' She pushed the duvet away and shuffled across the bed. 'But we know so little about him, and it's obvious you're invested and you want things to work out. I mean, look at you, you're all done up, for heaven's sake. I've never seen you this interested in a guy before. You're even wearing a lace bra. So I figured there was no harm in doing a little digging.'

Sofia's hand lifted to her neckline, wondering how her sister knew about the bra. 'Clearly there was some harm, as you found something,' she said, securing the wrap-dress a little tighter.

'I know, and part of me wishes I hadn't done it, but you need to know what I discovered.'

'Actually, I don't.' Sofia lifted her hands, blocking whatever Luisa was about to say. 'If there's something Connor needs to tell me, I'm sure he'll do so himself. I'm not relying on gossip and misinformation from the internet. Who knows if this stuff is even true? Or factually correct?'

'But what if it is true?' Luisa sat back on her heels. 'Wouldn't it be better to confront him and get an explanation before things go any further?'

Sofia suddenly felt too warm and lifted her hair away from her neck. 'You expect me to march in there and demand answers for something that's none of my business?

Things are already fragile between us, especially after everything that's happened this week. He's barely spoken to me since discovering I'm Elena's sister, and he's bound to feel conflicted over his brother being the opposing solicitor at the ET hearing. Interrogating him about his past would be the nail in the coffin. I'm not doing it.'

'He was charged with sexual assault, Sofia.' Luisa's words landed like a physical blow. Hard, fast, and sucking all the air from her lungs. 'There was a criminal investigation.'

Sofia wrung her hands, unsure what to do with herself. 'Which obviously resulted in a non-conviction, otherwise he'd be in prison, wouldn't he? So he was clearly innocent of the charges.'

'But still—'

'But nothing,' she snapped. Panic was making her edgy. 'I can't believe you overrode my wishes and told me what you'd found out, when I'd made it clear I didn't want to know.'

Luisa knelt up on the bed. 'This is serious stuff, Sofia.'

'And I thought you of all people would understand how hurtful it can be when people discriminate.'

Luisa flinched. 'Just ask him about it, please. Maybe there's a reasonable explanation.'

'And maybe the reason he's been so miserable of late is because he was unfairly accused of something he didn't do,' she said, throwing her hands in the air. 'Did you think of that?'

'In which case, he can tell you that.'

Tears were threatening, Sofia blinked rapidly to stem the flow. 'It's none of my business, and it's an invasion of his privacy.'

'Not if you want to be with him, it's not.' Luisa

clambered off the bed, her pyjamas hanging loose off of her thin frame. 'It's information you need to know to make an informed decision about whether he's the right guy for you.'

'He *is* the right guy for me.' Sofia knew she sounded defensive, but she had to make Luisa see how unfair she was being. 'Connor is the sweetest, most trustworthy, and kindest man I've ever met. I don't believe he's capable of hurting anyone, and I refuse to rely on information from untrusted sources rather than believing in my own judgement. I know Connor. He didn't do this.'

Luisa nodded slowly. 'I hope you're right.'

Sofia slid her feet into her boots and picked up the breakfast tray. 'I'm going to the community centre to complete my shift. Do you need anything before I go?'

'No ... are you mad with me?' Luisa looked frail and vulnerable standing there, and it clearly gave her no pleasure to be the bearer of bad news.

Sofia took a breath, trying to rein in her emotions. 'I know you mean well, Luisa, but I really wish you hadn't told me. In future, don't google people, okay?'

'Everyone does it. It's the norm these days.' Luisa gave a demoralised shrug as she clambered back into bed. 'Even prospective employers do a preliminary search on the internet before hiring. Everything's out there for the world to see.'

'Then no wonder there's so much misinformation being spread about.' Sofia headed for the door. 'And people wonder why we have trolling. I'll see you later.'

'Please don't be angry with me, Sofia. I love you. I don't want to see you get hurt.'

'I love you too.' Sofia forced a smile. 'Get some rest. I'll be back this afternoon. Call if you need me.'

Sofia had no idea what she was thinking or feeling as

she headed downstairs and got herself ready to leave the house to go to the community centre. It was as if her mind had switched to autopilot, refusing to allow Luisa's words to infiltrate her brain and derail her life plan.

Until a few minutes ago, she'd had a clear vision of her future for the first time in her life. She'd decided she wanted to work for a non-profit organisation, and she wanted to be with Connor. She'd never been more certain about anything, so to be hit by this unexpected curve-ball was a blow she hadn't seen coming, and she had no idea how to process it.

The numbness eased as she walked to the tube station and travelled to White City. Prior to Luisa's bombshell, she'd been excited to see Connor today and had spent an age getting ready. Her outfit wasn't exactly suitable for a tired and dusty community centre, but she'd wanted to make an effort—it wasn't every day you decided to throw caution to the wind and declare your feelings for someone. Now she was wondering if she should have worn something more sombre. Funeral black, maybe.

Keeping her head down, and unwilling to make eye-contact with any of the other passengers, she tried to assimilate her thoughts.

She'd known something bad had happened to Connor, he'd alluded to as much himself, but she couldn't have envisaged what Luisa had told her. It was all well and good to spout on about privacy rights and not believing information posted on the internet, but in reality, it didn't stop the negative thoughts from creeping in. There would be an explanation, she was sure if it. There had to be.

She exited the tube and walked steadily to the community centre.

Trusting someone wasn't something you made a

decision about. It was more gut instinct, and she trusted Connor, she knew inherently he was a good and decent person. This new information hadn't changed her opinion of him, but she'd be lying if she didn't acknowledge that Luisa might have stumbled across the reason why Connor had been suffering from such crippling depression. An accusation like that would be enough to derail anyone's life.

The annoying thing was, things between them had been improving of late, and when they'd danced together she'd felt a real connection. Like a spark of something had been ignited, and neither of them had wanted the flame to die out. It was a feeling she needed to keep hold of, and she was determined she wouldn't allow anything to derail it.

Connor was in the office and staring at the computer screen when she arrived at the community centre. His chin rested on his hands and the slump in his shoulders radiated acute unhappiness.

'Morning,' she said, hanging up her coat, determined to act in her usual friendly manner. 'Sorry I'm a bit late, I needed to deal with Luisa before I left.'

'I didn't realise you were late,' Connor replied, not looking away from the screen.

It was unusual for him not to look at her, and she felt a twinge of uneasiness. 'Everything okay?'

Connor's hair was a mess of dark curls, his hoodie was too big for him, and the spark of energy building in him of late had vanished. Silence hung in the air, heavy and foreboding.

Hanging up her bag, she moved next to him. 'I've been looking into card payment software. I think it's something we should introduce ahead of the café reopening. Many people don't carry cash these days, so we could be losing out on custom by not having another payment option.'

Still he didn't look at her. 'Sounds good.'

She pulled up a chair and sat down. 'Would you like me to show you the information?'

'That's okay. You go ahead and organise it. It sounds fine.' His gaze remained fixed on the generic screensaver.

She tried again. 'You don't want to check it first?'

'I'm not sure I'll be volunteering here much longer. So it won't be up to me.'

She prayed she'd misheard him. 'You're leaving? Why?'

'A few reasons.'

Panic crept up her neck, making her fidgety. 'But you love working here. It doesn't make sense.'

When he finally looked at her, his expression was tortured. 'It's for the best.'

'Has something happened?' She reached for his hand, but he withdrew it, preventing her from touching him. 'This isn't about the other night, is it? I appreciate things might be a little awkward with your brother, but—'

'A little awkward?' He looked incredulous. 'That's an understatement.'

'But it doesn't have to come between us. I'm probably going to lose the ET case anyway, regardless of who the opposing solicitor is. Please don't let that drive you away, it's really not an issue. Danny's just doing his job. I get that, and it's okay, really.'

Connor looked like someone had slapped him. 'Danny's the opposing solicitor?'

Sofia inwardly cursed. 'You didn't know?'

He shook his head. 'No, I didn't.'

As the colour drained from his face, she realised things were rapidly spiralling out of control, and she had to regroup. 'So, if that isn't the problem, then what is? Because I hate the idea of you stopping volunteering when I know how much you enjoy it.' She shifted her chair closer to him. 'And I'd also hate not seeing you all the time. I really like you, Connor. And I thought ... hoped ... you were starting to like me. It's not an easy thing for me to admit, but I like you ... a lot. And just to be clear, yes, I mean romantically. Not just friends, or work colleagues, but a couple. At least, that's what I'd like.'

She ignored the pleading note in her voice and focused instead on her bravery in admitting her feelings for this fragile, wounded man. To hell with it. Just like the ET hearing, she'd rather try and fail than be left wondering whether she should have taken a stand.

Connor eyelids fluttered closed. 'Please don't say that, it just makes things worse.'

She tried to swallow past the lump in her throat. 'You don't feel the same way?'

His hands covered his face. 'What I feel is irrelevant. Nothing can happen now, it's too late.'

'Why is it? I don't understand.' Her voice betrayed her and cracked slightly.

He lowered his hands. 'Danny and Elena are a couple. They're dating.'

It took Sofia a moment to absorb his words. Surely not? Elena hadn't divulged this information to her, and as far as she knew the pair of them mostly argued. Elena would have told her if things had developed. Wouldn't she? Maybe Connor had been misinformed? 'Are you sure?'

'Apparently so. It's the first time my dad's dated anyone since he became my guardian, so I don't want to complicate things for him by ...'

'Being with me?' She finished the sentence for him.

'It's not just that, Sofia. I'm damaged goods,' he said, jabbing himself in the chest. 'I'm messed up, and confused, and some days I feel so low I can't get out of bed. It wouldn't be fair on you, you deserve so much better than me.' The pain in his eyes was unbearable.

This was not how she'd imagined today would play out. She'd thought they were on the cusp of getting together, and now she was in danger of losing him for good. 'Isn't that for me to decide?'

His eyes fell away from hers. 'You're amazing, Sofia. Beautiful and special. I'd only drag you down.'

She grabbed his forearm and squeezed tightly, trying to cling hold of her last shred of hope. 'You've already told me about your depression, Connor. And I'm okay with it, truly. I understand.'

'No you don't. Not really.'

Stung, she withdrew her hand. 'So what are you going to do? Spend your entire life pushing people away if they get too close? Is that it? Because that's not a great plan, Connor. It's a lonely and sad existence, and a destructive one too. You say I deserve more, well so do you. If you don't want me, that's fine. But if you're pushing me away as some kind of punishment for something that's happened in the past, then that's unfair on both of us.'

There was a long, drawn-out moment before his gaze lifted to hers. 'You know, don't you?' She must have blushed, because he said, 'I heard some of the basketball lads talking about it. I figured you'd find out. You know what happened?'

She shook her head. 'Not really, not in any detail.'

He slumped back in his chair. 'What did you do, google me?' There was a tinge of harshness in his voice, and she knew he was upset.

'No, I didn't. That's something I'd never do. Luisa was looking at community centre stuff and apparently it led onto other stuff posted about you. I didn't look at anything myself, I promise you, and I honestly wished she hadn't told me.'

'I'll bet.' He rubbed the back of his neck.

She knew it was a lost cause, he'd never believe her, but she had to try and convince him. 'I wished she hadn't told me, because it's none of my business, Connor. And if you'd wanted me to know, you would've told me yourself. And I'm sure you would've done when the time was right. It wasn't right for her to pre-empt things. It wasn't fair on me, or you, and I'm so sorry this has happened. Please don't let it spoil things between us.'

He stood up. 'It already has.'

She tried to grab his hand. 'Connor, please. Don't leave.'

'I have to.' He gave her one last heart-wrenching look before opening the door. 'I'm sorry, Sofia.' The door closed shut behind him with a heavy thud, like the door was closing on her hope too.

'But I ... I'm falling in love with you,' she said to an empty space.

Unable to fight it, Sofia sank onto the desk and covered her head with her arms.

It was over.

It had never really begun.

Chapter Twenty-Two

DANNY

Thursday, 17th July

It felt strange not to be at work on a weekday, but Danny wasn't in the right frame of mind to deal with people today. More significantly, Elena. Avoiding her wasn't overly mature, but it was the safest option until he could work out his next move. His life was unravelling at an alarming speed and he needed to resolve things fast.

'Ever heard of the saying "a watched pot never boils"?'

Danny looked up at his best mate sitting across from him at the fancy breakfast counter with a wry smile on his face, sipping a strong espresso. 'Sorry?'

Hugh nodded to Danny's phone lying on the worktop. 'You've been staring at that all morning. It doesn't take a therapist to deduce you want to talk to Elena. She hasn't called you, so call her. Be an adult and take control of the situation. Resolve this.'

Danny ran a finger around his shirt collar, except he

wasn't wearing a shirt so his fingers met with bare neck above his long-sleeved T-shirt. 'She doesn't want to talk to me.'

Hugh took another sip of coffee. 'How do you know?'

Danny raised an eyebrow. 'How do I know? She yelled at me. She accused me of being an insensitive bastard and told me her first assessment of me had been correct. I'm a boring suit, apparently, rigid and uncaring. And to use your own analogy, it doesn't take a therapist to work out she hates me and she doesn't want to talk to me.'

'She doesn't hate you.' Hugh smiled indulgently. 'She was angry. You had a fight, it happens. It's what grown-ups do, in case you hadn't realised. I hate to break it to you, but if you're hoping for a relationship where you don't fight, then you'll die alone. Some fights are relationship ending, that's true. Others are a blip, a bump in the relationship road that needs careful navigating. This is not a relationship-ending argument. It's a blip.'

'It doesn't feel like a blip, and we're not in a relationship.' Danny got up and refilled his mug from the fancy machine that made a loud hissing noise when it dispensed coffee. 'It feels terminal.'

'That's because you're out of practice. When was the last time you fought with a woman?'

Danny rested his hip against the counter. 'Not since Maisie.'

'My point exactly.' Hugh swivelled on the high stool to face him. 'That was nearly two decades ago. View this as a learning curve. Face the issue head on and deal with it.' He held Danny's phone out to him. 'Call her.'

Danny shook his head. 'I can't.'

'Why not?'

'Because the problem hasn't gone away,' he said,

returning to the breakfast counter. 'I'm still representing Sofia's employers at the ET hearing. The minute she knows that she won't listen to anything else I have to say.'

Hugh tilted his head. 'Have you considered withdrawing from the case?'

'Of course I bloody well have, I've thought about little else.' So much so, it had kept him awake all night. 'Especially now I know Sofia's the woman Connor's interested in. Talk about rotten coincidences. I mean, what were the chances?'

'It's unfortunate, I agree, but surely the solution is simple. Withdraw from the case.' Hugh rested his forearms on the countertop. 'It's a conflict of interest, if nothing else.'

'It would be if I'd formally acted for Sofia, but I merely gave her some off-the-record advice about contacting ACAS,' Danny replied, morosely. 'I never discussed the details of her case and I wasn't ever appointed as her solicitor, so the grounds for claiming a conflict of interest are flimsy. I doubt a judge is going to appreciate my withdrawal based on the fact that I fancy the defendant's sister.'

Hugh sighed. 'It's a little more than that. It sounds like you're making excuses.'

'Maybe, but when you agree to a cancellation slot it's bad form to back out, you're obliged to continue with the case. If I quit now, I'll piss off the court staff, alienate my client and ACAS, and be liable for everyone's costs. Not to mention the damage it'll cause my professional reputation.'

'All irrelevances if you site a conflict of interest.' Hugh took another sip of coffee. 'Are you sure there isn't another reason?'

Danny folded his arms. 'Such as?'

'You've been on your own for a long time, Danny. You were resistant to dating. Being with someone is scary, and exposing, and it renders you vulnerable and open to heartbreak. You said it yourself, it's easier to live alone than be in a relationship. It's the safer option.'

'Your point?'

Hugh shrugged. 'Maybe this is your subconscious giving you a way out. You've listed the professional reasons why withdrawing from the case wouldn't be in your best interests, but what about the personal fallout? What impact will continuing with the case have on your relationship with Connor? And if Connor and Sofia become a couple, how do you think your actions will impact on the relationship you have with them? You risk losing not just Elena over this.' Hugh's expression turned serious. 'So, let me ask you this: which is more important, your career or your family?'

Danny glared at his best mate. 'You sound like Elena.'

Hugh smiled. 'Have you considered she might be right?'

Danny lifted his hands in the air, exasperated. 'Why d'you think I feel so crap?'

Hugh slid Danny's phone across to him. 'So call her. Resolve this.'

Danny rubbed his face, weary beyond belief. He felt trapped between two opposing decisions, damned either way.

The front door slammed and a flustered Connor appeared in the kitchen, looking upset. His hoodie seemed to swamp him, and he looked like a small child standing there, wounded and tearful.

Parental instinct kicked in, and Danny jumped up from the breakfast counter and raced over. 'Connor, what's wrong?'

Connor moved away before Danny could reach him, heading for the opposite side of the breakfast counter, creating a barrier between them. 'You're representing Sofia's employers at the ET hearing?'

A weight fill Danny's stomach. He'd hoped to break the news himself. 'I was planning on telling you—'

'When?' Connor was vibrating with anger. 'When were you going to tell me? After you'd won the case and ruined Sofia's chances of getting her job back?'

Danny flinched at the angst in Connor's voice. 'I was going to tell you today, after I'd worked out what to do about the case.'

'Worked out what to do?' Connor's hands laced into his wild curly hair. 'You mean you're considering going ahead? Even now you know who Sofia is?'

Danny glanced at Hugh, hoping for an ally, but Hugh's 'I told you so' expression left him in no doubt he was fighting this argument solo. 'It's complicated.'

'Complicated?' Connor began pacing. 'It's not complicated. It's cruel. You'd be deliberately hurting the woman I'm in love with.' His voice broke on the word love and he slumped against the counter.

Hugh leaned across and rubbed Connor's back, providing the comfort Danny wanted so desperately to offer but couldn't. He'd become the enemy. It wasn't a great feeling.

'You love her?' Danny's voice was barely a whisper.

Connor rubbed his eyes harshly. 'Not that it matters. It's over. She knows about what happened. Everything's ruined.' The sound of his sob broke Danny's heart.

Hugh continued to comfort Connor, offering soothing noises.

Danny wracked his brain, trying to work how to deal with the situation. 'Sofia knows? How did she find out, did you tell her?'

Connor shook his head. 'I never got the chance, her sister told her.'

Connor's words struck hard.

Elena had told her sister about Connor's past? After he'd specifically asked her not to and she'd promised to keep quiet? A buzzing sound began ringing in his ears, the pounding like a repetitive hammer striking over and over.

Connor leaned into Hugh for support, the only thing seemingly keeping him upright. 'I knew this would happen. She says she doesn't care, but how could she not? She'll never look at me the same way again. I've blown it.'

Hugh stood up and pulled Connor into a hug, rubbing his back and continuing with the soothing noises. 'It's okay, Connor. I'm sure if you talk to her and explain—'

'What's the point?' Connor pulled away. 'There's no chance she'll want me now, not after learning about the ET hearing.' He turned to Danny, his face drawn and tearstained. 'Besides, you're dating Elena. You don't need me complicating your life for you.'

'I'm not dating Elena,' Danny assured him, even though his brain was still tied up in knots trying to process Elena's betrayal. 'She ended things when she found out I was representing Sofia's employers at the ET hearing.'

'I'm not surprised!' Connor slapped his hand down on the countertop. 'You've upset Sofia. You've upset me, and now you've lost Elena. And you're still going through with it? Jesus! What's wrong with you?' He ran from the room and headed upstairs, hurdling the stairs two at a time.

The silence that followed was almost as bad as the yelling. It felt like a part of Danny had disappeared along with Connor upstairs. They never fought, not like this. It was torturous. And people wondered why he'd avoided dating? This is what happened when you let your guard down. Chaos ensued.

'It's okay, I'll deal with this.' Hugh followed Connor upstairs.

Danny let him go. He knew Connor needed space, his presence wouldn't help or reduce the tension, it would only inflame things further.

Besides, he had his own anger to deal with.

Grabbing his keys and phone, he left the house, his disgruntlement increasing with every step. Every second that ticked by, he sped up, reminded of what Elena had done. The anger bubbled inside of him, fuelling his outrage.

So much so, that by the time he reached the building where he worked, the pain of her betrayal had morphed from shock into full-blown rage.

So what if he was a suit? At least he'd never deliberately hurt anyone. If that was what being 'open' entailed, he'd rather stay closed off and rigid. It was safer that way.

He was in such a state, he hadn't thought through his actions, and it was only after he'd entered the building he realised Elena was on the second floor, and if he was going to confront her then he needed to use the elevator or climb the stairs.

Fine. Whatever it took.

He was so mad, he wasn't going to let his anxiety stop him.

Despite this show of rebellion, it didn't stop the onset of panic consuming him as he jabbed the button and waited for the elevator to arrive. The familiar clawing of unease prickled over his skin, sucking the air from his lungs and creating beads of sweat on his forehead.

In an effort to distract himself, he jogged on the spot

and shook his arms, like a boxer prepping for a fight. He was primed and ready for battle.

He was puffing heavily by the time the door pinged open. Without paying any attention to his surroundings, he propelled himself forwards and nearly collided with Elena as she stepped out of the elevator.

He swore loudly and careened backwards.

Elena dropped the heavy holdall she was carrying, which landed on her foot. 'What the hell, Danny? Watch where you're going!' She began hopping about, rubbing her foot.

As bad as he felt, there was no way he was going to let her take the high ground and steal his thunder. It was his turn to be mad. He'd earned this.

'I'm sorry about your foot,' he barked, not sounding sorry at all, and still jogging about trying to channel his anger. 'But that's what happens when you mess with people's lives. There are consequences. People get hurt!'

Elena drew back, looking somewhat confused. 'What are you on about?'

He pointed a finger at her. 'You had the audacity to barge into my office and accuse me of betraying you by representing Sofia's employers. Even though I had no say in the matter, and it's what I do. It's my damn job. But no, as far as you were concerned it was the biggest crime on the planet, and it warranted you calling me a *boring suit*. You accused me of being a lowlife and deliberately hurting you and your sister, which is absolute bollocks!'

'Whoa, calm down.' Elena lifted her hands and took another step backwards. 'Where's this rage coming from, Danny? I've said my piece, it's done. There's no need to go over it again. What's the point? We're over. Finished. Why are you bringing it up again?'

He was physically shaking. 'Because however much you think I betrayed you, it doesn't compare to the way you've betrayed me.'

Her eyes grew wide. 'How have I betrayed you?'

'You told Sofia about Connor's secret.' He could barely get the words out.

She looked shocked. 'I didn't—'

'Don't bother denying it. Connor's just told me. How could you, Elena?' His hands went into his hair. 'You know how fragile he's been, how he's struggled. How could you be so cruel?'

She flinched.

'And after I'd specifically asked you not to tell anyone. You go and tell the one person Connor feared finding out.'

'Danny, I didn't—'

'He's in love with her, did you know that?' He lowered his hands, rubbing his sweaty palms on his jeans. 'Connor is head over heels in love with Sofia, and I've just left him at the house bawling his bloody eyes out because you told Sofia about his past before he had the chance.'

Elena stepped forwards. 'Danny, I promise you—'

'I don't care that you betrayed me. I get it. You wanted payback. Fine. Do what you want to me, I can take it. But to hurt Connor like that is unforgivable.' He shook his head, trying to hold it together. 'What did you say me the other day? "When presented with the option to do the decent thing, you didn't take it." Well, neither did you, Elena. You've also displayed your *true self*, as you put it. And you're right, I am a boring suit.' He opened his arms. 'I don't like mess and drama and chaos in my life. You want to know why? Because someone I love always ends up getting hurt. And this time, it's Connor. And that's something I can never forgive you for.'

Leaving Elena looking dumbstruck, he turned and walked away, mostly because he'd choked on his final words and he feared he was about to mirror Connor and start crying. He hadn't cried since the night Connor had nearly died, and he had no desire to repeat the act now. Certainly not in front of the woman he'd stupidly fallen for.

This was why he avoided drama. It bloody hurt too much.

His phone pinged with a message from Hugh.

We have a problem. I can't find Connor. He left the house while I was in the loo and he hasn't taken his phone or keys with him. I'm worried.

Danny stopped walking.

His worst nightmare was happening all over again.

Chapter Twenty-Three

ELENA

Thursday, 17th July

Dealing with a bunch of unruly teenage rugby players was challenging at the best of times, but when your head was all over the place, it made the experience pure torture. Try as she might to concentrate on the stretching regime she'd devised for the team, her mind kept rerunning her argument with Danny.

She'd never seen Danny so unravelled before, so raw. If she wasn't so bruised, she might have seen the confrontation as a breakthrough. He'd finally unleashed all that bottled-up rage. Unfortunately for her, she'd been on the receiving end of his fury, and it wasn't a good feeling.

Elena waited until the carriage had emptied before hoisting up her heavy holdall and exiting the train. It had been a long day and she was bone-tired. That was the downside of being 'dramatic', as Danny referred to it. It was draining.

As she headed home, she replayed the argument again in her head, wondering why Danny thought she'd betrayed him and told Sofia about Connor's past. The fact he thought her capable of such an act stung. She'd never betray him like that.

Logically, she shouldn't care. They were done. She should shrug it off as a bad experience and move on, but for some reason she hated the idea of Danny thinking badly of her. Maybe because underneath all the outrage, she missed him.

It was a sad admission, but true. She'd never admit as much to him, and whatever her feelings, he was the one in the wrong, his name was still on those court papers. When it came to betrayal, he held the trump card.

It was dark by the time she arrived home, and as she opened the front door she heard muffled voices coming from the living room.

Dumping her jacket and holdall in the hallway, she went to investigate and discovered her sisters huddled together on the sofa. Luisa was wearing her giraffe onesie and a sparkly fairy headband, which bobbled about as she comforted a crying Sofia. It took Elena a moment to compute what was happening—it was usually Sofia supporting Luisa.

She rushed over. 'Oh my goodness. What's happened? What's wrong?'

'Everything's wrong.' Sofia's sobs were hard to hear.

Luisa stroked Sofia's loose hair. 'It's okay, sweetie. We're here for you.' She pulled a weird face at Elena. 'Quick recap. Connor discovered his brother is the opposing solicitor in Sofia's employment case. He wasn't happy.'

Elena frowned. 'We already knew this.'

'There's more.' Luisa glanced at Sofia. 'Connor also discovered you and Sofia are sisters.'

Elena sat back on her heels. 'Again, something we already knew.'

'But Connor didn't, not until the other night, anyway. And now he's told Sofia they can't be together, as it would be "too messy".' She mimed air quotations.

Sofia snatched a tissue from the box next to her. 'That's not the only reason.'

Luisa grimaced. 'There's also the minor issue of Sofia having found out about Connor's past. He kinda freaked out.'

Elena's sense of grievance rose to the surface once again. 'He isn't the only one. Danny's furious. He thinks I betrayed him, but I never said a word.' She placed a hand on Sofia's knee, noticing she was wearing her best Ghost dress. 'I'm really sorry this has happened, Sofia. And I'm sorry I didn't tell you about Connor, but until the other day, I honestly had no idea you and Connor even knew each other, let alone had feelings for each other. Danny told me about Connor's issues in confidence and asked me to keep the information private. It wouldn't have been appropriate for me to tell you.'

Sofia blew her nose. 'It's okay, I understand. You did the right thing.'

Luisa flinched. 'But I didn't, right? Come on guys, just say it. Let rip. I let the cat out of the bag, it was me who told Sofia about Connor. I'm the big bad wolf here.' She slapped her own cheek, making her fairy headband slip. 'But in my defence, it's serious stuff. I felt she should know.'

Elena dropped her head in her hands. So that's what had happened. Danny had the wrong sister. She wasn't sure whether this made her feel better or worse.

Regrouping, she looked up. 'How did you even find out about Connor?'

Luisa shrugged. 'I've been volunteering at the community centre with Sofia, helping to redecorate.'

Elena really had been out of the loop lately. 'Is that the secret art project you've been working on?'

Luisa nodded. 'Connor's lovely, and anyone can see they're made for each other.' She patted Sofia's back when her sister groaned. 'Sorry, but it's true. And I didn't mean to pry, I wasn't deliberately looking for dirt, I just stumbled across those articles on the internet when I was researching ideas for my mural about mindfulness. And then the articles were linked to all these social media posts.'

Elena sighed. 'Oh, Luisa, this was what Danny was afraid of. The stuff on the internet doesn't cover the whole story, and most of it is untrue and inflammatory.'

Luisa folded her arms defensively. 'Well, I get that now. But see it from my point of view: the guy your sister likes has a criminal record, she had a right to know.'

'But he doesn't have a criminal record.' Elena shifted position. 'The charges were dropped, it was a case of mistaken identity and Connor was wrongly accused. The police eventually found the real culprit and all charges were withdrawn.'

Luisa pushed her fairy headband back. 'Oh.'

Sofia grabbed a cushion and buried her face in it. 'I knew Connor was innocent!'

Elena moved to sit next to Sofia and put her arm around her. 'Sofia, listen to me. Danny and I are over. It's done, we're not dating. I hate the idea of you losing Connor over this, so let's focus on how we resolve things.'

Sofia lifted her tearstained face. 'I had no idea you and Danny had even started dating, why didn't you tell me?'

'Yeah, why didn't you tell us?' Luisa echoed, looking disgruntled. 'Bad form, Elena.'

'Because we hadn't been dating, not really. We hooked up that weekend we went away, and honestly, I thought it was a one-time thing. We're not exactly compatible. But he wanted more, and I wasn't sure, but I agreed to a date to see if things between us might develop, but the date never happened. I found out he was acting against Sofia at the ET hearing and called the whole thing off. It was over before it even began.'

Sofia looked puzzled. 'Why?'

'Why?' Elena raised an eyebrow. 'Because acting for the opposition would hurt my sister, that's why.'

'He's just doing his job,' Sofia said with a sigh. 'It's not personal.'

'Not personal?' Elena shook her head, wondering why Sofia wasn't more outraged—she should be furious. 'How can you say that? Of course it's personal. This could damage your future career prospects.'

'Honestly, Elena. It's just a job.' Sofia sniffed and wiped her eyes. 'I'm seriously not that invested in the outcome. I've decided to move on anyway, whatever happens. I don't want to work for a corporate any more. Working at the community centre has opened my eyes to so many other possibilities better suited to my temperament. So please don't let my issues damage your chances with Danny. If you like him, date him.'

Luisa adjusted her fairy headband. 'Good advice.'

Elena shook her head. 'I can't.'

Sofia sighed. 'Why not?'

'Because it's the Felix situation all over again. Danny's choosing his career over his personal life, and I'm not going down that route again. It hurt too much last time.' She swallowed past the lump in her throat, refusing to cry over Daniel bloody Jackson. 'And anyway, this is not about me. It's about you and Connor, and how we fix things.'

'In which case, I'll get the wine. We need stimulants if we're going to strategise.' Luisa disappeared into the kitchen, her fairy headband bouncing as she walked.

Sofia flopped against the sofa. 'I don't know that it can be fixed. I tried talking to him, but he says he's too damaged, and he'd only bring me down with him.'

Elena rested her hand over Sofia's. 'And what do you think?'

'I think he's wrong. I know things have been difficult for him, but he's worth it. He's the only man I want to be with.' Sofia rolled her head to look at Elena. 'I love him.'

Elena smiled, even though her chest ached like she was having a coronary. 'Well, newsflash, Sofia. He loves you too. And according to Danny, Connor's as distraught as you are.'

Sofia's eyes grew hopeful. 'Danny told you this?'

Elena winced at the memory. 'Shouted would be a more accurate description. But yes, he told me, and I believe him. So if Connor loves you, and you love him, then it would be crazy not to do something about it. Right?'

Sofia nodded. 'But I don't know how. He said he's stopping volunteering at the community centre, so I may never see him again. He loves that place, and he's invested so much time into improving things, I hate to think he's walking away because of me.'

Elena was about to respond, when her phone pinged with a message.

Seeing Danny's name flash up on the screen made her physically recoil. She wasn't in the mood for another yelling match. But any ill feeling vanished when she read the message.

Connor's gone missing. I can't find him. I'm panicking. Is he with Sofia?

Elena typed an immediate reply.

He's not with Sofia. Sorry. Hope you find him.

She regretted her terse reply the second after sending it. She should have been kinder, he must be out of his mind with worry.

She waited, but no further message popped up.

Luisa returned from the kitchen with a bottle of wine and three glasses. 'What's the deal? Are we hatching a plan?'

'Not right now.' With her mind in a whirl, Elena stood up. 'I need to head out for a while, something's come up. Luisa, can you stay with Sofia for me?'

Luisa lifted the wine bottle. 'You're not staying? We're in crisis here, Elena.'

'I know, and I wouldn't leave if I didn't have to. Trust me. I'll be back as soon as I can.' She kissed Sofia's cheek before making a hasty exit.

'Is everything okay?' Sofia called after her.

'Everything's fine!' Elena shouted back, grabbing her jacket and hoping she wasn't lying.

She couldn't sit back and let Danny search for Connor alone. She knew how much Connor meant to him, and how devastated he'd be if anything happened to him. Plus, her sister's happiness was on the line. She'd be shattered if anything happened to Connor, so like it or not, she had to help Danny find him. Sod being angry, family was more important.

She was almost out of the door when she saw Sofia's handbag on the hall table, a bunch of keys hanging from the opening.

Without pausing for thought, she grabbed the keys and

googled the address of the community centre as she ran from the house. If Connor loved the community centre as much as Sofia claimed, maybe that's where he'd be hiding out.

Elena left the house and headed for the tube station, knowing her plan might prove to be fruitless. But she had to do something. She didn't know Connor well enough to know where he might hang out, or who his friends were, so she just had to hope Danny and Hugh would have those bases covered. Part of her wondered if she should tell Danny she was joining in with the search, but the other part of her didn't want to get his hopes up.

It was hard to stay focused and not allow her thoughts to drift to the worst case scenario as she boarded the train for White City. If she was struggling to prevent negative thoughts, how must Danny be feeling? When he'd told her about the night Connor had almost taken his life, the ache in his voice had been awful, and she'd fully understood the depth of his pain. She'd experienced it enough times with Luisa, that sense of helplessness when someone you loved was suffering and there was nothing you could do about it. The idea Danny might be in as much distress made her chest ache even more.

She really hoped Connor would be found safe and well. The alternative didn't bear thinking about.

The White City area wasn't somewhere she was familiar with, and she had to use her maps app to locate the community centre. It wasn't the safest area to be wandering about late at night, but she often ran in the evenings, so she was used to staying alert and checking her surroundings.

There was a group of noisy kids messing around on bikes, and a couple of homeless people wrapped under tarpaulins. The traffic noise was heightened by the sound of police sirens in the distance and she prayed they weren't responding to an incident involving Connor.

At first, she wondered if the community centre was shut as there didn't appear to be any lights on, but as she approached, the door opened and a woman exited dressed in exercise gear. 'The step class has just finished,' she said, holding the door open.

'That's okay, I'm looking for Connor Jackson. Is he here?'

'I saw him heading into the meeting room at the back of the hall earlier. No idea if he's still around.'

Elena let out a breath. 'Thanks. I'll take a look.'

The woman said goodnight and let the door shut behind her.

The entrance lobby was chilly and led into a huge hall with a distinctive draft. It was an old building, with a musty smell and reverberating acoustics. Even in trainers, the sound of her footsteps echoed around her as she crossed the space.

'Hello!' she called out. 'Anyone here? Connor?'

No reply.

With only the security lights to guide her, she headed to the back of the hall and up a few steps leading to a corridor. Light shone from an open doorway, so she went over and peered around the door, her heart thudding in anticipation of what she might discover.

Connor was sitting cross-legged in the middle of the floor staring at the far wall. There were no signs of any blood or injury, and his posture seemed relaxed and calm. The relief she felt was almost as consuming as the panic she'd felt at being the one to find him.

Worried about startling him, she quietly cleared her throat. 'Hi, Connor. It's Elena.'

Connor twisted to look at her, his eyes widening with surprise. 'Elena?'

'Okay to come in?' She waited for his nod before heading over and sitting next to him. 'Not who you were expecting, right?'

'I wasn't expecting anyone,' he said, with a shrug. 'How did you know I was here?'

'Sofia mentioned how much this place meant to you. I thought it was worth a shot.'

He flinched at the mention of Sofia's name, his eyes drifting away.

'You do realise your brother's out looking for you? He's beside himself with worry.'

'I needed some space. He doesn't need to worry about me.'

'Except you don't have your phone with you.'

He seemed surprised by this. 'I don't?' His confusion switched to remorse as he patted his pockets and realised she was right. 'Shit.'

Elena rested her hand on his arm. 'Look at it from his perspective, you disappeared without a word and left your keys and phone behind. It's no wonder he's worried. I imagine this is a bit of a trigger for him.'

Connor turned to her. 'He told you about that night?'

Elena nodded. 'But in the strictest confidence.'

Connor closed his eyes. 'He should know I'm past that.'

'Logically, he knows that. Emotionally, he's still recovering. You can't blame him for being worried.'

Connor rubbed his forehead. 'Can you message him for me? Tell him I'm okay. I don't want him worrying, I just needed to be on my own. I hated arguing with him.'

Elena messaged Danny.

Connor's okay. He's at the community centre. I'm with

him. He's fine. He just needed some space. I'll make sure he gets home okay. You can stop panicking.

Danny's reply was immediate.

Can I come and get him?

Elena replied.

Better if you don't, give him time to calm down. I'll look after him, I promise.

Danny's reply was short and to the point.

Thanks.

Elena pocketed her phone to concentrate on Connor, who was staring at a large painted mural on the wall. It took a moment for her to recognise the style and quirky characteristics. The sight of a tap-dancing fairy sealed the deal. 'Did Luisa paint that?'

Connor nodded. 'Clever, isn't she? It's like she really gets it. The conflict of light and dark, both fighting for dominance. It's brutal, and yet hopeful, like she's captured the inside of my head.'

Elena stared at the mural, seeing all the elements of Luisa added into the design, the cartoon cherubs playing harps, the giant tree filled with lush green leaves masking the dying branches beneath. Connor was right, this was the good and bad of life captured in art form. Her sister was very clever indeed. 'I'd never thought about it like that before, but I think you're right. Luisa's a naturally happy and positive person dealing with a dark cloud constantly looming over her. It's a lot for someone to deal with.'

'I admire her. She makes me laugh.'

Elena smiled, a tightness forming in her throat. 'She makes me laugh too.'

He was silent for a while. 'I like Sofia too.'

Elena gave him a gentle nudge. 'You don't have to sound so morose about it. Newsflash, Connor, she likes you too.'

His chin dropped. 'I don't deserve her.'

Elena mulled over the best way to tackle the situation. Sofia liked Connor, he liked her too, why was it so hard for them to admit this and be together? She could ask herself the same question. She knew better than most how exterior factors could derail a blossoming romance. Intervention was needed.

She got to her feet. 'If we're going to have this conversation, then I need to move. This floor is flipping uncomfortable and it's filthy. The stains might never come out of my physio tunic.' She held her hand out. 'Come on, up you get.'

He gazed up at her, confused. 'Where are we going?'

'I'm taking you home. We can chat on the way. I have no idea where you live, so you'll need to lead the way.' She waited until he was off the floor before heading for the door. She was determined one of the Romero sisters would get a happy ending.

Connor remained rooted to the spot. 'I don't want to go home yet.'

She turned to him, hands on hips, making it clear this wasn't a negotiation. 'Connor, your brother's worried sick. He knows you're safe, but he won't be okay until he sees you in the flesh. I know you're angry with him, but surely you don't want him to suffer unnecessarily?'

He shook his head. 'Of course not.'

'Then do the adult thing and come home. We can chat on the way, and by the time you get home we'll have sorted things out, found a cure for cancer, and resolved world peace.'

He joined her by the door. 'That's a bit optimistic.'

'I like to think big.' She flicked off the wall light and followed him down the corridor leading to the main hall.

'So, you had a fight with Danny. I'm guessing it was about the ET hearing?'

Connor kept walking. 'Yep.'

She waited until they were outside and handed him Sofia's keys so he could lock up. It gave her time to formulate her thoughts. 'We had the same fight. Well, kind of. I called him a few names.'

Connor checked the door was secure. 'I'm sure he deserved it.'

'Maybe. We also fought about you.'

Connor turned to look at her. 'Me?'

She slid her arm through his and nudged him to start walking. 'He was livid when he found out someone had told Sofia about your past. He thought that someone was me and he wasn't happy about it. Actually, amend that statement, he was furious. He accused me of betraying him, and you. He's incredibly protective of you.'

Connor was frowning. 'Why did he think it was you?'

'Apparently you told him Sofia's sister told her about what happened. He assumed the sister was me. I guess it wouldn't have occurred to him to think it was Luisa, he doesn't know her.'

Connor sighed. 'Crap. He shouldn't have done that, I'm sorry.'

She encouraged him to keep walking when he slowed down. 'It's okay, it was quite enlightening to see him letting go of his emotions for once. Who knows, it might've expelled some of that internalised rage he carries inside of him. Do you know how rare it is to have someone stick up for you like that? He's a formidable ally to have. You're lucky to have him.'

Connor shrugged. 'I know.'

'Don't be too hard on him.' She tugged on his arm. 'He stuffed up, he knows that.'

They boarded the train, joining a carriage with a group of drunken football supporters. Their team obviously won, thank goodness. Morose football fans weren't something anyone wanted to encounter late at night.

When the train pulled away, Connor leaned closer. 'My dad representing Sofia's employers feels like a betrayal. I know it's his job, and I get he didn't know about the case until this week, but he shouldn't have accepted it.'

Elena agreed, but voicing her own disgruntlement wouldn't help heal the brothers' rift. 'To be fair, he didn't know about you and Sofia at the time, and whatever his decision moving forwards, he feels crap about it.' She glanced at him, wondering if she was helping or hindering. 'Has anything like this happened before?'

Connor shook his head. 'We never fight about anything. He has my back, always. I feel bad his life has been upturned because of me. He never complains about it, but it can't have been easy.'

Elena sighed. 'Probably not, but when you love someone you dig deep and find a way.'

Connor raised an eyebrow. 'Poetic.'

'It's a gift, I know.' The train pulled into Notting Hill Gate and the doors hissed open. 'Talking of which, we need to talk about Sofia.'

'No point, I've blown it,' he said, getting up from the seat. 'This is us.'

She followed him off of the train and through the exit turnstiles, knowing she only had once chance to make him see sense. 'If you think that then you don't know my sister. It'll take more than you getting cold feet to scare her away.'

They crossed the road and Elena resumed holding his arm, probably a subconscious device to prevent him running off. 'Sofia comes across as the sweet and calm one in the family, and she is, compared to me and Luisa anyway, but she's the most capable and resilient person I know. She's also incredibly kind and intelligent, and you'd be a fool to let her go.'

'You don't need to tell me how great she is.' He kicked a discarded beer can and sent it bouncing down the street.

'The thing is, people are always misjudging Sofia, assuming they know what she wants, but they don't. Sofia has no interest in money or status, and she loathes social media. She hates it when bolshy men flirt with her, and despite her very alluring appearance, she's actually quite shy. She values kindness and family loyalty. She's a real homebody, and she wants a man she feels comfortable with and can talk to. And that man is you.' She patted his hand. 'Honestly, Connor, this is the first time I've seen her like this. You're it for her.'

'I don't get it.' He looked genuinely confused. 'I've nothing to offer her.'

'You don't have to get it. You just have to thank your lucky stars and accept it. Don't question it, just jump in head first. And you've plenty to offer her, don't sell yourself short. For the record, she never once believed you were guilty of any of that stuff on the internet. She knew you were innocent.'

Connor slowed down. 'How?'

'Instinct. Sofia's an excellent judge of character and she's rarely wrong. She trusts you. She knows you. She sees exactly who you are and she loves you for it. Please don't walk away from that, you'll regret it if you do. At least talk to her. Have a proper discussion before making your mind up, you owe her that.'

Connor pointed to a street sign. 'This is us down here.'

They turned into a quiet mews, the traffic noise fading away with each step. 'Promise me you'll talk to her and be open to what she has to say?'

'I promise,' he said, with a resigned tone.

'Good, because you know first-hand how hurtful it can be when you're telling the truth and someone judges you wrongly. So when Sofia tells you how she feels, don't dismiss her feelings, okay? You'll crush her, and she doesn't deserve that. Believe what she's saying. My sister doesn't lie. You understand me?'

He nodded. 'I do.'

She realised he'd stopped walking and for the first time she took in her surroundings. They were in the posh part of Notting Hill. The *really* posh part, where only the über rich could afford to live. 'Is this where you live?'

Before Connor could answer, the door to one of the town houses swung open and a harassed-looking Danny flung himself at Connor. 'Thank god you're okay.'

Connor stumbled backwards. 'You're crushing me.'

'I'm sorry, but I was so worried.' Danny took Connor's face in his hands, his expression one of haunted relief. 'You scared the hell out of me.'

Connor looked remorseful. 'I didn't mean to leave my phone behind. I'm sorry I worried you, it wasn't intentional.'

'Okay, but don't frighten me like that again.' Danny pulled him into a hug. 'My heart can't take it. I love you.' He pulled back and ruffled Connor's hair. 'Now get inside. Hugh's ordered pizza.' He turned to Elena. 'Are you coming in?'

He looked quite the sight standing under the shadows of the street lamps, his hair a mess, barefoot, and his T-shirt untucked from his jeans. It was a far cry from his usual suited look. It took all her willpower not to run over and hug him. But then she remembered she was still mad with him and shook off the feeling.

'No, that's okay, I'd best get back to Sofia and Luisa.' She stepped away, knowing it wouldn't take much to tip her over the edge. She couldn't think straight with him looking at her like that, all dog-eyed and pleading.

He leaned against the doorframe. 'Thanks for finding Connor. You've no idea how grateful I am.' He was suddenly propelled into the street when Connor barged past him.

'Sorry, but I've just remembered something. You need to know it wasn't Elena who told Sofia about the stuff on the internet. It was Luisa.' Connor came over to Elena and hugged her. 'When you love someone you dig deep and find a way,' he whispered in her ear. 'Take your own advice, big shot.' He pulled away and headed back inside the house. 'Night, Elena.'

For a moment, her and Danny just stared at each other, unsure what this revelation meant for either of them, if anything.

Danny recovered first. 'Shit! Elena, I'm so—'

'It's fine, really.' She stopped his approach. 'No need to apologise. We both said stuff we regret. At least, I know I did. I'm just glad Connor's okay.' She forced a smile. 'I would say good luck for the hearing tomorrow, but I'd be lying. I hope you lose, in the nicest possible way.'

He ran a hand into his hair, a pained look on his face. 'Are you sure you won't come inside?'

She shook her head. 'You need time alone with Connor.'

He seemed to swallow awkwardly. 'Can I call you a cab? Hugh's here, he could drive you home.'

'Really, I'm fine walking.' She backed away, nearly slipping off the kerb. 'Thanks, though. I'm glad Connor's okay. Bye.'

She was almost running in her eagerness to escape. Her head was a whirl of jumbled thoughts, confusing her ability to think straight. There was so much to unravel. And then her phone pinged with a message. It was from Sofia.

Papi's home!!! Where are you??? xxx

Elena stopped running.

Papi was home?

Tears welled in her eyes and she started running again, this time at full speed.

Chapter Twenty-Four

SOFIA

Thursday, 24th July

Despite all the build-up and stress leading to the day, the employment hearing was over in a few hours. An intense few hours, in which Sofia's hands had shaken and her voice had wavered, but the result was worth it. She'd won her case. She still couldn't believe it.

The judge had refused her former employer's request to postpone the hearing as their solicitor had withdrawn from the case last minute, stating it would be a gross waste of tax payers' money. Despite their numerous objections, the case had proceeded as planned.

The relief she'd felt when she realised Danny had withdrawn was immense, and not just because of her own situation. However much she'd defended Danny's right to do his job, she also knew it would be the death of any chance of her sister being with him. Elena would never forgive him for putting work ahead of family.

In the end, the stern woman from her dismissal meeting, Rosemary Pitts, had been forced to present the employer's case and she'd made a complete hash of it. She was unable to find relevant papers, and failed to back up her arguments with actual legislation. Watching the woman grow increasingly agitated as the day had progressed highlighted the flaws in their case.

In the concluding summary, the judge found that Sofia's former employers to have been inconsistent in their assessment of the term 'carer', and that dismissing Sofia was not a 'proportionate response' to the circumstances. Instead 'reasonable adjustments' should have been made to allow her time off to care for her sister.

When the judge asked Sofia if she wanted her job back, she'd declined. He awarded her a financial settlement instead, full backpay from the date of dismissal, plus three months' salary to cover loss of future earnings. She was elated.

Being stuck inside a windowless room for so long meant she squinted as they emerged into bright sunlight at the end of the session.

Feeling a little shaky, Sofia was comforted by a steady hand on her shoulder. 'You won, *mi hija*.'

She smiled up at Papi, still overcome at having him home. His tanned, broad face smiled down at her, more lined than the last time she'd seen him, but less stricken with grief. 'It'll take a while to sink in.'

He squeezed her shoulder. 'A bold move to reject the job.'

'Maybe, but it feels right,' she said, leaning into his hard frame, strengthened by years of building work. 'I've lost respect for them as employers. There's no way I could go on working for them as though nothing's happened. Supposing Luisa gets ill again? I'd feel uncomfortable asking for more time off.'

He looked at her intently. 'I'm here now. You won't be in that position again.'

She searched his dark hooded eyes. 'Are you staying?'

He nodded. 'The business is sold. The properties are sold. This is where I need to be.'

Her head titled. 'Are you okay about that? I know you'll miss home.'

'*You* are my home,' he said, pulling her close for another hug, one of many since he'd arrived back. 'You and your sisters. I've been selfish. My grief took me away from you, but matters are now settled, financially and personally. I have said my goodbyes and made my peace. It's time to be a good Papi.'

Sofia blinked up at him. 'We missed you.'

He kissed the top of her head. 'Forgive me, *mi hija*.'

She pulled away and wiped her eyes. She felt drained from an emotional few days. 'What's next for you?'

He took her hands, swamping them with his calloused hands. 'The money from the property sales will provide a good income. I will be a builder again, but local, and only a few hours a day. My priority is looking after Luisa so you and Elena can be free to live your lives. It's time.'

'You can't get rid of us that easily,' she said, trying for a smile. 'But it's a relief to know you'll be here. She's a handful at times.'

One dark bushy eyebrow lifted. 'So was your mother.'

She laughed. 'That's true.'

'And I have a surprise for you.' There was a spark of light in his eyes, something that had been absent for so long. 'I won't be caring for Luisa alone. Yulitza will join us.'

'Yulitza?' Sofia couldn't believe it. Their old housekeeper was coming to the UK? 'You mean for a visit? Surely she's not staying?'

'Yes, she's coming to live with us. She missed you *chicas* after we left Colombia. She has worked for other families since, but she's older now, she wants less changing diapers and more relaxing time for herself.'

Sofia raised an eyebrow. 'You think looking after Luisa will be relaxing?'

He laughed, a sound she'd missed so much. 'Maybe not. But I think it will suit her. She has no family left in Venezuela and no ties in Colombia, so we will be her family now.'

'I can't believe it.' Sofia's mind was thrown back to messy baking sessions in their old kitchen, and curling up on the sofa in the afternoons to watch reruns of *Las Juanas*, Yulitza's favourite soap opera. The memories were still so clear, even after all these years. 'When does she arrive?'

'Tomorrow.' He rested his hands on her shoulders. 'This means freedom for you, *mi hija*. So what now for you?'

Her head was still whirling from all the changes in her life. 'Job hunting, for a start. I've been looking at the charity ads and non-profit organisations and there are a few positions I'm interested in.'

His gaze was intense. 'And *el amor*?'

'Love?' She silently crossed her fingers. 'Ask me again tonight. Hopefully I'll have an answer for you.'

'You tell me this boy's name and where he lives, Papi will deal with this.'

'That's the last thing I'm going to do. You'll scare him off.' It was a horrifying thought.

Papi tutted. 'Then he's not worthy of you.'

'Yes he is, Papi. I promise you.' She gave him a playful shove. 'I love you, but you're quite intimidating. I need to do this on my own. If things work out then I'll introduce you to him, but not yet.' She checked her watch. She was hoping to catch Connor before his shift at the community centre ended. If he truly was leaving, this might be her last chance. 'I'm going to see him now, so I'll update you later, okay?'

'Okay.' He kissed her hard, squeezing her shoulders. '*Vamos! Mi hija. El amor no esperará.*'

He was right, *love won't wait.*

Leaving Papi to head off and meet Elena after work for a dinner date and enjoy their own catch-up, Sofia prepared herself for the day's second challenge. She'd won her hearing, now all she had to do was convince Connor they should be together. It was the tougher of the two obstacles and something that would dictate the rest of her life. She couldn't blow her chance.

It had been a while since she'd worn formal workwear, so she felt a little unsteady on her heels as she headed for the tube station. Maybe she should have gone home to change first. A black suit and cream blouse didn't exactly scream romance, but she didn't want to waste any more time. Wearing a suit had given her confidence at the hearing, it might do the same when 'negotiating' her future with Connor.

Could she win him over? She was certainly going to try. She was done feeling shy and protective of her feelings. What did it matter if she made a fool of herself? The way things stood now she'd lost him anyway, she had nothing more to lose. Subtly hadn't got her anywhere, it was time for a more direct approach. She was going to lay everything on the line, and if he still didn't want her, then she'd be left with no regrets.

Well, maybe a few.

It wasn't late by the time she arrived at the community centre, so she was surprised to find the place in darkness. There were usually classes running and group sessions in the meeting room, which had now reopened following the renovation. The main door was unlocked, so someone must be inside. She headed through the dimly lit hall towards the back office, relieved when she saw the spill of light seeping from under the doorway.

Pausing to steady her nerves, she opened the door, hoping to find Connor inside. If she discovered one of cleaners, she'd be mightily disappointed.

Her fears were allayed when she saw Connor seated at the computer. He turned at the sound of the door opening and stood up.

'Hi,' he said, the catch in his voice indicating he was nervous. 'How did the hearing go?' His fingers were crossed and he looked hesitant. She'd never seen him wearing a smart shirt before. He looked adorable, even if the sleeves were slightly too long.

She smiled. 'I won.'

His hands flew into his hair. 'Thank fu– ... Sorry, I mean, that's great.' He moved back and forth like he wanted to hug her, but was undecided about what was appropriate.

She placed her handbag on top of the filing cabinet, needing her hands free in case a hug was coming further down the line. She hadn't given up hope just yet.

'Danny withdrawing from the case helped,' she said, removing her suit jacket. 'The woman who took over wasn't prepared and made the company seem a bit incompetent.

I'm grateful to him. He didn't have to do that, but I'm glad he did.'

Connor nodded. 'I'm glad he did too. I didn't like being angry with him.'

'It's done now, and I won, so please don't let this come between you, I'd hate that. I've accepted a decent settlement, which will tide me over until I find another job.'

Connor looked surprised. 'They didn't offer you your job back?'

'They did, but I turned it down. Volunteering here has made me realise this is the type of environment I want to work in. I feel excited and energised coming here. I never felt that about my other job.'

He let out a sigh. 'I'm so relieved you said that.'

She hung her jacket on the back of a chair. 'Why?'

'Because the trustees want to offer you the manager's job.' He smiled, even though his movements were still twitchy. 'They contacted me to say how impressed they'd been with everything you'd done, and they wanted my opinion on whether to offer you the job permanently. I told them you'd be amazing in the role.' He took a nervous step closer. 'I know the salary might not be what you're looking for, but even if you did it while you looked for something else, I think you'd really make a difference here. Even more than you have already.'

Sofia was stunned. She had a job offer already? And at the place she loved coming to, it was too much to believe. But then she realised what the job offer meant for Connor. 'But what about you? Don't you want the job? I wouldn't feel right taking it when you've done so much for the place.'

He shook his head. 'You don't need to worry about me.'

'But I do, Connor.' She reached for him, before thinking better of it and lowering her hand. 'You were here first, this is your project, your baby. You told me you didn't want to volunteer here anymore because of me. So honestly, I'd rather step back and let you run things than take the job.'

He was shaking his head. 'I meant, you don't need to worry about me because I've decided to finish my degree.'

She hadn't expected that. 'You're going back to university?'

'It's a way of reclaiming what I lost. I only dropped out because of what happened to me and the fallout. I've realised allowing it to derail the rest of my life would be like punishing myself for something I didn't do.'

She leaned on the chair, needing to steady her legs. 'I agree.'

'By finishing my degree, I think it'll help erase some of the resentment I feel.'

'That's great, Connor. Really.' She forced herself to appear happy for him ... and she was, but she was also sad about what this news meant for her. He'd be going away.

Connor ran a hand through his hair. 'I need to stop wallowing in self-pity and take control of my life. This is the first step.'

She wanted to reassure him that his unhappiness was justified and understandable, but it was all she could do to form a simple sentence. 'I'm really pleased for you,' she said, hating the tremble in her voice. She couldn't let him see how upset she was, not when he was taking such a positive step forwards and improving his wellbeing. She blinked away her tears. 'Which university will you be going to?'

'The Open University. That way, I don't have to leave home, and I can continue volunteering here ... with you.' He hesitated. 'If that's okay.'

His words landed in her brain, a jumble of shock and

joy. She was almost too afraid to ask, but she needed confirmation she wasn't dreaming. 'You're not leaving?'

He shook his head, watching her carefully. 'Are you interested in the job?'

'Very much.'

He looked hopeful. 'So you'll accept?'

'I will.'

His smile was all the answer she needed. He was genuinely happy for her. 'I'll text the chair now and let her know the good news.'

Overcome, Sofia closed her eyes and tried to assemble her thoughts. She had a job. Connor wasn't leaving. It was all she could wish for, almost. There was one last question yet to be answered.

When she opened her eyes, a flutter of red caught her attention and a butterfly appeared in the room as if from nowhere. It circled the space, before landing gently on her shoulder. She watched as it opened and closed its wings, not daring to move in case she frightened it.

Connor finished texting and was smiling at her. 'Mrs Hislop approves of your appointment as manager.'

'Is this her? The ghost of Mrs Hislop?' She inwardly groaned. 'What am I saying, of course it's not, that would be insane. There's no such thing as ghosts, that would be bonkers.'

He laughed. 'Sounds like something Luisa would say.'

She smiled. 'In this instance, it's apt.'

Connor's phone pinged. 'The chair's delighted,' he said, reading the message. 'She's going to contact you with a formal offer.'

On hearing that, the butterfly flew off, disappearing into the rafters, as if it had never existed. Sofia searched the room, but there was no sign of it.

'This has been a very strange day,' she said, shaking her head. 'My mind's playing tricks on me. I'm seeing butterflies, and now I can hear music.'

'That's not your imagination. The salsa class is starting in the hall.'

She frowned. 'But it's not salsa night?'

'It's a private booking.' He glanced nervously at her before moving towards the door. 'Come take a look.' He offered her a shaky hand.

She took his hand and let him lead her out of the office, wondering what was happening.

The dark hall was a glimmer of fairy lights. The central glitter ball was slowly spinning and catching the light, sending flickers of dancing light across the floor. Soft salsa music played in the background.

'What's all this?' she asked, looking around. 'And why isn't anybody here?'

'Like I said, it's a private booking.' Connor cleared his throat. 'For me—and you.'

She turned to him. 'You did this for me?'

His expression was shy. 'With a bit of help.'

'Don't mind me!' a voice called from the front of the hall. 'Pretend I'm not here!'

Sofia turned towards the voice. 'Luisa?' What on earth was her sister doing here?

'Who's Luisa?' came her sister's reply. 'No Luisa here, just an invisible fairy playing cupid. I'll be in the back room out of earshot, away from prying eyes, and absolutely not crouched behind the curtains watching you two doing whatever it is you're about to do. Ignore me. I'm gone. Look how I'm gone.' There was a thud. 'Nothing to see!'

Sofia shook her head. 'Why is my sister here? I'm confused.'

'It's Luisa's way of apologising for what she did. I should've known it would end in chaos,' he said, smiling. He was still holding her hand and he gently squeezed it, moving so he was facing her. 'Will you dance with me?'

She was still unsure what was happening. 'This is very unexpected.'

'Hugh told me I needed to make a big romantic gesture.'

'He did?'

'To show you how I really feel.' He waited, his eyes pleading, until she succumbed and began dancing with him. Only then did he smile. 'I'm just glad you came here after your hearing. It would have been embarrassing if you'd gone home. But Luisa assured me you'd come.'

So that's why Luisa had been texting asking where she was. She rested one hand on Connor's chest, as they slowly moved together. This was the moment of truth. She couldn't allow herself to hope until she knew for certain what this romantic gesture meant. 'Last time we spoke you told me we couldn't be together. Does this mean you've changed your mind?'

His thumb circled the back of her hand. 'I was scared and an idiot. I'm sorry.'

She met his eyes. 'Why were you scared?'

'I couldn't believe someone like you wanted someone like me. But I'm going to do better, I promise. I'm going to finish my degree and get a decent job, and I'll be the man who deserves you.' He hesitated. 'If that's still what you want?'

'You don't need to do anything for me, Connor. Finish your degree, if that's what's right for you, but please don't think you have to do anything for me, or be anything different than who you are. I just want you, as you are. I love you.'

He stopped dancing. 'You love me?'

'You think I'd have put myself through all of this if I didn't?' It was time for the truth, laid bare. 'I started falling in love with you before we'd even met, the first day I saw you on the train. I didn't think you'd ever notice me, so I couldn't believe my luck when the train broke down and you spoke to me that day. That's why Luisa and I showed up here to volunteer. It was because of you.'

His eyes had widened. 'I spent every train journey trying not to stare at you in case you thought I was a creep. And the whole time you wanted to talk to me?'

She nodded.

He closed his eyes. 'Remind me to thank Network Rail for unreliable trains.'

'Having made so much effort to get your attention, you can see why I was upset when you rejected me.'

'I didn't reject you,' he said, on a rush. 'Or, that's not how it felt. I think I was saving *myself* from being rejected, I couldn't believe you wanted to be with me. But when I spoke to Elena, she told me you'd never lie, and I should listen to you and trust what you say. So, that's what I'm doing. I'm putting my trust in you and praying you really do love me, because I'm completely and stupidly in love with you. Like totally in love with you.' He grimaced. 'I just said "totally". What am I, fifteen?'

Sofia laughed, but felt a catch in her throat. 'You love me?'

He nodded. 'I do.'

She felt her cheeks grow warm. 'Does this mean we can be together?'

His smile was the gentlest and softest she'd ever seen, a smile that made her insides melt. 'If that's okay with you?'

'How much longer are you two going to be!' Luisa

shouted from the front of the hall. 'I'm getting cramp! Just bloody kiss, will you!'

Taking her sister's advice, Sofia kissed Connor.

She knew she needed to take the lead, she'd be waiting all night for him to kiss her. It was up to her to show him she meant every word and she was in this for real. So she kissed him, unabashed, pulling him close, so he'd be certain this was what she wanted.

There was a brief hesitation on his part, a moment where his body flinched as if he was shocked into immobility, and then it was like someone had flicked a switch and he kissed her back, leaving her in no doubt as to how he felt.

He really did love her.

They continued kissing, and kissed some more, letting their bodies do the talking.

They continued kissing, even when Luisa started bowing to an imaginary audience and proclaimed, 'Thank you, ladies and gentleman, my work here is done.'

Chapter Twenty-Five

ELENA

Friday, 25th July

It took Elena a moment to recover from the shock of finding the door to Danny's office wide open and the space empty. She stepped inside and looked around. Everything had gone. His desk, the filing cabinets, and all his law books. There wasn't a trace of Daniel J Jackson left in the building, just his name stencilled on the glass panelled door.

A lump wedged in her throat, accompanied by a dull thumping in her chest. She should feel relieved. This was what she'd wanted, so why wasn't she happy? Instead of a good feeling, a heavy sickness filled her stomach—that feeling of dread when you realised too late you'd made a colossal mistake.

She'd wanted to come here in the hope of thanking him for withdrawing from Sofia's case, and to see if their connection could be repaired. Instead, she'd found him gone.

The walk home was slow and heavy. The onset of rain had the Portobello Road stallholders scurrying around, packing up their wares. The buzz of market activity usually made her smile, but not tonight. The chaos added to her misery, reflecting the torment she felt. She'd been out all day treating the residents of a care home, and only stopped off at work to dump her things and speak to Danny. Now she wished she hadn't. Her mood was even more morose than it had been before.

It was hard to believe she wouldn't see him every day. They wouldn't chat, or argue, or flirt. Her life would return to how it was before they'd met. What a depressing thought.

Rubbing her chest, she tried to soothe the ache in her ribs, but it refused to shift.

Even when she arrived home and found the Romero household in full 'party' mode, her mood didn't lift, despite the sound of loud Latin music assaulting her ears as she opened the front door.

An invite to Hugh's film-themed birthday party had given the whole family an excuse to dress up—as evidenced when she came across Princess Fiona doing the merengue with Indiana Jones in the lounge. Despite her despondency, she couldn't help smiling at the sight of Papi and a green-faced Yulitza dancing.

Yulitza's arrival from the airport last night had been met with excited screams, hugging, kissing, and an abundance of crying. After the loss of their mum, having Yulitza join the family was like a healing balm being spread over their collective grief.

Waving a greeting, Elena escaped upstairs to avoid

being coerced into joining in. She needed a moment to collect her thoughts.

Her quick escape was scuppered when Luisa appeared from her bedroom dressed in a sparkly pink ballgown and diamanté tiara. Her skin shimmered with glitter as she spun around, lifting her skirts to reveal bright pink trainers beneath.

'Welcome to Munchkinland!' Luisa sang, tap-dancing across the landing, wine bottle in one hand, fairy-wand in the other. 'I am Glinda, Good Witch of the North. Hurry now and get into costume, for the Wizard doesn't like to be kept waiting.' She skipped downstairs, slugging from the wine bottle.

Shaking her head, Elena went into her bedroom and flopped onto the bed.

A tap on the door ended any hope of a respite.

'Come in,' she said, resigned to having an audience while she changed.

It was a surprise when Papi entered. He was minus his Indiana Jones hat, but still had the bullwhip attached to his belt.

He came over and laid next to her, his big hand searching out hers. It was enough to bring her to tears. She wasn't sure why she was feeling so unsettled.

He rested on one elbow to look at her. 'Are you looking forward to the party?'

'Not really,' she admitted, too weary to bother lying.

'Why is that, *mi hija*? You normally like parties.'

'I'm not feeling very sociable right now.'

'Because of Danny?'

She inwardly cringed. 'Who told you?'

'No one needed to tell me, I can see the pain for myself.

Your sisters provided the man's name, that's all.' He watched her carefully. 'If it helps, I approve.'

'You've never met him.'

'I had lunch with him yesterday.'

Elena nearly gave herself whiplash twisting to look at him. 'You had lunch with Danny?'

He nodded. 'Connor wanted me to meet the man who'd raised him.'

Elena covered her face with a pillow in the hope it would smother her and end her suffering. 'You talked about me?'

'We talked about many things,' he said, removing the pillow from her face. 'Family, work, life. He's an honourable man. He has good principles and a kindness that is admirable. I like him. I liked him more when Sofia mentioned you and I saw the expression on his face. It was a look I recognised.'

'Telling me how great he is doesn't help, Papi. I'm painfully aware how wonderful Danny is, everyone keeps bloody-well telling me. It's me that's the problem. I'm the fly in the ointment.'

It was a moment before he spoke. 'Do you know the story of how I met your mother?'

Elena sighed. 'Yes, she was travelling South America and you had a holiday fling.'

'For me it was more than that.' His voice was so tender it forced her to look at him. 'By the time she returned home to the UK I was in love with her. My heart ached, and I feared I would never see her again. This beautiful woman, who had brought light and joy into my life, was leaving. I was at a crossroads. Stay and be safe, or take a risk. I borrowed money from your *abuela* and flew to London. I had never been abroad before. I didn't speak good English. It was very scary.'

It was hard to imagine Papi being afraid of anything, he always seemed so fearless—until their mum had died, anyway. Then he was a broken man.

'I turned up at your mother's house, and your grandfather opened the door, he did not look pleased to see me. He looked more unhappy when I proposed to your mother.'

'You proposed?' Elena blinked at him. 'After a couple of weeks? How come I never knew about this?'

'She said no.' He gave a nonchalant shrug. 'But she admitted she liked me, so I stayed for a few weeks. By the time I left, she was in love with me.' His grin had turned smug. 'I made sure of it. Next time I proposed, she said yes.'

Elena knew the rest of the story. 'And she moved country to be with you.'

'Your grandfather was very unhappy about that.'

'But it was what she wanted, you made her happy.'

'Yes, I did.' His expression turned serious. 'I worked hard to make her happy. Every day of our life together. Falling in love is the easy part. After that you have to make the decision to commit and show that love every day. It is not always easy, but it is always worth it.'

Elena kicked off her trainers and rolled to face him. 'Why are you telling me this?'

'Because I see that same look on this man's face.' He tucked her hair behind her ear. 'The look I had when your mother left. He is at a crossroads too.'

Elena shook her head. 'It's too late. He's already made his decision. Moving out of his office is a pretty definitive statement.'

'Maybe.' Papi shrugged. 'He will be at the party tonight. You must talk to him.'

'There's nothing left to say.' She stuffed the pillow under her head. 'I agree he's a good man, you don't need to tell me that. But is he the right man for me? I'm not so sure. We're so different. It feels like the Felix situation all over again.'

Papi frowned. 'Why do you say that?'

'I was more invested in the relationship than he was,' she said, hating the rise of humiliation she still felt at getting things so wrong. 'He put his career ahead of me. We liked different things. More than that, he actively disliked the way I behaved at times. It's not a great feeling knowing someone disapproves of you. Plus, he had no respect or understanding when it came to Luisa, or my need to be near her. There was a wedge between us.'

'This is true.' He nodded. 'He was not right for you. It was clear to see.'

Elena gave him a shove. 'Gee, thanks, Papi. You didn't think to tell me this?'

'Would you have listened?' He raised an eyebrow. 'A parent disliking their child's partner is not something that should be voiced. He was your choice, but he was not mine.'

Elena couldn't believe what she was hearing. 'You kept it well hidden. I knew Luisa didn't approve, but I had no idea you didn't like him either.' Although in hindsight, maybe she did have an inkling, she'd just chosen to ignore it.

'It wasn't that I didn't like him. He wasn't right for you. People are like planets, Elena. Independent and spinning in orbit, each one with a different climate and atmosphere. That is okay.' He tapped the end of her nose. 'You are an independent woman, this is good. But there are many planets in the sky, and sometimes gravity pulls us towards another life form. That can be a good thing too, to be co-dependent.'

'Have you been watching Brian Cox tutorials again?'

His gaze remained intense. 'Felix wasn't in the same universe as you. Your planets were not compatible to sustain life. Your love would have died.'

Brutal, but most probably true.

'Danny is different from you, yes. But his planet is compatible with yours. Your love would not die, it would last for infinity.'

She laughed, mostly to disguise the sudden lump in her throat. Annoyingly, he was right. Danny was the kind of man you would love forever. Maybe that's what scared her so much. 'You're a hopeless romantic, do you know that?'

'It is the key to a happy life, *mi hija*.' He kissed her forehead. 'Get ready for tonight's party. You are at a crossroads too. You have a decision to make.' He climbed off of the bed, pausing when he reached the doorway. 'Be brave, *mi hija. Solo tienes una vida*.'

Elena flopped back on the bed. *You only have one life.* Wasn't that the truth.

His words rattled through her brain on repeat like a hamster on a wheel as she showered and dressed for the party. By the time she'd clipped artificial hair buns to the sides of her head, and slipped into the long white Princess Leia dress, she was even more confused.

Even if Danny was her soulmate, she might be too late. Emptying his office had sent a clear message.

Heading downstairs, the sound of laughter grew louder, accompanied by incessant chatter and raucous music. The Romero family were in full party mode, drinking, dancing, and acting the fool. Elena paused at the bottom of the stairs to absorb the sight. It felt like a lifetime since the house had been filled with such happiness.

Sofia and Luisa were dancing together. Sofia was dressed as Morticia Addams, her long black dress accentuating her curves, her pouty red lips looking suitably sultry, and her long hair gleaming under the lights.

In contrast, Luisa was spinning around in her pink ballgown, waving her wand, and looking like Tinkerbell on speed.

It was great to see them so happy. Sofia had won her tribunal case and secured a job at the community centre, and Luisa was busy working on designs for redecorating the place. Both sisters were flourishing, and Elena couldn't be more pleased for them. They deserved the world.

Luisa spotted her and pirouetted over, losing her balance, most probably due to the consumption of too much wine. 'Elena, you look amazing. Come dance with us.'

The purple bruising on Luisa's arms was the only evidence of her illness. She was having a good spell, and they needed to make the most of it.

Their energetic dancing was interrupted when Papi clapped his hands. 'Miller is here. Let's go, *familia*! It's party time. *Vamos*!' He ushered them into the hallway and opened the front door to wave at his mate. '*Vamos, familia*! Let's go!'

The drive across town was thankfully short. Being squashed inside an SUV with Indiana Jones, Morticia Addams, Princess Fiona and The Good Witch of the North was a challenging test. Especially as everyone was talking and laughing and distracting poor Miller from driving.

As they exited the car at their destination, Luisa stepped on the back of Elena's dress and nearly ripped the garment from her body. Thankfully, the seams held firm and she didn't expose herself to the rest of the guests.

The party was in full swing, filled with people dressed in mostly recognisable film characters and determined to have a fun night.

Elena gasped when they entered the banqueting suite to find a giant circus tent had been erected. The large doors were open, leading onto the terrace, where fire eaters created long flames that disappeared into the sky. Jugglers circled the room, showing off their skills, and there was a man riding a unicycle. How he managed to stay upright, she had no idea.

A stage had been erected at one end where a cast of dancers performed the theme tune from The Greatest Showman. They were joined on stage by Hugh and James, who were both dressed as circus ringmasters, complete with red coats and top hats. They welcomed everyone to the party and insisted a good time was to be had by all.

Smiling, Elena scanned the room, spotting Hugh's parents, Virginia and Nigel, dressed as Bonnie and Clyde. Connor was with them. The moment he saw Sofia, his face lit up and he immediately headed over, his outfit of Gomez Addams a match for her Morticia.

His shyness only lasted a few seconds. All awkwardness disappeared when Sofia threw her arms around him and kissed him. He grinned like he was the luckiest man on the planet. And he was. They were so cute together, holding hands and staring at each other with soppy grins. It made Elena so happy to see them together.

The room was filled with people Elena mostly didn't know. She tried keeping her expression neutral as she searched for Danny, hoping to see him. Maybe Papi was right and it was time to stop overthinking and start paying attention to how she felt instead. She missed him. She hated the idea of not having him in her life. Maybe that was enough of a reason to let go of her resistance.

She was just wondering whether he'd decided not to attend when he appeared by her side, allaying her fears. She could stop panicking.

As she turned to look at him, she sucked in a sharp breath. He was dressed as Neo from The Matrix, and it was a look that hit her in all the right places. Who knew he'd look so good in black leather. His long coat almost touched the floor, and the addition of black sunglasses gave him a sexy edge.

It was a few seconds before he spoke. 'Dramatic enough for you?'

She couldn't help laughing.

'Nice suit,' she said, aiming for an air of nonchalance and not openly gawp. 'A change from your usual style.'

'Not sure how long the coat will last, I'm boiling up.'

She locked her hands, fighting the urge to touch him. 'Keep it on for a bit longer.'

He smiled at that, seeming to pick up on the heat in her voice. She couldn't see his eyes behind the dark glasses, but she could tell he was checking her out. 'Nice buns,' he said, nodding appreciatively.

She laughed. 'Nice buns?'

'I meant your hair.' He pointed to her hair pieces. 'What did you think I meant?'

She forced her gaze away from his flirtatious one, needing a moment to compose herself. 'Cool party.'

He joined her in watching an acrobat climb a rope and swing above them. 'Hugh certainly knows how to host an event. I thought you'd appreciate a chance to dress up.' He nodded to the dance floor. 'Your family seem to be having fun.'

Elena smiled as she watched Papi and Yulitza flailing about to a Dua Lipa song. Luisa was flirting with one of the acrobats, a topless man with impressive abs, and Sofia and Connor were huddled together away from prying eyes. 'They don't need much encouragement.'

There was a long pause before she felt him look at her. 'How long do I have to make small talk for before we can clear the air?'

She smiled. 'Not really a suitable place for a heart-to-heart. I can barely hear you above the music.'

'I agree.' Before she knew what was happening, he'd taken her hand and she was being led towards the exit.

Danny paused by the doorway and turned to wave at Hugh, who gave him a thumbs up. She had no idea what was going on.

'Through here,' he said, leading her into an adjacent room, partitioned off from the main hall. 'It's quieter in here.'

It was a dimly lit space filled with stacks of chairs and tables.

Danny turned to her, his movements animated. 'Can I go first?'

Seeing as she was clueless as to what was happening, her answer was easy. 'Sure.'

He tucked his sunglasses inside his coat pocket, before positioning himself in front of her. 'I'm sorry I didn't make the decision to withdraw from Sofia's tribunal case earlier. I should've done, and I'm sorry for the distress my actions caused.'

She waited, his raised hand an indication he wasn't done.

'I'm also sorry I accused you of telling Sofia about Connor's past. I jumped to the wrong conclusion, and I acted impulsively. It was wrong of me, and I feel bad about the things I said to you. I should've known you'd never betray my trust, and on reflection, I think it was born out of panic. A way of sabotaging any chance of a relationship with you, because I was scared shitless of the way I felt about you. I've had time to analyse this and I realise my mistake. I'm sorry. Please can you forgive me?' He was staring at her intently.

She nodded. 'Yes.'

He tilted his head, as if he expected more. 'Yes? That's it? That's all it took?'

'That's all it took.' She gave a little shrug. 'Why, is there more?'

'Well ... yes, there is, actually.' He began pacing, clearly building up the courage to say something else. 'You've accused me on several occasions of being a boring suit, and that's not something I'm going to apologise for. I am a boring suit. I can't change who I am. I'm not demonstrative, or a risk-taker, and maybe that's a turn-off for you.' His voice wavered a little and he coughed to clear it. 'But being a suit also makes me dependable, trustworthy, and honest. I'm committed to making a decent career, not because it's the most important thing in my life, but because it allows me to provide for Connor, who *is* the most important thing in my life. Stability and security, and consistency, are essential values to have, and I won't apologise for that.' His expression turned almost steely. 'So, if that's not what you want, and you don't find those qualities attractive, then maybe you're right, we shouldn't be together, because I'm not about to change who I am.'

God, she wanted to kiss him. 'Good.'

His eyebrows lifted. 'Good?'

'I agree with everything you've just said. You are all those things. They make you the man you are, and you shouldn't have to change that for anyone, least of all me.' She took a breath, allowing her gut instinct to take control of her next words. 'I've also had time to reflect. And like you, I was trying to protect myself. Telling myself you weren't the right man for me was safer than admitting how I truly felt.'

She watched his Adam's apple bob. 'I thought you were supposed to be the brave one.'

'Not in this instance. So, I'm also sorry. I'm sorry for being mean to you, and for accusing you of being a boring suit, when in truth, you're ...' she trailed off, searching for the right word.

He looked worried. 'I'm what?'

'Quite edgy, actually.' Her eyes scanned his leather outfit. 'Especially dressed like that.'

He cleared his throat. 'So how *do* you feel? You know, about me?'

'I'm not sure it's relevant anymore.'

He looked crushed. 'Why would you say that?'

'Because you're leaving.' She felt the weight of her words, heavy and morose. 'Left, in fact. Your office is empty. I took that as a sign that you were done with me. You'd had enough and moved out.'

'I'm not done with you, Elena. Are you kidding me?' He took her by the shoulders. 'I'm crazy about you. Why else would I have spent today with Hugh lugging furniture up to his office so you could move your clinic downstairs. I even used the damned bloody elevator. *Several* times. It was torture. That's how much I love you. I used a sodding elevator.'

Her heart sped up. 'You moved offices for me?'

'Yes.'

She blinked several times. 'You love me?'

'It would appear so.' His eyes dipped to her mouth. 'Any more questions?'

'Just the one.' She slid her arms around his waist. 'How long is your outfit on hire for?'

He grinned. 'All night.'

'And do you have a room booked?'

'I do.'

She was about to kiss him when his phone pinged.

'Hold that thought.' He tapped a reply, before pocketing his phone. When he was done, his eyes returned to hers, filled with the promise of what was to come. 'So, can we go on that date now?'

She reached up on tiptoes. 'I think we can skip dating and jump to the good stuff.'

Maybe it was the dimly lit space, or the clandestine hideaway, or the effect of his leather outfit, but the kiss hit the jackpot first time of asking. She couldn't get enough of this man, and she was determined to let him know that. There was nothing holding her back now, all doubt had vanished. He was her planet, and she wanted to spin in his orbit for eternity, or whatever the metaphor was that Papi had confused her with.

The kiss deepened and became slightly frantic, filled with relief and wanting and unspoken apologies. Maybe they communicated better when they weren't actually talking. Whatever the reason, it was a kiss that stripped away any lasting barriers. Who knew where the kiss may have led, if the partition doors hadn't slid open.

Loud screaming and applause hit Elena like a tornado. It was enough to break the kiss, dragging her away from Danny and to the sight of the entire party facing them and cheering. Above was a lit-up neon sign that said, *Danny & Elena are dating!*

She turned to Danny. 'Seriously? You planned this?'

His expression was deadpan. 'Dramatic enough for you?'

She burst out laughing.

And then she kissed him again. It seemed fitting.

So much for being a boring suit. Daniel J Jackson was anything but.

'And just so you know,' she said, breaking the kiss and holding his adorable face in her hands. 'I love you too.'

His smile was breath-taking. 'You know, something tells me my luck might be about to change.'

She matched his smile. 'You'd better believe it.'

At which point they were rugby tackled by her entire family, including Virginia and Nigel, Hugh and James, and the shirtless acrobat.

This was her new life. Her new family.

Well, apart from the shirtless acrobat.

Although, judging by the way Luisa was looking at him, maybe she was wrong about that.

Afterword

Three decades ago, the average person with Cystic Fibrosis would only live to the age of thirty, but now fifty years is typical, and some patients with CF live into their eighties. The character of Luisa is based on a good friend of mine, Louise, who sadly died of complications resulting from the disease in 2006. She was only thirty-two. The situations depicted in this book relate to her experiences only and my viewpoint as her friend, they do not reflect the stories of everyone living with CF. Each person has a different journey and thankfully the advances in medical science mean that someone diagnosed with Cystic Fibrosis can now expect to live a full life.

Acknowledgments

This story has taken me a while to write, so thank you for your patience. I can't tell you what it means to me to receive messages from readers asking when the next book will be released. Well, here it is! Various changes in my life have contributed to the delay – like everyone, stuff happens, and it can derail the best of plans. So this book is something of a celebration in getting back to being creative and doing what I love – making stuff up.

I've always wanted to write a story about a character with Cystic Fibrosis as a tribute to my dear friend, Louise. She was the funniest, kindest, and most looney friend anyone could ask for, and working with her was such joy. The Tap-Dancing Fairy was her invention – something she would do to make us laugh during a particularly dull day at work. All would be quiet in the office and then Louise would randomly start tap-dancing around the office, singing made-up songs about fairies, and disappearing into the corridor, leaving her co-workers shaking their heads and smiling. Her life was curtailed by Cystic Fibrosis, and watching some of the things she endured was heartbreaking, and yet she would bounce back each time with more hilarity and more tap-dancing. She was a true inspiration and I hope I've done the character of Luisa justice in displaying her strength, humour, and craziness. I just wish she was still around to read the book.

I'd also like to thank my partner, Simon, for supporting

my writing dreams. For a man with no interest in romance, fiction, or tap-dancing fairies, he has a surprising talent for solving plot problems. He also makes a superb cup of tea.

Most of my previous books feature a dog. This has been my way of manifesting one into my life for many years, but now I finally have one of my own. We rehomed Poppy from the RSPCA in early 2025 and I can't imagine how I lived without her. Unlike Simon, she stares blankly at me when I talk through my plot ideas with her, but she makes up for it with cuddles and licks. She's a shinning example of unconditional love and I adore her.

This book would not have been possible without a team to support me, so I'd like to thank the following people: Cover design: Diane Meacham, Blog Tour: Rachel's Random Resources, and Editing: Mary Hargreaves.

A special mention to the wonderful author and my dear friend, Rosanna Ley, for reading an early draft of *The Love Dilemma* and steering me in the right direction. If you haven't read her books, I'd encourage you to do so, she's an amazing author.

Finally, thank you to all the fabulous readers, bloggers and fellow authors for supporting my journey, sharing posts, posting reviews and generally being wonderful people. In particular, my wonderful family and drama friends, who are always the first to read my books, leave reviews and recommend them to their friends. It's incredibly humbling. Thank you!

If you'd like to follow me on social media or make contact, then I'd love to hear from you:

Instagram: @tracyacorbett

Facebook: @tracyacorbettauthor

Website: www.tracycorbettauthor.co.uk

About the Author

Tracy is an award-winning author who lives in rural Surrey with her motorbike-loving partner and her little rescue dog, Poppy. After a long career with Citizens Advice, Tracy is now a full-time author. She describes her writing style as modern tales of romance, with engaging quirky characters, who overcome adversity, grow as people and conclude in satisfying optimistic endings.

Also by Tracy Corbett

Someone Like You

Someone To Love

Someone For Everyone

A Winter's Wish

Only For Christmas

Copyright © 2026 by Tracy Corbett

All rights reserved.

No part of this book may be reproduced in any form or by any electronic or mechanical means, including information storage and retrieval systems, without written permission from the author, except for the use of brief quotations in a book review.

Formatted with Vellum

www.ingramcontent.com/pod-product-compliance
Ingram Content Group UK Ltd.
Pitfield, Milton Keynes, MK11 3LW, UK
UKHW010915040326
468628UK00002B/140

9 781919 343419